THE BLITHEDALE ROMANCE

NATHANIEL HAWTHORNE was born in Salem, Massachu-setts, a descendant of the William Hathorne who had emigrated to New England with the first generation of Puritan settlers in 1630. Hawthorne's interest in the history and legend of his region was revealed in his early stories, which began to appear in print in the 1830s. New England Puritanism and its legacy provided Hawthorne with the means of exploring many of the themes that concerned him deeply, among them the conflict between patriarchal authority and the impulse to a variety of freedoms, including the freedom of the artist. Though he immersed himself in the early literature of New England, Hawthorne's own writings are peculiarly modern in some of their leading characteristics. One is the self-reflexiveness of narratives which make the telling a part of the tale. Another is the concern with signifying practices, with the relationships between objects (a Red Cross, a Black Veil, a Scarlet Letter) and what they come to signify.

Never willing to submit to the conventions of the realist novel, when he abandoned the short story and the sketch for longer works, Hawthorne claimed the imaginative freedom of the romance. His first—*The Scarlet Letter*—was published in 1850 and brought him immediate critical recognition, if not financial success. In quick succession he completed two more romances—*The House of the Seven Gables* (1851) and *The Blithedale Romance* (1852)—and con-solidated his position as a major writer of his day. After his appointment as consul at Liverpool and Manchester in 1853 Hawthorne produced no more fiction until 1860, when *The Marble Faun* was published. Returning to Massachusetts in that year after travels in France and Italy, he struggled to finish other romances but left them uncompleted at his death in 1864.

TONY TANNER is a Fellow of King's College, Cambridge. His books on American literature include *The Reign of Wonder*, *City of Words*, and *Scenes of Nature, Signs of Men*. For the Oxford World's Classics he has edited Melville's *Moby Dick*, *The Confidence Man*, and *White-Jacket*, and (also with John Dugdale) two novels by William Dean Howells, *Indian Summer* and *A Hazard of New Fortunes*.

JOHN DUGDALE is the author of a study of the novelist Thomas Pynchon.

OXFORD WORLD'S CLASSICS

For over 100 years Oxford World's Classics have brought readers closer to the world's great literature. Now with over 700 titles—from the 4,000-year-old myths of Mesopotamia to the twentieth century's greatest novels—the series makes available lesser-known as well as celebrated writing.

The pocket-sized hardbacks of the early years contained introductions by Virginia Woolf, T. S. Eliot, Graham Greene, and other literary figures which enriched the experience of reading. Today the series is recognized for its fine scholarship and reliability in texts that span world literature, drama and poetry, religion, philosophy and politics. Each edition includes perceptive commentary and essential background information to meet the changing needs of readers.

OXFORD WORLD'S CLASSICS

NATHANIEL HAWTHORNE

The Blithedale Romance

With an Introduction by
TONY TANNER

and Explanatory Notes by
JOHN DUGDALE

OXFORD
UNIVERSITY PRESS

OXFORD
UNIVERSITY PRESS

Great Clarendon Street, Oxford OX2 6DP

Oxford University Press is a department of the University of Oxford.
It furthers the University's objective of excellence in research, scholarship,
and education by publishing worldwide in

Oxford New York

Athens Auckland Bangkok Bogotá Buenos Aires Calcutta
Cape Town Chennai Dar es Salaam Delhi Florence Hong Kong Istanbul
Karachi Kuala Lumpur Madrid Melbourne Mexico City Mumbai
Nairobi Paris São Paulo Singapore Taipei Tokyo Toronto Warsaw

with associated companies in Berlin Ibadan

Oxford is a registered trade mark of Oxford University Press
in the UK and in certain other countries

Published in the United States
by Oxford University Press Inc., New York

Database right Oxford University Press (maker)

First published as a World's Classics paperback 1991
Reissued as an Oxford World's Classics paperback 1998

British Library Cataloguing in Publication Data

Data available

Library of Congress Cataloging in Publication Data
Hawthorne, Nathaniel, 1804–1864.
The Blithedale romance/Nathaniel Hawthorne with an introduction by
Tony Tanner and explanatory notes by John Dugdale
p. cm.—(Oxford world's classics)
Includes bibliographical references
[I. Title. II. Series.]
PS1855.A2T36 1991 813'.3—dc20 90-25303

ISBN 0–19–283697–8

5 7 9 10 8 6 4

Printed in Great Britain by
Cox & Wyman Ltd.
Reading, Berkshire

CONTENTS

CONTENTS

INTRODUCTION

It would probably be advisable to read the text of the novel before reading this
Introduction, since inevitably, in discussing the novel, I indirectly reveal much of
the plot.

True; if you look at it in one way, it had been only a summer in the
country. But, considered in a profounder relation, it was part of
another age, a different state of society, a segment of an existence
peculiar in its aims and methods, a leaf of some mysterious volume,
interpolated into the current history which Time was writing off. At
one moment, the very circumstances now surrounding me—my coal-
fire, and the dingy room in the bustling hotel—appeared far off and
intangible. The next instant, Blithedale looked vague, as if it were at
a distance both in time and space, and so shadowy, that a question
might be raised whether the whole affair had been anything more
than the thoughts of a speculative man. I had never before experienced a mood that so robbed the actual world of its solidity. It
nevertheless involved a charm, on which—a devoted epicure of my
own emotions—I resolved to pause, and enjoy the moral sillabub
until quite dissolved away. (p. 146)

BY the end of this passage it is not entirely clear whether the
'dissolving away' refers to the sillabub or the writer himself.
Certainly in a text in which the word 'melt' endlessly recurs
and where dematerialization, attenuation, liquidation, vapor-
ization, and other modes of desubstantiation seem variously
to dominate the changing atmosphere, the facility with which
a sweet dessert or a sentimental author might come to share in
the prevailing tendency to fade, no matter how stickily, away
could well come to seem about equal. We are certainly invited
to consider what kind of writer, and what kind of writing, are
here involved. Yes, it is, from one point of view, all based on
'a summer in the country'—the summer of 1841, to be
precise, which Hawthorne himself spent at or in the experi-
mental socialist (Utopian? perhaps Fourierist)[1] community at
Brook Farm. But, looked at another way, and thus written
another way, it might become 'a leaf of some mysterious
volume, interpolated into the current history which Time was

---

[1] See explanatory note to p. 52, Charles Fourier.

writing off'. It is a somewhat curious formulation and one
might wonder—who is doing the writing here? Does Time
both write current history and write it off at the same time? Is
history somehow at once inscribed and erased? But Time
only writes by a metaphor (though I suppose we would have
to say that it erases in good earnest). The writing here is being
done by the narrator, Miles Coverdale, and, in likening his
summer experiences to 'a leaf of some mysterious volume'
interpolated into the, presumably, unmysterious history
being written, and written off, by Time, he must be suggesting that, whatever it is he is now writing, it is not history—
or not history as currently conceived. And indeed he calls
his non-historical history of that summer in the country a
Romance. Hawthorne and Romance is a subject to drown in,
but for the moment I want to make only a restricted point.
Why is Miles Coverdale *not* writing history? Why does he,
gesturally, leave that to Time or whatever? Or perhaps it is a
more mysterious kind of history he is writing—devious,
surreptitious, interpolatory? The matter is important
because, as I shall try to suggest, problems involved in
writing American history, the history of America (and in *not*
writing it—writing off, writing out), are central to this novel.
And whatever his relationship—non-relationship, sly-rela-
tionship—to history might be, the narrator has here reached a
state of extreme reality-deprivation in which the 'actual
world' has lost its solidity and he is collapsing into a state of
solipsism—not to say infantilism—in which he has un-
ashamed recourse to a kind of primal orality in which he sucks
contentedly away on the (moral!) sillabub of the dissolving
self.

What *is* Hawthorne doing?

When he returns to Blithedale after his sojourn in the city,
Coverdale confessedly indulges in 'odd and extravagant conjectures' (p. 206). The conjectures are 'spectral' and are all
concerned with the evacuation of the real.

Either there was no such place as Blithedale, nor ever had been, nor
any brotherhood of thoughtful laborers . . . or else it was all changed,
during my absence. It had been nothing but dream-work and
enchantment. I should seek in vain for the old farm-house . . . and for

all that configuration of the land which I had imagined. It would be another spot, and an utter strangeness. (p. 206)

There is a peculiarly American nightmare or dread summed up in that last sentence—a sudden sense of the *complete* defamiliarization of a site or terrain thought to be known and amenable. Coverdale looks for something to anchor him and finds it in the farm. 'That, surely, was something real' (p. 206). (On another occasion he describes his determination to force Zenobia out of what he takes to be her continual acting. 'She should be compelled to give me a glimpse of something true; some nature, some passion, no matter whether right or wrong, provided it were real' (p. 405). It is that same urgent need and desire for 'something real'. As in Frost's famous poem 'For once, then, something' (1923) which ends: 'What was that whiteness? | Truth? A pebble of quartz? For once, then, something.') The reality he finds is the very earth of the farm where, for a while, he had worked. 'I could have knelt down, and have laid my breast against that soil' (p. 206). I am prompted to invoke Robert Frost again, and his powerful poem 'To Earthward' (1923), which ends:

When stiff and sore and scarred
I take away my hand
From leaning on it hard
In grass and sand,
The hurt is not enough:
I long for weight and strength
To feel the earth as rough
To all my length.

—though it would have to be said that this longing stems from more powerful feelings than animate the always potentially dilettante Coverdale. Nor could the sybaritic Coverdale declare with the same authority as the austerely ascetic Thoreau—'Be it life or death, we crave only Reality.'[2] But it is an important aspect of him that he should at least intermittently experience this hunger for the real, undeveloped and undernourished an appetite as it may be. What might

[2] H. D. Thoreau, *Walden* (1854; New York: Library of America edn.), 400.

constitute the real or the Real are questions hardly to be
addressed in this book, where reality, whatever and wherever
it may be, is—it would appear—mainly to be known by the
conviction that you have not got it.

What Coverdale does get, as he prowls around Blithedale
looking for something real, is a 'concourse of strange figures'
(p. 209) appearing and vanishing 'confusedly', consisting of,
among others, an Indian chief, the goddess Diana, a Bavarian
broom girl, a negro 'of the Jim Crow order', a Kentucky
woodsman, a Shaker, Shepherds of Arcadia, grim Puritans,
gay Cavaliers, Revolutionary officers, a gypsy, a witch, and so
on—a disorderly medley of mythical and literary figures,
national types, or stereotypes, and historical representatives.
The chapter is called 'The Masqueraders' and that is what
they are. The atmosphere of Blithedale has been saturated
with artifice of all kinds from the start, as when Coverdale
feels that the presence of Zenobia 'caused our heroic enterprise to show like an illusion, a masquerade, a pastoral, a
counterfeit Arcadia, in which we grown-up men and women
were making a play-day of the years that were given us to live
in' (p. 21). Noting the word 'counterfeit' we may just observe
that all this pseudo-'masquerading' reveals itself to be piti-
fully self-conscious, juvenile, and fragile. Is *this* what has
become of the deeply resonant pastoral and Arcadian images
and visions of old Europe, when transplanted to the New
World? It is a sort of ultimate trivialization, and here the
simple presence of the Yankee farmer Silas Foster, with his
'shrewd, acrid observation', is enough to 'disenchant the
scene' (p. 210). And yet there was a strong line of thought, or
a persistent dream, that America might be the last best chance
of, if not literalizing Arcadia, then realizing—Real-izing—
Utopia. And that, surely, is not a trivial aspiration. I shall
return to these matters.

Fleeing from 'the whole fantastic rabble' (p. 211) of masqueraders—'like a mad poet hunted by chimaeras', he rather
extravagantly puts it, given that it seems more like a romp at a
picnic—Coverdale finally finds himself alone and effectively
lost deep in the woods where

I stumbled over a heap of logs and sticks that had been cut for firewood, a great while ago, by some former possessor of the soil, and piled up square, in order to be carted or sledded away to the farmhouse. But, being forgotten, they had lain there, perhaps fifty years, and possibly much longer; until, by the accumulation of moss, and leaves falling over them and decaying there, from autumn to autumn, a green mound was formed, in which the softened outline of the wood-pile was still perceptible. In the fitful mood that then swayed my mind, I found something strangely affecting in this simple circumstance. I imagined the long-dead woodman, and his long-dead wife and children, coming out of their chill graves, and essaying to make a fire with this heap of mossy fuel. (p. 212)

This is, for me, one of the key moments of the book and to explain why I think so I want, once again, to invoke some lines by Frost from a poem called, indeed, 'The Wood-Pile' (1914). Frost describes going out for a walk in the woods and deciding at a certain point that, rather than turning back for home, he will 'go on farther'—a very Frostian moment. Soon he finds himself unable to 'mark or name a place' or 'say for certain I was here|Or somewhere else'. He is not exactly lost—'I was just far from home.' And then he comes upon a pile of wood.

> It was a cord of maple, cut and split
> And piled—and measured, four by four by eight.
> And not another like it could I see.
> No runner tracks in this year's snow looped near it.
> And it was older sure than this year's cutting,
> Or even last year's or the year's before.
> The wood was grey and the bark warping off it
> And the pile somewhat sunken. . . .
>
> . . . .
>   I thought that only
> Someone who lived in turning to fresh tasks
> Could so forget his handiwork on which
> He spent himself, the labour of his axe,
> And leave it there far from a useful fireplace
> To warm the frozen swamp as best it could
> With the slow smokeless burning of decay.

The two American poets—Coverdale is a poet, albeit a minor one—both find something almost namelessly pregnant and suggestive when they come across an abandoned wood-pile. Their somewhat disoriented, non-orientated state recapitulates in little—echoes if you like—the ontological situation of the original settlers of the land who would have found themselves, not lost exactly, but, with names and markers not yet affixed, definitely and definitively 'far from home', perhaps having to develop a sense of where they were from the knowledge of where they were not. The wood-pile, marked in both cases by 'decay', serves as both a sort of commemorial mound to 'some former possessor of the soil', and a reminder of the labour, the 'tasks', involved in the settling and domesticating (fuel essential for the 'useful fireplace'—the home) of the land. The 'axe' is the prime symbol of the pioneer and the advancing frontier. As an intentional object—in both cases the wood has been 'cut' and 'piled up square'—the wood-pile is a sign of culture in the wilderness; but a sign already mouldering away and being reclaimed by, reabsorbed into, nature, suggesting, a little, the pathos, transience, and ephemerality of the residual testimonies to the presence of human effort and constructive work. The wood-piles are inexplicably abandoned, suggesting that death—or distraction—always comes too soon; that man is everywhere outlasted by the poignant traces of his labour, leaving sundry edifices which he can no longer either tend or use. And with the 'softened outline' of the 'green mound', the pile is beginning—more specifically in Hawthorne—to resemble a grave. And it is this and all that it implies—call it mortality, call it mutability—which Coverdale has to face and his text, if it can, absorb. ET IN ARCADIA EGO.

In a much earlier scene, talking, somewhat banteringly, to Hollingworth about the future of their new Community, Coverdale says:

I shall never feel as if this were a real, practical, as well as poetical system of human life, until someone has sanctified it by death. . . . Let us choose the rudest, roughest, most uncultivatable spot, for Death's garden-ground; and Death shall teach us to beautify it, grave by grave. By our sweet, calm way of dying, and the airy elegance out of which we will shape our funeral rites, and the cheerful allegories which we will model into tombstones, the final scene shall lose its terrors . . . (p. 130)

and more in the same vein. His tone as always tends uncon-
trollably towards the facetious, so that, even if he wants to
take something seriously, by the time he has finished talking
about it he has either undermined, ridiculed, banalized, or
vaporized it. In this scene, it is quite understandable that the
grim, humourless Hollingsworth is irritated by what he feels
is Coverdale's 'nonsense'. I will come to Coverdale and his
hapless, or worse, errancies of tone. Here I just want to stress
that, although the tone of this speech is all wrong, the content
is half right. What he touches on banteringly, another American poet, Louis Simpson, formulates with more appropriate
seriousness in the last stanza of his poem 'To the Western
World' (1955):

> The treasures of Cathay were never found.
> In this America, this wilderness
> Where the axe echoes with a lonely sound,
> The generations labor to possess
> And grave by grave we civilize the ground.

The treasures of Cathay, the fields of Arcadia, the phalansteries[3] of Utopia—alike, never found—or founded. Though
some people may have been the better for the searching.
Maybe better, and then again maybe worse. That is a part of
what this book is about. What Coverdale has to confront—
and not as a matter for banter, or light literary conceits, or the
pale, etiolated images of a Puvis de Chavannes—is that, yes it
is 'grave by grave' (his phrase as well as Simpson's) that we
civilize the ground; that *death* is 'the real'; and that only by
properly assimilating that will he—will we—find the real in
anything else. By the end, of course, Blithedale has its grave.
It contains the body of Zenobia, the figure accorded most
physical, sexual, reality by Coverdale's account. Judging by
the concluding chapter which follows her burial, she effectively, for Coverdale, takes 'the real' into the grave with her.

In Coverdale's story his primary involvement—if that is
the word for his self-retentive, self-protective proximities to
other people—is with Hollingsworth, Zenobia, and Priscilla.
But he has a crucial conversation with the shadowy figure of

---

[3] See explanatory note to p. 19.

Old Moodie, who is indeed the first person who speaks to Coverdale (with a request which Coverdale characteristically shrinks from complying with). The shadowy Moodie turns out to be the father, by different mothers (one brilliant and voluptuous, the other a 'poor phantom') of the allegorically opposed half-sisters, Zenobia and Priscilla. Late in the book, in a saloon (and I shall return to this setting), Moodie tells Coverdale his life story, which Coverdale then reconstitutes and writes down, with his customary speculative largesse ('my pen has perhaps allowed itself a trifle of romantic and legendary license' (p. 181)). For the purposes of his story—one might, following Melville's use of the phrase, term it an 'inside narrative'—Coverdale rebaptizes Moodie and mystifies his origin. 'Five-and-twenty years ago . . . there dwelt, in one of the middle states, a man whom we shall call Fauntleroy . . .' (p. 182). Coverdale has a rather coy way with names which I shall look at later, but here I want to pause on the pseudonym—or is it the true name *behind* the name (but then what *is* a *true* name?)—he has chosen.

And first I want to point to an important word he deploys on just two occasions. After recounting Zenobia's passionate words spoken at Eliot's Pulpit, Coverdale wonders if they amounted to no more than a 'stage declamation'. 'Were they formed of a material lighter than common air? Or, supposing them to bear *sterling* weight, was it not a perilous and dreadful wrong, which she was meditating towards herself and Hollingsworth?' (p. 127; my italics). After they have recovered the corpse of Zenobia, rigid in an attitude of prayer but now disfigured and mutilated, Coverdale writes: 'A reflection occurs to me, that will show ludicrously, I doubt not, on my page, but must come in, for its *sterling* truth' (p. 236; my italics). The reflection is that if she could have foreseen what a horrid spectacle she would present when recovered from the river, she would no more have done it than she would have appeared in public wearing a badly fitting garment—that is to say, that she was 'not quite simple in her death', that it contained 'some tint of Arcadian affectation' (p. 237); acting, or counterfeiting, to the end we might say. 'Sterling' is of course the legal tender of what Hawthorne referred to as 'Our

Old Home' (1863), and by extension came to be an epithet meaning 'authentic'. In using the word in these two contexts, Coverdale implicitly raises the question of the problem of authenticity of both spoken and written words. How can we know if *any* words are, as it were, good currency, reliable 'scrip(t)'?

Now, 'Fauntleroy', it appeared, committed a crime which led him to flee to New England and live the shady, shadowy life of Old Moodie. And this crime 'was just the sort of crime, growing out of its artificial state, which society (unless it should change its entire constitution for this man's unworthy state) neither could nor ought to pardon. More safely might it pardon murder' (p. 183). This heinous crime would seem to be literally unspeakable, or unwritable, since Coverdale never names it. But, since the appearance of an article by Charles Swann,[4] there can be no doubt that the crime was forgery. Henry Fauntleroy (1785–1824), a London banker who was also a spendthrift forger, became what one writer described as 'the prototypal forger for his contemporaries'. He was caught and executed, though there was a rumour that he had mysteriously escaped death (by inserting a silver tube in his throat to avoid strangulation) and gone abroad, where he lived for many years. All this was reported at length in the *Gentleman's Magazine*, which we know Hawthorne read (he was in any case an avid reader of newspaper accounts of criminal cases), and it is marvellously to his purpose. By seeming to pluck a pseudonym out of the air at random and actually fastening on the—at the time well-known—name of a notorious English forger, Coverdale releases suggestive resonances which permeate the whole book he is writing.

The worryingly close similarity between writing fiction (or coining images) and counterfeiting the currency on which society depends (which is why the crime was regarded as more socially undermining than murder since it abuses the trust—ruins by falsifying and thus depreciating the 'value'— which enables social exchange and coherence) has often occurred to artists. What is a 'true' copy? How can you tell

---

[4] C. Swann, 'A Note on *The Blithedale Romance* or "Call him Fauntleroy"', *Journal of American Studies*, 10 (1976), 103–4.

the difference between 'forging' the uncreated conscience of your race, and the kind of forgery the police hunt down? You can, of course, but to a certain kind of writer it can seem that, at a certain level, both 'forgers' work by putting falsities/ fictions into circulation. The matter has certainly worried more than one American writer (cf. *The Recognitions* by William Gaddis). But Hawthorne is effectively doing more than throw ironic light on the possible dubiety of his own writerly activity. Fauntleroy is a quintessentially European name, literally containing a recognition of that royalty (*le roi*) which America had violently repudiated in the process of asserting its own identity. Perhaps if Henry Fauntleroy *had* somehow escaped and come to live abroad—and where more obvious than America for his long declining years (he was thirty-nine when he was 'executed' and would have been fifty-six when the Blithedalers were forgathering)?—he would indeed be indistinguishable from Old Moodie. And *that* might suggest that, in addition to all the obvious beliefs and practices—in religion, law, literature—which America had inherited, or transplanted, from Our Old Home, it had latterly received a more sinister and unforeseen bequest— fakery. Dissimulation on an unknowably large scale. Or perhaps America replicated the English Fauntleroy with its own version engendered in those vague 'middle states'. Either way, Mr Fauntleroy has bequeathed to society, in the form of his children, not the customary patriarchal law and authority, but something catastrophically opposite—the seeds of paternal inauthenticity. Priscilla is more a void than a value (victim, too, perhaps): that she should 'triumph' or at least be the main survivor of the Blithedale experiment is by no means an unequivocally felicitous conclusion. While Zenobia, with her 'uncomfortable surplus of vitality' (p. 96), seemed to be the force which helped to drive Blithedale, Lady of the Revels, Queen of Arcadia. Was she all counterfeit? Was there *no* 'sterling' there? If so, the implications do not bear too much pondering—for that way lies the sort of scepticism, or distrust, which terminates in the nihilism of Billy Budd's posthumous rhetorical question—'aren't it all a sham?'[5] This is

[5] H. Melville, *Billy Budd, Foretopman* (1924; New York: Library of America, 1989), 1435.

the other end—or is it the other side?—of the quest for the Real.

All this goes some way to explaining Coverdale's, and the book's, obsession with veils and veilings of all kinds. But before addressing that, I want to revert to Coverdale's slightly teasing, slightly uncomfortable, way with 'names'. We may start with a short, jocular exchange between Coverdale and Old Moodie before he settles down to hear the life story or confessional reminiscences of the great forger—not that he is going to name *that*—to be recounted by, call him Fauntleroy, in the local saloon. A bottle of claret arrives. '"It should be good wine," I remarked, "if it have any right to its label." "You cannot suppose, sir," said Moodie, with a sigh, "that a poor old fellow, like me, knows any difference in wines"' (p. 180). Nor any differencies in currencies, in view of the story he is about to tell. More interesting is Coverdale's, perhaps habitual, suspicion. Does anything—anyone—have a 'right to its label'? What is it—what could it be—to have a *right* to a label? Take 'Zenobia'. What is the relationship between that 'label' and the intoxicatingly full-bodied wine of a woman who pours through these pages?

In Chapter II Coverdale says, or writes, to us, concerning 'Zenobia':

This (as the reader, if at all acquainted with our literary biography, need scarcely be told) was not her real name. She had assumed it, in the first instance, as her magazine signature; and as it accorded well with something imperial which her friends attributed to this lady's figure and deportment, they, half-laughingly, adopted it in their familiar intercourse with her. She took the appellation in good part, and even encouraged its constant use ... (p. 13)

Real name? Where might we find that? Not in this book, certainly. When Westervelt comes to Blithedale seeking information concerning 'Zenobia', Coverdale somewhat ineffectually hedges by replying: '"That is her name in literature ... a name, too, which possibly she may permit her private friends to know and address her by;—but not one which they feel at liberty to recognize, when used of her, personally, by a stranger or casual acquaintance."' As it transpires, Westervelt is no stranger or casual acquaintance—though whether he is/was Zenobia's lover or husband is never named, or, perhaps we should say, spelled out—and here he replies, '"I am willing to know her by any cognomen that you may suggest."' Appellation, cognomen—what is the real name for a 'name'? Disliking Westervelt and wishing to get rid of him, Coverdale writes: 'I mentioned Zenobia's real name' (p. 93). Mentions it to Westervelt, but never to us. You could say that Zenobia's real name in real life was Margaret Fuller[6] and that Hawthorne, in his characteristically enigmatic way, is effectively saying: he who runs may read. But in terms of the novel as novel, that simply will not do. Coverdale as narrator is showing us that he is keeping something back—cover-ing it indeed—leaving us with a very uncertain sense of the relationship, in his story, between labels and bottles, people and names. Call him Fauntleroy: call her Zenobia. This, after a famous neighbour had started a great novel: 'Call me Ishmael'. Westervelt admits to Coverdale that '"my business is private, personal, and somewhat peculiar"' (p. 93). I think Coverdale, as writer, could say the same.

But the most interesting play with names occurs when a committee is formed 'for providing our infant Community with an appropriate name'. It is a more revealing moment than covering Coverdale lets on.

Blithedale was neither good nor bad. We should have resumed the old Indian name of the premises, had it possessed the oil-and-honey flow which the aborigines were so often happy in communicating to their local appellations; but it chanced to be a harsh, ill-connected, and interminable word, which seemed to fill the mouth with a mixture of very stiff clay and very crumbly pebbles. Zenobia suggested 'Sunny Glimpse' . . . too fine and sentimental a name . . . I ventured to whisper 'Utopia', which, however, was unanimously scouted down . . . Some were for calling our institution 'The Oasis,' . . . others insited on a proviso for reconsidering the matter, at a twelvemonth's end; when a final decision might be had, whether to name it 'The Oasis,' or 'Saharah.' So, at last, finding it impracticable to hammer out anything better, we resolved that the spot should still be Blithedale, as being of good augury enough. (p. 37)

The alternatives are anodyne and cosy enough—the sort of names you could doubtless see on some middle-class homes

---

[6] See explanatory note to p. 52, Miss Margaret Fuller.

and, in due course, on motels. But I wonder what that harsh and interminable 'old Indian name' was, the name given to the place by the, after all, ab-original inhabitants? That surely might be a label which, as it were, had a right to its bottle. Here we must 'go behind' a little, an activity particularly justified by this book, as I hope to show.

John Eliot, the famous apostle to the Indians and a leading founding Puritan, is a very important name in the book; more of that later. Crucially, he undertook to learn the language of the Indians, the better to preach to them. In *Magnalia Christi Americana*—almost a founding volume for America and one which not only Hawthorne but many of his readers would have known—Cotton Mather wrote the 'Life of John Eliot' and in particular animadverted on the great difficulties involved in mastering the Indian language:

but if their *Alphabet* be *short*, I am sure the *Words* composed of it are long enough to trie the Patience of any Scholar in the World; they are *Sesquidipedalia Verba*, of which their *Lingua* is composed; one would think, they had been growing ever since *Babel*, unto the Dimensions to which they are now extended. For instance, if my reader will count how many Letters there are in this one Word, *Nummatchekodtantamooonganunnonash*, when he has done, for his Reward I'll tell him, it signifies no more in *English*, than *our lusts*, and if I were to translate, *our Loves*; it must be nothing shorter than *Noowomantammooonkanunonnash*. Or, to give my Reader a longer Word than either of these, *Kummogkodonattoottummooetiteaongannunnonash*, is, in English, *Our Question*: But I pray, Sir, count the Letters! ... This tedious Language, our *Eliot* (the anagram of whose name was TOILE) quickly became a master of...[7]

Hellish difficult: why, says Mather, I tried it out on the *Daemons* of a possessed woman, and, although they had no trouble with Greek and Hebrew, they just could not cope with Indian. (Another justification, perhaps, for eliminating these tedious Lewis Carrolls of the forest.) Now perhaps the 'real name' of Blithedale was just such an 'ill-connected and interminable word' as the ones cited by Cotton Mather. Somewhat too harsh for the genteel New Englanders. Better

[7] C. Mather, *The Puritans*, ed. P. Miller and T. H. Johnson (New York, 1939), ii. 506.

change the label—something more soft and sweet. Something, too, which gets rid of the grating (and potentially embarrassing—whose Utopia was this?) otherness and Indianness of the original name. As a result, somehow the wrong book is being written. As a matter of fact, 'Our Lusts, Our Loves, Our Question' would have been no bad name for the site of this story, no bad title for the novel itself. I am suggesting, quite improperly, that the book we *should* have would have been *The History of Nummatchekodtantamooonganunnonash, Noowomantammooonkanunonnash, and Kummogkodonattoottummooetiteaongannunnonash* by Nathaniel Hawthorne. Instead we have *The Blithedale Romance* by Miles Coverdale—a sentimental over-writing of an earlier, uglier and harsher reality which is unpronounceable, unhandlable, unwritable. The Devil himself would not understand it. 'Blithedale' is a cover: indeed it is a 'Coverdale'—the narrator is peculiarly well named.

Names then, or names as Coverdale and some of his characters use them, are veils (and I have added the suggestion that the book itself is a kind of veil). An article by Frank Davidson[8] scrupulously notes the prolific references to veils and veilings throughout the novel. It has to be said, it would be hard *not* to notice them. The novel opens with a description of 'the wonderful exhibition of the Veiled Lady' (p. 5), and, in one way or another, the whole novel is a 'veiled exhibition'. In Frank Davidson's words, 'Almost everything in the romance except "the naked exposure" in Westervelt "of something that ought not to be left prominent" is partially hidden or totally obscured by a veiling medium or mask.'[9] Literal veils, false names, mysterious and mystified life histories (the whole Old Moodie/Fauntleroy family has an unpenetrated and perhaps impenetrable past—perhaps, in this, like America itself), and a general disposition towards 'screening' of all kinds—these are the hallmarks of the book. Old Moodie himself is, fittingly enough, particularly and literally self-effacing, as one might say—'He had a queer

[8] F. Davidson, 'Toward a Revaluation of *The Blithedale Romance*', *New England Quarterly*, 25/3 (1952), 374–83.
[9] Ibid. 376.

appearance of hiding himself behind the patch on his left eye' (p. 82); 'his upper part was mostly hidden behind the shrubbery' (p. 83); in the tavern Coverdale 'recognized his hand and arm, protruding from behind a screen' (p. 178)—but his is only the most extreme case of a general tendency to lead a masked life.

The case of Westervelt is interesting. One should note that the characters seem to have differing ontological statuses—more real and less real in differing ways—and he is at once the most masked and the most exposed. Like his teeth, the man is *manifestly* 'a sham'—he is all 'humbug'; his face might be 'removeable like a mask'; there is 'nothing genuine about him', his visage is like 'polished steel' (pp. 95, 173) (reminding me of a Faulkner character whose face has 'the depthless brutality of stamped tin'). He leaves the tale as he enters it—mysteriously, independently, his power unassailed. Coverdale, in one of his frequent less than charitable moods, dismisses him, hoping that Heaven will 'annihilate him. He was altogether earthy, worldly, made for time and its gross objects, and incapable ... of so much as one spiritual idea' (p. 241). That is all very well, except that there is precious little 'idealism' in the book that is not badly compromised by the end. In all his fakery and falsity there is, nevertheless, that 'naked exposure of something that ought not to be left prominent' (p. 92)—unlike the river with its 'broad, black inscrutable depth, keeping its secrets from the eye of man' (p. 232).

Coverdale does not attempt to put a name to that naked something Westervelt leaves indecently showing (he would rather cover than name), but we can perhaps suggest it is his shameless appetite and will-to-power. Although Hollingsworth rescues Priscilla from him, Westervelt—on his own terms—is the most powerful figure in the book. Of the male figures, it is only he, so we are allowed to gather, who has possessed Zenobia sexually. Man of mask he may be, but, looked at from one point of view, there is more *to* him than to the narrator. Coverdale's description of Christ as 'One, who merely veiled himself in mortal and masculine shape, but was, in truth, divine' (p. 121) suggests that corporeality, sheer or mere physicality, is the unreal for Coverdale, an orthodox enough Transcendentalist tenet. Yet he is strangely drawn to the farm's pigs, 'involved, and almost stifled, and buried alive, in their own corporeal substance', and ponders 'the ponderous and fat satisfaction of their existence' (p. 144). Hawthorne particularly disliked fat on women (you should be allowed to cut it off, he, let us hope jocularly, maintained), and perhaps some of his ambivalence to flesh and fleshliness has got into Coverdale, but it is hard to find in the book any very deep conviction of the existence of any divine, spiritual, or ideal realm of Reality. Perhaps the corporeal veil is all we have got—not a thought for Coverdale, or even Hawthorne, to be easy with. Zenobia's farewell declaration concludes: '"When you next hear of Zenobia, her face will be behind the black veil . . ."' (p. 228). In the event it will be the black veil of the river, which now has another secret to keep.

More than anything else, veils ask to be looked behind, and Coverdale, who takes a 'back-room' in the hotel in town, makes a speciality of looking behind. Literally.

Bewitching to my fancy are all those nooks and crannies, where Nature, like a stray partridge, hides her head among the long-established haunts of men! It is likewise to be remarked, as a general rule, that there is far more of the picturesque, more truth to native and characteristic tendencies, and vastly greater suggestiveness, in the back view of a residence, whether in town or country, than in its front. The latter is always artificial; it is meant for the world's eye, and is therefore a veil and a concealment. Realities keep in the rear, and put forward an advance-guard of show and humbug. (p. 149)

Realities keep in the rear. Coverdale is interested (and excited by) 'posterior aspects' (p. 149)—in every sense, we may say. He announces his predilection—unambiguously enough we might feel—for getting acquainted with 'the backside of the universe' (p. 148). His curiosity, not least his sexual curiosity, is high and easily inflamed. In his last recorded comment on Hawthorne (in a letter of 1904) Henry James summed up what he admired about Hawthorne with apt words: he saw 'the interest *behind* the interest'.[10] In an essay of 1896 he had spelt it out at greater length.

[10] H. James, *Essays on Literature, American Writers, English Writers* (New York, 1984), 471.

It was a question of looking behind and beneath for the suggestive idea, the artistic motive . . . This ingenuity grew alert and irrepressible as it manoeuvred for the back view and turned up the under side of common aspects,—the laws secretly broken, the impulses secretly felt, the hidden passions, the double lives, the dark corners, the closed rooms, the skeletons in the cupboard and at the feast.[11]

'Behind and beneath' became one of James's favourite phrases as he grew more and more fascinated with 'the things *behind*', and one of the things behind was, awesomely and sometimes seemingly ubiquitously, the sexual.

Realities keep in the rear. All Coverdale's compulsive 'looking behind'—literally of houses, speculatively of people, their motives, their pasts, their relationships—suggests that, effete voyeur though he himself is, he has more than half a notion that he might find 'the real' in the sexual. Though, being the man he is, he is certainly not going to write like D. H. Lawrence! But he likes to imagine Zenobia naked and brood lasciviously on her past: '"Zenobia is a wife! Zenobia has lived, and loved! There is no folded petal, no latent dewdrop, in this perfectly developed rose"' (p. 47). And, talking of petals and roses, what is one to make of such a passage as the following, describing Priscilla's silk purses:

Their peculiar excellence, besides the great delicacy and beauty of the manufacture, lay in the almost impossibility that any uninitiated person should discover the aperture; although, to a practised touch, they would open as wide as charity or prodigality might wish. I wondered if it were not a symbol of Priscilla's own mystery. (p. 35)

One can only wonder at the sort of tacit cultural collusion which could maintain that no possibility of any *double entendre* and thus nothing remotely lubricious should attach to such writing, while being constantly ready to recoil in real or simulated horror if matters pertaining to sexual actualities were explicitly named. Coverdale, self-cosseting bachelor that he is, is not a passionate man, but he is a mighty prurient one; he is also a shameless fetishist: after Zenobia's corpse is recovered, he eagerly takes one of her shoes and has 'kept it ever since' (p. 232). The original Coverdale was the first translator of the Bible, in a version reputedly pretty inaccurate

[11] Ibid. 459.

but with some sudden arresting felicities. The same could be said of this Coverdale book, though what he translates is Fourier (likewise inaccurately if the one example we are given is anything to go by). Fourierism at that time was a code-word for free love and a byword for promiscuity—such as Coverdale more than hints obtained at Blithedale. (More than fifty Fourierist communities sprang up in America between 1840 and 1860, not all, of course, emphasizing the need for the multiple sexual servicing of their members.)[12] He admits to a certain male grossness of imagination, and, while we may choose not to place much credence on the concluding line of the book in which he claims that he was in love with Priscilla all along (a line opportunistically added by Hawthorne the day he dispatched the manuscript), we can feel fairly sure that he would not be above fantasizing about fingering and opening the aperture to Priscilla's purse, running more to prodigality than to charity perhaps.

When he is outlining what they hoped to erect and achieve at Blithedale, Coverdale undermines the formulaic and pro-grammatic optimism of their original intentions and ex-pectations with an unusual metaphor.

Altogether, by projecting our minds outward, we had imparted a show of novelty to existence, and contemplated it as hopefully as if the soil, beneath our feet, had not been fathom-deep with the dust of deluded generations, on every one of which, as on ourselves, the world had imposed itself as a hitherto unwedded bride. (p. 128)

It is, characteristically, an erotic image; but it reveals much more than that. In an important essay Lauren Berlant glosses the passage as follows:

This 'people', according to Coverdale, sees the present moment as a hopeful fore-gleam of a future luminescence. But the scene of utopian fantasy is founded on the repression of histories that would, presumably, challenge the 'fact' of our present existence: Coverdale notes that his follow workers act as if they are the land's first tillers and, by association, the nation's first utopians. But the community's historical amnesia with respect to the utopian projects that have preceded it reveals that American history has never been written or

[12] See explanatory note to p. 52, Charles Fourier.

even thought. It has only been repressed, buried by new 'dirt,' new stories. America, in this view, is always distinctively post-Utopian, but has never 'known' it.[13]

The image of the 'unwedded bride' suggests that Utopian dreams, hopes, and desires are dependent on, perhaps a function of, 'virginity' in every sense.

But when historical and sexual knowledge comes, when 'the world had imposed itself' upon us, we lose the clarity of utopian, libidinal perfection. The postvirginal bride who weds her demystifying knowledge to us is simultaneously the source of our historical consciousness, our historical amnesia, and our personal nostalgia for those moments before her 'knowledge' atomized our whole bodies and destroyed our utopian collective dreams.[14]

A striking example of such historical amnesia is given by Coverdale himself when Hollingsworth, describing his 'visionary edifice' for the reform of criminals, says: '"But I offer my edifice as a spectacle to the world . . . that it may take example and build many another like it. Therefore I mean to set it on the open hill-side"' (p. 80). The echo of John Winthrop's 'city on a hill' speech—a sort of foundational American declaration—could hardly be clearer. But it is lost on Coverdale. 'Twist these words how I might, they offered no very satisfactory import' (p. 80). If he can forget *that*, what may not an American writer forget? And yet Coverdale sees the Blithedale venture as both a recapitulation and an extension of the first Puritan errand into the wilderness, and he and his friends as 'the descendants of the Pilgrims, whose high enterprise, as we sometimes flattered ourselves, we had taken up, and were carrying it onward and aloft, to a point which they never dreamed of attaining' (p. 117). One may wonder if he has that original 'high enterprise' very clearly in his mind—and what it entailed for the original inhabitants.

This is the point of one of the slyest barbs, which Hawthorne releases through Coverdale when he describes the site of Eliot's Pulpit: 'as wild a tract of woodland as the great-

---

[13] L. Berlant, 'Fantasies of Utopia in *The Blithedale Romance*', *American Literary History*, 1/1 (1989), 30–62; pp. 31–2

[14] Ibid. 32.

great-great-great grandson of one of Eliot's Indians (had any such posterity been in existence) could have desired, for the site and shelter of his wigwam' (p. 118). As here quite literally, the Indians have everywhere been 'bracketed out' of American history. This is why the name of John Eliot is important in the book. He was a figure who, as it were, tried to bracket the Indians *in*—even while his contemporaries continued the work of dispossession. He set up 'praying towns' for numbers of Indians, and there is no reason to doubt the sincerity of his desire to transform, reclaim by converting, the manifestly un-Elect Indians. Coverdale 'romanticizes' Eliot—that, after all, is what he is writing: 'I used to see the holy Apostle of the Indians, with the sunlight flickering down upon him through the leaves, and glorifying his figure as with the half-perceptible glow of a transfiguration' (p. 119). If he had historicized Eliot, Coverdale might have brought to mind, and written in, the fact that Eliot created in his Christianized Indians vulnerable hybrids who could never survive. They were wiped out in King Philip's War (1673–5), not least because they were not yet fully trusted by the whites, and no longer trusted by the Indians. This must be marked up as another Utopian project which ended in disastrous failure. Or rather, not marked up but left out. Coverdale takes (makes) the Romance—the saint in the wilderness;—and forgets the history—the subsequent victims. Eliot trying to convert his Indians is clearly replicated in some way by Hollingsworth dedicated to reforming his criminals, another too fanatical attempt to assimilate the marginalized, or—to use a phrase of Bernard Schlurick—'le verrouillage de l'autre dans le même' (the locking up of the other in the same).[15] It is another massive failure. No criminals are reclaimed; instead Hollingsworth feels he has been criminalized by causing Zenobia's suicide.

I am not, in this introduction, going to discuss the characters and characterization. Henry James's summary in the essay of 1896 can hardly be bettered.

---

[15] Personal communication.

The idea that he most tangibly presents is that of the unconscious way in which the search for the common good may cover a hundred interested impulses and personal motives; the suggestion that such a company could only be bound together more by its delusions, its mutual suspicions and frictions, than by any successful surrender of the self.[16]

Psychologically, Hawthorne was clearly still interested in how relationships could in fact be power struggles, contests of adverse wills, as he dramatized most clearly in Chapter XIII of *The House of the Seven Gables*, 'Alice Pyncheon', in which Matthew Maule literally mesmerizes the proud Alice in an agonistic contest of the eyes. 'She instinctively knew, it may be, that some sinister or evil potency was now striving to pass her barriers; nor would she decline the contest. So Alice put woman's might against man's might; a match not often equal on the part of the woman.'[17] Indeed not. Matthew achieves total dominion, domination, saying to himself, '"She is mine! ... Mine, by the right of the strongest spirit."'[18] Hawthorne had a strikingly adversarial and appropriative sense of human relationships—'sharkish', Melville might have said—and this is again in evidence in the struggles between Hollingsworth and Zenobia, Hollingsworth and Coverdale, and the struggles over Priscilla. All this is clear enough in the book. But a word should be said about one of its central concerns—Reform.

'In the history of the world the doctrine of Reform had never such scope as at the present hour'—thus Emerson in 1841 in 'Man the Reformer'.[19] There was an extraordinary proliferation, explosion indeed, of reform literature and movements in antebellum America. In his very interesting work, *Beneath the American Renaissance*, David Reynolds describes this vast literature and suggests very plausibly how it affected the now-regarded major writers. Initially this reform literature was conventional.

---

[16] James, *Essays*, p. 464.
[17] N. Hawthorne, *The House of the Seven Gables* (1851; New York: Library of America, 1983), 527.
[18] Ibid. 529.
[19] *Emerson* (New York: Library of America, 1983), 135.

As time passed, however, there arose a strong subversive element, seen in a succession of vociferous reformers whose loudly announced goal was to stamp out various behavioral sins or social iniquities—intemperance, licentiousness, urban poverty, chattel and wage slavery, poor prison conditions, and so forth—but who described vice in such lurid detail that they were branded as dangerously immoral and sacrilegious. The *immoral* or *dark reformers*, as I call them, used didactic rhetoric as a protective shield for highly unconventional explorations of tabooed psychological and spiritual areas. ... for both Hawthorne and Melville contemporary reform devices and themes provided an inroad toward literary ambiguity.[20]

'The dark reformers are largely responsible for transforming a culture of morality into a culture of ambiguity.'[21] The flood of this literature would seem to have had a destabilizing effect on the old certainties, even the old ontologies. Reynolds quotes from *The Quaker City* by George Lippard (1845), in which a character, bewildered by the instabilities and amoralities surrounding him, complains: '"Every thing fleeting and nothing stable, everything shifting and changing, and nothing substantial!"'[22] Reynolds comments: 'each of the major authors at one time or another expressed puzzlement and terror over the relativism implied by this fluid reform environment'.[23]

As we have seen at the start, this is certainly true of Coverdale, and he, of course, is surrounded by—up to his neck (though not his heart) in—reform movements of all kinds: prison reform, Associationism, temperance, feminism, spiritualism, mesmerism. Perhaps he does not directly confront the implication of his own writing (and non-writing)—namely that you cannot hope, and perhaps should hardly seek, to build a Utopia on a land stained by genocide and already replete with the dust of earlier failures. There is much talk of 'systems' in the book—throwing off old systems, devising new ones—but Coverdale finally finds that this talk is moving him towards a kind of vertigo of unreality.

[20] D. Reynolds, *Beneath the American Renaissance* (Cambridge, Mass., 1988), 55–6.
[21] Ibid. 59.
[22] Quoted in ibid. 84.
[23] Ibid. 85.

I was beginning to lose the sense of what kind of world it was, among innumerable schemes of what it might or ought to be. It was impossible, situated as we were, not to imbibe the idea that everything in nature and human existence was fluid, or fast becoming so; that the crust of the Earth, in many places, was broken, and its whole surface portentously upheaving; that it was a day of crisis, and that we ourselves were in the critical vortex. Our great globe floated in the atmosphere of infinite space like an unsubstantial bubble. No sagacious man will long retain his sagacity, if he lives exclusively among reformers and progressive people, without periodically returning into a settled system of things, to correct himself by a new observation from that old stand-point. (pp. 140–1)

After a quick good-bye to the pigs, he heads for town and some restabilizing talk with a few Cambridge conservatives. So we may return to our opening question. What *is* Hawthorne doing with—through—Miles Coverdale?

From the start, commentators on the book have noted and stressed that, whatever else he is, Coverdale is pre-eminently an observer.

Coverdale is a picture of the contemplative, observant, analytic nature, nursing its fancies, and yet, thanks to an element of strong good sense, not bringing them up to be spoiled children; having little at stake in life, at any given moment, and yet indulging, in imagination, in a good many adventures; a portrait of a man, in a word, whose passions are slender, whose imagination is active, and whose happiness lies, not in doing, but in perceiving—half a poet, half a critic, and all a spectator.[24]

Thus Henry James, seeing Coverdale, we might think, in the most generous possible light. Not, perhaps, surprisingly, since his own subsequent work would turn out to be well-populated with just such slender-passioned imaginative spectators as he here describes. Writing nearly one hundred years later, Richard Poirier is more diagnostic and critical:

one consequence of an idealism gone sour can be the self-absorbed fastidiousness of a character like Coverdale . . . A somewhat sickly, somewhat even masturbatory quality in Coverdale's self-regarding retreat is evident even in the images describing it. It is as if he were retreating into a state not of heightened consciousness but of death

[24] James, *Essays*, p. 419.

... Hawthorne is here showing us the transformations of a sort of Emersonian man into a Dandy. ... a man incapable of human fellowship.[25]

James thought that Hawthorne had put himself into Coverdale ('Miles Coverdale is evidently as much Hawthorne as he is any one else in particular'), but that is necessarily imponderable. What is clear is that Hawthorne is attempting a kind of self-revelatory portrait of an American artist at a particular, and particularly problematic, moment of time—rather, artist *manqué*, just as Coverdale is also a lover *manqué*, idealist *manqué*, Utopianist *manqué*, communalist *manqué*, farmer *manqué*, citizen both of country and world *manqué*, arguably human *manqué* who comes to rest in metaphorical sillabubs and actual sherry-cobblers. After diaries of nobodies and confessions of superfluous men, not to mention notes from underground and men without qualities, we are quite familiar with self-marginalizing, self-deprecating, even self-immolating narrators. But there is no narrator like him in earlier American literature (or in English, come to that) and I just want to ponder some of the possible implications of Hawthorne's handing over the telling of his novel to such a figure.

He is, we may say, bricked-in, bricked-up, from the start: 'a lodger—like myself—in one of the midmost houses of a brick-block; each house partaking of the warmth of all the rest' (p. 10). Since he is a 'frosty bachelor' (p. 9), this generalized, anonymous communal warmth is no doubt welcome to him, and I shall return to his ambiguous need for heat. Here I want to note that Coverdale is in fact a generic 'lodger'. He is most at home in apartments, hotel rooms, taverns—places of transience. Even at Blithedale, for all his simulated commitment, he was only ever, really, passing through. He has a cat-like knack of making himself comfortable, particularly in his own apartment, but he is truly at home nowhere. Taking the word with its broadest implications, the 'lodger' as failed artist, or the failed artist as 'lodger', was a new figure for Hawthorne to have introduced into American literature. And I think it has something to do with the spread of the 'brick-

[25] R. Poirier, *A World Elsewhere* (London, 1967), 116–22.

block'—let us call it the suburbanization of America. I take the word from a very important sentence in the novel. It concerns the audience at the village Lyceum-hall where the (melo-)drama of the 'Veiled Lady' is to be enacted. Coverdale lists the varied occupations of this audience—farmers, shop-keepers, lawyers, students, and so on—and comments: 'all looking rather suburban than rural. In these days, there is absolutely no rusticity, except when the actual labor of the soil leaves its earth-mould on the person' (p. 197). It was in quest of some such absolute 'rusticity' that Coverdale went to Blithedale, even to the extent of indeed getting 'earth-mould' on his person. And what he discovered is that it cannot be done. The attempt is *bound* to seem affected, factitious. The suburban lodger can never, despite or perhaps because of his sentimental pastoral nostalgia, reachieve or rediscover any absolute 'rusticity'—always supposing, of course, that there ever was such a thing. Suburban, not urban—suburbia as that indeterminate, homogenizing area between the true town and the real country, which seeks to combine the comforts and amenities of the one with the beauties and felicities of the other, arguably, in the process, losing contact with the differing, dynamic energies of both. Hawthorne was astute enough to see that it was becoming increasingly difficult to avoid—ontologically, let us say—some variant of the sub-urban condition. Lodgers—in a sense—all, or most, of us.

This is why Coverdale's tone is so uncertain, veering always towards self-defeating facetiousness. He says he might join an Exploring Expedition up the Nile, or go and fight for Kossuth in Hungary, but just to formulate the notional possibilities is to become aware of their absurd unrealizabil-ity. 'Suburbanized' self-consciousness seems to corrode in advance any possibility of significant action and commitment. (In this, Coverdale is remarkably similar to the narrator figures of the poetry of Arthur Hugh Clough.) He tries to throw himself into Blithedale, and even seems to undergo some temporary re-birth there, but very soon he finds that he has, as it were, come out on the other side, floundering among failed hyperboles, bitter scepticism, and bathetic self-ridi-cule. But *is* there a right tone for Blithedale? Is it not from the

start an impossible and doomed project? Economically—
'I very soon became sensible, that, as regarded society at
large, we stood in a position of new hostility, rather than new
brotherhood' (p. 20)—and socially; it seems soon to disin-
tegrate into the centrifugality of unaligned power-plays—it is
something of a disaster. Everybody is, more or less, posing
(leaving aside Priscilla, who has something of an object
status) and at least Coverdale *knows* he is posing. The motives
of some of the other leading figures at Blithedale would not
stand much scrutiny—particularly Hollingsworth's—and we
may want to look again at Coverdale's motives, for at least he
seems to have the virtue, even if it has curiously deleterious
effects, of refusing to succumb to the lures of self-deception.
At Blithedale and after, he is, indeed, the less—the least—
deceived.

One thing he is not is an 'unreliable narrator', if by that we
mean a narrator who, we somehow gather, is seeking to
deceive the reader and probably him or her self, by dis-
ingenuousness, editing out, reformulation, or whatever (there
are distinct traces of this in the narrative account of Gatsby
by Nick Carraway, who otherwise is the American narrator
who bears the greatest resemblance to Coverdale). Coverdale
readily admits, when he does not positively flaunt the fact,
that he has endless recourse to supplementation, speculation,
fabrication, imagination, fantasy—the lot, you might say.
'I hardly could make out an intelligible sentence, on either
side. What I seem to remember, I yet suspect may have been
patched together by my fancy, in brooding over the matter,
afterwards' (p. 104)—this is a characteristic admission. He is
usually too far away in some sense or another—up the tree of
his 'hermitage', in a distant hotel room looking through
windows over which curtains are suddenly drawn—out of
earshot and eyeshot. When he returns to Blithedale, he says:
'Had it been evening, I would have stolen to some lighted
window of the old farm-house, and peeped darkling in . . .'
(p. 207)—a dark peeper, and a peeper usually in the dark.
Such is the darkling voyeur who nevertheless writes—fabric-
ates, forges—a narrative of some considerable length concerning matters of some considerable importance. Of himself,

he writes in the last chapter: 'But what, after all, have I to tell? Nothing, nothing, nothing!' (p. 245). But, though there is a feeling of vacancy, vacuity, at the end, Coverdale has in fact told us a great deal about himself—not only his unreconstructible bachelorhood predilections, but the motivations behind his enquiry, his narrative.

That these motivations are deeply ambiguous he is well aware. The start of Chapter IX is a long meditation on the unhealthiness of devoting oneself 'too exclusively to the study of individual men and women' (p. 69). He makes the acute observation that, if we 'put a friend under our microscope, we thereby insulate him from many of his true relations, magnify his peculiarities, inevitably tear him into parts' (p. 69) and Coverdale knows that he may be doing Hollingsworth 'a great wrong by prying into his character . . . *But I could not help it*' (p. 69; my italics). Blithedale and its inhabitants comprise both a 'problem' which it is his 'business', his 'vocation' (p. 97), to solve and also 'my private theatre' (p. 70), at once an obligation and a pastime. He often makes statements such as 'making my prey of peoples' individualities, as my custom was' (p. 84), and he can recognize that 'That cold tendency, between instinct and intellect, which made me pry with a speculative interest into people's passions and impulses, appeared to have gone far towards unhumanizing my heart' (p. 154). Peep, pry, prey—these are not very pleasant words, and it becomes something of a question whether Coverdale can justify his uncontrollable speculative curiosity—he cannot help it, and will not—even to himself. When he talks about his 'experiments' on people, and collecting them as 'specimens' (p. 160), he is, morally speaking, in the most dangerous of areas as far as Hawthorne is concerned. Zenobia is quite certain of the culpability of his pursuits. '"You know not what you do! It is dangerous, sir, believe me, to tamper thus with earnest human passions, out of your own mere idleness, and for your sport"' (p. 170). She says she will hold him 'responsible' for any future 'mischief' that may follow, on account of his 'interference'. Since the main mischief will be her suicide, the charge is, in effect, a capital one. Again, when he spies on her in town, she indicts him for '"following up your game, groping for human emotions in the dark corners of the heart"' (p. 214). But what she calls his 'game', he also claims is his 'duty'. His main defence of his uncontrollable curiosity and obsessive observation is as follows:

For, was mine a mere vulgar curiosity? Zenobia should have known me better than to suppose it. She should have been able to appreciate that quality of the intellect and the heart, which impelled me (often against my own will, and to the detriment of my own comfort) to live in other lives, and to endeavour—by generous sympathies, by delicate intuitions, by taking note of things too slight for record, and by bringing my human spirit into manifold accordance with the companions whom God assigned me—to learn the secret which was hidden even from themselves. (p. 160)

This, we may think, is to make the best possible case for his compulsions—though there is a bit of a sting in the tail with the last words raising the matter of prying and preying. More generally, it reads like an artist's defence or apologia. The key claim is that the inquisitive spectatorial compulsion derives from, or crucially involves, 'generous sympathy'. It is Hawthorne's achievement, through Coverdale, to suggest just how many other derivations may be involved, what an inextricable cluster of motives may be determining the compulsion to watch, speculate, and 'narrativize'—or peep, pry, and prey.

An obvious comparison with Coverdale is the unnamed first-person narrator (*very* rare in Henry James) of *The Sacred Fount*, who is indeed James's Coverdale. To remind you, this narrator is a weekend guest at a country house party and he spends the time quite frantically speculating about the possible sexual relations—and their effects—among the guests. He may be right and he may be, as some think him, 'mad'. Whatever else, he is undoubtedly obsessive. I will run together some of his statements or claims.

My extraordinary interest in my fellow-creatures. I have more than most men. I've never really seen anyone with half so much. That breeds observation, and observation breeds ideas. . . .

the best example I can give of the intensity of amusement I had at last enabled my private madness to yield me. . . .

the common fault of minds for which the vision of life is an obsession. The obsession pays, if one will; but to pay it has to borrow. . . .

it justified my indiscreet curiosity; it crowned my underhand process with beauty. . . .

I alone was magnificently and absurdly aware—everyone else was benightedly out of it. . . .

I struck myself as knowing again the joy of the intellectual mastery of things unamenable, that joy of determining, almost of creating results. . . .

Light or darkness, my imagination rides me. . . .

The satisfaction of my curiosity is the pacification of my mind. . . .

I couldn't save Mrs. Server, and I couldn't save poor Briss; I *could*, however, guard to the last grain of gold, my precious sense of their loss, their disintegration and their doom.[26]

The key notion here is that of *guardianship*—not of the people involved, since they may be on their unarrestable way to doom and disintegration, but of the observer's *sense* of their experience, which is, by comparison, pure gold. It is, in Jamesian translation, the translator Coverdale's claim. It is somewhat akin to the Conradian notion of art as a constant act of salvage from the perpetual wreckage of life. To this extent, Coverdale, in all his ambiguity, hesitations, mixed motives, and uncertainties of tone, embodies a flawed stance and articulates an equivocal defence which would become increasingly discernible and audible in the art, and among the artists, of the next hundred years. He also reveals some of the dangers which attach to the observer–speculator–empathizer stance.

I had given up my heart and soul to interests that were not mine. What had I ever had to do with them? And why, being now free, should I take this thraldom on me, once again? It was both sad and dangerous . . . to be in too close affinity with the passions, the errors, and misfortunes, of individuals who stood within a circle of their own, into which, if I stept at all, it must be as an intruder, and at a peril that I could not estimate. (p. 206)

[26] H. James, *The Sacred Fount* (1901; New York: Grove Press, 1953), 147, 162, 23, 128, 177, 214, 276, 287, 273.

The artist as 'intruder' is another fine adumbration on
Hawthorne's part. And, while the figures he watches have
'absorbed my life into themselves' (p. 194), he has also
vaporized reality by too much thinking about it. 'I spent
painful hours in recalling these trifles, and rendering them
more misty and unsubstantial than at first, by the quality of
speculative musing, thus kneaded in with them' (p. 194).
Why do it? Why all this kneading and losing? Why incur such
pain and sadness? Why risk such danger? Because he cannot
help it. No wonder James spoke of 'the madness of art'.[27]

In his self-confessed 'frostiness', Coverdale clearly needs
something to warm him up. There are many grateful references to actual domestic fires—his own apartment, we may
infer, was warm even to fugginess—though even here a note
of wariness enters, as when, at Blithedale, he speaks of
enjoying 'the warm and radiant luxury of a *somewhat too
abundant* fire' (p. 23; my italics). Sex, not to put too fine a
point upon it, would also seem to offer the possibility of
thermal consolation, but here again a note of caution enters,
as when, in reference to Zenobia, even Westervelt speaks of
'her *uncomfortable surplus* of vitality' (p. 96; my italics). Just
as Coverdale is drawn to, he draws back from, any heat which
threatens to lead to excess, to involve him in a surplus
abundance. At a, perhaps, higher level, the Transcendentalist
excitations and Utopian warmth of Blithedale seem to hold
out 'delectable visions of the spiritualization of labor' (p. 65).
But materiality remains coldly resistant. 'The clods of earth,
which we so constantly belabored and turned over and over,
were never etherealized into thought. Our thoughts, on the
contrary, were fast becoming cloddish. Our labor symbolized
nothing . . .' (p. 66). This is only a disillusioning deflation if
you feel it must symbolize *something* or else, in Melville's
words, be of little worth. In an admittedly very diluted and
attenuated way, Coverdale is still a late product of that
Puritan–Transcendentalist line of American thought which
requires a second order of justifying meaning behind the
merely materially visible and palpable. If earth is only

[27] *The Complete Tales of Henry James*, ix (London, 1964), 75.

'cloddish', if pigs in the 'fat satisfaction of their existence' (p. 144), have, as it were, got it right—well, says this kind of mentality, what really is it all about? Blithedale might turn out to be a cold comfort farm indeed.

But there is one thing which is guaranteed, and can be relied on, to afford an instant warmth, without involving the difficulties of engaging with other people or bothering about proto-religious convictions—'a sherry-cobbler'. And, away from Blithedale, Coverdale seldom enters his apartment, or a hotel or tavern, without procuring one. Which makes his reference to himself, in the tavern scene, as 'we temperance people' a singular piece of effrontery. That scene (Chapter XXI) again marks an innovation, for I can think of no earlier serious work of American fiction which situates one of its most important scenes in a tavern (temperance tracts with sensationalist accounts of the results of drink already abounded, as David Reynolds has documented,[28] but that is not quite the same thing; and T. S. Arthur's influential *Ten Nights in a Barroom* (1854) was still three years away). Coverdale's mild—let us assume—solitary tippling perhaps only tells us something about his somewhat regressive, oral, narcissistic character—sucking on sillabubs, various. But references to alcohol play an important part in this novel. This is no place to attempt a brief history of alcohol. Suffice it here to remind ourselves that the word itself is Arabic and refers to the paint used to cover the eyelids of the dead—thus having connections with the 'spirit' world—and that in the early years of distilling alcohol in Europe (the fifteenth and sixteenth centuries) it was often closely associated with alchemy, which was involved in the attempts to distil other 'essences', and thus the attempt to produce what we call 'spirits' in some vague way carried overtones of a quest for higher 'spirit-ual' things, even when the searches set themselves in direct opposition.

It is these overtones which Hawthorne exploits. He will deliberately mix realms, as when, for instance, Coverdale imagines Zenobia's death-moment—'her soul, bubbling out

[28] See Reynolds, *Beneath the American Renaissance*.

through her lips, may be' (p. 235). Since we have had not a few references to the bubbles of sparkling wine previously, it is hard to say whether she died a Christian penitent, or went out like a bottle of opened champagne. Quite so, Hawthorne might say: not hard—*impossible*. Twice Coverdale comes across strangely—strangely in New England—luxuriant grape vines. There are grapes in his hermitage 'in abundant clusters of the deepest purple' (p. 228), and they provoke him to almost Dionysiac reveries.

Methinks a wine might be pressed out of them, possessing a passionate zest, and endowed with a new kind of intoxicating quality, attended with such bacchanalian ecstasies as the tamer grapes of Madeira, France, and the Rhine, are inadequate to produce. And I longed to quaff a great goblet of it, at that moment. (p. 228)

Methinks, if he was actually offered any such goblet, he would demur and settle for a sherry-cobbler, not being one actually to capitulate to bacchanalian ecstasies—as opposed to fantasizing about them. In the tavern scene Coverdale attempts a cautious and measured defence of wine, if not of spirits: 'Human nature, in my opinion, has a naughty instinct that approves of wine, if not of stronger liquor' (p. 175). (This sentence was crossed out, possibly by Sophia Hawthorne, so you can see what he was up against, and, in his sly Hawthorne way, writing against.)[29]

There are various paintings on the walls of the tavern, all concerned with representations of food and drink, or drinking, and this permits Coverdale, and doubtless Hawthorne, to meditate on varying modes of representation, from low mimetic realism to a more etherealizing kind of art. By situating the book's main discussion of *art* in a *tavern* Hawthorne is again doing something rather novel, or, rather, raising an old problem in a new way. Since the paintings concern food, drink, and 'revelling' (wenching?), we may say that in their varying ways—gross, life-like, noble, ideal, *too* real—they engage with our basic hungers and desires. Which implicitly points to the larger problem: what is, what can be, what should be, the relationship between art and appetite?

[29] See explanatory notes to pp. 10, 17, and 175.

Do such representations pander to our lowest, most basic and most powerful, wants and desires, courting and inflaming them? Or, by transposing such appetites and objects of desire into another medium, can such representations ideal-ize and spirit-ualize them? Hawthorne would not be one to resolve such a potentially infinite debate: characteristically, inasmuch as he hopes the latter, he fears the former—and vice versa. And, anyway, it is all just 'painted canvas'. But on this occasion, and in this setting, meditations about why men paint lead on to a discussion of why men drink. Art shades into alcohol. And Coverdale has a most interesting subversive thought. There is a fountain in the tavern and the basin or 'lakelet' in which it stands contains several 'gold-fishes'. Coverdale indulges a fancy.

Never before, I imagine, did a company of water-drinkers remain so entirely uncontaminated by the bad example around them, nor could I help wondering that it had not occurred to any freakish inebriate, to empty a glass of liquor into their lakelet. What a delightful idea! Who would not be a fish, if he could inhale jollity with the essential element of his existence! (p. 178)

Is the artist, perhaps, just such a 'freakish inebriate', subtly introducing his potent stimulants into the very cultural air his unsuspecting compatriots breathe? Is it a beneficence ('bringing warmth and cheer'), or a treachery ('intoxicating' people secretly and against their will)? Inasmuch as alcohol is known temporarily to raise the 'spirits', it may, with an ironic turn, be said to 'spiritualize' the consumer. But, despite its undoubted properties of bringing temporary consolation, short-lived feelings of gladness and hope, a brief illusion of restored 'youth and vigour' (p. 178), alcohol is far more likely to bestialize the one who turns to it too often. What clearly worried or preoccupied Hawthorne was the extent to which the questions and considerations raised in those last two sentences might exactly be applied to art.

Very near the end, Coverdale draws a 'moral' from what Hollingsworth's 'ruling passion' has done to him.

It ruins, or is fearfully apt to ruin, the heart; the rich juices of which God never meant should be pressed violently out, and distilled into

alcoholic liquor, by an unnatural process; but should render life
sweet, bland, and gently beneficent, and sensibly influence other
hearts and other lives to the same blessed end. (p. 243)

A nice distinction, particularly in view of all the references to
alcoholic drinks which have preceded it. Our heart's juices
were not meant to be 'distilled' into strong liquor—certainly
an unnatural and, if you will, a violent process; rather they
should simply render life 'sweet' and 'bland'—a sherry-
cobbler of a life (sherry is fortified but not distilled—a
suitably equivocal potion), a sillabub existence. Coverdale is
truly not a man of, or for, strong spirit(s)—in *every* sense of
the word. But the most crucial play with this word occurs in
the closing words of the narrative (excluding here the last
short chapter which is a sort of postscript). Coverdale muses
that, while Zenobia was alive, 'Nature was proud of her'.
Now she is dead, will not 'Nature shed a tear?' (p. 244).

Ah, no! She adopts the calamity at once into her system, and is just as
well pleased, for aught we can see, with the tuft of ranker vegetation
that grew out of Zenobia's heart, as with all the beauty which has
bequeathed us no earthly representative, except in this crop of
weeds. It is because the spirit is inestimable, that the lifeless body is
so little valued. (p. 244)

Nature is the system which absorbs *all* the other systems, the
provisional, partial, and ephemeral structures and social
orderings which man attempts to erect. Nature simply waits
for all human signs to fail, and Zenobia, like Conrad's
Decoud, is 'swallowed up in the immense indifference of
things'.[30] That being so, 'the spirit is inestimable'—but by
this end-point of the book what on earth, literally on that
cloddish earth, can 'spirit' signify? Throughout, Coverdale
has revealed himself to be adrift in a lexicon of failed
transcendence; a 'strayed reveller' (in Matthew Arnold's
phrase) who has indeed lost his way, his home, his sense of
history, his grasp of the real, any access to any ideal realm.
That last appearance of the word 'spirit' gestures both
pathetically to the final vagueness of a fading religious sense,
and bathetically to those always available sherry-cobblers.
Inasmuch as he sees him as a true product of America, in his

[30] J. Conrad, *Nostromo* (London, 1904), 501.

disorientation, amnesia, and general sense of loss—*that* is what Hawthorne is doing with Coverdale. Saying to American society, American history, American religion and culture: *this* is the artist you have produced—intruder, lodger, spy.

As Michael Colacurcio[31] and Richard Brodhead[32] have very well demonstrated, Hawthorne could use his fiction brilliantly to reinsert aspects of the American past which had been, or were being, assiduously left out and erased in the official versions—writing back *on*, as it were, what triumphalist American historiography was busy 'writing *off*'. But in *The Blithedale Romance*, though he does make his point about the occlusion and elimination of the Indians, he shows us an artist forgetting the American past, while being disablingly sceptical about the American present. Always dubious, undecided, ambiguous, about the ultimate validity or value of 'fiction' and art in general, Hawthorne has written that uncertainty all through this book. Indeed one could say that he has taken that uncertainty, and a very far-reaching anatomy of it, and made it *into* a book. A curious dividend of this enterprise is that the book has more of the American nineteenth century in it than any other novel I know, and contains innumerable unforeseen and unforeseeable profundities and insights. In all its idiosyncratic inconsistencies of tone, its narrative vacillations and swerves, its inconclusiveness and loose ends, its unpredictable ranging through incongruously contiguous settings and scenes, its collocation of wildly dissimilar characters—in all these features, and indeed because of them, it is, almost despite itself, undoubtedly one of the great American novels. And, in its way, one of the saddest and most pessimistic. For by the end clearly America itself has become for Coverdale 'another spot, and an utter strangeness' (p. 206). Perhaps for Hawthorne, too. For it was one of Henry James's late and considered characterizations of him that 'He is outside of everything, and an alien everywhere.'[33]

---

[31] M. Colacurcio, *The Province of Piety: Moral History in Hawthorne's Early Tales* (London and Cambridge, Mass., 1984).

[32] R. Brodhead, *The School of Hawthorne* (Oxford and New York, 1986).

[33] James, *Essays*, p. 467.

NOTE ON THE TEXT

The text of this volume is that of *The Blithedale Romance*, Volume III of the *Centenary Edition of the Works of Nathaniel Hawthorne*, published in 1964 by the Ohio State University Press for the Ohio State University Center for Textual Studies. The Centenary text was established by the application of bibliographical and analytical criticism to the evidence of the various documentary forms in which the text had appeared. It is a critical, unmodernized reconstruction of Hawthorne's text, and is approved by the Center for Editions of the Modern Language Association of America.

SELECT BIBLIOGRAPHY

LETTERS AND NOTEBOOKS

The Letters 1813–1843 (Centenary Edition of the Works of Nathaniel Hawthorne, 25; Columbus, Ohio, 1984).

The American Notebooks (Centenary Edition, 8; Columbus, Ohio, 1972).

Love Letters of Nathaniel Hawthorne (2 vols., Chicago, 1907).

BIOGRAPHY

Hawthorne, Julian, *Nathaniel Hawthorne and his Wife* (2 vols., Boston, 1884).

Mellow, James, *Nathaniel Hawthorne in his Times* (Boston, 1980).

Stewart, Randall, *Nathaniel Hawthorne: A Biography* (New Haven, 1948).

Turner, Arlin, *Nathaniel Hawthorne: A Biography* (New York and Oxford, 1980).

CRITICISM: GENERAL

Baym, Nina, 'Thwarted Nature: Hawthorne as Feminist', in Fritz Fleischmann (ed.), *American Novelists Revisited: Essays in Feminist Criticism* (Boston, 1982), 55–77.

—— *The Shape of Hawthorne's Career* (Ithaca and London, 1976).

—— 'The Significance of Plot in Hawthorne's Romances', in G. R. Thompson and V. L. Lokke (eds.), *Ruined Eden of the Present* (West Lafayette, Ind., 1981), 49–70.

Bloom, Harold (ed.), *Nathaniel Hawthorne* (New York, 1986).

Brodhead, Richard, *Hawthorne, Melville, and the Novel* (Chicago, 1976).

—— *The School of Hawthorne* (Oxford and New York, 1986).

Cameron, Sharon, *The Corporeal Self: Allegories of the Body in Melville and Hawthorne* (Baltimore and London, 1979).

Cohen, Bernard (ed.), *The Recognition of Nathaniel Hawthorne: Selected Criticism Since 1828* (Ann Arbor, Mich., 1969).

Colacurcio, M., *The Province of Piety: Moral History in Hawthorne's Early Tales* (London and Cambridge, Mass., 1984).

Crane, Teresa, *The Hawthorne Heritage* (London, 1988).

Crews, Frederick, *The Sins of the Fathers: Hawthorne's Psychological Themes* (New York, 1966).

Crowley, J. Donald (ed.), *Hawthorne: The Critical Heritage* (London, 1970).

DeSalvo, Louise, *Nathaniel Hawthorne* (Brighton, 1987).

Dryden, Edgar, *Nathaniel Hawthorne: The Poetics of Enchantment* (Ithaca, NY, 1977).

James, Henry, *Hawthorne* (1879; repr. Ithaca, New York, 1956).

Lee, A. R. (ed.), *Nathaniel Hawthorne: New Critical Essays* (London, 1982).

Lloyd Smith, Allan Gardner, *Eve Tempted: Writing and Sexuality in Hawthorne's Fiction* (Sydney and London, 1984).

Martin, Terence, *Nathaniel Hawthorne* (rev. edn., New York, 1983).

Pearce, Roy Harvey (ed.), *Hawthorne: Centenary Essays* (Columbus, Ohio, 1964).

Poirier, Richard, *A World Elsewhere* (London, 1967).

CRITICISM: 'THE BLITHEDALE ROMANCE'

Berlant, L., 'Fantasies of Utopia in *The Blithedale Romance*'. *American Literary History*, 1/1 (1989), 30–62.

Carabine, Keith, '"Bitter Honey": Miles Coverdale as Narrator in *The Blithedale Romance*', in A. R. Lee (ed.), *Nathaniel Hawthorne: New Critical Essays* (London, 1982), 110–130.

Crews, Frederick, 'A New Reading of *The Blithedale Romance*', *American Literature*, 29 (May 1957), 147–70.

Davidson, F., 'Toward a Revaluation of *The Blithedale Romance*', *New England Quarterly*, 25/3 (1952), 374–83.

Eliot, George, review in *Westminster Review*, 58 (1852), 592–8; repr. in J. Donald Crowley (ed.), *Hawthorne: The Critical Heritage* (London, 1970), 259–64.

Elliott, Robert C., '*The Blithedale Romance*', in Roy Harvey Pearce (ed.), *Hawthorne: Centenary Essays* (Columbus, Ohio, 1964), 103–17.

Fryer, Judith, *The Faces of Eve: Women in the Nineteenth Century American Novel* (New York, 1976).

Garrett, J. C., *Hope or Disillusion: Three Versions of Utopia: Nathaniel Hawthorne, Samuel Butler, George Orwell* (Christchurch, New Zealand, 1984).

Griffith, Kelley, Jr., 'Form in *The Blithedale Romance*', *American Literature*, 40 (1968), 15–26.

Gross, Seymour, and Murphy, Rosalie (eds.), *The Blithedale Romance* (Norton Critical Edition; New York, 1978).

Howe, Irving, 'Hawthorne—Pastoral and Politics', in *Politics and the Novel* (New York, 1957), 163–75.

Justin, James, 'Hawthorne's Coverdale: Character and Art in *The Blithedale Romance*', *American Literature*, 47 (1975), 21–36.

Kolodny, Annette, Introduction to Penguin edition (Harmondsworth, 1983).

Lefcowitz, A., and Lefcowitz, B., 'Some Rents in the Veil: New Light on Priscilla and Zenobia in *The Blithedale Romance*', *Nineteenth Century Fiction*, 21/3 (1966), 263–75.

Stoehr, T., 'Art vs. Utopia: The Case of Nathaniel Hawthorne and Brook Farm', *Antioch Review*, 36/1 (1978), 89–102.

Swann, C., 'A Note on *The Blithedale Romance* or "Call him Fauntleroy"', *Journal of American Studies*, 10 (1976), 103–4.

Turner, Arlin, Introduction to Norton edition (New York, 1958).

Winslow, Joan, 'New Light on Hawthorne's Miles Coverdale', *Journal of Narrative Technique*, 7 (1977), 189–99.

ON RELATED SUBJECTS

Flaxner, E., *Century of Struggle: The Women's Rights Movement in the USA* (Cambridge, Mass., 1975).

Fuller, Margaret, *Memories of Margaret Fuller* (Boston, 1852).

—— *Women in the Nineteenth Century*, ed. A. D. Fuller (1864; repr. Greenwood, New York, 1968).

—— *Writings of Margaret Fuller*, ed. M. Wade (Clifton, 1973).

Goldfarb, Clare, and Goldfarb, Russell, *Spiritualism and Nineteenth Century Letters* (London, 1978).

Miller, Perry (ed.), *The Transcendentalists* (Cambridge, Mass., 1971).

Reynolds, D., *Beneath the American Renaissance* (Cambridge, Mass., 1988).

Tatar, Maria, *Spellbound: Studies on Mesmerism and Literature* (Princeton, 1978).

Tharp, L. H., *The Peabody Sisters of Salem* (Boston, 1950).

Wilson, Edmund, *To The Finland Station* [sections on nineteenth-century Utopian communities] (1942; London, 1974).

BIBLIOGRAPHIES

Boswell, Jeanetta, *Nathaniel Hawthorne and the Critics: A Checklist of Criticism, 1900–1978* (Methuchen, NJ, and London, 1982).

Browne, Nina, *A Bibliography of Nathaniel Hawthorne* (1905; New York, 1968).

Frazer Clark, C. E., Jr., *Nathaniel Hawthorne: A Descriptive Bibliography* (Pittsburgh, 1978); 'limited to writings by Hawthorne'.

Ricks, Beatrice, Adams, Joseph D., and Hazelrig, Jack O., *Nathaniel Hawthorne: A Reference Bibliography, 1900–1971* (Boston, 1972).

For more recent criticism, see the annual MLA Bibliographies, and the periodical *Nathaniel Hawthorne Review*.

A CHRONOLOGY OF
NATHANIEL HAWTHORNE

1804   4 July: born in Salem, Massachusetts, second of three children of Elizabeth (*née* Manning) and Nathaniel Hathorne.

1808   Father, a ship's captain, dies of yellow fever at Surinam (Dutch Guiana). The Hathornes move to the Manning family home in Salem.

1813   November: a foot injury causes lameness and keeps Nathaniel from school for fourteen months.

1818   October: the Hathorne family moves to Raymond, Maine, which is still a wilderness area. Nathaniel hunts, fishes, and runs wild.

1819   July: Nathaniel returns to Salem to live with his mother's family, under the guardianship of his uncle Robert Manning. His mother stays in Maine.

1820   Prepares for college under Benjamin L. Oliver in Salem.

1821   October: enters Bowdoin College, Brunswick, Maine. College friendships with Horatio Bridge, Franklin Pierce, Jonathan Cilley.

1822   H. W. Longfellow enters Bowdoin. He and Hawthorne meet.

1825   September: graduates from Bowdoin. Returns to live with family in Salem. According to his sister Elizabeth, Nathaniel has completed 'Seven Tales of My Native Land' by the time he graduates from Bowdoin.

1828   October: *Fanshawe* published anonymously and at the author's expense. By now Nathaniel has added the 'w' to his family name.

1829   Plans a second collection of stories, to be called 'Provincial Tales', and submits manuscript to S. G. Goodrich, editor of *The Token*, an annual.

1830   12 November and 21 December: 'The Hollow of the Three Hills' and 'An Old Woman's Tale'—Hawthorne's first known tales to appear in print—published in *Salem Gazette*.

1831   Releases some tales intended for 'Provincial Tales' for publication in *The Token*, dated 1832: 'The Gentle Boy', 'The Wives of the Dead', 'Roger Malvin's Burial', 'My Kinsman, Major Molineux'.

1832   Plans a third collection, to be called 'The Story Teller'. September–October: makes extensive journeys in Vermont and New York State, gathering literary materials.

1834   November and December: 'The Story Teller, Nos I and II' published in *New England Magazine*.

1835   'The Minister's Black Veil', 'The Maypole of Merry Mount', and 'The Wedding-Knell' published in *The Token* for 1836.

1836   January: moves to Boston to edit *American Magazine of Useful and Entertaining Knowledge*. March: first issue with Nathaniel Hawthorne as editor. His salary is not paid. Magazine goes bankrupt in May. May to September: writes—with the help of Elizabeth—*Peter Parley's Universal History, on the Basis of Geography*.

1837   March: *Twice-told Tales* published. Unknown to Hawthorne, Horatio Bridge has given financial guarantee to publisher. July: Longfellow's highly favourable review of *Twice-told Tales* appears in the *North American Review*. November: meets Sophia Amelia Peabody. October: begins his association with John L. O'Sullivan's *Democratic Review*. Eight Hawthorne pieces appear there in fifteen months.

1838   July–September: begins three months of seclusion in North Adams, Massachusetts, with trips to the Berkshires, upstate New York, Vermont, Connecticut.

1839   January: takes up appointment as measurer in the Boston Custom House. 6 March: writes first surviving love-letter to Sophia Peabody.

1840   November: resigns from Custom House with effect from 1 January 1841. December: *Grandfather's Chair* published, dated 1841, a children's history of New England.

1841   January: returns to Salem. *Famous Old People* published. March: *The Liberty Tree* published. April: joins the Brook Farm Associationist experiment at West Roxbury, near Boston, as working member. Becomes a paying boarder at the Farm, with no work commitments, in the autumn.

September: buys two shares in the Brook Farm project, planning to bring Sophia to live there when they are married. October: leaves the Farm for Boston.

1842   January: second edition of *Twice-told Tales* published, with additional volume containing sixteen recent tales and sketches together with five that antedate the 1837 collection. 9 July: Hawthorne and Sophia Peabody married. They move to Concord, Mass., where they rent the Old Manse. October: withdraws from the Brook Farm project and requests return of his stock.

1844   3 March: daughter (Una) born.

1845   January–April: edits Horatio Bridge's *Journal of an African Cruiser*. October: the Hawthornes move to Herbert Street, Salem, as the owner wants Old Manse.

1846   9 April: sworn in a surveyor at Salem Custom House, having been nominated by President Polk, the new Democratic President. June: *Mosses from an Old Manse* published in two volumes. A critical, but not a financial, success. 22 June: Julian Hawthorne born. August: Hawthornes move to Salem.

1848   November: becomes manager and corresponding secretary of Salem Lyceum. Invites Emerson, Thoreau, Theodore Parker, Horace Mann, Louis Agassiz to lecture.

1849   7 June: removed from office in Custom House, following election of Whig President, Zachary Taylor, in 1848. 31 July: Mother dies. September: begins writing *The Scarlet Letter* and 'The Custom-House'.

1850   16 March: *The Scarlet Letter* published in edition of 2,500 copies. April: second edition published. May: Hawthornes move to 'Red Cottage', Lenox, Massachusetts. 5 August: Hawthorne meets Melville at a literary picnic. August: begins *The House of the Seven Gables*. 17 and 24 August: Melville's 'Hawthorne and His Mosses' appears anonymously in *The Literary World*. November: *True Stories* (reissue of *Grandfather's Chair* and *Biographical Stories*) published, dated 1851.

1851   April: *The House of the Seven Gables* published. March: third edition of *Twice-told Tales* published, with preface. 20 May: Rose Hawthorne born. November: *A Wonder Book for Girls and Boys* published, dated 1852. December: *The Snow-Image* published, dated 1852.

1852   April: buys the Alcott House in Concord, naming it 'The Wayside'. July: *The Blithedale Romance* published. September: *Life of Franklin Pierce*—a campaign biography of the Presidential candidate—published.

1853   March: nominated to consulship at Liverpool and Manchester by President Pierce. Appointment confirmed by US Senate. July: sails for England with family. September: *Tanglewood Tales* published.

1853–7 While working as consul, Hawthorne keeps notebooks in which he records his English experiences and impressions.

1854   Revised edition of *Mosses* published.

1856   November: Melville visits Hawthorne in Liverpool on way to the Holy Land. He also meets Hawthorne briefly on return journey in May 1857.

1857   October: gives up consulship.

1858   January: travels to Italy by way of France. Takes up residence in Rome. Keeps notebooks on his Italian experiences and begins work on an English romance, never to be completed, but published posthumously as *The Ancestral Footstep*. May to October: the Hawthornes live in Florence. He begins work on romance with an Italian theme.

1859   June: returns to England, where he rewrites the Italian romance.

1860   February: *The Transformation* published in England; in March the romance is published in America with the title *The Marble Faun*. June: returns to America and settles at 'The Wayside', Concord, where he begins work on a second version of his English romance.

1861   Abandons the romance, after making seven studies for the story. The fragment is published posthumously as *Dr Grimshaw's Secret*. Autumn: begins work on series of English essays. Begins a new romance on theme of the elixir of life but abandons this in 1862. Set at the time of the Revolution, the fragment is published posthumously as *Septimius Felton*.

1863   September: *Our Old Home* published—the collected essays on England—most of which had appeared separately in the *Atlantic Monthly*.

1864   19 May: dies at Plymouth, New Hampshire, having written three chapters of another romance about the elixir of life, which is posthumously published as *The Dolliver Romance*.

THE BLITHEDALE ROMANCE

PREFACE

I N THE 'BLITHEDALE' of this volume, many readers will
probably suspect a faint and not very faithful shadowing
of BROOK FARM,* in Roxbury, which (now a little more
than ten years ago) was occupied and cultivated by a company
of socialists. The Author does not wish to deny, that he had
this Community in his mind, and that (having had the good
fortune, for a time, to be personally connected with it) he
has occasionally availed himself of his actual reminiscences,
in the hope of giving a more lifelike tint to the fancy-sketch*
in the following pages. He begs it to be understood, however,
that he has considered the Institution itself as not less fairly
the subject of fictitious handling, than the imaginary personages whom he has introduced there. His whole treatment of
the affair is altogether incidental to the main purpose of the
Romance; nor does he put forward the slightest pretensions
to illustrate a theory, or elicit a conclusion, favorable or otherwise, in respect to Socialism.

In short, his present concern with the Socialist Community
is merely to establish a theatre, a little removed from the
highway of ordinary travel, where the creatures of his brain
may play their phantasmagorical antics, without exposing
them to too close a comparison with the actual events of real
lives. In the old countries, with which Fiction has long been

conversant, a certain conventional privilege seems to be awarded to the romancer; his work is not put exactly side by side with nature; and he is allowed a license with regard to every-day Probability, in view of the improved effects which he is bound to produce thereby. Among ourselves, on the contrary, there is as yet no such Faery Land, so like the real world, that, in a suitable remoteness, one cannot well tell the difference, but with an atmosphere of strange enchantment, beheld through which the inhabitants have a propriety of their own. This atmosphere is what the American romancer* needs. In its absence, the beings of imagination are compelled to show themselves in the same category as actually living mortals; a necessity that generally renders the paint and pasteboard of their composition but too painfully discernible. With the idea of partially obviating this difficulty, (the sense of which has always pressed very heavily upon him,) the Author has ventured to make free with his old, and affectionately remembered home, at BROOK FARM, as being, certainly, the most romantic episode of his own life—essentially a daydream, and yet a fact—and thus offering an available foothold between fiction and reality. Furthermore, the scene was in good keeping with the personages whom he desired to introduce.

These characters, he feels it right to say, are entirely fictitious. It would, indeed, (considering how few amiable qualities he distributes among his imaginary progeny,) be a most grievous wrong to his former excellent associates, were the Author to allow it to be supposed that he has been sketching any of their likenesses. Had he attempted it, they would at least have recognized the touches of a friendly pencil. But he has done nothing of the kind. The self-concentrated Philanthropist; the high-spirited Woman, bruising herself against the narrow limitations of her sex; the weakly Maiden, whose tremulous nerves endow her with Sibylline* attributes; the Minor Poet, beginning life with strenuous aspirations, which die out with his youthful fervor —all these might have been looked for, at BROOK FARM, but, by some accident, never made their appearance there.

The Author cannot close his reference to this subject, without expressing a most earnest wish that some one of the many cultivated and philosophic minds, which took an interest in that enterprise, might now give the world its history. Ripley, with whom rests the honorable paternity of the Institution, Dana, Dwight, Channing, Burton, Parker,* for instance—with others, whom he dares not name, because they veil themselves from the public eye—among these is the ability to convey both the outward narrative and the inner truth and spirit of the whole affair, together with the lessons which those years of thought and toil must have elaborated, for the behoof of future experimentalists. Even the brilliant Howadji* might find as rich a theme in his youthful reminiscenses of BROOK FARM, and a more novel one—close at hand as it lies—than those which he has since made so distant a pilgrimage to seek, in Syria, and along the current of the Nile.

CONCORD (Mass.), May, 1852.

THE BLITHEDALE ROMANCE

I

OLD MOODIE

T HE EVENING before my departure for Blithedale, I
was returning to my bachelor-apartments, after attend-
ing the wonderful exhibition of the Veiled Lady, when
an elderly-man of rather shabby appearance met me in an
obscure part of the street.

"Mr. Coverdale,"*said he, softly, "can I speak with you a
moment?"

As I have casually alluded to the Veiled Lady, it may not
be amiss to mention, for the benefit of such of my readers as
are unacquainted with her now forgotten celebrity, that she
was a phenomenon in the mesmeric line;*one of the earliest
that had indicated the birth of a new science, or the revival
of an old humbug. Since those times, her sisterhood have
grown too numerous to attract much individual notice; nor,
in fact, has any one of them ever come before the public
under such skilfully contrived circumstances of stage-effect,
as those which at once mystified and illuminated the remarkable performances of the lady in question. Now-a-days, in
the management of his 'subject,' 'clairvoyant,' or 'medium,'
the exhibitor affects the simplicity and openness of scientific
experiment; and even if he profess to tread a step or two
across the boundaries of the spiritual world, yet carries with
him the laws of our actual life, and extends them over his

preternatural conquests. Twelve or fifteen years ago, on the contrary, all the arts of mysterious arrangement, of picturesque disposition, and artistically contrasted light and shade, were made available in order to set the apparent miracle in the strongest attitude of opposition to ordinary facts. In the case of the Veiled Lady, moreover, the interest of the spectator was further wrought up by the enigma of her identity, and an absurd rumor (probably set afloat by the exhibitor, and at one time very prevalent) that a beautiful young lady, of family and fortune, was enshrouded within the misty drapery of the veil. It was white, with somewhat of a subdued silver sheen, like the sunny side of a cloud; and falling over the wearer, from head to foot, was supposed to insulate her from the material world, from time and space, and to endow her with many of the privileges of a disembodied spirit.

Her pretensions, however, whether miraculous or otherwise, have little to do with the present narrative; except, indeed, that I had propounded, for the Veiled Lady's prophetic solution, a query as to the success of our Blithedale enterprise. The response, by-the-by, was of the true Sibylline stamp, nonsensical in its first aspect, yet, on closer study, unfolding a variety of interpretations, one of which has certainly accorded with the event. I was turning over this riddle in my mind, and trying to catch its slippery purport by the tail, when the old man, above-mentioned, interrupted me.

"Mr. Coverdale!—Mr. Coverdale!" said he, repeating my name twice, in order to make up for the hesitating and ineffectual way in which he uttered it—"I ask your pardon, sir—but I hear you are going to Blithedale tomorrow?"

I knew the pale, elderly face, with the red-tipt nose, and the patch over one eye, and likewise saw something characteristic in the old fellow's way of standing under the arch of a gate, only revealing enough of himself to make me recognize him as an acquaintance. He was a very shy personage, this Mr. Moodie; and the trait was the more singular, as his mode of getting his bread necessarily brought him into the stir and hubbub of the world, more than the generality of men.

"Yes, Mr. Moodie," I answered, wondering what interest he could take in the fact, "it is my intention to go to Blithedale tomorrow. Can I be of any service to you, before my departure?"

"If you pleased, Mr. Coverdale," said he, "you might do me a very great favor."

"A very great one!" repeated I, in a tone that must have expressed but little alacrity of beneficence, although I was ready to do the old man any amount of kindness involving no special trouble to myself. "A very great favor, do you say? My time is brief, Mr. Moodie, and I have a good many preparations to make. But be good enough to tell me what you wish."

"Ah, sir," replied old Moodie, "I don't quite like to do that; and, on further thoughts, Mr. Coverdale, perhaps I had better apply to some older gentleman, or to some lady, if you would have the kindness to make me known to one, who may happen to be going to Blithedale. You are a young man, sir!"

"Does that fact lessen my availability for your purpose?" asked I. "However, if an older man will suit you better, there is Mr. Hollingsworth, who has three or four years the advantage of me in age, and is a much more solid character, and a philanthropist to boot. I am only a poet, and, so the critics tell me, no great affair at that! But what can this business be, Mr. Moodie? It begins to interest me; especially since your hint that a lady's influence might be found desirable. Come; I am really anxious to be of service to you."

But the old fellow, in his civil and demure manner, was both freakish and obstinate; and he had now taken some notion or other into his head that made him hesitate in his former design.

"I wonder, sir," said he, "whether you know a lady whom they call Zenobia?"*

"Not personally," I answered, "although I expect that pleasure tomorrow, as she has got the start of the rest of us, and is already a resident at Blithedale. But have you a literary turn, Mr. Moodie?—or have you taken up the advocacy of women's rights?—or what else can have interested you in this lady? Zenobia, by-the-by, as I suppose you know, is merely her public name; a sort of mask in which she comes before the world, retaining all the privileges of privacy—a contrivance, in short, like the white drapery of the Veiled Lady, only a little more transparent. But it is late! Will you tell me what I can do for you?"

"Please to excuse me to-night, Mr. Coverdale," said Moodie. "You are very kind; but I am afraid I have troubled you, when, after all, there may be no need. Perhaps, with your good leave, I will come to your lodgings tomorrow-morning, before you set out for Blithedale. I wish you a good-night, sir, and beg pardon for stopping you."

And so he slipt away; and, as he did not show himself, the next morning, it was only through subsequent events that I ever arrived at a plausible conjecture as to what his business could have been. Arriving at my room, I threw a lump of cannel coal*upon the grate, lighted a cigar, and spent an hour in musings of every hue, from the brightest to the most sombre; being, in truth, not so very confident as at some former periods, that this final step, which would mix me up irrevocably with the Blithedale affair, was the wisest that could possibly be taken. It was nothing short of midnight when I went to bed, after drinking a glass of particularly fine Sherry, on which I used to pride myself, in those days. It was the very last bottle; and I finished it, with a friend, the next forenoon, before setting out for Blithedale.

II

BLITHEDALE

THERE can hardly remain for me, (who am really getting to be a frosty bachelor, with another white hair, every week or so, in my moustache,) there can hardly flicker up again so cheery a blaze upon the hearth, as that which I remember, the next day, at Blithedale. It was a wood-fire, in the parlor of an old farm-house, on an April afternoon, but with the fitful gusts of a wintry snow-storm roaring in the chimney. Vividly does that fireside re-create itself, as I rake away the ashes from the embers in my memory, and blow them up with a sigh, for lack of more inspiring breath. Vividly, for an instant, but, anon, with the dimmest gleam, and with just as little fervency for my heart as for my finger-ends! The staunch oaken-logs were long ago burnt out. Their genial glow must be represented, if at all, by the merest phosphoric glimmer, like that which exudes, rather than shines, from damp fragments of decayed trees, deluding the benighted wanderer through a forest. Around such chill mockery of a fire, some few of us might sit on the withered leaves, spreading out each a palm towards the imaginary warmth, and talk over our exploded scheme for beginning the life of Paradise anew.

Paradise, indeed! Nobody else in the world, I am bold to affirm—nobody, at least, in our bleak little world of New

England—had dreamed of Paradise, that day, except as the pole suggests the tropic. Nor, with such materials as were at hand, could the most skilful architect have constructed any better imitation of Eve's bower, than might be seen in the snow-hut of an Esquimaux.* But we made a summer of it, in spite of the wild drifts.

It was an April day, as already hinted, and well towards the middle of the month. When morning dawned upon me, in town, its temperature was mild enough to be pronounced even balmy, by a lodger—like myself—in one of the midmost houses of a brick-block; each house partaking of the warmth of all the rest, besides the sultriness of its individual furnace-heat. But, towards noon, there had come snow, driven along the street by a north-easterly blast, and whitening the roofs and sidewalks with a business-like perseverance that would have done credit to our severest January tempest. It set about its task, apparently as much in earnest as if it had been guaranteed from a thaw, for months to come. The greater, surely, was my heroism, when, puffing out a final whiff of cigar-smoke, I quitted my cosey pair of bachelor-rooms—with a good fire burning in the grate, and a closet right at hand, where there was still a bottle or two in the champagne-basket, and a residuum of claret in a box, and somewhat of proof in the concavity of a big demijohn*—quitted, I say, these comfortable quarters, and plunged into the heart of the pitiless snow-storm, in quest of a better life.

The better life! Possibly, it would hardly look so, now; it is enough if it looked so, then. The greatest obstacle to being heroic, is the doubt whether one may not be going to prove one's self a fool; the truest heroism is, to resist the doubt—and the profoundest wisdom, to know when it ought to be resisted, and when to be obeyed.

Yet, after all, let us acknowledge it wiser, if not more sagacious, to follow out one's day-dream to its natural consummation, although, if the vision have been worth the having, it is certain never to be consummated otherwise than by a failure. And what of that! Its airiest fragments, impalpable as they may be, will possess a value that lurks not in the most ponderous realities of any practicable scheme. They are not the rubbish of the mind. Whatever else I may repent of, therefore, let it be reckoned neither among my sins nor follies, that I once had faith and force enough to form generous hopes of the world's destiny—yes!—and to do what in me lay for their accomplishment; even to the extent of quitting a warm fireside, flinging away a freshly lighted cigar, and travelling far beyond the strike of city-clocks, through a drifting snow-storm.

There were four of us who rode together through the storm; and Hollingsworth, who had agreed to be of the number, was accidentally delayed, and set forth at a later hour, alone. As we threaded the streets, I remember how the buildings, on either side, seemed to press too closely upon us, insomuch that our mighty hearts found barely room enough to throb between them. The snow-fall, too, looked inexpressibly dreary, (I had almost called it dingy,) coming down through an atmosphere of city-smoke, and alighting on the sidewalk, only to be moulded into the impress of somebody's patched boot or over-shoe. Thus, the track of an old conventionalism was visible on what was freshest from the sky. But—when we left the pavements, and our muffled hoof-tramps beat upon a desolate extent of country-road, and were effaced by the unfettered blast, as soon as stamped—then, there was better air to breathe. Air, that had not been breathed, once and again! Air, that had not been spoken into words of falsehood, formality, and error, like all the air of the dusky city!

"How pleasant it is!" remarked I, while the snow-flakes flew into my mouth, the moment it was opened. "How very mild and balmy is this country-air!"

"Ah, Coverdale, don't laugh at what little enthusiasm you

have left," said one of my companions. "I maintain that this nitrous atmosphere is really exhilarating; and, at any rate, we can never call ourselves regenerated men, till a February north-easter shall be as grateful to us as the softest breeze of June."

So we all of us took courage, riding fleetly and merrily along, by stone-fences that were half-buried in the wave-like drifts; and through patches of woodland, where the tree-trunks opposed a snow-encrusted side towards the north-east; and within ken of deserted villas, with no foot-prints in their avenues; and past scattered dwellings, whence puffed the smoke of country fires, strongly impregnated with the pungent aroma of burning peat. Sometimes, encountering a traveller, we shouted a friendly greeting; and he, unmuffling his ears to the bluster and the snow-spray, and listening eagerly, appeared to think our courtesy worth less than the trouble which it cost him. The churl! He understood the shrill whistle of the blast, but had no intelligence for our blithe tones of brotherhood. This lack of faith in our cordial sympathy, on the traveller's part, was one among the innumerable tokens how difficult a task we had in hand, for the reformation of the world. We rode on, however, with still unflagging spirits, and made such good companionship with the tempest, that, at our journey's end, we professed ourselves almost loth to bid the rude blusterer good bye. But, to own the truth, I was little better than an icicle, and began to be suspicious that I had caught a fearful cold.

And, now, we were seated by the brisk fireside of the old farm-house; the same fire that glimmers so faintly among my reminiscences, at the beginning of this chapter. There we sat, with the snow melting out of our hair and beards, and our faces all a-blaze, what with the past inclemency and present warmth. It was, indeed, a right good fire that we found awaiting us, built up of great, rough logs, and knotty limbs, and splintered fragments of an oak-tree, such as farmers are

wont to keep for their own hearths; since these crooked and
unmanageable boughs could never be measured into mer-
chantable cords for the market. A family of the old Pilgrims
might have swung their kettle over precisely such a fire as
this, only, no doubt, a bigger one; and, contrasting it with
my coal-grate, I felt, so much the more, that we had trans-
ported ourselves a world-wide distance from the system of
society that shackled us at breakfast-time.

Good, comfortable Mrs. Foster (the wife of stout Silas
Foster, who was to manage the farm, at a fair stipend, and
be our tutor in the art of husbandry) bade us a hearty
welcome. At her back—a back of generous breadth—appeared
two young women, smiling most hospitably, but looking
rather awkward withal, as not well knowing what was to be
their position in our new arrangement of the world. We
shook hands affectionately, all round, and congratulated ourselves that the blessed state of brotherhood and sisterhood, at
which we aimed, might fairly be dated from this moment.
Our greetings were hardly concluded, when the door opened,
and Zenobia—whom I had never before seen, important as
was her place in our enterprise—Zenobia entered the parlor.

This (as the reader, if at all acquainted with our literary
biography, need scarcely be told) was not her real name.
She had assumed it, in the first instance, as her magazine-
signature; and as it accorded well with something imperial
which her friends attributed to this lady's figure and deportment, they, half-laughingly, adopted it in their familiar intercourse with her. She took the appellation in good part, and
even encouraged its constant use, which, in fact, was thus far
appropriate, that our Zenobia—however humble looked her
new philosophy—had as much native pride as any queen
would have known what to do with.

III

A KNOT OF DREAMERS

ZENOBIA bade us welcome, in a fine, frank, mellow voice, and gave each of us her hand, which was very soft and warm. She had something appropriate, I recollect, to say to every individual; and what she said to myself was this:—

"I have long wished to know you, Mr. Coverdale, and to thank you for your beautiful poetry, some of which I have learned by heart;—or, rather, it has stolen into my memory, without my exercising any choice or volition about the matter. Of course—permit me to say—you do not think of relinquishing an occupation in which you have done yourself so much credit. I would almost rather give you up, as an associate, than that the world should lose one of its true poets!"

"Ah, no; there will not be the slightest danger of that, especially after this inestimable praise from Zenobia!" said I, smiling and blushing, no doubt, with excess of pleasure. "I hope, on the contrary, now, to produce something that shall really deserve to be called poetry—true, strong, natural, and sweet, as is the life which we are going to lead—something that shall have the notes of wild-birds twittering through it, or a strain like the wind-anthems in the woods, as the case may be!"

"Is it irksome to you to hear your own verses sung?" asked

Zenobia, with a gracious smile. "If so, I am very sorry; for you will certainly hear me singing them, sometimes, in the summer evenings."

"Of all things," answered I, "that is what will delight me most."

While this passed, and while she spoke to my companions, I was taking note of Zenobia's aspect; and it impressed itself on me so distinctly, that I can now summon her up like a ghost, a little wanner than the life, but otherwise identical with it. She was dressed as simply as possible, in an American print, (I think the dry-goods people* call it so,) but with a silken kerchief, between which and her gown there was one glimpse of a white shoulder. It struck me as a great piece of good-fortune that there should be just that glimpse. Her hair —which was dark, glossy, and of singular abundance—was put up rather soberly and primly, without curls, or other ornament, except a single flower. It was an exotic, of rare beauty, and as fresh as if the hot-house gardener had just clipt it from the stem. That flower has struck deep root into my memory. I can both see it and smell it, at this moment. So brilliant, so rare, so costly as it must have been, and yet enduring only for a day, it was more indicative of the pride and pomp, which had a luxuriant growth in Zenobia's character, than if a great diamond had sparkled among her hair.

Her hand, though very soft, was larger than most women would like to have—or than they could afford to have—though not a whit too large in proportion with the spacious plan of Zenobia's entire development. It did one good to see a fine intellect (as hers really was, although its natural tendency lay in another direction than towards literature) so fitly cased. She was, indeed, an admirable figure of a woman, just on the hither verge of her richest maturity, with a combination of features which it is safe to call remarkably beautiful, even if some fastidious persons might pronounce them a little deficient in softness and delicacy. But we find enough of those attributes, everywhere. Preferable—by way of variety, at least —was Zenobia's bloom, health, and vigor, which she possessed in such overflow that a man might well have fallen in love with her for their sake only. In her quiet moods, she seemed rather indolent; but when really in earnest, particularly if there were a spice of bitter feeling, she grew all alive, to her finger-tips.

"I am the first-comer," Zenobia went on to say, while her smile beamed warmth upon us all; "so I take the part of hostess, for to-day, and welcome you as if to my own fireside. You shall be my guests, too, at supper. Tomorrow, if you please, we will be brethren and sisters, and begin our new life from day-break."

"Have we our various parts assigned?" asked some one.

"Oh, we of the softer sex," responded Zenobia, with her mellow, almost broad laugh—most delectable to hear, but not in the least like an ordinary woman's laugh—"we women (there are four of us here, already) will take the domestic and indoor part of the business, as a matter of course. To bake, to boil, to roast, to fry, to stew—to wash, and iron, and scrub, and sweep, and, at our idler intervals, to repose ourselves on knitting and sewing—these, I suppose, must be feminine occupations for the present. By-and-by, perhaps, when our individual adaptations begin to develop themselves, it may be that some of us, who wear the petticoat, will go afield, and leave the weaker brethren to take our places in the kitchen!"

"What a pity," I remarked, "that the kitchen, and the house-work generally, cannot be left out of our system altogether! It is odd enough, that the kind of labor which falls to the lot of women is just that which chiefly distinguishes artificial life—the life of degenerated mortals—from the life of Paradise. Eve had no dinner-pot, and no clothes to mend, and no washing-day."

"I am afraid," said Zenobia, with mirth gleaming out of

her eyes, "we shall find some difficulty in adopting the Paradisiacal system, for at least a month to come. Look at that snow-drift sweeping past the window! Are there any figs ripe, do you think? Have the pine-apples been gathered, to-day? Would you like a bread-fruit, or a cocoa-nut? Shall I run out and pluck you some roses? No, no, Mr. Coverdale, the only flower hereabouts is the one in my hair, which I got out of a green-house, this morning. As for the garb of Eden," added she, shivering playfully, "I shall not assume it till after May-day!"

Assuredly, Zenobia could not have intended it—the fault must have been entirely in my imagination—but these last words, together with something in her manner, irresistibly brought up a picture of that fine, perfectly developed figure, in Eve's earliest garment. I almost fancied myself actually beholding it.* Her free, careless, generous modes of expression often had this effect of creating images which, though pure, are hardly felt to be quite decorous, when born of a thought that passes between man and woman. I imputed it, at that time, to Zenobia's noble courage, conscious of no harm, and scorning the petty restraints which take the life and color out of other women's conversation. There was another peculiarity about her. We seldom meet with women, now-a-days, and in this country, who impress us as being women at all; their sex fades away and goes for nothing, in ordinary intercourse. Not so with Zenobia. One felt an influence breathing out of her, such as we might suppose to come from Eve, when she was just made, and her Creator brought her to Adam, saying— 'Behold, here is a woman!' Not that I would convey the idea of especial gentleness, grace, modesty, and shyness, but of a certain warm and rich characteristic, which seems, for the most part, to have been refined away out of the feminine system.

"And now," continued Zenobia, "I must go and help get supper. Do you think you can be content—instead of figs, pine-apples, and all the other delicacies of Adam's supper-table—with tea and toast, and a certain modest supply of ham and tongue, which, with the instinct of a housewife, I brought hither in a basket? And there shall be bread-and-milk, too, if the innocence of your taste demands it."

The whole sisterhood now went about their domestic avocations, utterly declining our offers to assist, farther than by bringing wood, for the kitchen-fire, from a huge pile in the back-yard. After heaping up more than a sufficient quantity, we returned to the sitting-room, drew our chairs closer to the hearth, and began to talk over our prospects. Soon, with a tremendous stamping in the entry, appeared Silas Foster, lank, stalwart, uncouth, and grisly-bearded. He came from foddering the cattle, in the barn, and from the field, where he had been ploughing, until the depth of the snow rendered it impossible to draw a furrow. He greeted us in pretty much the same tone as if he were speaking to his oxen, took a quid from his iron tobacco-box, pulled off his wet cow-hide boots, and sat down before the fire in his stocking-feet. The steam arose from his soaked garments, so that the stout yeoman looked vaporous and spectre-like.

"Well, folks," remarked Silas, "you'll be wishing yourselves back to town again, if this weather holds!"

And, true enough, there was a look of gloom, as the twilight fell silently and sadly out of the sky, its gray or sable flakes intermingling themselves with the fast descending snow. The storm, in its evening aspect, was decidedly dreary. It seemed to have arisen for our especial behoof; a symbol of the cold, desolate, distrustful phantoms that invariably haunt the mind, on the eve of adventurous enterprises, to warn us back within the boundaries of ordinary life.

But our courage did not quail. We would not allow ourselves to be depressed by the snow-drift, trailing past the window, any more than if it had been the sigh of a summer wind among rustling boughs. There have been few brighter seasons for us, than that. If ever men might lawfully dream awake, and give utterance to their wildest visions, without dread of laughter or scorn on the part of the audience—yes, and speak of earthly happiness, for themselves and mankind, as an object to be hopefully striven for, and probably attained —we, who made that little semi-circle round the blazing fire, were those very men. We had left the rusty iron frame-work of society behind us. We had broken through many hindrances that are powerful enough to keep most people on the weary tread-mill of the established system, even while they feel its irksomeness almost as intolerable as we did. We had stept down from the pulpit; we had flung aside the pen; we had shut up the ledger; we had thrown off that sweet, bewitching, enervating indolence, which is better, after all, than most of the enjoyments within mortal grasp. It was our purpose—a generous one, certainly, and absurd, no doubt, in full proportion with its generosity—to give up whatever we had heretofore attained, for the sake of showing mankind the example of a life governed by other than the false and cruel principles, on which human society has all along been based.

And, first of all, we had divorced ourselves from Pride, and were striving to supply its place with familiar love. We meant to lessen the laboring man's great burthen of toil, by performing our due share of it at the cost of our own thews and sinews. We sought our profit by mutual aid, instead of wresting it by the strong hand from an enemy, or filching it craftily from those less shrewd than ourselves, (if, indeed, there were any such, in New England,) or winning it by selfish competition with a neighbor; in one or another of which fashions, every son of woman both perpetrates and suffers his share of the common evil, whether he chooses it or no. And, as the basis of our institution, we purposed to offer up the earnest toil of our bodies, as a prayer, no less than an effort, for the advancement of our race.

Therefore, if we built splendid castles (phalansteries,*

perhaps, they might be more fitly called,) and pictured beautiful scenes, among the fervid coals of the hearth around which we were clustering—and if all went to rack with the crumbling embers, and have never since arisen out of the ashes—let us take to ourselves no shame. In my own behalf, I rejoice that I could once think better of the world's improvability than it deserved. It is a mistake into which men seldom fall twice, in a lifetime; or, if so, the rarer and higher is the nature that can thus magnanimously persist in error.

Stout Silas Foster mingled little in our conversation; but when he did speak, it was very much to some practical purpose. For instance:—

"Which man among you," quoth he, "is the best judge of swine? Some of us must go to the next Brighton fair, and buy half-a-dozen pigs!"

Pigs! Good heavens, had we come out from among the swinish multitude, for this? And again, in reference to some discussion about raising early vegetables for the market:—

"We shall never make any hand at market-gardening," said Silas Foster, "unless the women-folks will undertake to do all the weeding. We haven't team enough for that and the regular farm-work, reckoning three of you city-folks as worth one common field-hand. No, no, I tell you, we should have to get up a little too early in the morning, to compete with the market-gardeners round Boston!"

It struck me as rather odd, that one of the first questions raised, after our separation from the greedy, struggling, self-seeking world, should relate to the possibility of getting the advantage over the outside barbarians, in their own field of labor. But, to own the truth, I very soon became sensible, that, as regarded society at large, we stood in a position of new hostility, rather than new brotherhood. Nor could this fail to be the case, in some degree, until the bigger and better half of society should range itself on our side. Constituting so pitiful a minority as now, we were inevitably estranged from the rest of mankind, in pretty fair proportion with the strictness of our mutual bond among ourselves.

This dawning idea, however, was driven back into my inner consciousness by the entrance of Zenobia. She came with the welcome intelligence that supper was on the table. Looking at herself in the glass, and perceiving that her one magnificent flower had grown rather languid, (probably by being exposed to the fervency of the kitchen-fire,) she flung it on the floor, as unconcernedly as a village-girl would throw away a faded violet. The action seemed proper to her character; although, methought, it would still more have befitted the bounteous nature of this beautiful woman to scatter fresh flowers from her hand, and to revive faded ones by her touch. Nevertheless—it was a singular, but irresistible effect—the presence of Zenobia caused our heroic enterprise to show like an illusion, a masquerade, a pastoral, a counterfeit Arcadia,* in which we grown-up men and women were making a play-day of the years that were given us to live in. I tried to analyze this impression, but not with much success.

"It really vexes me," observed Zenobia, as we left the room, "that Mr. Hollingsworth should be such a laggard. I should not have thought him at all the sort of person to be turned back by a puff of contrary wind, or a few snow-flakes drifting into his face."

"Do you know Hollingsworth personally?" I inquired.

"No; only as an auditor—auditress, I mean—of some of his lectures," said she. "What a voice he has! And what a man he is! Yet not so much an intellectual man, I should say, as a great heart; at least, he moved me more deeply than I think myself capable of being moved, except by the stroke of a true, strong heart against my own. It is a sad pity that he should have devoted his glorious powers to such a grimy, unbeautiful, and positively hopeless object as this reformation of criminals, about which he makes himself and his wretchedly small audiences so very miserable. To tell you a secret, I never could tolerate a philanthropist, before. Could you?"

"By no means," I answered; "neither can I now!"

"They are, indeed, an odiously disagreeable set of mortals," continued Zenobia. "I should like Mr. Hollingsworth a great deal better, if the philanthropy had been left out. At all events, as a mere matter of taste, I wish he would let the bad people alone, and try to benefit those who are not already past his help. Do you suppose he will be content to spend his life—or even a few months of it—among tolerably virtuous and comfortable individuals, like ourselves?"

"Upon my word, I doubt it," said I. "If we wish to keep him with us, we must systematically commit at least one crime apiece! Mere peccadillos will not satisfy him."

Zenobia turned, sidelong, a strange kind of a glance upon me; but, before I could make out what it meant, we had entered the kitchen, where, in accordance with the rustic simplicity of our new life, the supper-table was spread.

IV

THE SUPPER-TABLE

T HE PLEASANT firelight! I must still keep harping
on it.

The kitchen-hearth had an old-fashioned breadth,
depth, and spaciousness, far within which lay what seemed
the butt of a good-sized oak-tree, with the moisture bubbling
merrily out of both ends. It was now half-an-hour beyond
dusk. The blaze from an armfull of substantial sticks, rendered
more combustible by brush-wood and pine, flickered powerfully on the smoke-blackened walls, and so cheered our spirits
that we cared not what inclemency might rage and roar, on
the other side of our illuminated windows. A yet sultrier
warmth was bestowed by a goodly quantity of peat, which was
crumbling to white ashes among the burning brands, and
incensed the kitchen with its not ungrateful fragrance. The
exuberance of this household fire would alone have sufficed
to bespeak us no true farmers; for the New England yeoman,
if he have the misfortune to dwell within practicable distance
of a wood-market, is as niggardly of each stick as if it were a
bar of California gold.*

But it was fortunate for us, on that wintry eve of our untried
life, to enjoy the warm and radiant luxury of a somewhat too
abundant fire. If it served no other purpose, it made the men
look so full of youth, warm blood, and hope, and the women—

such of them, at least, as were anywise convertible by its magic
—so very beautiful, that I would cheerfully have spent my
last dollar to prolong the blaze. As for Zenobia, there was a
glow in her cheeks that made me think of Pandora,* fresh
from Vulcan's workshop, and full of the celestial warmth by
dint of which he had tempered and moulded her.

"Take your places, my dear friends all," cried she; "seat
yourselves without ceremony—and you shall be made happy
with such tea as not many of the world's working-people,
except yourselves, will find in their cups to-night. After this
one supper, you may drink butter-milk, if you please.
To-night, we will quaff this nectar, which, I assure you,
could not be bought with gold."

We all sat down—grisly Silas Foster, his rotund helpmate,
and the two bouncing handmaidens, included—and looked at
one another in a friendly, but rather awkward way. It was the
first practical trial of our theories of equal brotherhood and
sisterhood; and we people of superior cultivation and refine-
ment (for as such, I presume, we unhesitatingly reckoned
ourselves) felt as if something were already accomplished
towards the millennium of love.* The truth is, however, that
the laboring oar was with our unpolished companions; it being
far easier to condescend, than to accept of condescension.
Neither did I refrain from questioning, in secret, whether
some of us—and Zenobia among the rest—would so quietly
have taken our places among these good people, save for the
cherished consciousness that it was not by necessity, but
choice. Though we saw fit to drink our tea out of earthen
cups to-night, and in earthen company, it was at our own
option to use pictured porcelain and handle silver forks again,
tomorrow. This same salvo, as to the power of regaining our
former position, contributed much, I fear, to the equanimity
with which we subsequently bore many of the hardships and
humiliations of a life of toil. If ever I have deserved—(which
has not often been the case, and, I think, never)—but if ever

I did deserve to be soundly cuffed by a fellow-mortal, for secretly putting weight upon some imaginary social advantage, it must have been while I was striving to prove myself ostentatiously his equal, and no more. It was while I sat beside him on his cobbler's bench, or clinked my hoe against his own, in the cornfield, or broke the same crust of bread, my earth-grimed hand to his, at our noontide lunch. The poor, proud man should look at both sides of sympathy like this.

The silence, which followed upon our sitting down to table, grew rather oppressive; indeed, it was hardly broken by a word, during the first round of Zenobia's fragrant tea.

"I hope," said I, at last, "that our blazing windows will be visible a great way off. There is nothing so pleasant and encouraging to a solitary traveller, on a stormy night, as a flood of firelight, seen amid the gloom. These ruddy window-panes cannot fail to cheer the hearts of all that look at them. Are they not warm and bright with the beacon-fire which we have kindled for humanity?"

"The blaze of that brush-wood will only last a minute or two longer," observed Silas Foster; but whether he meant to insinuate that our moral illumination would have as brief a term, I cannot say.

"Meantime," said Zenobia, "it may serve to guide some wayfarer to a shelter."

And, just as she said this, there came a knock at the house-door.

"There is one of the world's wayfarers!" said I.

"Aye, aye, just so!" quoth Silas Foster. "Our firelight will draw stragglers, just as a candle draws dor-bugs, on a summer night."

Whether to enjoy a dramatic suspense, or that we were selfishly contrasting our own comfort with the chill and dreary situation of the unknown person at the threshold—or that some of us city-folk felt a little startled at the knock which came so unseasonably, through night and storm, to the door of the lonely farm-house—so it happened, that nobody, for an instant or two, arose to answer the summons. Pretty soon, there came another knock. The first had been moderately loud; the second was smitten so forcibly that the knuckles of the applicant must have left their mark in the door-panel.

"He knocks as if he had a right to come in," said Zenobia, laughing. "And what are we thinking of? It must be Mr. Hollingsworth!"

Hereupon, I went to the door, unbolted, and flung it wide open. There, sure enough, stood Hollingsworth, his shaggy great-coat all covered with snow; so that he looked quite as much like a polar bear as a modern philanthropist.

"Sluggish hospitality, this!" said he, in those deep tones of his, which seemed to come out of a chest as capacious as a barrel. "It would have served you right if I had lain down and spent the night on the door-step, just for the sake of putting you to shame. But here is a guest, who will need a warmer and softer bed."

And stepping back to the wagon, in which he had journeyed hither, Hollingsworth received into his arms, and deposited on the door-step, a figure enveloped in a cloak. It was evidently a woman; or rather—judging from the ease with which he lifted her, and the little space which she seemed to fill in his arms—a slim and unsubstantial girl. As she showed some hesitation about entering the door, Hollingsworth, with his usual directness and lack of ceremony, urged her forward, not merely within the entry, but into the warm and strongly lighted kitchen.

"Who is this?" whispered I, remaining behind with him, while he was taking off his great-coat.

"Who? Really, I don't know," answered Hollingsworth, looking at me with some surprise. "It is a young person who belongs here, however; and, no doubt, she has been expected. Zenobia, or some of the women-folks, can tell you all about it."

"I think not," said I, glancing towards the new-comer and

the other occupants of the kitchen. "Nobody seems to welcome her. I should hardly judge that she was an expected
guest."

"Well, well," said Hollingsworth, quietly. "We'll make
it right."

The stranger, or whatever she were, remained standing
precisely on that spot of the kitchen-floor, to which Hollingsworth's kindly hand had impelled her. The cloak falling partly
off, she was seen to be a very young woman, dressed in a
poor, but decent gown, made high in the neck, and without
any regard to fashion or smartness. Her brown hair fell down
from beneath a hood, not in curls, but with only a slight
wave; her face was of a wan, almost sickly hue, betokening
habitual seclusion from the sun and free atmosphere, like a
flower-shrub that had done its best to blossom in too scanty
light. To complete the pitiableness of her aspect, she shivered either with cold, or fear, or nervous excitement, so that
you might have beheld her shadow vibrating on the fire-
lighted wall. In short, there has seldom been seen so depressed
and sad a figure as this young girl's; and it was hardly possible
to help being angry with her, from mere despair of doing
anything for her comfort. The fantasy occurred to me, that
she was some desolate kind of a creature, doomed to wander
about in snow-storms, and that, though the ruddiness of our
window-panes had tempted her into a human dwelling, she
would not remain long enough to melt the icicles out of
her hair.

Another conjecture likewise came into my mind. Recollecting Hollingsworth's sphere of philanthropic action, I deemed
it possible that he might have brought one of his guilty
patients, to be wrought upon, and restored to spiritual health,
by the pure influences which our mode of life would create.

As yet, the girl had not stirred. She stood near the door,
fixing a pair of large, brown, melancholy eyes upon Zenobia—
only upon Zenobia!—she evidently saw nothing else in the

room, save that bright, fair, rosy, beautiful woman. It was
the strangest look I ever witnessed; long a mystery to me,
and forever a memory. Once, she seemed about to move forward and greet her—I know not with what warmth, or with
what words;—but, finally, instead of doing so, she drooped
down upon her knees, clasped her hands, and gazed piteously
into Zenobia's face. Meeting no kindly reception, her head
fell on her bosom.

I never thoroughly forgave Zenobia for her conduct on this
occasion. But women are always more cautious, in their casual
hospitalities, than men.

"What does the girl mean?" cried she, in rather a sharp
tone. "Is she crazy? Has she no tongue?"

And here Hollingsworth stept forward.

"No wonder if the poor child's tongue is frozen in her
mouth," said he—and I think he positively frowned at Zenobia
—"The very heart will be frozen in her bosom, unless you
women can warm it, among you, with the warmth that ought
to be in your own!"

Hollingsworth's appearance was very striking, at this
moment. He was then about thirty years old, but looked
several years older, with his great shaggy head, his heavy
brow, his dark complexion, his abundant beard, and the rude
strength with which his features seemed to have been hammered out of iron, rather than chiselled or moulded from any
finer or softer material. His figure was not tall, but massive
and brawny, and well befitting his original occupation, which
—as the reader probably knows—was that of a blacksmith. As
for external polish, or mere courtesy of manner, he never possessed more than a tolerably educated bear; although, in his
gentler moods, there was a tenderness in his voice, eyes,
mouth, in his gesture, and in every indescribable manifestation, which few men could resist, and no woman. But he now
looked stern and reproachful; and it was with that inauspicious

meaning in his glance, that Hollingsworth first met Zenobia's eyes, and began his influence upon her life.

To my surprise, Zenobia—of whose haughty spirit I had been told so many examples—absolutely changed color, and seemed mortified and confused.

"You do not quite do me justice, Mr. Hollingsworth," said she, almost humbly. "I am willing to be kind to the poor girl. Is she a protégée of yours? What can I do for her?"

"Have you anything to ask of this lady?" said Hollingsworth, kindly, to the girl. "I remember you mentioned her name, before we left town."

"Only that she will shelter me," replied the girl, tremulously. "Only that she will let me be always near her!"

"Well, indeed," exclaimed Zenobia, recovering herself, and laughing, "this is an adventure, and well worthy to be the first incident in our life of love and free-heartedness! But I accept it, for the present, without further question—only," added she, "it would be a convenience if we knew your name!"

"Priscilla," said the girl; and it appeared to me that she hesitated whether to add anything more, and decided in the negative. "Pray do not ask me my other name—at least, not yet—if you will be so kind to a forlorn creature."

Priscilla! Priscilla! I repeated the name to myself, three or four times; and, in that little space, this quaint and prim cognomen had so amalgamated itself with my idea of the girl, that it seemed as if no other name could have adhered to her for a moment. Heretofore, the poor thing had not shed any tears; but now that she found herself received, and at least temporarily established, the big drops began to ooze out from beneath her eyelids, as if she were full of them. Perhaps it showed the iron substance of my heart, that I could not help smiling at this odd scene of unknown and unaccountable calamity, into which our cheerful party had been entrapped, without the liberty of choosing whether to sympathize or no.

Hollingsworth's behavior was certainly a great deal more creditable than mine.

"Let us not pry farther into her secrets," he said to Zenobia and the rest of us, apart—and his dark, shaggy face looked really beautiful with its expression of thoughtful benevolence —"Let us conclude that Providence has sent her to us, as the first fruits of the world, which we have undertaken to make happier than we find it. Let us warm her poor, shivering body with this good fire, and her poor, shivering heart with our best kindness. Let us feed her, and make her one of us. As we do by this friendless girl, so shall we prosper! And, in good time, whatever is desirable for us to know will be melted out of her, as inevitably as those tears which we see now."

"At least," remarked I, "you may tell us how and where you met with her."

"An old man brought her to my lodgings," answered Hollingsworth, "and begged me to convey her to Blithedale, where—so I understood him—she had friends. And this is positively all I know about the matter."

Grim Silas Foster, all this while, had been busy at the supper-table, pouring out his own tea, and gulping it down with no more sense of its exquisiteness than if it were a decoction of catnip; helping himself to pieces of dipt toast on the flat of his knife-blade, and dropping half of it on the table-cloth; using the same serviceable implement to cut slice after slice of ham; perpetrating terrible enormities with the butter-plate; and, in all other respects, behaving less like a civilized Christian than the worst kind of an ogre. Being, by this time, fully gorged, he crowned his amiable exploits with a draught from the water-pitcher, and then favored us with his opinion about the business in hand. And, certainly, though they proceeded out of an unwiped mouth, his expressions did him honor.

"Give the girl a hot cup of tea, and a thick slice of this first-rate bacon," said Silas, like a sensible man as he was. "That's what she wants. Let her stay with us as long as she likes, and help in the kitchen, and take the cow-breath at milking-time; and, in a week or two, she'll begin to look like a creature of this world!"

So we sat down again to supper, and Priscilla along with us.

V

UNTIL BEDTIME

S ILAS FOSTER, by the time we concluded our meal, had
stript off his coat and planted himself on a low chair
by the kitchen-fire, with a lap-stone, a hammer, a piece
of sole-leather, and some waxed ends, in order to cobble an
old pair of cow-hide boots; he being, in his own phrase,
'something of a dab' (whatever degree of skill that may imply)
at the shoemaking-business. We heard the tap of his hammer,
at intervals, for the rest of the evening. The remainder of the
party adjourned to the sitting-room. Good Mrs. Foster took
her knitting-work, and soon fell fast asleep, still keeping her
needles in brisk movement, and, to the best of my observation,
absolutely footing a stocking out of the texture of a dream.
And a very substantial stocking it seemed to be. One of the
two handmaidens hemmed a towel, and the other appeared
to be making a ruffle, for her Sunday's wear, out of a little
bit of embroidered muslin, which Zenobia had probably
given her.

It was curious to observe how trustingly, and yet how
timidly, our poor Priscilla betook herself into the shadow of
Zenobia's protection. She sat beside her on a stool, looking
up, every now and then, with an expression of humble
delight at her new friend's beauty. A brilliant woman is
often an object of the devoted admiration—it might almost be

termed worship, or idolatry—of some young girl, who perhaps
beholds the cynosure only at an awful distance, and has as
little hope of personal intercourse as of climbing among the
stars of heaven. We men are too gross to comprehend it. Even
a woman, of mature age, despises or laughs at such a passion.
There occurred to me no mode of accounting for Priscilla's
behavior, except by supposing that she had read some of
Zenobia's stories, (as such literature goes everywhere,) or
her tracts in defence of the sex, and had come hither with the
one purpose of being her slave. There is nothing parallel to
this, I believe—nothing so foolishly disinterested, and hardly
anything so beautiful—in the masculine nature, at whatever
epoch of life; or, if there be, a fine and rare development of
character might reasonably be looked for, from the youth who
should prove himself capable of such self-forgetful affection.

Zenobia happening to change her seat, I took the opportunity, in an under tone, to suggest some such notion as
the above.

"Since you see the young woman in so poetical a light,"
replied she, in the same tone, "you had better turn the affair
into a ballad. It is a grand subject, and worthy of supernatural
machinery. The storm, the startling knock at the door, the
entrance of the sable knight Hollingsworth and this shadowy
snow-maiden, who, precisely at the stroke of midnight, shall
melt away at my feet, in a pool of ice-cold water, and give me
my death with a pair of wet slippers! And when the verses
are written, and polished quite to your mind, I will favor you
with my idea as to what the girl really is."

"Pray let me have it now," said I. "It shall be woven into
the ballad."

"She is neither more nor less," answered Zenobia, "than
a seamstress from the city,* and she has probably no more
transcendental purpose than to do my miscellaneous sewing;
for I suppose she will hardly expect to make my dresses."

"How can you decide upon her so easily?" I inquired.

"Oh, we women judge one another by tokens that escape the obtuseness of masculine perceptions," said Zenobia. "There is no proof, which you would be likely to appreciate, except the needle marks on the tip of her forefinger. Then, my supposition perfectly accounts for her paleness, her nervousness, and her wretched fragility. Poor thing! She has been stifled with the heat of a salamander-stove,* in a small, close room, and has drunk coffee, and fed upon dough-nuts, raisins, candy, and all such trash, till she is scarcely half-alive; and so, as she has hardly any physique, a poet, like Mr. Miles Coverdale, may be allowed to think her spiritual!"

"Look at her now!" whispered I.

Priscilla was gazing towards us, with an inexpressible sorrow in her wan face, and great tears running down her cheeks. It was difficult to resist the impression, that, cautiously as we had lowered our voices, she must have overheard and been wounded by Zenobia's scornful estimate of her character and purposes.

"What ears the girl must have!" whispered Zenobia, with a look of vexation, partly comic and partly real. "I will confess to you that I cannot quite make her out. However, I am positively not an ill-natured person, unless when very grievously provoked; and as you, and especially Mr. Hollingsworth, take so much interest in this odd creature—and as she knocks, with a very slight tap, against my own heart, likewise—why, I mean to let her in! From this moment, I will be reasonably kind to her. There is no pleasure in tormenting a person of one's own sex, even if she do favor one with a little more love than one can conveniently dispose of;—and that, let me say, Mr. Coverdale, is the most troublesome offence you can offer to a woman."

"Thank you!" said I, smiling. "I don't mean to be guilty of it."

She went towards Priscilla, took her hand, and passed her own rosy finger-tips, with a pretty, caressing movement, over the girl's hair. The touch had a magical effect. So vivid a look of joy flushed up beneath those fingers, that it seemed as if the sad and wan Priscilla had been snatched away, and another kind of creature substituted in her place. This one caress, bestowed voluntarily by Zenobia, was evidently received as a pledge of all that the stranger sought from her, whatever the unuttered boon might be. From that instant, too, she melted in quietly amongst us, and was no longer a foreign element. Though always an object of peculiar interest, a riddle, and a theme of frequent discussion, her tenure at Blithedale was thenceforth fixed; we no more thought of questioning it, than if Priscilla had been recognized as a domestic sprite, who had haunted the rustic fireside, of old, before we had ever been warmed by its blaze.

She now produced, out of a work-bag that she had with her, some little wooden instruments, (what they are called, I never knew,) and proceeded to knit, or net, an article which ultimately took the shape of a silk purse. As the work went on, I remembered to have seen just such purses, before. Indeed, I was the possessor of one. Their peculiar excellence, besides the great delicacy and beauty of the manufacture, lay in the almost impossibility that any uninitiated person should discover the aperture; although, to a practised touch, they would open as wide as charity or prodigality might wish. I wondered if it were not a symbol of Priscilla's own mystery.

Notwithstanding the new confidence with which Zenobia had inspired her, our guest showed herself disquieted by the storm. When the strong puffs of wind spattered the snow against the windows, and made the oaken frame of the farm-house creak, she looked at us apprehensively, as if to inquire whether these tempestuous outbreaks did not betoken some unusual mischief in the shrieking blast. She had been bred up, no doubt, in some close nook, some inauspiciously sheltered court of the city, where the uttermost rage of a tempest, though it might scatter down the slates of the roof into the bricked area, could not shake the casement of her little room. The sense of vast, undefined space, pressing from the outside against the black panes of our uncurtained windows, was fearful to the poor girl, heretofore accustomed to the narrowness of human limits, with the lamps of neighboring tenements glimmering across the street. The house probably seemed to her adrift on the great ocean of the night. A little parallelogram of sky was all that she had hitherto known of nature; so that she felt the awfulness that really exists in its limitless extent. Once, while the blast was bellowing, she caught hold of Zenobia's robe, with precisely the air of one who hears her own name spoken, at a distance, but is unutterably reluctant to obey the call.

We spent rather an incommunicative evening. Hollingsworth hardly said a word, unless when repeatedly and pertinaciously addressed. Then, indeed, he would glare upon us from the thick shrubbery of his meditations, like a tiger out of a jungle, make the briefest reply possible, and betake himself back into the solitude of his heart and mind. The poor fellow had contracted this ungracious habit from the intensity with which he contemplated his own ideas, and the infrequent sympathy which they met with from his auditors; a circumstance that seemed only to strengthen the implicit confidence that he awarded to them. His heart, I imagine, was never really interested in our socialist scheme, but was forever busy with his strange, and, as most people thought it, impracticable plan for the reformation of criminals, through an appeal to their higher instincts. Much as I liked Hollingsworth, it cost me many a groan to tolerate him on this point. He ought to have commenced his investigation of the subject by perpetrating some huge sin, in his proper person, and examining the condition of his higher instincts, afterwards.

The rest of us formed ourselves into a committee for providing our infant Community with an appropriate name; a matter of greatly more difficulty than the uninitiated reader would suppose. Blithedale*was neither good nor bad. We should have resumed the old Indian name of the premises, had it possessed the oil-and-honey flow which the aborigines were so often happy in communicating to their local appellations; but it chanced to be a harsh, ill-connected, and interminable word, which seemed to fill the mouth with a mixture of very stiff clay and very crumbly pebbles. Zenobia suggested 'Sunny Glimpse,' as expressive of a vista into a better system of society. This we turned over and over, for awhile, acknowledging its prettiness, but concluded it to be rather too fine and sentimental a name (a fault inevitable by literary ladies, in such attempts) for sun-burnt men to work under. I ventured to whisper 'Utopia,' which, however, was unanimously scouted down, and the proposer very harshly maltreated, as if he had intended a latent satire. Some were for calling our institution 'The Oasis,' in view of its being the one green spot in the moral sand-waste of the world; but others insisted on a proviso for reconsidering the matter, at a twelvemonth's end; when a final decision might be had, whether to name it 'The Oasis,' or 'Saharah.' So, at last, finding it impracticable to hammer out anything better, we resolved that the spot should still be Blithedale, as being of good augury enough.

The evening wore on, and the outer solitude looked in upon us through the windows, gloomy, wild, and vague, like another state of existence, close beside the littler sphere of warmth and light in which we were the prattlers and bustlers of a moment. By-and-by, the door was opened by Silas Foster, with a cotton handkerchief about his head, and a tallow candle in his hand.

"Take my advice, brother-farmers," said he, with a great, broad, bottomless yawn, "and get to bed as soon as you can. I shall sound the horn at day-break; and we've got the cattle to fodder, and nine cows to milk, and a dozen other things to do, before breakfast."

Thus ended the first evening at Blithedale. I went shivering to my fireless chamber, with the miserable consciousness (which had been growing upon me for several hours past) that I had caught a tremendous cold, and should probably awaken, at the blast of the horn, a fit subject for a hospital. The night proved a feverish one. During the greater part of it, I was in that vilest of states when a fixed idea remains in the mind, like the nail in Sisera's brain,* while innumerable other ideas go and come, and flutter to-and-fro, combining constant transition with intolerable sameness. Had I made a record of that night's half-waking dreams, it is my belief that it would have anticipated several of the chief incidents of this narrative, including a dim shadow of its catastrophe. Starting up in bed, at length, I saw that the storm was past, and the moon was shining on the snowy landscape, which looked like a lifeless copy of the world in marble.

From the bank of the distant river, which was shimmering in the moonlight, came the black shadow of the only cloud in heaven, driven swiftly by the wind, and passing over meadow and hillock—vanishing amid tufts of leafless trees, but reappearing on the hither side—until it swept across our door-step.

How cold an Arcadia* was this!

VI

COVERDALE'S SICK-CHAMBER

THE HORN sounded at day-break, as Silas Foster had forewarned us, harsh, uproarious, inexorably drawn out, and as sleep-dispelling as if this hard-hearted old yeoman had got hold of the trump of doom.

On all sides, I could hear the creaking of the bedsteads, as the brethren of Blithedale started from slumber, and thrust themselves into their habiliments, all awry, no doubt, in their haste to begin the reformation of the world. Zenobia put her head into the entry, and besought Silas Foster to cease his clamor, and to be kind enough to leave an armful of firewood and a pail of water at her chamber-door. Of the whole household—unless, indeed, it were Priscilla, for whose habits, in this particular, I cannot vouch—of all our apostolic society, whose mission was to bless mankind, Hollingsworth, I apprehend, was the only one who began the enterprise with prayer. My sleeping-room being but thinly partitioned from his, the solemn murmur of his voice made its way to my ears, compelling me to be an auditor of his awful privacy with the Creator. It affected me with a deep reverence for Hollingsworth, which no familiarity then existing, or that afterwards grew more intimate between us—no, nor my subsequent perception of his own great errors—ever quite effaced. It is so rare, in these times, to meet with a man of prayerful habits, (except, of course, in the pulpit,) that such an one is decidedly marked out by a light of transfiguration, shed upon him in the divine interview from which he passes into his daily life.

As for me, I lay abed, and, if I said my prayers, it was backward, cursing my day as bitterly as patient Job himself. The truth was, the hot-house warmth of a town-residence, and the luxurious life in which I indulged myself, had taken much of the pith out of my physical system; and the wintry blast of the preceding day, together with the general chill of our airy old farm-house, had got fairly into my heart and the marrow of my bones. In this predicament, I seriously wished—selfish as it may appear—that the reformation of society had been postponed about half-a-century, or at all events, to such a date as should have put my intermeddling with it entirely out of the question.

What, in the name of common-sense, had I to do with any better society than I had always lived in! It had satisfied me well enough. My pleasant bachelor-parlor, sunny and shadowy, curtained and carpeted, with the bed-chamber adjoining; my centre-table, strewn with books and periodicals; my writing-desk, with a half-finished poem in a stanza of my own contrivance; my morning lounge at the reading-room or picture-gallery; my noontide walk along the cheery pavement, with the suggestive succession of human faces, and the brisk throb of human life, in which I shared; my dinner at the Albion, where I had a hundred dishes at command, and could banquet as delicately as the wizard Michael Scott,* when the devil fed him from the King of France's kitchen; my evening at the billiard-club, the concert, the theatre, or at somebody's party, if I pleased:—what could be better than all this? Was it better to hoe, to mow, to toil and moil amidst the accumulations of a barn-yard, to be the chambermaid of two yoke of oxen and a dozen cows, to eat salt-beef and earn it with the sweat of my brow, and thereby take the tough morsel out of some wretch's mouth, into whose vocation I had thrust myself? Above all, was it better to have a fever, and die blaspheming, as I was like to do?

In this wretched plight, with a furnace in my heart, and another in my head, by the heat of which I was kept constantly at the boiling point—yet shivering at the bare idea of extruding so much as a finger into the icy atmosphere of the room—I kept my bed until breakfast-time, when Hollingsworth knocked at the door, and entered.

"Well, Coverdale," cried he, "you bid fair to make an admirable farmer! Don't you mean to get up to-day?"

"Neither to-day nor tomorrow," said I, hopelessly. "I doubt if I ever rise again!"

"What is the matter now?" he asked.

I told him my piteous case, and besought him to send me back to town, in a close carriage.

"No, no!" said Hollingsworth, with kindly seriousness. "If you are really sick, we must take care of you."

Accordingly, he built a fire in my chamber, and having little else to do while the snow lay on the ground, established himself as my nurse. A doctor was sent for, who, being homeopathic,* gave me as much medicine, in the course of a fortnight's attendance, as would have lain on the point of a needle. They fed me on water-gruel, and I speedily became a skeleton above ground. But, after all, I have many precious recollections connected with that fit of sickness.

Hollingsworth's more than brotherly attendance gave me inexpressible comfort. Most men—and, certainly, I could not always claim to be one of the exceptions—have a natural indifference, if not an absolutely hostile feeling, towards those whom disease, or weakness, or calamity of any kind, causes to faulter and faint amid the rude jostle of our selfish existence. The education of Christianity, it is true, the sympathy of a like experience, and the example of women, may soften, and possibly subvert, this ugly characteristic of our sex. But it is originally there, and has likewise its analogy in the practice of our brute brethren, who hunt the sick or disabled member of the herd from among them, as an enemy. It is for this reason that the stricken deer goes apart, and the sick lion grimly withdraws himself into his den. Except in love, or the attachments of kindred, or other very long and habitual affection, we really have no tenderness. But there was something of the woman moulded into the great, stalwart frame of Hollingsworth; nor was he ashamed of it, as men often are of what is best in them, nor seemed ever to know that there was such a soft place in his heart. I knew it well, however, at that time; although, afterwards, it came nigh to be forgotten. Methought there could not be two such men alive, as Hollingsworth. There never was any blaze of a fireside that warmed and cheered me, in the down-sinkings and shiverings of my spirit, so effectually as did the light out of those eyes, which lay so deep and dark under his shaggy brows.

· Happy the man that has such a friend beside him, when he comes to die! And unless a friend like Hollingsworth be at hand, as most probably there will not, he had better make up his mind to die alone. How many men, I wonder, does one meet with, in a lifetime, whom he would choose for his death-bed companions! At the crisis of my fever, I besought Hollingsworth to let nobody else enter the room, but continually to make me sensible of his own presence by a grasp of the hand, a word—a prayer, if he thought good to utter it—and that then he should be the witness how courageously I would encounter the worst. It still impresses me as almost a matter of regret, that I did not die, then, when I had tolerably made up my mind to it; for Hollingsworth would have gone with me to the hither verge of life, and have sent his friendly and hopeful accents far over on the other side, while I should be treading the unknown path. Now, were I to send for him, he would hardly come to my bedside; nor should I depart the easier, for his presence.

"You are not going to die, this time," said he, gravely smiling. "You know nothing about sickness, and think your case a great deal more desperate than it is."

"Death should take me while I am in the mood," replied I, with a little of my customary levity.

"Have you nothing to do in life," asked Hollingsworth, "that you fancy yourself so ready to leave it?"

"Nothing," answered I—"nothing, that I know of, unless to make pretty verses, and play a part, with Zenobia and the rest of the amateurs, in our pastoral. It seems but an unsubstantial sort of business, as viewed through a mist of fever. But, dear Hollingsworth, your own vocation is evidently to be a priest, and to spend your days and nights in helping your fellow-creatures to draw peaceful dying-breaths."

"And by which of my qualities," inquired he, "can you suppose me fitted for this awful ministry?"

"By your tenderness," I said. "It seems to me the reflection of God's own love."

"And you call me tender!" repeated Hollingsworth, thoughtfully. "I should rather say, that the most marked trait in my character is an inflexible severity of purpose. Mortal man has no right to be so inflexible, as it is my nature and necessity to be!"

"I do not believe it," I replied.

But, in due time, I remembered what he said.

Probably, as Hollingsworth suggested, my disorder was never so serious as, in my ignorance of such matters, I was inclined to consider it. After so much tragical preparation, it was positively rather mortifying to find myself on the mending hand.

All the other members of the Community showed me kindness, according to the full measure of their capacity. Zenobia brought me my gruel, every day, made by her own hands, (not very skilfully, if the truth must be told,) and, whenever I seemed inclined to converse, would sit by my bedside, and talk with so much vivacity as to add several gratuitous throbs to my pulse. Her poor little stories and tracts never half did justice to her intellect; it was only the lack of a fitter avenue that drove her to seek development in literature. She was made (among a thousand other things that she might have been) for a stump-oratress. I recognized no severe culture in Zenobia; her mind was full of weeds. It startled me, sometimes, in my state of moral, as well as bodily faint-heartedness, to observe the hardihood of her philosophy; she made no scruple of oversetting all human institutions, and scattering them as with a breeze from her fan. A female reformer, in her attacks upon society, has an instinctive sense of where the life lies, and is inclined to aim directly at that spot. Especially, the relation between the sexes is naturally among the earliest to attract her notice.

Zenobia was truly a magnificent woman. The homely simplicity of her dress could not conceal, nor scarcely diminish, the queenliness of her presence. The image of her form and face should have been multiplied all over the earth. It was wronging the rest of mankind, to retain her as the spectacle of only a few. The stage would have been her proper sphere. She should have made it a point of duty, moreover, to sit endlessly to painters and sculptors, and preferably to the latter; because the cold decorum of the marble would consist with the utmost scantiness of drapery, so that the eye might chastely be gladdened with her material perfection, in its entirety. I know not well how to express, that the native glow of coloring in her cheeks, and even the flesh-warmth over her round arms, and what was visible of her full bust—in a word, her womanliness incarnated—compelled me sometimes to close my eyes, as if it were not quite the privilege of modesty to gaze at her. Illness and exhaustion, no doubt, had made me morbidly sensitive.

I noticed—and wondered how Zenobia contrived it—that she had always a new flower in her hair. And still it was a hot-house flower—an outlandish flower—a flower of the tropics, such as appeared to have sprung passionately out of a soil, the very weeds of which would be fervid and spicy. Unlike as was the flower of each successive day to the preceding one, it yet so assimilated its richness to the rich beauty of the woman, that I thought it the only flower fit to be worn; so fit, indeed, that Nature had evidently created this floral gem, in a happy exuberance, for the one purpose of worthily adorning Zenobia's head. It might be, that my feverish fantasies clustered themselves about this peculiarity, and caused it to look more gorgeous and wonderful than if beheld with temperate eyes. In the height of my illness, as I well recollect, I went so far as to pronounce it preternatural.

"Zenobia is an enchantress!" whispered I once to Hollingsworth. "She is a sister of the Veiled Lady! That flower in her hair is a talisman. If you were to snatch it away, she would vanish; or be transformed into something else!"

"What does he say?" asked Zenobia.

"Nothing that has an atom of sense in it," answered Hollingsworth. "He is a little beside himself, I believe, and talks about your being a witch, and of some magical property in the flower that you wear in your hair."

"It is an idea worthy of a feverish poet," said she, laughing, rather compassionately, and taking out the flower. "I scorn to owe anything to magic. Here, Mr. Hollingsworth:—you may keep the spell, while it has any virtue in it; but I cannot promise you not to appear with a new one, tomorrow. It is the one relic of my more brilliant, my happier days!"

The most curious part of the matter was, that, long after my slight delirium had passed away—as long, indeed, as I continued to know this remarkable woman—her daily flower affected my imagination, though more slightly, yet in very much the same way. The reason must have been, that, whether intentionally on her part, or not, this favorite ornament was actually a subtile expression of Zenobia's character.

One subject, about which—very impertinently, moreover—
I perplexed myself with a great many conjectures, was,
whether Zenobia had ever been married. The idea, it must
be understood, was unauthorized by any circumstance or
suggestion that had made its way to my ears. So young as
I beheld her, and the freshest and rosiest woman of a
thousand, there was certainly no need of imputing to her a
destiny already accomplished; the probability was far greater,
that her coming years had all life's richest gifts to bring. If
the great event of a woman's existence had been consummated, the world knew nothing of it, although the world
seemed to know Zenobia well. It was a ridiculous piece of
romance, undoubtedly, to imagine that this beautiful personage, wealthy as she was, and holding a position that might
fairly enough be called distinguished, could have given herself
away so privately, but that some whisper and suspicion, and,
by degrees, a full understanding of the fact, would eventually
be blown abroad. But, then, as I failed not to consider, her
original home was at a distance of many hundred miles.
Rumors might fill the social atmosphere, or might once have
filled it, there, which would travel but slowly, against the
wind, towards our north-eastern metropolis, and perhaps melt
into thin air before reaching it.

There was not, and I distinctly repeat it, the slightest
foundation in my knowledge for any surmise of the kind.
But there is a species of intuition—either a spiritual lie, or
the subtle recognition of a fact—which comes to us in a
reduced state of the corporeal system. The soul gets the better
of the body, after wasting illness, or when a vegetable diet*
may have mingled too much ether in the blood. Vapors then
rise up to the brain, and take shapes that often image falsehood, but sometimes truth. The spheres of our companions
have, at such periods, a vastly greater influence upon our
own, than when robust health gives us a repellent and self-
defensive energy. Zenobia's sphere, I imagine, impressed itself

powerfully on mine, and transformed me, during this period of my weakness, into something like a mesmerical clairvoyant.

Then, also, as anybody could observe, the freedom of her deportment (though, to some tastes, it might commend itself as the utmost perfection of manner, in a youthful widow, or a blooming matron) was not exactly maidenlike. What girl had ever laughed as Zenobia did! What girl had ever spoken in her mellow tones! Her unconstrained and inevitable manifestation, I said often to myself, was that of a woman to whom wedlock had thrown wide the gates of mystery. Yet, sometimes, I strove to be ashamed of these conjectures. I acknowledged it as a masculine grossness—a sin of wicked interpretation, of which man is often guilty towards the other sex—thus to mistake the sweet, liberal, but womanly frankness of a noble and generous disposition. Still, it was of no avail to reason with myself, nor to upbraid myself. Pertinaciously the thought—'Zenobia is a wife! Zenobia has lived, and loved! There is no folded petal, no latent dew-drop, in this perfectly developed rose!'—irresistibly that thought drove out all other conclusions, as often as my mind reverted to the subject.

Zenobia was conscious of my observation, though not, I presume, of the point to which it led me.

"Mr. Coverdale," said she, one day, as she saw me watching her, while she arranged my gruel on the table, "I have been exposed to a great deal of eye-shot in the few years of my mixing in the world, but never, I think, to precisely such glances as you are in the habit of favoring me with. I seem to interest you very much; and yet—or else a woman's instinct is for once deceived—I cannot reckon you as an admirer. What are you seeking to discover in me?"

"The mystery of your life," answered I, surprised into the truth by the unexpectedness of her attack. "And you will never tell me."

She bent her head towards me, and let me look into her

eyes, as if challenging me to drop a plummet-line down into the depths of her consciousness.

"I see nothing now," said I, closing my own eyes, "unless it be the face of a sprite, laughing at me from the bottom of a deep well."

A bachelor always feels himself defrauded, when he knows, or suspects, that any woman of his acquaintance has given herself away. Otherwise, the matter could have been no concern of mine. It was purely speculative; for I should not, under any circumstances, have fallen in love with Zenobia. The riddle made me so nervous, however, in my sensitive condition of mind and body, that I most ungratefully began to wish that she would let me alone. Then, too, her gruel was very wretched stuff, with almost invariably the smell of pine-smoke upon it, like the evil taste that is said to mix itself up with a witch's best concocted dainties. Why could not she have allowed one of the other women to take the gruel in charge? Whatever else might be her gifts, Nature certainly never intended Zenobia for a cook. Or, if so, she should have meddled only with the richest and spiciest dishes, and such as are to be tasted at banquets, between draughts of intoxicating wine.

VII

THE CONVALESCENT

AS SOON as my incommodities allowed me to think of past occurrences, I failed not to inquire what had become of the odd little guest, whom Hollingsworth had been the medium of introducing among us. It now appeared, that poor Priscilla had not so literally fallen out of the clouds, as we were at first inclined to suppose. A letter, which should have introduced her, had since been received from one of the city-missionaries, containing a certificate of character, and an allusion to circumstances which, in the writer's judgment, made it especially desirable that she should find shelter in our Community. There was a hint, not very intelligible, implying either that Priscilla had recently escaped from some particular peril, or irksomeness of position, or else that she was still liable to this danger or difficulty, whatever it might be. We should ill have deserved the reputation of a benevolent fraternity, had we hesitated to entertain a petitioner in such need, and so strongly recommended to our kindness; not to mention, moreover, that the strange maiden had set herself diligently to work, and was doing good service with her needle. But a slight mist of uncertainty still floated about Priscilla, and kept her, as yet, from taking a very decided place among creatures of flesh and blood.

The mysterious attraction, which, from her first entrance

on our scene, she evinced for Zenobia, had lost nothing of its
force. I often heard her footsteps, soft and low, accompanying
the light, but decided tread of the latter, up the staircase,
stealing along the passage-way by her new friend's side, and
pausing while Zenobia entered my chamber. Occasionally,
Zenobia would be a little annoyed by Priscilla's too close
attendance. In an authoritative and not very kindly tone, she
would advise her to breathe the pleasant air in a walk, or to
go with her work into the barn, holding out half a promise to
come and sit on the hay with her, when at leisure. Evidently,
Priscilla found but scanty requital for her love. Hollingsworth
was likewise a great favorite with her. For several minutes
together, sometimes, while my auditory nerves retained the
susceptibility of delicate health, I used to hear a low, pleasant
murmur, ascending from the room below, and at last ascertained it to be Priscilla's voice, babbling like a little brook to
Hollingsworth. She talked more largely and freely with him
than with Zenobia, towards whom, indeed, her feelings
seemed not so much to be confidence, as involuntary affection.
I should have thought all the better of my own qualities, had
Priscilla marked me out for the third place in her regards.
But, though she appeared to like me tolerably well, I could
never flatter myself with being distinguished by her, as
Hollingsworth and Zenobia were.

One forenoon, during my convalescence, there came a
gentle tap at my chamber-door. I immediately said—"Come
in, Priscilla!"—with an acute sense of the applicant's identity.
Nor was I deceived. It was really Priscilla, a pale, large-eyed
little woman, (for she had gone far enough into her teens
to be, at least, on the outer limit of girlhood,) but much less
wan than at my previous view of her, and far better condi-
tioned both as to health and spirits. As I first saw her, she
had reminded me of plants that one sometimes observes doing
their best to vegetate among the bricks of an enclosed court,

where there is scanty soil, and never any sunshine. At present, though with no approach to bloom, there were indications that the girl had human blood in her veins.

Priscilla came softly to my bedside, and held out an article of snow-white linen, very carefully and smoothly ironed. She did not seem bashful, nor anywise embarrassed. My weakly condition, I suppose, supplied a medium in which she could approach me.

"Do not you need this?" asked she. "I have made it for you."

It was a night-cap!

"My dear Priscilla," said I, smiling, "I never had on a night-cap in my life! But perhaps it will be better for me to wear one, now that I am a miserable invalid. How admirably you have done it! No, no; I never can think of wearing such an exquisitely wrought night-cap as this, unless it be in the day-time, when I sit up to receive company!"

"It is for use, not beauty," answered Priscilla. "I could have embroidered it and made it much prettier, if I pleased."

While holding up the night-cap, and admiring the fine needle-work, I perceived that Priscilla had a sealed letter, which she was waiting for me to take. It had arrived from the village post-office, that morning. As I did not immediately offer to receive the letter, she drew it back, and held it against her bosom, with both hands clasped over it, in a way that had probably grown habitual to her. Now, on turning my eyes from the night-cap to Priscilla, it forcibly struck me that her air, though not her figure, and the expression of her face, but not its features, had a resemblance to what I had often seen in a friend of mine, one of the most gifted women of the age. I cannot describe it. The points, easiest to convey to the reader, were, a certain curve of the shoulders, and a partial closing of the eyes, which seemed to look more penetratingly into my own eyes, through the narrowed apertures, than if they had been open at full width. It was a singular anomaly of likeness co-existing with perfect dissimilitude.

"Will you give me the letter, Priscilla?" said I.

She started, put the letter into my hand, and quite lost the look that had drawn my notice.

"Priscilla," I inquired, "did you ever see Miss Margaret Fuller?"*

"No," she answered.

"Because," said I, "you reminded me of her, just now, and it happens, strangely enough, that this very letter is from her!"

Priscilla, for whatever reason, looked very much discomposed.

"I wish people would not fancy such odd things in me!" she said, rather petulantly. "How could I possibly make myself resemble this lady, merely by holding her letter in my hand?"

"Certainly, Priscilla, it would puzzle me to explain it," I replied. "Nor do I suppose that the letter had anything to do with it. It was just a coincidence—nothing more."

She hastened out of the room; and this was the last that I saw of Priscilla, until I ceased to be an invalid.

Being much alone, during my recovery, I read interminably in Mr. Emerson's Essays, the Dial, Carlyle's works, George Sand's romances,* (lent me by Zenobia,) and other books which one or another of the brethren or sisterhood had brought with them. Agreeing in little else, most of these utterances were like the cry of some solitary sentinel, whose station was on the outposts of the advance-guard of human progression; or, sometimes, the voice came sadly from among the shattered ruins of the past, but yet had a hopeful echo in the future. They were well adapted (better, at least, than any other intellectual products, the volatile essence of which had heretofore tinctured a printed page) to pilgrims like ourselves, whose present bivouâc was considerably farther into the waste of chaos than any mortal army of crusaders had ever marched before. Fourier's* works, also, in a series of horribly tedious volumes, attracted a good deal of my attention, from the analogy which I could not but recognize between his system and our own. There was far less resemblance, it is true, than the world chose to imagine; inasmuch as the two theories differed, as widely as the zenith from the nadir, in their main principles.

I talked about Fourier to Hollingsworth, and translated, for his benefit, some of the passages that chiefly impressed me.

"When, as a consequence of human improvement," said I, "the globe shall arrive at its final perfection, the great ocean is to be converted into a particular kind of lemonade, such as was fashionable at Paris in Fourier's time. He calls it *limonade à cèdre.* It is positively a fact! Just imagine the city-docks filled, every day, with a flood-tide of this delectable beverage!"

"Why did not the Frenchman make punch of it, at once?" asked Hollingsworth. "The jack-tars would be delighted to go down in ships, and do business in such an element."

I further proceeded to explain, as well as I modestly could, several points of Fourier's system, illustrating them with here and there a page or two, and asking Hollingsworth's opinion as to the expediency of introducing these beautiful peculiarities into our own practice.

"Let me hear no more of it!" cried he, in utter disgust. "I never will forgive this fellow! He has committed the Unpardonable Sin! For what more monstrous iniquity could the Devil himself contrive, than to choose the selfish principle* —the principle of all human wrong, the very blackness of man's heart, the portion of ourselves which we shudder at, and which it is the whole aim of spiritual discipline to eradicate—to choose it as the master-workman of his system? To seize upon and foster whatever vile, petty, sordid, filthy, bestial, and abominable corruptions have cankered into our nature, to be the efficient instruments of his infernal regeneration! And his consummated Paradise, as he pictures it, would be worthy of the agency which he counts upon for establishing it. The nauseous villain!"

"Nevertheless," remarked I, "in consideration of the promised delights of his system—so very proper, as they certainly are, to be appreciated by Fourier's countrymen—I cannot but wonder that universal France did not adopt his theory, at a moment's warning. But is there not something very characteristic of his nation in Fourier's manner of putting forth his views? He makes no claim to inspiration. He has not persuaded himself—as Swedenborg* did, and as any other than a Frenchman would, with a mission of like importance to communicate—that he speaks with authority from above. He promulgates his system, so far as I can perceive, entirely on his own responsibility. He has searched out and discovered the whole counsel of the Almighty, in respect to mankind, pást, present, and for exactly seventy thousand years to come, by the mere force and cunning of his individual intellect!"

"Take the book out of my sight!" said Hollingsworth, with great virulence of expression, "or, I tell you fairly, I shall fling it in the fire! And as for Fourier, let him make a Paradise, if he can, of Gehenna,* where, as I conscientiously believe, he is floundering at this moment!"

"And bellowing, I suppose," said I—not that I felt any ill-will towards Fourier, but merely wanted to give the finishing touch to Hollingsworth's image—"bellowing for the least drop of his beloved *limonade à cèdre!*"

There is but little profit to be expected in attempting to argue with a man who allows himself to declaim in this manner; so I dropt the subject, and never took it up again.

But had the system, at which he was so enraged, combined almost any amount of human wisdom, spiritual insight, and imaginative beauty, I question whether Hollingsworth's mind was in a fit condition to receive it. I began to discern that he had come among us, actuated by no real sympathy with our feelings and our hopes, but chiefly because we were estranging ourselves from the world, with which his lonely and exclusive object in life had already put him at odds. Hollingsworth must have been originally endowed with a great spirit of benevolence, deep enough, and warm enough, to be the source of as much disinterested good, as Providence often allows a human being the privilege of conferring upon his fellows. This native instinct yet lived within him. I myself had profited by it, in my necessity. It was seen, too, in his treatment of Priscilla. Such casual circumstances, as were here involved, would quicken his divine power of sympathy, and make him seem, while their influence lasted, the tenderest man and the truest friend on earth. But, by-and-by, you missed the tenderness of yesterday, and grew drearily conscious that Hollingsworth had a closer friend than ever you could be. And this friend was the cold, spectral monster which he had himself conjured up, and on which he was wasting all the warmth of his heart, and of which, at last—as these men of a mighty purpose so invariably do—he had grown to be the bond-slave. It was his philanthropic theory!

This was a result exceedingly sad to contemplate, considering that it had been mainly brought about by the very ardor and exuberance of his philanthropy. Sad, indeed, but by no means unusual. He had taught his benevolence to pour its warm tide exclusively through one channel; so that there was nothing to spare for other great manifestations of love to man, nor scarcely for the nutriment of individual attachments, unless they could minister, in some way, to the terrible egotism which he mistook for an angel of God. Had Hollingsworth's education been more enlarged, he might not so inevitably have stumbled into this pit-fall. But this identical pursuit had educated him. He knew absolutely nothing, except in a single direction, where he had thought so energetically, and felt to such a depth, that, no doubt, the entire reason and justice of the universe appeared to be concentrated thither-ward.

It is my private opinion, that, at this period of his life, Hollingsworth was fast going mad; and, as with other crazy people, (among whom I include humorists of every degree,) it required all the constancy of friendship to restrain his associates from pronouncing him an intolerable bore. Such prolonged fiddling upon one string; such multiform presentation of one idea! His specific object (of which he made the public more than sufficiently aware, through the medium of lectures and pamphlets) was to obtain funds for the construction of an edifice, with a sort of collegiate endowment. On this foundation, he purposed to devote himself and a few disciples to the reform and mental culture of our criminal brethren. His visionary edifice was Hollingsworth's one castle in the air; it was the material type, in which his philanthropic dream strove to embody itself; and he made the scheme more definite, and caught hold of it the more strongly, and kept his clutch the more pertinaciously, by rendering it visible to the bodily eye. I have seen him, a hundred times, with a pencil and sheet of paper, sketching the façade, the side-view, or the rear of the structure, or planning the internal arrangements, as lovingly as another man might plan those of the projected home, where he meant to be happy with his wife and children. I have known him to begin a model of the building with little stones, gathered at the brookside, whither we had gone to cool ourselves in the sultry noon of haying-time. Unlike all other ghosts, his spirit haunted an edifice which, instead of being time-worn, and full of storied love, and joy, and sorrow, had never yet come into existence.

"Dear friend," said I, once, to Hollingsworth, before leaving my sick-chamber, "I heartily wish that I could make your schemes my schemes, because it would be so great a happiness to find myself treading the same path with you. But I am afraid there is not stuff in me stern enough for a philanthropist

—or not in this peculiar direction—or, at all events, not solely in this. Can you bear with me, if such should prove to be the case?"

"I will, at least, wait awhile," answered Hollingsworth, gazing at me sternly and gloomily. "But how can you be my life-long friend, except you strive with me towards the great object of my life?"

Heaven forgive me! A horrible suspicion crept into my heart, and stung the very core of it as with the fangs of an adder. I wondered whether it were possible that Hollingsworth could have watched by my bedside, with all that devoted care, only for the ulterior purpose of making me a proselyte to his views!

VIII

A MODERN ARCADIA

MAY-DAY—I forget whether by Zenobia's sole decree, or by the unanimous vote of our Community—had been declared a moveable festival. It was deferred until the sun should have had a reasonable time to clear away the snow-drifts, along the lee of the stone-walls, and bring out a few of the readiest wild-flowers. On the forenoon of the substituted day, after admitting some of the balmy air into my chamber, I decided that it was nonsense and effeminacy to keep myself a prisoner any longer. So I descended to the sitting-room, and finding nobody there, proceeded to the barn, whence I had already heard Zenobia's voice, and along with it a girlish laugh, which was not so certainly recognizable. Arriving at the spot, it a little surprised me to discover that these merry outbreaks came from Priscilla.

The two had been a-maying together. They had found anemones in abundance, houstonias* by the handfull, some columbines, a few long-stalked violets, and a quantity of white everlasting-flowers, and had filled up their basket with the delicate spray of shrubs and trees. None were prettier than the maple-twigs, the leaf of which looks like a scarlet-bud, in May, and like a plate of vegetable gold in October. Zenobia—who showed no conscience in such matters—had also rifled a cherry-tree of one of its blossomed boughs; and, with all this variety of sylvan ornament, had been decking out Priscilla. Being done with a good deal of taste, it made her look more charming than I should have thought possible, with my recollection of the wan, frost-nipt girl, as heretofore described. Nevertheless, among those fragrant blossoms, and conspicuously, too, had been stuck a weed of evil odor and ugly aspect, which, as soon as I detected it, destroyed the effect of all the rest. There was a gleam of latent mischief—not to call it deviltry—in Zenobia's eye, which seemed to indicate a slightly malicious purpose in the arrangement.

As for herself, she scorned the rural buds and leaflets, and wore nothing but her invariable flower of the tropics.

"What do you think of Priscilla now, Mr. Coverdale?" asked she, surveying her as a child does its doll. "Is not she worth a verse or two?"

"There is only one thing amiss," answered I.

Zenobia laughed, and flung the malignant weed away.

"Yes; she deserves some verses now," said I, "and from a better poet than myself. She is the very picture of the New England spring, subdued in tint, and rather cool, but with a capacity of sunshine, and bringing us a few alpine blossoms, as earnest of something richer, though hardly more beautiful, hereafter. The best type of her is one of those anemones."

"What I find most singular in Priscilla, as her health improves," observed Zenobia, "is her wildness. Such a quiet little body as she seemed, one would not have expected that! Why, as we strolled the woods together, I could hardly keep her from scrambling up the trees like a squirrel! She has never before known what it is to live in the free air, and so it intoxicates her as if she were sipping wine. And she thinks it such a Paradise here, and all of us, particularly Mr. Hollingsworth and myself, such angels! It is quite ridiculous, and provokes one's malice, almost, to see a creature so happy—especially a feminine creature."

"They are always happier than male creatures," said I.

"You must correct that opinion, Mr. Coverdale," replied Zenobia, contemptuously, "or I shall think you lack the poetic insight. Did you ever see a happy woman in your life? Of course, I do not mean a girl—like Priscilla, and a thousand others, for they are all alike, while on the sunny side of experience—but a grown woman. How can she be happy, after discovering that fate has assigned her but one single event, which she must contrive to make the substance of her whole life? A man has his choice of innumerable events."

"A woman, I suppose," answered I, "by constant repetition of her one event, may compensate for the lack of variety."

"Indeed!" said Zenobia.

While we were talking, Priscilla caught sight of Hollingsworth, at a distance, in a blue frock*and with a hoe over his shoulder, returning from the field. She immediately set out to meet him, running and skipping, with spirits as light as the breeze of the May-morning, but with limbs too little exercised to be quite responsive; she clapt her hands, too, with great exuberance of gesture, as is the custom of young girls, when their electricity overcharges them. But, all at once, midway to Hollingsworth, she paused, looked round about her, towards the river, the road, the woods, and back towards us, appearing to listen, as if she heard some one calling her name, and knew not precisely in what direction.

"Have you bewitched her?" I exclaimed.

"It is no sorcery of mine," said Zenobia. "But I have seen the girl do that identical thing, once or twice before. Can you imagine what is the matter with her?"

"No; unless," said I, "she has the gift of hearing those 'airy tongues that syllable men's names'*—which Milton tells about."

From whatever cause, Priscilla's animation seemed entirely to have deserted her. She seated herself on a rock, and remained there until Hollingsworth came up; and when he took her hand and led her back to us, she rather resembled

my original image of the wan and spiritless Priscilla, than
the flowery May Queen of a few moments ago. These sudden
transformations, only to be accounted for by an extreme
nervous susceptibility, always continued to characterize the
girl, though with diminished frequency, as her health progres-
sively grew more robust.

I was now on my legs again. My fit of illness had been
an avenue between two existences; the low-arched and dark-
some doorway, through which I crept out of a life of old conventionalisms, on my hands and knees, as it were, and gained
admittance into the freer region that lay beyond. In this
respect, it was like death. And, as with death, too, it was
good to have gone through it. No otherwise could I have rid
myself of a thousand follies, fripperies, prejudices, habits,
and other such worldly dust as inevitably settles upon the
crowd along the broad highway, giving them all one sordid
aspect, before noontime, however freshly they may have
begun their pilgrimage, in the dewy morning. The very
substance upon my bones had not been fit to live with, in
any better, truer, or more energetic mode than that to which
I was accustomed. So it was taken off me and flung aside,
like any other worn out or unseasonable garment; and, after
shivering a little while in my skeleton, I began to be clothed
anew, and much more satisfactorily than in my previous suit.
In literal and physical truth, I was quite another man. I had
a lively sense of the exultation with which the spirit will
enter on the next stage of its eternal progress, after leaving
the heavy burthen of its mortality in an earthly grave, with as
little concern for what may become of it, as now affected me
for the flesh which I had lost.

Emerging into the genial sunshine, I half fancied that
the labors of the brotherhood had already realized some of
Fourier's predictions. Their enlightened culture of the soil,
and the virtues with which they sanctified their life, had
begun to produce an effect upon the material world and its

climate. In my new enthusiasm, man looked strong and stately!—and woman, oh, how beautiful!—and the earth, a green garden, blossoming with many-colored delights! Thus Nature, whose laws I had broken in various artificial ways, comported herself towards me as a strict, but loving mother, who uses the rod upon her little boy for his naughtiness, and then gives him a smile, a kiss, and some pretty playthings, to console the urchin for her severity.

In the interval of my seclusion, there had been a number of recruits to our little army of saints and martyrs. They were mostly individuals who had gone through such an experience as to disgust them with ordinary pursuits, but who were not yet so old, nor had suffered so deeply, as to lose their faith in the better time to come. On comparing their minds, one with another, they often discovered that this idea of a Community had been growing up, in silent and unknown sympathy, for years. Thoughtful, strongly-lined faces were among them, sombre brows, but eyes that did not require spectacles, unless prematurely dimmed by the student's lamplight, and hair that seldom showed a thread of silver. Age, wedded to the past, incrusted over with a stony layer of habits, and retaining nothing fluid in its possibilities, would have been absurdly out of place in an enterprise like this. Youth, too, in its early dawn, was hardly more adapted to our purpose; for it would behold the morning radiance of its own spirit beaming over the very same spots of withered grass and barren sand, whence most of us had seen it vanish. We had very young people with us, it is true—downy lads, rosy girls in their first teens, and children of all heights above one's knee;—but these had chiefly been sent hither for education, which it was one of the objects and methods of our institution to supply. Then we had boarders, from town and elsewhere, who lived with us in a familiar way, sympathized more or less in our theories, and sometimes shared in our labors.

On the whole, it was a society such as has seldom met

together; nor, perhaps, could it reasonably be expected to hold together long. Persons of marked individuality—crooked sticks, as some of us might be called—are not exactly the easiest to bind up into a faggot. But, so long as our union should subsist, a man of intellect and feeling, with a free nature in him, might have sought far and near, without finding so many points of attraction as would allure him hitherward. We were of all creeds and opinions, and generally tolerant of all, on every imaginable subject. Our bond, it seems to me, was not affirmative, but negative. We had individually found one thing or another to quarrel with, in our past life, and were pretty well agreed as to the inexpediency of lumbering along with the old system any farther. As to what should be substituted, there was much less unanimity. We did not greatly care—at least, I never did—for the written constitution under which our millennium had commenced. My hope was, that, between theory and practice, a true and available mode of life might be struck out, and that, even should we ultimately fail, the months or years spent in the trial would not have been wasted, either as regarded passing enjoyment, or the experience which makes men wise.

Arcadians though we were, our costume bore no resemblance to the be-ribboned doublets, silk breeches and stockings, and slippers fastened with artificial roses, that distinguish the pastoral people of poetry and the stage. In outward show, I humbly conceive, we looked rather like a gang of beggars or banditti, than either a company of honest laboring men or a conclave of philosophers. Whatever might be our points of difference, we all of us seemed to have come to Blithedale with the one thrifty and laudable idea of wearing out our old clothes. Such garments as had an airing, whenever we strode afield! Coats with high collars, and with no collars, broadskirted or swallow-tailed, and with the waist at every point between the hip and armpit; pantaloons of a dozen successive epochs, and greatly defaced at the knees by the humiliations of the wearer before his lady-love;—in short, we were a living epitome of defunct fashions, and the very raggedest present-ment of men who had seen better days. It was gentility in tatters. Often retaining a scholarlike or clerical air, you might have taken us for the denizens of Grub-street,* intent on getting a comfortable livelihood by agricultural labor; or Coleridge's projected Pantisocracy,* in full experiment; or Candide*and his motley associates, at work in their cabbage-garden; or anything else that was miserably out at elbows, and most clumsily patched in the rear. We might have been sworn comrades to Falstaff's* ragged regiment. Little skill as we boasted in other points of husbandry, every mother's son of us would have served admirably to stick up for a scarecrow. And the worst of the matter was, that the first energetic move-ment, essential to one downright stroke of real labor, was sure to put a finish to these poor habiliments. So we gradually flung them all aside, and took to honest homespun and linsey-woolsey,* as preferable, on the whole, to the plan recom-mended, I think, by Virgil—'Ara nudus; sere nudus'—which, as Silas Foster remarked when I translated the maxim, would be apt to astonish the women-folks.

After a reasonable training, the yeoman-life throve well with us. Our faces took the sunburn kindly; our chests gained in compass, and our shoulders in breadth and squareness; our great brown fists looked as if they had never been capable of kid gloves. The plough, the hoe, the scythe, and the hay-fork, grew familiar to our grasp. The oxen responded to our voices. We could do almost as fair a day's work as Silas Foster himself, sleep dreamlessly after it, and awake at daybreak with only a little stiffness of the joints, which was usually quite gone by breakfast-time.

To be sure, our next neighbors pretended to be incredulous as to our real proficiency in the business which we had taken in hand. They told slanderous fables about our inability to yoke our own oxen, or to drive them afield, when yoked, or to release the poor brutes from their conjugal bond at nightfall. They had the face to say, too, that the cows laughed at our awkwardness at milking-time, and invariably kicked over the pails; partly in consequence of our putting the stool on the wrong side, and partly because, taking offence at the whisking of their tails, we were in the habit of holding these natural flyflappers with one hand, and milking with the other. They further averred, that we hoed up whole acres of Indian corn and other crops, and drew the earth carefully about the weeds; and that we raised five hundred tufts of burdock, mistaking them for cabbages; and that, by dint of unskilful planting, few of our seeds ever came up at all, or if they did come up, it was stern foremost, and that we spent the better part of the month of June in reversing a field of beans, which had thrust themselves out of the ground in this unseemly way. They quoted it as nothing more than an ordinary occurrence for one or other of us to crop off two or three fingers, of a morning, by our clumsy use of the hay-cutter. Finally, and as an ultimate catastrophe, these mendacious rogues circulated a report that we Communitarians were exterminated, to the last man, by severing ourselves asunder with the sweep of our own scythes!—and that the world had lost nothing by this little accident.

But this was pure envy and malice on the part of the neighboring farmers. The peril of our new way of life was not lest we should fail in becoming practical agriculturalists, but that we should probably cease to be anything else. While our enterprise lay all in theory, we had pleased ourselves with delectable visions of the spiritualization of labor. It was to be our form of prayer, and ceremonial of worship. Each stroke of the hoe was to uncover some aromatic root of wisdom, heretofore hidden from the sun. Pausing in the field, to let the wind exhale the moisture from our foreheads, we were to look upward, and catch glimpses into the far-off soul of truth. In this point of view, matters did not turn out quite so well as we anticipated. It is very true, that, sometimes, gazing casually around me, out of the midst of my toil, I used to discern a richer picturesqueness in the visible scene of earth and sky. There was, at such moments, a novelty, an unwonted aspect on the face of Nature, as if she had been taken by surprise and seen at unawares, with no opportunity to put off her real look, and assume the mask with which she mysteriously hides herself from mortals. But this was all. The clods of earth, which we so constantly belabored and turned over and over, were never etherealized into thought. Our thoughts, on the contrary, were fast becoming cloddish. Our labor symbolized nothing, and left us mentally sluggish in the dusk of the evening. Intellectual activity is incompatible with any large amount of bodily exercise. The yeoman and the scholar—the yeoman and the man of finest moral culture, though not the man of sturdiest sense and integrity—are two distinct individuals, and can never be melted or welded into one substance.

Zenobia soon saw this truth, and gibed me about it, one evening, as Hollingsworth and I lay on the grass, after a hard day's work.

"I am afraid you did not make a song, to-day, while loading the hay-cart," said she, "as Burns did, when he was reaping barley."

"Burns never made a song in haying-time," I answered, very positively. "He was no poet while a farmer, and no farmer while a poet."

"And, on the whole, which of the two characters do you like best?" asked Zenobia. "For I have an idea that you cannot combine them, any better than Burns did. Ah, I see, in my mind's eye, what sort of an individual you are to be, two or three years hence! Grim Silas Foster is your prototype, with his palm of sole-leather, and his joints of rusty iron, (which, all through summer, keep the stiffness of what he calls his winter's rheumatize,) and his brain of—I don't know what his brain is made of, unless it be a Savoy cabbage; but yours may be cauliflower, as a rather more delicate variety. Your physical man will be transmuted into salt-beef and fried pork, at the rate, I should imagine, of a pound and a half a day; that being about the average which we find necessary in the kitchen. You will make your toilet for the day (still like this delightful Silas Foster) by rinsing your fingers and the front part of your face in a little tin-pan of water, at the door-step, and teasing your hair with a wooden pocket-comb, before a seven-by-nine-inch looking-glass. Your only pastime will be, to smoke some very vile tobacco in the black stump of a pipe!"

"Pray spare me!" cried I. "But the pipe is not Silas's only mode of solacing himself with the weed."

"Your literature," continued Zenobia, apparently delighted with her description, "will be the Farmer's Almanac; for, I observe, our friend Foster never gets so far as the newspaper. When you happen to sit down, at odd moments, you will fall asleep, and make nasal proclamation of the fact, as he does; and invariably you must be jogged out of a nap, after supper, by the future Mrs. Coverdale, and persuaded to go regularly to bed. And on Sundays; when you put on a blue coat with brass buttons, you will think of nothing else to do, but to go and lounge over the stone-walls and rail-fences, and stare at the corn growing. And you will look with a knowing eye at oxen, and will have a tendency to clamber over into pig-sties, and feel of the hogs, and give a guess how much they will weigh, after you shall have stuck and dressed them. Already, I have noticed, you begin to speak through your nose, and with a drawl. Pray, if you really did make any poetry to-day, let us hear it in that kind of utterance!"

"Coverdale has given up making verses, now," said Hollingsworth, who never had the slightest appreciation of my poetry. "Just think of him penning a sonnet, with a fist like that! There is at least this good in a life of toil, that it takes the nonsense and fancy-work out of a man, and leaves nothing but what truly belongs to him. If a farmer can make poetry at the plough-tail, it must be because his nature insists on it; and if that be the case, let him make it, in Heaven's name!"

"And how is it with you?" asked Zenobia, in a different voice; for she never laughed at Hollingsworth, as she often did at me.—"You, I think, cannot have ceased to live a life of thought and feeling."

"I have always been in earnest," answered Hollingsworth. "I have hammered thought out of iron, after heating the iron in my heart! It matters little what my outward toil may be. Were I a slave at the bottom of a mine, I should keep the same purpose—the same faith in its ultimate accomplishment— that I do now. Miles Coverdale is not in earnest, either as a poet or a laborer."

"You give me hard measure, Hollingsworth," said I, a little hurt. "I have kept pace with you in the field; and my bones feel as if I had been in earnest, whatever may be the case with my brain!"

"I cannot conceive," observed Zenobia, with great emphasis—and, no doubt, she spoke fairly the feeling of the moment—"I cannot conceive of being, so continually as Mr. Coverdale is, within the sphere of a strong and noble nature, without being strengthened and enobled by its influence!"

This amiable remark of the fair Zenobia confirmed me in what I had already begun to suspect—that Hollingsworth, like many other illustrious prophets, reformers, and philanthropists, was likely to make at least two proselytes, among the women, to one among the men. Zenobia and Priscilla! These, I believe, (unless my unworthy self might be reckoned for a third,) were the only disciples of his mission; and I spent a great deal of time, uselessly, in trying to conjecture what Hollingsworth meant to do with them—and they with him!

IX

HOLLINGSWORTH, ZENOBIA, PRISCILLA

I T IS not, I apprehend, a healthy kind of mental occupation, to devote ourselves too exclusively to the study of individual men and women. If the person under examination be one's self, the result is pretty certain to be diseased action of the heart, almost before we can snatch a second glance. Or, if we take the freedom to put a friend under our microscope, we thereby insulate him from many of his true relations, magnify his peculiarities, inevitably tear him into parts, and, of course, patch him very clumsily together again. What wonder, then, should we be frightened by the aspect of a monster, which, after all—though we can point to every feature of his deformity in the real personage—may be said to have been created mainly by ourselves!

Thus, as my conscience has often whispered me, I did Hollingsworth a great wrong by prying into his character, and am perhaps doing him as great a one, at this moment, by putting faith in the discoveries which I seemed to make. But I could not help it. Had I loved him less, I might have used him better. He—and Zenobia and Priscilla, both for their own sakes and as connected with him—were separated from the rest of the Community, to my imagination, and stood forth as the indices of a problem which it was my business to solve. Other associates had a portion of my time; other matters amused me; passing occurrences carried me along with them, while they lasted. But here was the vortex of my meditations around which they revolved, and whitherward they too continually tended. In the midst of cheerful society, I had often a feeling of loneliness. For it was impossible not to be sensible, that, while these three characters figured so largely on my private theatre, I—though probably reckoned as a friend by all—was at best but a secondary or tertiary personage with either of them.

I loved Hollingsworth, as has already been enough expressed. But it impressed me, more and more, that there was a stern and dreadful peculiarity in this man, such as could not prove otherwise than pernicious to the happiness of those who should be drawn into too intimate a connection with him. He was not altogether human. There was something else in Hollingsworth, besides flesh and blood, and sympathies and affections, and celestial spirit.

This is always true of those men who have surrendered themselves to an over-ruling purpose. It does not so much impel them from without, nor even operate as a motive power within, but grows incorporate with all that they think and feel, and finally converts them into little else save that one principle. When such begins to be the predicament, it is not cowardice, but wisdom, to avoid these victims. They have no heart, no sympathy, no reason, no conscience. They will keep no friend, unless he make himself the mirror of their purpose; they will smite and slay you, and trample your dead corpse under foot, all the more readily, if you take the first step with them, and cannot take the second, and the third, and every other step of their terribly straight path. They have an idol, to which they consecrate themselves high-priest, and deem it holy work to offer sacrifices of whatever is most precious, and never once seem to suspect—so cunning has the Devil been with them—that this false deity, in whose iron features, immitigable to all the rest of mankind, they see only benignity and love, is but a spectrum of the very priest himself, projected upon the surrounding darkness. And the higher and purer the original object, and the more unselfishly it may have been taken up, the slighter is the probability that they can be led to recognize the process, by which godlike benevolence has been debased into all-devouring egotism.

Of course, I am perfectly aware that the above statement is exaggerated, in the attempt to make it adequate. Professed philanthropists have gone far; but no originally good man, I presume, ever went quite so far as this. Let the reader abate whatever he deems fit. The paragraph may remain, however, both for its truth and its exaggeration, as strongly expressive of the tendencies which were really operative in Hollingsworth, and as exemplifying the kind of error into which my mode of observation was calculated to lead me. The issue was, that, in solitude, I often shuddered at my friend. In my recollection of his dark and impressive countenance, the features grew more sternly prominent than the reality, duskier in their depth and shadow, and more lurid in their light; the frown, that had merely flitted across his brow, seemed to have contorted it with an adamantine wrinkle. On meeting him again, I was often filled with remorse, when his deep eyes beamed kindly upon me, as with the glow of a household fire that was burning in a cave.—"He is a man, after all!" thought I—"his Maker's own truest image, a philanthropic man!—not that steel engine of the Devil's contrivance, a philanthropist!"—But, in my wood-walks, and in my silent chamber, the dark face frowned at me again.

When a young girl comes within the sphere of such a man, she is as perilously situated as the maiden whom, in the old classical myths, the people used to expose to a dragon. If I had any duty whatever, in reference to Hollingsworth, it was, to endeavor to save Priscilla from that kind of personal worship which her sex is generally prone to lavish upon saints and heroes. It often requires but one smile, out of the hero's

eyes into the girl's or woman's heart, to transform this devotion, from a sentiment of the highest approval and confidence,
into passionate love. Now, Hollingsworth smiled much upon
Priscilla; more than upon any other person. If she thought
him beautiful, it was no wonder. I often thought him so,
with the expression of tender, human care, and gentlest sympathy, which she alone seemed to have power to call out upon
his features. Zenobia, I suspect, would have given her eyes,
bright as they were, for such a look; it was the least that our
poor Priscilla could do, to give her heart for a great many of
them. There was the more danger of this, inasmuch as the
footing, on which we all associated at Blithedale, was widely
different from that of conventional society. While inclining
us to the soft affections of the Golden Age,* it seemed to
authorize any individual, of either sex, to fall in love with any
other, regardless of what would elsewhere be judged suitable
and prudent. Accordingly, the tender passion was very rife
among us, in various degrees of mildness or virulence, but
mostly passing away with the state of things that had given
it origin. This was all well enough; but, for a girl like Priscilla,
and a woman like Zenobia, to jostle one another in their love
of a man like Hollingsworth, was likely to be no child's play.

Had I been as cold-hearted as I sometimes thought myself,
nothing would have interested me more than to witness the
play of passions that must thus have been evolved. But, in
honest truth, I would really have gone far to save Priscilla, at
least, from the catastrophe in which such a drama would be
apt to terminate.

Priscilla had now grown to be a very pretty girl, and still
kept budding and blossoming, and daily putting on some new
charm, which you no sooner became sensible of, than you
thought it worth all that she had previously possessed. So
unformed, vague, and without substance, as she had come to
us, it seemed as if we could see Nature shaping out a woman
before our very eyes, and yet had only a more reverential sense

of the mystery of a woman's soul and frame. Yesterday, her
cheek was pale; to-day, it had a bloom. Priscilla's smile, like
a baby's first one, was a wondrous novelty. Her imperfections
and short-comings affected me with a kind of playful pathos,
which was as absolutely bewitching a sensation as ever I
experienced. After she had been a month or two at Blithedale,
her animal spirits waxed high, and kept her pretty constantly
in a state of bubble and ferment, impelling her to far more
bodily activity than she had yet strength to endure. She was
very fond of playing with the other girls, out-of-doors. There
is hardly another sight in the world so pretty, as that of a
company of young girls, almost women grown, at play, and
so giving themselves up to their airy impulse that their
tiptoes barely touch the ground.

Girls are incomparably wilder and more effervescent than
boys, more untameable, and regardless of rule and limit, with
an ever-shifting variety, breaking continually into new modes
of fun, yet with a harmonious propriety through all. Their
steps, their voices, appear free as the wind, but keep conso-
nance with a strain of music, inaudible to us. Young men and
boys, on the other hand, play according to recognized law,
old, traditionary games, permitting no caprioles* of fancy, but
with scope enough for the outbreak of savage instincts. For,
young or old, in play or in earnest, man is prone to be a brute.

Especially is it delightful to see a vigorous young girl run
a race, with her head thrown back, her limbs moving more
friskily than they need, and an air between that of a bird
and a young colt. But Priscilla's peculiar charm, in a foot-race,
was the weakness and irregularity with which she ran. Growing up without exercise, except to her poor little fingers, she
had never yet acquired the perfect use of her legs. Setting
buoyantly forth, therefore, as if no rival less swift than
Atalanta* could compete with her, she ran faulteringly, and
often tumbled on the grass. Such an incident—though it
seems too slight to think of—was a thing to laugh at, but

which brought the water into one's eyes, and lingered in the memory after far greater joys and sorrows were swept out of it, as antiquated trash. Priscilla's life, as I beheld it, was full of trifles that affected me in just this way.

When she had come to be quite at home among us, I used to fancy that Priscilla played more pranks, and perpetrated more mischief, than any other girl in the Community. For example, I once heard Silas Foster, in a very gruff voice, threatening to rivet three horse-shoes round Priscilla's neck and chain her to a post, because she, with some other young people, had clambered upon a load of hay and caused it to slide off the cart. How she made her peace, I never knew; but very soon afterwards, I saw old Silas, with his brawny hands round Priscilla's waist, swinging her to-and-fro and finally depositing her on one of the oxen, to take her first lesson in riding. She met with terrible mishaps in her efforts to milk a cow; she let the poultry into the garden; she generally spoilt whatever part of the dinner she took in charge; she broke crockery; she dropt our biggest pitcher into the well; and—except with her needle, and those little wooden instruments for purse-making—was as unserviceable a member of society as any young lady in the land. There was no other sort of efficiency about her. Yet everybody was kind to Priscilla; everybody loved her, and laughed at her, to her face, and did not laugh, behind her back; everybody would have given her half of his last crust, or the bigger share of his plum-cake. These were pretty certain indications that we were all conscious of a pleasant weakness in the girl, and considered her not quite able to look after her own interests, or fight her battle with the world. And Hollingsworth—perhaps because he had been the means of introducing Priscilla to her new abode—appeared to recognize her as his own especial charge.

Her simple, careless, childish flow of spirits often made me sad. She seemed to me like a butterfly, at play in a flickering bit of sunshine, and mistaking it for a broad and eternal summer. We sometimes hold mirth to a stricter accountability than sorrow; it must show good cause, or the echo of its laughter comes back drearily. Priscilla's gaiety, moreover, was of a nature that showed me how delicate an instrument she was, and what fragile harp-strings were her nerves. As they made sweet music at the airiest touch, it would require but a stronger one to burst them all asunder. Absurd as it might be, I tried to reason with her, and persuade her not to be so joyous, thinking that, if she would draw less lavishly upon her fund of happiness, it would last the longer. I remember doing so, one summer evening, when we tired laborers sat looking on, like Goldsmith's old folks*under the village thorn-tree, while the young people were at their sports.

"What is the use or sense of being so very gay?" I said to Priscilla, while she was taking breath after a great frolic. "I love to see a sufficient cause for everything; and I can see none for this. Pray tell me, now, what kind of a world you imagine this to be, which you are so merry in?"

"I never think about it at all," answered Priscilla, laughing. "But this I am sure of—that it is a world where everybody is kind to me, and where I love everybody. My heart keeps dancing within me; and all the foolish things, which you see me do, are only the motions of my heart. How can I be dismal, if my heart will not let me?"

"Have you nothing dismal to remember?" I suggested. "If not, then, indeed, you are very fortunate!"

"Ah!" said Priscilla, slowly.

And then came that unintelligible gesture, when she seemed to be listening to a distant voice.

"For my part," I continued, beneficently seeking to over-shadow her with my own sombre humor, "my past life has been a tiresome one enough; yet I would rather look backward ten times, than forward once. For, little as we know of our life to come, we may be very sure, for one thing, that the good we aim at will not be attained. People never do get just the good they seek. If it come at all, it is something else, which they never dreamed of, and did not particularly want. Then, again, we may rest certain that our friends of to-day will not be our friends of a few years hence; but, if we keep one of them, it will be at the expense of the others—and, most probably, we shall keep none. To be sure, there are more to be had! But who cares about making a new set of friends, even should they be better than those around us?"

"Not I!" said Priscilla. "I will live and die with these!"

"Well; but let the future go!" resumed I. "As for the present moment, if we could look into the hearts where we wish to be most valued, what should you expect to see? One's own likeness, in the innermost, holiest niche? Ah, I don't know! It may not be there at all. It may be a dusty image, thrust aside into a corner, and by-and-by to be flung out-of-doors, where any foot may trample upon it. If not to-day, then tomorrow! And so, Priscilla, I do not see much wisdom in being so very merry in this kind of a world!"

It had taken me nearly seven years of worldly life, to hive up the bitter honey which I here offered to Priscilla. And she rejected it!

"I don't believe one word of what you say!" she replied, laughing anew. "You made me sad, for a minute, by talking about the past. But the past never comes back again. Do we dream the same dream twice? There is nothing else that I am afraid of."

So away she ran, and fell down on the green grass, as it was often her luck to do, but got up again without any harm.

"Priscilla, Priscilla!" cried Hollingsworth, who was sitting on the door-step. "You had better not run any more to-night. You will weary yourself too much. And do not sit down out of doors; for there is a heavy dew beginning to fall!"

At his first word, she went and sat down under the porch, at Hollingsworth's feet, entirely contented and happy. What charm was there, in his rude massiveness, that so attracted and soothed this shadowlike girl? It appeared to me—who have always been curious in such matters—that Priscilla's vague and seemingly causeless flow of felicitous feeling was that with which love blesses inexperienced hearts, before they begin to suspect what is going on within them. It transports them to the seventh heaven; and if you ask what brought them thither, they neither can tell nor care to learn, but cherish an ecstatic faith that there they shall abide forever.

Zenobia was in the door-way, not far from Hollingsworth. She gazed at Priscilla, in a very singular way. Indeed, it was a sight worth gazing at, and a beautiful sight too, as the fair girl sat at the feet of that dark, powerful figure. Her air, while perfectly modest, delicate, and virginlike, denoted her as swayed by Hollingsworth, attracted to him, and unconsciously seeking to rest upon his strength. I could not turn away my own eyes, but hoped that nobody, save Zenobia and myself, were witnessing this picture. It is before me now, with the evening twilight a little deepened by the dusk of memory.

"Come hither, Priscilla!" said Zenobia. "I have something to say to you!"

She spoke in little more than a whisper. But it is strange how expressive of moods a whisper may often be. Priscilla felt at once that something had gone wrong.

"Are you angry with me?" she asked, rising slowly and standing before Zenobia in a drooping attitude. "What have I done? I hope you are not angry!"

"No, no, Priscilla!" said Hollingsworth, smiling. "I will answer for it, she is not. You are the one little person in the world, with whom nobody can be angry!"

"Angry with you, child? What a silly idea!" exclaimed Zenobia, laughing. "No, indeed! But, my dear Priscilla, you are getting to be so very pretty that you absolutely need a duenna; and as I am older than you, and have had my own little experience of life, and think myself exceedingly sage, I intend to fill the place of a maiden-aunt. Every day, I shall give you a lecture, a quarter-of-an-hour in length, on the morals, manners, and proprieties of social life. When our pastoral shall be quite played out, Priscilla, my worldly wisdom may stand you in good stead!"

"I am afraid you are angry with me," repeated Priscilla, sadly; for, while she seemed as impressible as wax, the girl often showed a persistency in her own ideas, as stubborn as it was gentle.

"Dear me, what can I say to the child!" cried Zenobia, in a tone of humorous vexation. "Well, well; since you insist on my being angry, come to my room, this moment, and let me beat you!"

Zenobia bade Hollingsworth good night very sweetly, and nodded to me with a smile. But, just as she turned aside with Priscilla into the dimness of the porch, I caught another glance at her countenance. It would have made the fortune of a tragic actress, could she have borrowed it for the moment when she fumbles in her bosom for the concealed dagger, or the exceedingly sharp bodkin, or mingles the ratsbane in her lover's bowl of 'wine, or her rival's cup of tea. Not that I in the least anticipated any such catastrophe; it being a remarkable truth, that custom has in no one point a greater sway than over our modes of wreaking our wild passions. And, besides, had we been in Italy, instead of New England, it was hardly yet a crisis for the dagger or the bowl.

It often amazed me, however, that Hollingsworth should show himself so recklessly tender towards Priscilla, and never once seem to think of the effect which it might have upon her heart. But the man, as I have endeavored to explain, was thrown completely off his moral balance, and quite bewildered as to his personal relations, by his great excrescence of a philanthropic scheme. I used to see, or fancy, indications that he was not altogether obtuse to Zenobia's influence as a woman. No doubt, however, he had a still more exquisite enjoyment of Priscilla's silent sympathy with his purposes, so unalloyed with criticism, and therefore more grateful than any intellectual approbation, which always involves a possible reserve of latent censure. A man—poet, prophet, or whatever he may be—readily persuades himself of his right to all the worship that is voluntarily tendered. In requital of so rich benefits as he was to confer upon mankind, it would have been hard to deny Hollingsworth the simple solace of a young girl's heart, which he held in his hand, and smelled to, like a rosebud. But what if, while pressing out its fragrance, he should crush the tender rosebud in his grasp!

As for Zenobia, I saw no occasion to give myself any trouble. With her native strength, and her experience of the world, she could not be supposed to need any help of mine. Nevertheless, I was really generous enough to feel some little interest likewise for Zenobia. With all her faults, (which might have been a great many, besides the abundance that I knew of,) she possessed noble traits, and a heart which must at least have been valuable while new. And she seemed ready to fling it away, as uncalculatingly as Priscilla herself. I could not but suspect, that, if merely at play with Hollingsworth, she was sporting with a power which she did not fully estimate. Or, if in earnest, it might chance, between Zenobia's passionate force and his dark, self-delusive egotism, to turn out such earnest as would develop itself in some sufficiently tragic catastrophe, though the dagger and the bowl should go for nothing in it.

Meantime, the gossip of the Community set them down as a pair of lovers. They took walks together, and were not seldom encountered in the wood-paths; Hollingsworth deeply discoursing, in tones solemn and sternly pathetic. Zenobia, with a rich glow on her cheeks, and her eyes softened from their ordinary brightness, looked so beautiful, that, had her companion been ten times a philanthropist, it seemed impossible but that one glance should melt him back into a man. Oftener than anywhere else, they went to a certain point on the slope of a pasture, commanding nearly the whole of our own domain, besides a view of the river and an airy prospect of many distant hills. The bond of our Community was such, that the members had the privilege of building cottages for their own residence, within our precincts, thus laying a hearth-stone and fencing in a home, private and peculiar, to all desirable extent; while yet the inhabitants should continue to share the advantages of an associated life. It was inferred, that Hollingsworth and Zenobia intended to rear their dwelling on this favorite spot.

I mentioned these rumors to Hollingsworth in a playful way.

"Had you consulted me," I went on to observe, "I should have recommended a site further to the left, just a little withdrawn into the wood, with two or three peeps at the prospect, among the trees. You will be in the shady vale of years, long before you can raise any better kind of shade around your cottage, if you build it on this bare slope."

"But I offer my edifice as a spectacle to the world," said Hollingsworth, "that it may take example and build many another like it. Therefore I mean to set it on the open hill-side."

Twist these words how I might, they offered no very satisfactory import. It seemed hardly probable that Hollingsworth should care about educating the public taste in the department of cottage-architecture, desirable as such improvement certainly was.

X

A VISITOR FROM TOWN

HOLLINGSWORTH and I—we had been hoeing potatoes, that forenoon, while the rest of the fraternity were engaged in a distant quarter of the farm —sat· under a clump of maples, eating our eleven o'clock lunch, when we saw a stranger approaching along the edge of the field. He had admitted himself from the road-side, through a turnstile, and seemed to have a purpose of speaking with us.

And, by-the-by, we were favored with many visits at Blithedale; especially from people who sympathized with our theories, and perhaps held themselves ready to unite in our actual experiment, as soon as there should appear a reliable promise of its success. It was rather ludicrous, indeed, (to me, at least, whose enthusiasm had insensibly been exhaled, together with the perspiration of many a hard day's toil,) it was absolutely funny, therefore, to observe what a glory was shed about our life and labors, in the imagination of these longing proselytes. In their view, we were as poetical as Arcadians, besides being as practical as the hardest-fisted husbandmen in Massachusetts. We did not, it is true, spend much time in piping to our sheep, or warbling our innocent loves to the sisterhood. But they gave us credit for imbuing the ordinary rustic occupations with a kind of religious poetry, insomuch that our very cow-yards and pig-sties were as delightfully fragrant as a flower-garden. Nothing used to please me more than to see one of these lay enthusiasts snatch up a hoe, as they were very prone to do, and set to work with a vigor that perhaps carried him through about a dozen ill-directed strokes. Men are wonderfully soon satisfied, in this day of shameful bodily enervation, when, from one end of life to the other, such multitudes never taste the sweet weariness that follows accustomed toil. I seldom saw the new enthusiasm that did not grow as flimsy and flaccid as the proselyte's moistened shirt-collar, with a quarter-of-an-hour's active labor, under a July sun.

But the person, now at hand, had not at all the air of one of these amiable visionaries. He was an elderly man, dressed rather shabbily, yet decently enough, in a gray frock-coat, faded towards a brown hue, and wore a broad-brimmed white hat, of the fashion of several years gone by. His hair was perfect silver, without a dark thread in the whole of it; his nose, though it had a scarlet tip, by no means indicated the jollity of which a red nose is the generally admitted symbol. He was a subdued, undemonstrative old man, who would doubtless drink a glass of liquor, now and then, and probably more than was good for him; not, however, with a purpose of undue exhilaration, but in the hope of bringing his spirits up to the ordinary level of the world's cheerfulness. Drawing nearer, there was a shy look about him, as if he were ashamed of his poverty, or, at any rate, for some reason or other, would rather have us glance at him sidelong than take a full-front view. He had a queer appearance of hiding himself behind the patch on his left eye.

"I know this old gentleman," said I to Hollingsworth, as we sat observing him—"that is, I have met him a hundred times, in town, and have often amused my fancy with wondering what he was, before he came to be what he is. He haunts restaurants and such places, and has an odd way of lurking in corners or getting behind a door, whenever practicable, and holding out his hand, with some little article in it, which he wishes you to buy. The eye of the world seems to trouble him, although he necessarily lives so much in it. I never expected to see him in an open field."

"Have you learned anything of his history?" asked Hollingsworth.

"Not a circumstance," I answered. "But there must be something curious in it. I take him to be a harmless sort of a person, and a tolerably honest one; but his manners, being so furtive, remind me of those of a rat—a rat without the mischief, the fierce eye, the teeth to bite with, or the desire to bite. See, now! He means to skulk along that fringe of bushes, and approach us on the other side of our clump of maples."

We soon heard the old man's velvet tread on the grass, indicating that he had arrived within a few feet of where we sat.

"Good morning, Mr. Moodie," said Hollingsworth, addressing the stranger as an acquaintance. "You must have had a hot and tiresome walk from the city. Sit down, and take a morsel of our bread and cheese!"

The visitor made a grateful little murmur of acquiescence, and sat down in a spot somewhat removed; so that, glancing round, I could see his gray pantaloons and dusty shoes, while his upper part was mostly hidden behind the shrubbery. Nor did he come forth from this retirement during the whole of the interview that followed. We handed him such food as we had, together with a brown jug of molasses-and-water, (would that it had been brandy, or something better, for the sake of his chill old heart!) like priests offering dainty sacrifice to an enshrined and invisible idol. I have no idea that he really lacked sustenance; but it was quite touching, nevertheless, to hear him nibbling away at our crusts.

"Mr. Moodie," said I, "do you remember selling me one

of those very pretty little silk purses, of which you seem to have a monopoly in the market? I keep it, to this day, I can assure you."

"Ah, thank you!" said our guest. "Yes, Mr. Coverdale, I used to sell a good many of those little purses."

He spoke languidly, and only those few words, like a watch with an inelastic spring, that just ticks, a moment or two, and stops again. He seemed a very forlorn old man. In the wantonness of youth, strength, and comfortable condition—making my prey of people's individualities, as my custom was—I tried to identify my mind with the old fellow's, and take his view of the world, as if looking through a smoke-blackened glass at the sun. It robbed the landscape of all its life. Those pleasantly swelling slopes of our farm, descending towards the wide meadows, through which sluggishly circled the brimfull tide of the Charles, bathing the long sedges on its hither and farther shores; the broad, sunny gleam over the winding water; that peculiar picturesqueness of the scene, where capes and headlands put themselves boldly forth upon the perfect level of the meadow, as into a green lake, with inlets between the promontories; the shadowy woodland, with twinkling showers of light falling into its depths; the sultry heat-vapor, which rose everywhere like incense, and in which my soul delighted, as indicating so rich a fervor in the passionate day, and in the earth that was burning with its love:—I beheld all these things as through old Moodie's eyes. When my eyes are dimmer than they have yet come to be, I will go thither again, and see if I did not catch the tone of his mind aright, and if the cold and lifeless tint of his perceptions be not then repeated in my own.

Yet it was unaccountable to myself, the interest that I felt in him.

"Have you any objection," said I, "to telling me who made those little purses?"

"Gentlemen have often asked me that," said Moodie,

slowly; "but I shake my head, and say little or nothing, and creep out of the way, as well as I can. I am a man of few words; and if gentlemen were to be told one thing, they would be very apt, I suppose, to ask me another. But it happens, just now, Mr. Coverdale, that you can tell me more about the maker of those little purses, than I can tell you."

"Why do you trouble him with needless questions, Coverdale?" interrupted Hollingsworth. "You must have known, long ago, that it was Priscilla. And so, my good friend, you have come to see her? Well, I am glad of it. You will find her altered very much for the better, since that wintry evening when you put her into my charge. Why, Priscilla has a bloom in her cheeks, now!"

"Has my pale little girl a bloom?" repeated Moodie, with a kind of slow wonder. "Priscilla with a bloom in her cheeks! Ah, I am afraid I shall not know my little girl. And is she happy?"

"Just as happy as a bird," answered Hollingsworth.

"Then, gentlemen," said our guest, apprehensively, "I don't think it well for me to go any further. I crept hitherward only to ask about Priscilla; and now that you have told me such good news, perhaps I can do no better than to creep back again. If she were to see this old face of mine, the child would remember some very sad times which we have spent together. Some very sad times indeed! She has forgotten them, I know—them and me—else she could not be so happy, nor have a bloom in her cheeks. Yes—yes—yes," continued he, still with the same torpid utterance; "with many thanks to you, Mr. Hollingsworth, I will creep back to town again."

"You shall do no such thing, Mr. Moodie!" said Hollingsworth, bluffly. "Priscilla often speaks of you; and if there lacks anything to make her cheeks bloom like two damask roses, I'll venture to say, it is just the sight of your face. Come; we will go and find her."

"Mr. Hollingsworth!" said the old man, in his hesitating way.

"Well!" answered Hollingsworth.

"Has there been any call for Priscilla?" asked Moodie; and though his face was hidden from us, his tone gave a sure indication of the mysterious nod and wink with which he put the question. "You know, I think, sir, what I mean."

"I have not the remotest suspicion what you mean, Mr. Moodie," replied Hollingsworth. "Nobody, to my knowledge, has called for Priscilla, except yourself. But, come; we are losing time, and I have several things to say to you, by the way."

"And, Mr. Hollingsworth!" repeated Moodie.

"Well, again!" cried my friend, rather impatiently. "What now?"

"There is a lady here," said the old man; and his voice lost some of its wearisome hesitation. "You will account it a very strange matter for me to talk about; but I chanced to know this lady, when she was but a little child. If I am rightly informed, she has grown to be a very fine woman, and makes a brilliant figure in the world, with her beauty, and her talents, and her noble way of spending her riches. I should recognize this lady, so people tell me, by a magnificent flower in her hair!"

"What a rich tinge it gives to his colorless ideas, when he speaks of Zenobia!" I whispered to Hollingsworth. "But how can there possibly be any interest or connecting link between him and her?"

"The old man, for years past," whispered Hollingsworth, "has been a little out of his right mind, as you probably see."

"What I would inquire," resumed Moodie, "is, whether this beautiful lady is kind to my poor Priscilla."

"Very kind," said Hollingsworth.

"Does she love her?" asked Moodie.

"It should seem so," answered my friend. "They are always together."

"Like a gentlewoman and her maid servant, I fancy?" suggested the old man.

There was something so singular in his way of saying this, that I could not resist the impulse to turn quite round, so as to catch a glimpse of his face; almost imagining that I should see another person than old Moodie. But there he sat, with the patched side of his face towards me.

"Like an elder and younger sister, rather," replied Hollingsworth.

"Ah," said Moodie, more complaisantly—for his latter tones had harshness and acidity in them—"it would gladden my old heart to witness that. If one thing would make me happier than another, Mr. Hollingsworth, it would be, to see that beautiful lady holding my little girl by the hand."

"Come along," said Hollingsworth, "and perhaps you may."

After a little more delay on the part of our freakish visitor, they set forth together; old Moodie keeping a step or two behind Hollingsworth, so that the latter could not very conveniently look him in the face. I remained under the tuft of maples, doing my utmost to draw an inference from the scene that had just passed. In spite of Hollingsworth's off-hand explanation, it did not strike me that our strange guest was really beside himself, but only that his mind needed screwing up, like an instrument long out of tune, the strings of which have ceased to vibrate smartly and sharply. Methought it would be profitable for us, projectors of a happy life, to welcome this old gray shadow, and cherish him as one of us, and let him creep about our domain, in order that he might be a little merrier for our sakes, and we, sometimes, a little sadder for his. Human destinies look ominous, without some perceptible intermixture of the sable or the gray. And then, too, should any of our fraternity grow feverish with an over-exulting sense of prosperity, it would be a sort of cooling

regimen to slink off into the woods, and spend an hour, or a
day, or as many days as might be requisite to the cure, in
uninterrupted communion with this deplorable old Moodie!

Going homeward to dinner, I had a glimpse of him behind
the trunk of a tree, gazing earnestly towards a particular window of the farm-house. And, by-and-by, Priscilla appeared at
this window, playfully drawing along Zenobia, who looked
as bright as the very day that was blazing down upon us,
only not, by many degrees, so well advanced towards her
noon. I was convinced that this pretty sight must have been
purposely arranged by Priscilla, for the old man to see. But
either the girl held her too long, or her fondness was resented
as too great a freedom; for Zenobia suddenly put Priscilla
decidedly away, and gave her a haughty look, as from a mistress to a dependant. Old Moodie shook his head—and again,
and again, I saw him shake it, as he withdrew along the
road—and, at the last point whence the farm-house was visible,
he turned, and shook his uplifted staff.

XI

THE WOOD-PATH

NOT LONG after the preceding incident, in order to get the ache of too constant labor out of my bones, and to relieve my spirit of the irksomeness of a settled routine, I took a holiday. It was my purpose to spend it, all alone, from breakfast-time till twilight, in the deepest wood-seclusion that lay anywhere around us. Though fond of society, I was so constituted as to need these occasional retirements, even in a life like that of Blithedale, which was itself characterized by a remoteness from the world. Unless renewed by a yet farther withdrawal towards the inner circle of self-communion, I lost the better part of my individuality. My thoughts became of little worth, and my sensibilities grew as arid as a tuft of moss, (a thing whose life is in the shade, the rain, or the noontide dew,) crumbling in the sunshine, after long expectance of a shower. So, with my heart full of a drowsy pleasure, and cautious not to dissipate my mood by previous intercourse with any one, I hurried away, and was soon pacing a wood-path, arched overhead with boughs, and dusky brown beneath my feet.

At first, I walked very swiftly, as if the heavy floodtide of social life were roaring at my heels, and would outstrip and overwhelm me, without all the better diligence in my escape. But, threading the more distant windings of the track, I abated

my pace and looked about me for some side-aisle, that should
admit me into the innermost sanctuary of this green cathedral;
just as, in human acquaintanceship, a casual opening sometimes lets us, all of a sudden, into the long-sought intimacy of
a mysterious heart. So much was I absorbed in my reflections—or rather, in my mood, the substance of which was as
yet too shapeless to be called thought—that footsteps rustled
on the leaves, and a figure passed me by, almost without
impressing either the sound or sight upon my consciousness.

A moment afterwards, I heard a voice at a little distance
behind me, speaking so sharply and impertinently that it
made a complete discord with my spiritual state, and caused
the latter to vanish, as abruptly as when you thrust a finger
into a soap-bubble.

"Halloo, friend!" cried this most unseasonable voice. "Stop
a moment, I say! I must have a word with you!"

I turned about, in a humor ludicrously irate. In the first
place, the interruption, at any rate, was a grievous injury;
then, the tone displeased me. And, finally, unless there be
real affection in his heart, a man cannot—such is the bad
state to which the world has brought itself—cannot more effectually show his contempt for a brother-mortal, nor more gall-
ingly assume a position of superiority, than by addressing him
as 'friend.' Especially does the misapplication of this phrase
bring out that latent hostility, which is sure to animate peculiar sects, and those who, with however generous a purpose,
have sequestered themselves from the crowd; a feeling, it is
true, which may be hidden in some dog-kennel of the heart,
grumbling there in the darkness, but is never quite extinct,
until the dissenting party have gained power and scope
enough to treat the world generously. For my part, I should
have taken it as far less an insult to be styled 'fellow,' 'clown,'
or 'bumpkin.' To either of these appellations, my rustic garb
(it was a linen blouse, with checked shirt and striped pantaloons, a chip-hat on my head, and a rough hickory-stick in

my hand) very fairly entitled me. As the case stood, my temper darted at once to the opposite pole; not friend, but enemy!

"What do you want with me?" said I, facing about.

"Come a little nearer, friend!" said the stranger, beckoning.

"No," answered I. "If I can do anything for you, without too much trouble to myself, say so. But recollect, if you please, that you are not speaking to an acquaintance, much less a friend!"

"Upon my word, I believe not!" retorted he, looking at me with some curiosity; and lifting his hat, he made me a salute, which had enough of sarcasm to be offensive, and just enough of doubtful courtesy to render any resentment of it absurd.— "But I ask your pardon! I recognize a little mistake. If I may take the liberty to suppose it, you, sir, are probably one of the Æsthetic—or shall I rather say ecstatic?—laborers, who have planted themselves hereabouts. This is your forest of Arden;* and you are either the banished Duke, in person, or one of the chief nobles in his train. The melancholy Jacques, perhaps? Be it so! In that case, you can probably do me a favor."

I never, in my life, felt less inclined to confer a favor on any man.

"I am busy!" said I.

So unexpectedly had the stranger made me sensible of his presence, that he had almost the effect of an apparition, and certainly a less appropriate one (taking into view the dim woodland solitude about us) than if the salvage man* of antiquity, hirsute and cinctured with a leafy girdle, had started out of a thicket. He was still young, seemingly a little under thirty, of a tall and well-developed figure, and as handsome a man as ever I beheld. The style of his beauty, however, though a masculine style, did not at all commend itself to my taste. His countenance—I hardly know how to describe the peculiarity—had an indecorum in it, a kind of rudeness, a hard, coarse, forth-putting freedom of expression, which no degree of external polish could have abated, one single jot. Not that it was vulgar. But he had no fineness of nature; there was in his eyes (although they might have artifice enough of another sort) the naked exposure of something that ought not to be left prominent. With these vague allusions to what I have seen in other faces, as well as his, I leave the quality to be comprehended best—because with an intuitive repugnance—by those who possess least of it.

His hair, as well as his beard and moustache, was coal-black; his eyes, too, were black and sparkling, and his teeth remarkably brilliant. He was rather carelessly, but well and fashionably dressed, in a summer-morning costume. There was a gold chain, exquisitely wrought, across his vest. I never saw a smoother or whiter gloss than that upon his shirt-bosom, which had a pin in it, set with a gem that glimmered, in the leafy shadow where he stood, like a living tip of fire. He carried a stick with a wooden head, carved in vivid imitation of that of a serpent. I hated him, partly, I do believe, from a comparison of my own homely garb with his well-ordered foppishness.

"Well, sir," said I, a little ashamed of my first irritation, but still with no waste of civility, "be pleased to speak at once, as I have my own business in hand."

"I regret that my mode of addressing you was a little unfortunate," said the stranger, smiling; for he seemed a very acute sort of person, and saw, in some degree, how I stood affected towards him. "I intended no offence, and shall certainly comport myself with due ceremony hereafter. I merely wish to make a few inquiries respecting a lady, formerly of my acquaintance, who is now resident in your Community, and, I believe, largely concerned in your social enterprise. You call her, I think, Zenobia."

"That is her name in literature," observed I—"a name, too, which possibly she may permit her private friends to know and address her by;—but not one which they feel at liberty to recognize, when used of her, personally, by a stranger or casual acquaintance."

"Indeed!" answered this disagreeable person; and he turned aside his face, for an instant, with a brief laugh, which struck me as a noteworthy expression of his character. "Perhaps I might put forward a claim, on your own grounds, to call the lady by a name so appropriate to her splendid qualities. But I am willing to know her by any cognomen that you may suggest."

Heartily wishing that he would be either a little more offensive, or a good deal less so, or break off our intercourse altogether, I mentioned Zenobia's real name.

"True," said he; "and, in general society, I have never heard her called otherwise. And, after all, our discussion of the point has been gratuitous. My object is only to inquire when, where, and how, this lady may most conveniently be seen?"

"At her present residence, of course," I replied. "You have but to go thither and ask for her. This very path will lead you within sight of the house;—so I wish you good morning."

"One moment, if you please," said the stranger. "The course you indicate would certainly be the proper one, in an ordinary morning-call. But my business is private, personal, and somewhat peculiar. Now, in a Community like this, I should judge that any little occurrence is likely to be discussed rather more minutely than would quite suit my views. I refer solely to myself, you understand, and without intimating that it would be other than a matter of entire indifference to the lady. In short, I especially desire to see her in private. If her habits are such as I have known them, she is probably often to be met with in the woods, or by the river-side; and I think you could do me the favor to point out some favorite walk, where, about this hour, I might be fortunate enough to gain an interview."

I reflected, that it would be quite a super-erogatory piece of quixotism,* in me, to undertake the guardianship of Zenobia, who, for my pains, would only make me the butt of endless ridicule, should the fact ever come to her knowledge. I therefore described a spot which, as often as any other, was Zenobia's resort, at this period of the day; nor was it so remote from the farm-house as to leave her in much peril, whatever might be the stranger's character.

"A single word more!" said he; and his black eyes sparkled at me, whether with fun or malice I knew not, but certainly as if the Devil were peeping out of them. "Among your fraternity, I understand, there is a certain holy and benevolent blacksmith; a man of iron, in more senses than one; a rough, cross-grained, well-meaning individual, rather boorish in his manners—as might be expected—and by no means of the highest intellectual cultivation. He is a philanthropical lecturer, with two or three disciples, and a scheme of his own, the preliminary step in which involves a large purchase of land, and the erection of a spacious edifice, at an expense considerably beyond his means; inasmuch as these are to be reckoned in copper or old iron, much more conveniently than in gold or silver. He hammers away upon his one topic, as lustily as ever he did upon a horse-shoe! Do you know such a person?"

I shook my head, and was turning away.

"Our friend," he continued, "is described to me as a brawny, shaggy, grim, and ill-favored personage, not particularly well-calculated, one would say, to insinuate himself with the softer sex. Yet, so far has this honest fellow succeeded with one lady, whom we wot of, that he anticipates, from her abundant resources, the necessary funds for realizing his plan in brick and mortar!"

Here the stranger seemed to be so much amused with his sketch of Hollingsworth's character and purposes, that he burst into a fit of merriment, of the same nature as the brief, metallic laugh already alluded to, but immensely prolonged and enlarged. In the excess of his delight, he opened his mouth wide, and disclosed a gold band around the upper part of his teeth; thereby making it apparent that every one of his brilliant grinders and incisors was a sham. This discovery affected me very oddly. I felt as if the whole man were a moral and physical humbug; his wonderful beauty of face, for aught I knew, might be removeable like a mask; and, tall and comely as his figure looked, he was perhaps but a wizened little elf, gray and decrepit, with nothing genuine about him, save the wicked expression of his grin. The fantasy of his spectral character so wrought upon me, together with the contagion of his strange mirth on my sympathies, that I soon began to laugh as loudly as himself.

By-and-by, he paused, all at once; so suddenly, indeed, that my own cachinnation lasted a moment longer.

"Ah, excuse me!" said he. "Our interview seems to proceed more merrily than it began."

"It ends here," answered I. "And I take shame to myself, that my folly has lost me the right of resenting your ridicule of a friend."

"Pray allow me," said the stranger, approaching a step nearer, and laying his gloved hand on my sleeve. "One other favor I must ask of you. You have a young person, here at Blithedale, of whom I have heard—whom, perhaps, I have known—and in whom, at all events, I take a peculiar interest. She is one of those delicate, nervous young creatures, not uncommon in New England, and whom I suppose to have become what we find them by the gradual refining away of the physical system, among your women. Some philosophers choose to glorify this habit of body by terming it spiritual; but, in my opinion, it is rather the effect of unwholesome food, bad air, lack of out-door exercise, and neglect of bathing, on the part of these damsels and their female progenitors; all resulting in a kind of hereditary dyspepsia. Zenobia, even with her uncomfortable surplus of vitality, is far the better model of womanhood. But—to revert again to this young person—she goes among you by the name of Priscilla. Could you possibly afford me the means of speaking with her?"

"You have made so many inquiries of me," I observed, "that I may at least trouble you with one. What is your name?"

He offered me a card, with 'Professor Westervelt' engraved on it. At the same time, as if to vindicate his claim to the professorial dignity, so often assumed on very questionable grounds, he put on a pair of spectacles, which so altered the character of his face that I hardly knew him again. But I liked the present aspect no better than the former one.

"I must decline any further connection with your affairs," said I, drawing back. "I have told you where to find Zenobia. As for Priscilla, she has closer friends than myself, through whom, if they see fit, you can gain access to her."

"In that case," returned the Professor, ceremoniously raising his hat, "good morning to you."

He took his departure, and was soon out of sight among the windings of the wood-path. But, after a little reflection, I could not help regretting that I had so peremptorily broken off the interview, while the stranger seemed inclined to continue it. His evident knowledge of matters, affecting my three friends, might have led to disclosures, or inferences, that would perhaps have been serviceable. I was particularly struck with the fact, that, ever since the appearance of Priscilla, it had been the tendency of events to suggest and establish a connection between Zenobia and her. She had come, in the first instance, as if with the sole purpose of claiming Zenobia's protection. Old Moodie's visit, it appeared, was chiefly to ascertain whether this object had been accomplished. And here, to-day, was the questionable Professor, linking one with the other in his inquiries, and seeking communication with both.

Meanwhile, my inclination for a ramble having been baulked, I lingered in the vicinity of the farm, with perhaps a vague idea that some new event would grow out of Westervelt's proposed interview with Zenobia. My own part, in these transactions, was singularly subordinate. It resembled that of the Chorus* in a classic play, which seems to be set aloof from the possibility of personal concernment, and bestows the whole measure of its hope or fear, its exultation or sorrow, on the fortunes of others, between whom and itself this sympathy is the only bond. Destiny, it may be—the most skilful of stage-managers—seldom chooses to arrange its scenes, and carry forward its drama, without securing the presence of at least one calm observer. It is his office to give applause, when due, and sometimes an inevitable tear, to detect the final fitness of incident to character, and distil, in his long-brooding thought, the whole morality of the performance.

Not to be out of the way, in case there were need of me in my vocation, and, at the same time, to avoid thrusting myself where neither Destiny nor mortals might desire my presence, I remained pretty near the verge of the woodlands. My position was off the track of Zenobia's customary walk, yet not so remote but that a recognized occasion might speedily have brought me thither.

XII

COVERDALE'S HERMITAGE

LONG since, in this part of our circumjacent wood, I had found out for myself a little hermitage. It was a kind of leafy cave, high upward into the air, among the midmost branches of a white-pine tree. A wild grape-vine, of unusual size and luxuriance, had twined and twisted itself up into the tree, and, after wreathing the entanglement of its tendrils around almost every bough, had caught hold of three or four neighboring trees, and married the whole clump with a perfectly inextricable knot of polygamy. Once, while sheltering myself from a summer shower, the fancy had taken me to clamber up into this seemingly impervious mass of foliage. The branches yielded me a passage, and closed again, beneath, as if only a squirrel or a bird had passed. Far aloft, around the stem of the central pine, behold, a perfect nest for Robinson Crusoe* or King Charles!* A hollow chamber, of rare seclusion, had been formed by the decay of some of the pine-branches, which the vine had lovingly strangled with its embrace, burying them from the light of day in an aerial sepulchre of its own leaves. It cost me but little ingenuity to enlarge the interior, and open loop-holes through the verdant walls. Had it ever been my fortune to spend a honey-moon, I should have thought seriously of inviting my bride up thither, where our next neighbors would have been two orioles in another part of the clump.

It was an admirable place to make verses, tuning the rhythm to the breezy symphony that so often stirred among the vine-leaves; or to meditate an essay for the Dial, in which the many tongues of Nature whispered mysteries, and seemed to ask only a little stronger puff of wind, to speak out the solution of its riddle. Being so pervious to air-currents, it was just the nook, too, for the enjoyment of a cigar. This hermitage was my one exclusive possession, while I counted myself a brother of the socialists. It symbolized my individuality, and aided me in keeping it inviolate. None ever found me out in it, except, once, a squirrel. I brought thither no guest, because, after Hollingsworth failed me, there was no longer the man alive with whom I could think of sharing all. So there I used to sit, owl-like, yet not without liberal and hospitable thoughts. I counted the innumerable clusters of my vine, and fore-reckoned the abundance of my vintage. It gladdened me to anticipate the surprise of the Community, when, like an allegorical figure of rich October,* I should make my appearance, with shoulders bent beneath the burthen of ripe grapes, and some of the crushed ones crimsoning my brow as with a blood-stain.

Ascending into this natural turret, I peeped, in turn, out of several of its small windows. The pine-tree, being ancient, rose high above the rest of the wood, which was of comparatively recent growth. Even where I sat, about midway between the root and the topmost bough, my position was lofty enough to serve as an observatory, not for starry investigations, but for those sublunary matters in which lay a lore as infinite as that of the planets. Through one loop-hole, I saw the river lapsing calmly onward, while, in the meadow near its brink, a few of the brethren were digging peat for our winter's fuel. On the interior cart-road of our farm, I discerned Hollingsworth, with a yoke of oxen hitched to a drag of stones, that were to be piled into a fence, on which we employed ourselves at the odd intervals of other labor. The harsh tones of his voice, shouting to the sluggish steers, made me sensible, even at such a distance, that he was ill at ease, and that the baulked philanthropist had the battle-spirit in his heart.

"Haw Buck!" quoth he. "Come along there, ye lazy ones! What are ye about now? Gee!"

"Mankind, in Hollingsworth's opinion," thought I, "is but another yoke of oxen, as stubborn, stupid, and sluggish, as our old Brown and Bright. He vituperates us aloud, and curses us in his heart, and will begin to prick us with the goad stick, by-and-by. But, are we his oxen? And what right has he to be the driver? And why, when there is enough else to do, should we waste our strength in dragging home the ponderous load of his philanthropic absurdities? At my height above the earth, the whole matter looks ridiculous!"

Turning towards the farm-house, I saw Priscilla (for, though a great way off, the eye of faith assured me that it was she) sitting at Zenobia's window, and making little purses, I suppose, or perhaps mending the Community's old linen. A bird flew past my tree; and as it clove its way onward into the sunny atmosphere, I flung it a message for Priscilla.

"Tell her," said I, "that her fragile thread of life has inextricably knotted itself with other and tougher threads, and most likely it will be broken. Tell her that Zenobia will not be long her friend. Say that Hollingsworth's heart is on fire with his own purpose, but icy for all human affection, and that, if she has given him her love, it is like casting a flower into a sepulchre. And say, that, if any mortal really cares for her, it is myself, and not even I, for her realities—poor little seamstress, as Zenobia rightly called her!—but for the fancy-work*with which I have idly decked her out!"

The pleasant scent of the wood, evolved by the hot sun, stole up to my nostrils, as if I had been an idol in its niche. Many trees mingled their fragrance into a thousand-fold odor. Possibly, there was a sensual influence in the broad light of noon that lay beneath me. It may have been the cause, in part, that I suddenly found myself possessed by a mood of disbelief in moral beauty or heroism, and a conviction of the folly of attempting to benefit the world. Our especial scheme of reform, which, from my observatory, I could take in with the bodily eye, looked so ridiculous that it was impossible not to laugh aloud.

"But the joke is a little too heavy," thought I. "If I were wise, I should get out of the scrape, with all diligence, and then laugh at my companions for remaining in it!"

While thus musing, I heard, with perfect distinctness, somewhere in the wood beneath, the peculiar laugh, which I have described as one of the disagreeable characteristics of Professor Westervelt. It brought my thoughts back to our recent interview. I recognized, as chiefly due to this man's influence, the sceptical and sneering view which, just now, had filled my mental vision in regard to all life's better purposes. And it was through his eyes, more than my own, that I was looking at Hollingsworth, with his glorious, if impracticable dream, and at the noble earthliness of Zenobia's character, and even at Priscilla, whose impalpable grace lay so singularly between disease and beauty. The essential charm of each had vanished. There are some spheres, the contact with which inevitably degrades the high, debases the pure, deforms the beautiful. It must be a mind of uncommon strength, and little impressibility, that can permit itself the habit of such intercourse, and not be permanently deteriorated; and yet the Professor's tone represented that of worldly society at large, where a cold scepticism smothers what it can of our spiritual aspirations, and makes the rest ridiculous.

I detested this kind of man, and all the more, because a part of my own nature showed itself responsive to him.

Voices were now approaching, through the region of the wood which lay in the vicinity of my tree. Soon, I caught glimpses of two figures—a woman and a man—Zenobia and the stranger—earnestly talking together as they advanced.

Zenobia had a rich, though varying color. It was, most of the while, a flame, and anon a sudden paleness. Her eyes glowed, so that their light sometimes flashed upward to me, as when the sun throws a dazzle from some bright object on the ground. Her gestures were free, and strikingly impressive. The whole woman was alive with a passionate intensity, which I now perceived to be the phase in which her beauty culminated. Any passion would have become her well, and passionate love, perhaps, the best of all. This was not love, but anger, largely intermixed with scorn. Yet the idea strangely forced itself upon me, that there was a sort of familiarity between these two companions, necessarily the result of an intimate love—on Zenobia's part, at least—in days gone by, but which had prolonged itself into as intimate a hatred, for all futurity. As they passed among the trees, reckless as her movement was, she took good heed that even the hem of her garment should not brush against the stranger's person. I wondered whether there had always been a chasm, guarded so religiously, betwixt these two.

As for Westervelt, he was not a whit more warmed by Zenobia's passion, than a salamander by the heat of its native furnace. He would have been absolutely statuesque, save for a look of slight perplexity tinctured strongly with derision. It was a crisis in which his intellectual perceptions could not altogether help him out. He failed to comprehend, and cared but little for comprehending, why Zenobia should put herself into such a fume; but satisfied his mind that it was all folly, and only another shape of a woman's manifold absurdity, which men can never understand. How many a woman's evil fate has yoked her with a man like this! Nature thrusts some of us into the world miserably incomplete, on the emotional side, with hardly any sensibilities except what pertain to us as animals. No passion, save of the senses; no holy tenderness, nor the delicacy that results from this. Externally, they bear a close resemblance to other men, and have perhaps all save the finest grace; but when a woman wrecks herself on such a being, she ultimately finds that the real womanhood, within her, has no corresponding part in him. Her deepest voice lacks a response; the deeper her cry, the more dead his silence. The fault may be none of his; he cannot give her what never lived within his soul. But the wretchedness, on her side, and the moral deterioration attendant on a false and shallow life, without strength enough to keep itself sweet, are among the most pitiable wrongs that mortals suffer.

Now, as I looked down from my upper region at this man and woman—outwardly so fair a sight, and wandering like two lovers in the wood—I imagined that Zenobia, at an earlier period of youth, might have fallen into the misfortune above indicated. And when her passionate womanhood, as was inevitable, had discovered its mistake, there had ensued the character of eccentricity and defiance, which distinguished the more public portion of her life.

Seeing how aptly matters had chanced, thus far, I began to think it the design of fate to let me into all Zenobia's secrets, and that therefore the couple would sit down beneath my tree, and carry on a conversation which would leave me nothing to inquire. No doubt, however, had it so happened, I should have deemed myself honorably bound to warn them of a listener's presence by flinging down a handful of unripe grapes; or by sending an unearthly groan out of my hiding-place, as if this were one of the trees of Dante's ghostly forest.*

But real life never arranges itself exactly like a romance. In the first place, they did not sit down at all. Secondly, even while they passed beneath the tree, Zenobia's utterance was so hasty and broken, and Westervelt's so cool and low, that I hardly could make out an intelligible sentence, on either side. What I seem to remember, I yet suspect may have been patched together by my fancy, in brooding over the matter, afterwards.

"Why not fling the girl off," said Westervelt, "and let her go?"

"She clung to me from the first," replied Zenobia. "I neither know nor care what it is in me that so attaches her. But she loves me, and I will not fail her."

"She will plague you, then," said he, "in more ways than one."

"The poor child!" exclaimed Zenobia. "She can do me neither good nor harm. How should she?"

I know not what reply Westervelt whispered; nor did Zenobia's subsequent exclamation give me any clue, except that it evidently inspired her with horror and disgust.

"With what kind of a being am I linked!" cried she. "If my Creator cares aught for my soul, let him release me from this miserable bond!"

"I did not think it weighed so heavily," said her companion.

"Nevertheless," answered Zenobia, "it will strangle me at last!"

And then I heard her utter a helpless sort of moan; a sound which, struggling out of the heart of a person of her pride and strength, affected me more than if she had made the wood dolorously vocal with a thousand shrieks and wails.

Other mysterious words, besides what are above-written, they spoke together; but I understood no more, and even question whether I fairly understood so much as this. By long brooding over our recollections, we subtilize them into something akin to imaginary stuff, and hardly capable of being distinguished from it. In a few moments, they were completely beyond ear-shot. A breeze stirred after them, and awoke the leafy tongues of the surrounding trees, which forthwith began to babble, as if innumerable gossips had all at once got wind of Zenobia's secret. But, as the breeze grew stronger, its voice among the branches was as if it said—'Hush! Hush!'—and I resolved that to no mortal would I disclose what I had heard. And, though there might be room for casuistry, such, I conceive, is the most equitable rule in all similar conjunctures.

XIII

ZENOBIA'S LEGEND

THE illustrious Society of Blithedale, though it toiled in downright earnest for the good of mankind, yet not unfrequently illuminated its laborious life with an afternoon or evening of pastime. Pic-nics under the trees were considerably in vogue; and, within doors, fragmentary bits of theatrical performance, such as single acts of tragedy or comedy, or dramatic proverbs and charades. Zenobia, besides, was fond of giving us readings from Shakspeare, and often with a depth of tragic power, or breadth of comic effect, that made one feel it an intolerable wrong to the world, that she did not at once go upon the stage. *Tableaux vivants**were another of our occasional modes of amusement, in which scarlet shawls, old silken robes, ruffs, velvets, furs, and all kinds of miscellaneous trumpery, converted our familiar companions into the people of a pictorial world. We had been thus engaged, on the evening after the incident narrated in the last chapter. Several splendid works of art—either arranged after engravings from the Old Masters, or original illustrations of scenes in history or romance—had been presented, and we were earnestly entreating Zenobia for more.

She stood, with a meditative air, holding a large piece of gauze, or some such ethereal stuff, as if considering what picture should next occupy the frame; while at her feet lay a heap of many-colored garments, which her quick fancy and magic skill could so easily convert into gorgeous draperies for heroes and princesses.

"I am getting weary of this," said she, after a moment's thought. "Our own features, and our own figures and airs, show a little too intrusively through all the characters we assume. We have so much familiarity with one another's realities, that we cannot remove ourselves, at pleasure, into an imaginary sphere. Let us have no more pictures, to-night; but, to make you what poor amends I can, how would you like to have me trump up a wild, spectral legend, on the spur of the moment?"

Zenobia had the gift of telling a fanciful little story, off hand, in a way that made it greatly more effective, than it was usually found to be, when she afterwards elaborated the same production with her pen. Her proposal, therefore, was greeted with acclamation.

"Oh, a story, a story, by all means!" cried the young girls. "No matter how marvellous, we will believe it, every word! And let it be a ghost-story, if you please!"

"No; not exactly a ghost-story," answered Zenobia; "but something so nearly like it that you shall hardly tell the difference. And, Priscilla, stand you before me, where I may look at you, and get my inspiration out of your eyes. They are very deep and dreamy, to-night!"

I know not whether the following version of her story will retain any portion of its pristine character. But, as Zenobia told it, wildly and rapidly, hesitating at no extravagance, and dashing at absurdities which I am too timorous to repeat— giving it the varied emphasis of her inimitable voice, and the pictorial illustration of her mobile face, while, through it all, we caught the freshest aroma of the thoughts, as they came bubbling out of her mind—thus narrated, and thus heard, the legend seemed quite a remarkable affair. I scarcely knew, at the time, whether she intended us to laugh, or be more seriously impressed. From beginning to end it was undeniable nonsense, but not necessarily the worse for that.

THE SILVERY VEIL

You have heard, my dear friends, of the Veiled Lady, who grew suddenly so very famous, a few months ago. And have you never thought how remarkable it was, that this marvellous creature should vanish, all at once, while her renown was on the increase, before the public had grown weary of her, and when the enigma of her character, instead of being solved, presented itself more mystically at every exhibition? Her last appearance, as you know, was before a crowded audience. The next evening—although the bills had announced her, at the corner of every street, in red letters of a gigantic size—there was no Veiled Lady to be seen! Now, listen to my simple little tale; and you shall hear the very latest incident in the known life—(if life it may be called, which seemed to have no more reality than the candlelight image of one's self, which peeps at us outside of a dark window-pane)—the life of this shadowy phenomenon.

A party of young gentlemen, you are to understand, were enjoying themselves, one afternoon, as young gentlemen are sometimes fond of doing, over a bottle or two of champagne; and—among other ladies less mysterious—the subject of the Veiled Lady, as was very natural, happened to come up before them for discussion. She rose, as it were, with the sparkling effervescence of their wine, and appeared in a more airy and fantastic light, on account of the medium through which they saw her. They repeated to one another, between jest and earnest, all the wild stories that were in vogue; nor, I presume, did they hesitate to add any small circumstance that the inventive whim of the moment might suggest, to heighten the marvellousness of their theme.

"But what an audacious report was that," observed one, "which pretended to assert the identity of this strange creature with a young lady"—and here he mentioned her name—"the daughter of one of our most distinguished families!"

"Ah, there is more in that story than can well be accounted for!" remarked another. "I have it on good authority, that the young lady in question is invariably out of sight, and not to be traced, even by her own family, at the hours when the Veiled Lady is before the public; nor can any satisfactory explanation be given of her disappearance. And just look at the thing! Her brother is a young fellow of spirit. He cannot but be aware of these rumors in reference to his sister. Why, then, does he not come forward to defend her character, unless he is conscious that an investigation would only make the matter worse?"

It is essential to the purposes of my legend to distinguish one of these young gentlemen from his companions; so, for the sake of a soft and pretty name, (such as we, of the literary sisterhood, invariably bestow upon our heroes,) I deem it fit to call him 'Theodore.'

"Pshaw!" exclaimed Theodore. "Her brother is no such fool! Nobody, unless his brain be as full of bubbles as this wine, can seriously think of crediting that ridiculous rumor. Why, if my senses did not play me false, (which never was the case yet,) I affirm that I saw that very lady, last evening, at the exhibition, while this veiled phenomenon was playing off her juggling tricks! What can you say to that?"

"Oh, it was a spectral illusion that you saw!" replied his friends, with a general laugh. "The Veiled Lady is quite up to such a thing."

However, as the above-mentioned fable could not hold its ground against Theodore's downright refutation, they went on to speak of other stories, which the wild babble of the town had set afloat. Some upheld, that the veil covered the most beautiful countenance in the world; others—and certainly with more reason, considering the sex of the Veiled

Lady—that the face was the most hideous and horrible, and that this was her sole motive for hiding it. It was the face of a corpse; it was the head of a skeleton; it was a monstrous visage, with snaky locks, like Medusa's,* and one great red eye in the centre of the forehead. Again, it was affirmed, that there was no single and unchangeable set of features, beneath the veil, but that whosoever should be bold enough to lift it, would behold the features of that person, in all the world, who was destined to be his fate; perhaps he would be greeted by the tender smile of the woman whom he loved; or, quite as probably, the deadly scowl of his bitterest enemy would throw a blight over his life. They quoted, moreover, this startling explanation of the whole affair:—that the Magician (who exhibited the Veiled Lady, and who, by-the-by, was the handsomest man in the whole world) had bartered his own soul for seven years' possession of a familiar fiend, and that the last year of the contract was wearing towards its close.

If it were worth our while, I could keep you till an hour beyond midnight, listening to a thousand such absurdities as these. But, finally, our friend Theodore, who prided himself upon his common-sense, found the matter getting quite beyond his patience.

"I offer any wager you like," cried he, setting down his glass so forcibly as to break the stem of it, "that, this very evening, I find out the mystery of the Veiled Lady!"

Young men, I am told, boggle at nothing, over their wine. So, after a little more talk, a wager of considerable amount was actually laid, the money staked, and Theodore left to choose his own method of settling the dispute.

How he managed it, I know not, nor is it of any great importance to this veracious legend; the most natural way, to be sure, was by bribing the door-keeper, or, possibly, he preferred clambering in at the window. But, at any rate, that very evening, while the exhibition was going forward in the hall, Theodore contrived to gain admittance into the private withdrawing-room, whither the Veiled Lady was accustomed to retire, at the close of her performances. There he waited, listening, I suppose, to the stifled hum of the great audience; and, no doubt, he could distinguish the deep tones of the Magician, causing the wonders that he wrought to appear more dark and intricate, by his mystic pretence of an explanation; perhaps, too, in the intervals of the wild, breezy music which accompanied the exhibition, he might hear the low voice of the Veiled Lady, conveying her Sibylline responses. Firm as Theodore's nerves might be, and much as he prided himself on his sturdy perception of realities, I should not be surprised if his heart throbbed at a little more than its ordinary rate!

Theodore concealed himself behind a screen. In due time, the performance was brought to a close; and whether the door was softly opened, or whether her bodiless presence came through the wall, is more than I can say; but, all at once, without the young man's knowing how it happened, a veiled figure stood in the centre of the room. It was one thing to be in presence of this mystery, in the hall of exhibition, where the warm, dense life of hundreds of other mortals kept up the beholder's courage, and distributed her influence among so many; it was another thing to be quite alone with her, and that, too, with a hostile, or, at least, an unauthorized and unjustifiable purpose. I rather imagine that Theodore now began to be sensible of something more serious in his enterprise than he had been quite aware of, while he sat with his boon-companions over their sparkling wine.

Very strange, it must be confessed, was the movement with which the figure floated to-and-fro over the carpet, with the silvery veil covering her from head to foot; so impalpable, so ethereal, so without substance, as the texture seemed, yet hiding her every outline in an impenetrability like that of midnight. Surely, she did not walk! She floated, and flitted, and hovered about the room;—no sound of a footstep, no perceptible motion of a limb;—it was as if a wandering breeze wafted her before it, at its own wild and gentle pleasure. But, by-and-by, a purpose began to be discernible, throughout the seeming vagueness of her unrest. She was in quest of something! Could it be, that a subtile presentiment had informed her of the young man's presence? And, if so, did the Veiled Lady seek, or did she shun him? The doubt in Theodore's mind was speedily resolved; for, after a moment or two of these erratic flutterings, she advanced, more decidedly, and stood motionless before the screen.

"Thou art here!" said a soft, low voice. "Come forth, Theodore!"

Thus summoned by his name, Theodore, as a man of courage, had no choice. He emerged from his concealment, and presented himself before the Veiled Lady, with the wine-flush, it may be, quite gone out of his cheeks.

"What wouldst thou with me?" she inquired, with the same gentle composure that was in her former utterance.

"Mysterious creature," replied Theodore, "I would know who and what you are!"

"My lips are forbidden to betray the secret!" said the Veiled Lady.

"At whatever risk, I must discover it!" rejoined Theodore.

"Then," said the Mystery, "there is no way, save to lift my veil!"

And Theodore, partly recovering his audacity, stept forward, on the instant, to do as the Veiled Lady had suggested. But she floated backward to the opposite side of the room, as if the young man's breath had possessed power enough to waft her away.

"Pause, one little instant," said the soft, low voice, "and learn the conditions of what thou art so bold to undertake! Thou canst go hence, and think of me no more; or, at thy option, thou canst lift this mysterious veil, beneath which I am a sad and lonely prisoner, in a bondage which is worse to me than death. But, before raising it, I entreat thee, in all maiden modesty, to bend forward, and impress a kiss, where my breath stirs the veil; and my virgin lips shall come forward to meet thy lips; and from that instant, Theodore, thou shalt be mine, and I thine, with never more a veil between us! And all the felicity of earth and of the future world shall be thine and mine together. So much may a maiden say behind the veil! If thou shrinkest from this, there is yet another way."

"And what is that?" asked Theodore.

"Dost thou hesitate," said the Veiled Lady, "to pledge thyself to me, by meeting these lips of mine, while the veil yet hides my face? Has not thy heart recognized me? Dost thou come hither, not in holy faith, nor with a pure and generous purpose, but in scornful scepticism and idle curiosity? Still, thou mayst lift the veil! But from that instant, Theodore, I am doomed to be thy evil fate; nor wilt thou ever taste another breath of happiness!"

There was a shade of inexpressible sadness in the utterance of these last words. But Theodore, whose natural tendency was towards scepticism, felt himself almost injured and insulted by the Veiled Lady's proposal that he should pledge himself, for life and eternity, to so questionable a creature as herself; or even that she should suggest an inconsequential kiss, taking into view the probability that her face was none of the most bewitching. A delightful idea, truly, that he should salute the lips of a dead girl, or the jaws of a skeleton, or the grinning cavity of a monster's mouth! Even should she prove a comely maiden enough, in other respects, the odds were ten to one that her teeth were defective; a terrible drawback on the delectableness of a kiss!

"Excuse me, fair lady," said Theodore—and I think he nearly burst into a laugh—"if I prefer to lift the veil first; and for this affair of the kiss, we may decide upon it, afterwards!"

"Thou hast made thy choice," said the sweet, sad voice, behind the veil; and there seemed a tender, but unresentful sense of wrong done to womanhood by the young man's contemptuous interpretation of her offer. "I must not counsel thee to pause; although thy fate is still in thine own hand!"

Grasping at the veil, he flung it upward, and caught a glimpse of a pale, lovely face, beneath; just one momentary glimpse; and then the apparition vanished, and the silvery veil fluttered slowly down, and lay upon the floor. Theodore was alone. Our legend leaves him there. His retribution was, to pine, forever and ever, for another sight of that dim, mournful face—which might have been his life-long, household, fireside joy—to desire, and waste life in a feverish quest, and never meet it more!

But what, in good sooth, had become of the Veiled Lady? Had all her existence been comprehended within that mysterious veil, and was she now annihilated? Or was she a spirit, with a heavenly essence, but which might have been tamed down to human bliss, had Theodore been brave and true enough to claim her? Hearken, my sweet friends—and hearken, dear Priscilla—and you shall learn the little more that Zenobia can tell you!

Just at the moment, so far as can be ascertained, when the Veiled Lady vanished, a maiden, pale and shadowy, rose up amid a knot of visionary people, who were seeking for the better life. She was so gentle and so sad—a nameless melancholy gave her such hold upon their sympathies—that they never thought of questioning whence she came. She might have heretofore existed; or her thin substance might have been moulded out of air, at the very instant when they first beheld her. It was all one to them; they took her to their hearts. Among them was a lady, to whom, more than to all the rest, this pale, mysterious girl attached herself.

But, one morning, the lady was wandering in the woods, and there met her a figure in an Oriental robe, with a dark beard, and holding in his hand a silvery veil. He motioned her to stay. Being a woman of some nerve, she did not shriek, nor run away, nor faint, as many ladies would have been apt to do, but stood quietly, and bade him speak. The truth was, she had seen his face before, but had never feared it, although she knew him to be a terrible magician.

"Lady," said he, with a warning gesture, "you are in peril!"

"Peril!" she exclaimed. "And of what nature?"

"There is a certain maiden," replied the Magician, "who has come out of the realm of Mystery, and made herself your most intimate companion. Now, the fates have so ordained it, that, whether by her own will, or no, this stranger is your deadliest enemy. In love, in worldly fortune, in all your pursuit of happiness, she is doomed to fling a blight over your prospects. There is but one possibility of thwarting her disastrous influence."

"Then, tell me that one method," said the lady.

"Take this veil!" he answered, holding forth the silvery texture. "It is a spell; it is a powerful enchantment, which I wrought for her sake, and beneath which she was once my prisoner. Throw it, at unawares, over the head of this secret foe, stamp your foot, and cry—'Arise, Magician, here is the Veiled Lady'—and immediately I will rise up through the earth, and seize her. And from that moment, you are safe!"

So the lady took the silvery veil, which was like woven air, or like some substance airier than nothing, and that would float upward and be lost among the clouds, were she once to let it go. Returning homeward, she found the shadowy girl, amid the knot of visionary transcendentalists,* who were still seeking for the better life. She was joyous, now, and had a rose-bloom in her cheeks, and was one of the prettiest creatures, and seemed one of the happiest, that the world could show. But the lady stole noiselessly behind her, and threw the veil over her head. As the slight, ethereal texture sank inevitably down over her figure, the poor girl strove to raise it, and met her dear friend's eyes with one glance of mortal terror, and deep, deep reproach. It could not change her purpose.

"Arise, Magician!" she exclaimed, stamping her foot upon the earth. "Here is the Veiled Lady!"

At the word, uprose the bearded man in the Oriental robes—the beautiful!—the dark Magician, who had bartered away his soul! He threw his arms around the Veiled Lady; and she was his bond-slave, forever more!

———————

Zenobia, all this while, had been holding the piece of gauze, and so managed it as greatly to increase the dramatic effect of the legend, at those points where the magic veil was to be described. Arriving at the catastrophe, and uttering the fatal words, she flung the gauze over Priscilla's head; and, for an instant, her auditors held their breath, half expecting, I verily believe, that the Magician would start up through the floor, and carry off our poor little friend, before our eyes.

As for Priscilla, she stood, droopingly, in the midst of us, making no attempt to remove the veil.

"How do you find yourself, my love?" said Zenobia, lifting a corner of the gauze, and peeping beneath it, with a mischievous smile. "Ah, the dear little soul! Why, she is really going to faint! Mr. Coverdale, Mr. Coverdale, pray bring a glass of water!"

Her nerves being none of the strongest, Priscilla hardly recovered her equanimity during the rest of the evening. This, to be sure, was a great pity; but, nevertheless, we thought it a very bright idea of Zenobia's, to bring her legend to so effective a conclusion.

XIV

ELIOT'S PULPIT

O UR SUNDAYS, at Blithedale, were not ordinarily
kept with such rigid observance as might have befitted
the descendants of the Pilgrims, whose high enterprise, as we sometimes flattered ourselves, we had taken up,
and were carrying it onward and aloft, to a point which they
never dreamed of attaining.

On that hallowed day, it is true, we rested from our labors.
Our oxen, relieved from their week-day yoke, roamed at large
through the pasture; each yoke-fellow, however, keeping close
beside his mate, and continuing to acknowledge, from the
force of habit and sluggish sympathy, the union which the
taskmaster had imposed for his own hard ends. As for us,
human yoke-fellows, chosen companions of toil, whose hoes
had clinked together throughout the week, we wandered off,
in various directions, to enjoy our interval of repose. Some, I
believe, went devoutly to the village-church. Others, it may
be, ascended a city or a country-pulpit, wearing the clerical
robe with so much dignity that you would scarcely have suspected the yeoman's frock to have been flung off, only since
milking-time. Others took long rambles among the rustic
lanes and by-paths, pausing to look at black, old farm-houses,
with their sloping roofs; and at the modern cottage, so like
a plaything that it seemed as if real joy or sorrow could have

no scope within; and at the more pretending villa, with its range of wooden columns, supporting the needless insolence of a great portico. Some betook themselves into the wide, dusky barn, and lay there, for hours together, on the odorous hay; while the sunstreaks and the shadows strove together— these to make the barn solemn, those to make it cheerful—and both were conquerors; and the swallows twittered a cheery anthem, flashing into sight, or vanishing, as they darted to-and-fro among the golden rules of sunshine. And others went a little way into the woods, and threw themselves on Mother Earth, pillowing their heads on a heap of moss, the green decay of an old log; and dropping asleep, the humble-bees and musquitoes sung and buzzed about their ears, causing the slumberers to twitch and start, without awakening.

With Hollingsworth, Zenobia, Priscilla, and myself, it grew to be a custom to spend the Sabbath-afternoon at a certain rock. It was known to us under the name of Eliot's pulpit, from a tradition that the venerable Apostle Eliot* had preached there, two centuries gone by, to an Indian auditory. The old pine-forest, through which the Apostle's voice was wont to sound, had fallen, an immemorial time ago. But the soil, being of the rudest and most broken surface, had apparently never been brought under tillage; other growths, maple, and beech, and birch, had succeeded to the primeval trees; so that it was still as wild a tract of woodland as the great-great-great-great grandson of one of Eliot's Indians (had any such posterity been in existence) could have desired, for the site and shelter of his wigwam. These after-growths, indeed, lose the stately solemnity of the original forest. If left in due neglect, however, they run into an entanglement of softer wildness, among the rustling leaves of which the sun can scatter cheerfulness, as it never could among the dark-browed pines.

The rock itself rose some twenty or thirty feet, a shattered granite boulder, or heap of boulders, with an irregular outline and many fissures, out of which sprang shrubs, bushes, and even trees; as if the scanty soil, within those crevices, were sweeter to their roots than any other earth. At the base of the pulpit, the broken boulders inclined towards each other, so as to form a shallow cave, within which our little party had sometimes found protection from a summer shower. On the threshold, or just across it, grew a tuft of pale columbines, in their season, and violets, sad and shadowy recluses, such as Priscilla was, when we first knew her; children of the sun, who had never seen their father, but dwelt among damp mosses, though not akin to them. At the summit, the rock was overshadowed by the canopy of a birch-tree, which served as a sounding-board for the pulpit. Beneath this shade, (with my eyes of sense half shut, and those of the imagination widely opened,) I used to see the holy Apostle of the Indians, with the sunlight flickering down upon him through the leaves, and glorifying his figure as with the half-perceptible glow of a transfiguration.

I the more minutely describe the rock, and this little Sabbath solitude, because Hollingsworth, at our solicitation, often ascended Eliot's pulpit, and—not exactly preached—but talked to us, his few disciples, in a strain that rose and fell as naturally as the wind's breath among the leaves of the birch-tree. No other speech of man has ever moved me like some of those discourses. It seemed most pitiful—a positive calamity to the world—that a treasury of golden thoughts should thus be scattered, by the liberal handful, down among us three, when a thousand hearers might have been the richer for them; and Hollingsworth the richer, likewise, by the sympathy of multitudes. After speaking much or little, as might happen, he would descend from his gray pulpit, and generally fling himself at full length on the ground, face downward. Meanwhile, we talked around him, on such topics as were suggested by the discourse.

Since her interview with Westervelt, Zenobia's continual

inequalities of temper had been rather difficult for her friends to bear. On the first Sunday after that incident, when Hollingsworth had clambered down from Eliot's pulpit, she declaimed with great earnestness and passion, nothing short of anger, on the injustice which the world did to women, and equally to itself, by not allowing them, in freedom and honor, and with the fullest welcome, their natural utterance in public.

"It shall not always be so!" cried she. "If I live another year, I will lift up my own voice, in behalf of woman's wider liberty."

She, perhaps, saw me smile.

"What matter of ridicule do you find in this, Miles Coverdale?" exclaimed Zenobia, with a flash of anger in her eyes. "That smile, permit me to say, makes me suspicious of a low tone of feeling, and shallow thought. It is my belief—yes, and my prophecy, should I die before it happens—that, when my sex shall achieve its rights, there will be ten eloquent women, where there is now one eloquent man. Thus far, no woman in the world has ever once spoken out her whole heart and her whole mind. The mistrust and disapproval of the vast bulk of society throttles us, as with two gigantic hands at our throats! We mumble a few weak words, and leave a thousand better ones unsaid. You let us write a little, it is true, on a limited range of subjects. But the pen is not for woman. Her power is too natural and immediate. It is with the living voice, alone, that she can compel the world to recognize the light of her intellect and the depth of her heart!"

Now—though I could not well say so to Zenobia—I had not smiled from any unworthy estimate of woman, or in denial of the claims which she is beginning to put forth. What amused and puzzled me, was the fact, that women, however intellectually superior, so seldom disquiet themselves about the rights or wrongs of their sex, unless their own individual affections chance to lie in idleness, or to be ill at ease. They are not natural reformers, but become such by the pressure of exceptional misfortune. I could measure Zenobia's inward trouble, by the animosity with which she now took up the general quarrel of woman against man.

"I will give you leave, Zenobia," replied I, "to fling your utmost scorn upon me, if you ever hear me utter a sentiment unfavorable to the widest liberty which woman has yet dreamed of. I would give her all she asks, and add a great deal more, which she will not be the party to demand, but which men, if they were generous and wise, would grant of their own free motion. For instance, I should love dearly—for the next thousand years, at least—to have all government devolve into the hands of women. I hate to be ruled by my own sex; it excites my jealousy and wounds my pride. It is the iron sway of bodily force, which abases us, in our compelled submission. But, how sweet the free, generous courtesy, with which I would kneel before a woman-ruler!"

"Yes; if she were young and beautiful," said Zenobia, laughing. "But how if she were sixty, and a fright?"

"Ah; it is you that rate womanhood low," said I. "But let me go on. I have never found it possible to suffer a bearded priest so near my heart and conscience, as to do me any spiritual good. I blush at the very thought! Oh, in the better order of things, Heaven grant that the ministry of souls may be left in charge of women! The gates of the Blessed City will be thronged with the multitude that enter in, when that day comes! The task belongs to woman. God meant it for her. He has endowed her with the religious sentiment in its utmost depth and purity, refined from that gross, intellectual alloy, with which every masculine theologist—save only One, who merely veiled Himself in mortal and masculine shape, but was, in truth, divine—has been prone to mingle it. I have always envied the Catholics their faith in that sweet, sacred Virgin Mother, who stands between them and the Deity, intercepting somewhat of His awful splendor, but permitting His love to stream upon the worshipper, more intelligibly to human comprehension, through the medium of a woman's tenderness. Have I not said enough, Zenobia?"

"I cannot think that this is true," observed Priscilla, who had been gazing at me with great, disapproving eyes. "And I am sure I do not wish it to be true!"

"Poor child!" exclaimed Zenobia, rather contemptuously. "She is the type of womanhood, such as man has spent centuries in making it. He is never content, unless he can degrade himself by stooping towards what he loves. In denying us our rights, he betrays even more blindness to his own interests, than profligate disregard of ours!"

"Is this true?" asked Priscilla, with simplicity, turning to Hollingsworth. "Is it all true that Mr. Coverdale and Zenobia have been saying?"

"No, Priscilla," answered Hollingsworth, with his customary bluntness. "They have neither of them spoken one true word yet."

"Do you despise woman?" said Zenobia. "Ah, Hollingsworth, that would be most ungrateful!"

"Despise her?—No!" cried Hollingsworth, lifting his great shaggy head and shaking it at us, while his eyes glowed almost fiercely. "She is the most admirable handiwork of God, in her true place and character. Her place is at man's side. Her office, that of the Sympathizer; the unreserved, unquestioning Believer; the Recognition, withheld in every other manner, but given, in pity, through woman's heart, lest man should utterly lose faith in himself; the Echo of God's own voice, pronouncing—'It is well done!' All the separate action of woman is, and ever has been, and always shall be, false, foolish, vain, destructive of her own best and holiest qualities, void of every good effect, and productive of intolerable mischiefs! Man is a wretch without woman; but woman is a monster—and, thank Heaven, an almost impossible and

hitherto imaginary monster—without man, as her acknowledged principal! As true as I had once a mother, whom I
loved, were there any possible prospect of woman's taking
the social stand which some of them—poor, miserable, abortive
creatures, who only dream of such things because they have
missed woman's peculiar happiness, or because Nature made
them really neither man nor woman!—if there were a chance
of their attaining the end which these petticoated monstrosities
have in view, I would call upon my own sex to use its physical
force, that unmistakeable evidence of sovereignty, to scourge
them back within their proper bounds! But it will not be
needful. The heart of true womanhood knows where its own
sphere is, and never seeks to stray beyond it!"

Never was mortal blessed—if blessing it were—with a glance
of such entire acquiescence and unquestioning faith, happy
in its completeness, as our little Priscilla unconsciously bestowed on Hollingsworth. She seemed to take the sentiment
from his lips into her heart, and brood over it in perfect
content. The very woman whom he pictured—the gentle
parasite, the soft reflection of a more powerful existence—sat
there at his feet.

I looked at Zenobia, however, fully expecting her to resent
—as I felt, by the indignant ebullition of my own blood, that
she ought—this outrageous affirmation of what struck me as
the intensity of masculine egotism. It centred everything in
itself, and deprived woman of her very soul, her inexpressible
and unfathomable all, to make it a mere incident in the great
sum of man. Hollingsworth had boldly uttered what he, and
millions of despots like him, really felt. Without intending
it, he had disclosed the well-spring of all these troubled
waters. Now, if ever, it surely behoved Zenobia to be the
champion of her sex.

But, to my surprise, and indignation too, she only looked
humbled. Some tears sparkled in her eyes, but they were
wholly of grief, not anger.

"Well; be it so," was all she said. "I, at least, have deep cause to think you right. Let man be but manly and godlike, and woman is only too ready to become to him what you say!"

I smiled—somewhat bitterly, it is true—in contemplation of my own ill-luck. How little did these two women care for me, who had freely conceded all their claims, and a great deal more, out of the fulness of my heart; while Hollingsworth, by some necromancy of his horrible injustice, seemed to have brought them both to his feet!

"Women almost invariably behave thus!" thought I. "What does the fact mean? Is it their nature? Or is it, at last, the result of ages of compelled degradation? And, in either case, will it be possible ever to redeem them?"

An intuition now appeared to possess all the party, that, for this time, at least, there was no more to be said. With one accord, we arose from the ground, and made our way through the tangled undergrowth towards one of those pleasant wood-paths, that wound among the over-arching trees. Some of the branches hung so low as partly to conceal the figures that went before, from those who followed. Priscilla had leaped up more lightly than the rest of us, and ran along in advance, with as much airy activity of spirit as was typified in the motion of a bird, which chanced to be flitting from tree to tree, in the same direction as herself. Never did she seem so happy as that afternoon. She skipt, and could not help it, from very playfulness of heart.

Zenobia and Hollingsworth went next, in close contiguity, but not with arm in arm. Now, just when they had passed the impending bough of a birch-tree, I plainly saw Zenobia take the hand of Hollingsworth in both her own, press it to her bosom, and let it fall again!

The gesture was sudden and full of passion; the impulse had evidently taken her by surprise; it expressed all! Had Zenobia knelt before him, or flung herself upon his breast, and gasped out—'I love you, Hollingsworth!'—I could not have been more certain of what it meant. They then walked onward, as before. But, methought, as the declining sun threw Zenobia's magnified shadow along the path, I beheld it tremulous; and the delicate stem of the flower, which she wore in her hair, was likewise responsive to her agitation.

Priscilla—through the medium of her eyes, at least—could not possibly have been aware of the gesture above-described. Yet, at that instant, I saw her droop. The buoyancy, which just before had been so birdlike, was utterly departed; the life seemed to pass out of her, and even the substance of her figure to grow thin and gray. I almost imagined her a shadow, fading gradually into the dimness of the wood. Her pace became so slow, that Hollingsworth and Zenobia passed by, and I, without hastening my footsteps, overtook her.

"Come, Priscilla," said I, looking her intently in the face, which was very pale and sorrowful, "we must make haste after our friends. Do you feel suddenly ill? A moment ago, you flitted along so lightly that I was comparing you to a bird. Now, on the contrary, it is as if you had a heavy heart, and very little strength to bear it with. Pray take my arm!"

"No," said Priscilla, "I do not think it would help me. It is my heart, as you say, that makes me heavy; and I know not why. Just now, I felt very happy."

No doubt, it was a kind of sacrilege in me to attempt to come within her maidenly mystery. But as she appeared to be tossed aside by her other friends, or carelessly let fall, like a flower which they had done with, I could not resist the impulse to take just one peep beneath her folded petals.

"Zenobia and yourself are dear friends, of late," I remarked. "At first—that first evening when you came to us—she did not receive you quite so warmly as might have been wished."

"I remember it," said Priscilla. "No wonder she hesitated to love me, who was then a stranger to her, and a girl of no grace or beauty; she being herself so beautiful!"

"But she loves you now, of course," suggested I. "And, at this very instant, you feel her to be your dearest friend?"

"Why do you ask me that question?" exclaimed Priscilla, as if frightened at the scrutiny into her feelings which I compelled her to make. "It somehow puts strange thoughts into my mind. But I do love Zenobia dearly! If she only loves me half as well, I shall be happy!"

"How is it possible to doubt that, Priscilla?" I rejoined. "But, observe how pleasantly and happily Zenobia and Hollingsworth are walking together! I call it a delightful spectacle. It truly rejoices me that Hollingsworth has found so fit and affectionate a friend! So many people in the world mistrust him—so many disbelieve and ridicule, while hardly any do him justice, or acknowledge him for the wonderful man he is—that it is really a blessed thing for him to have won the sympathy of such a woman as Zenobia. Any man might be proud of that. Any man, even if he be as great as Hollingsworth, might love so magnificent a woman. How very beautiful Zenobia is! And Hollingsworth knows it, too!"

There may have been some petty malice in what I said. Generosity is a very fine thing, at a proper time, and within due limits. But it is an insufferable bore, to see one man engrossing every thought of all the women, and leaving his friend to shiver in outer seclusion, without even the alternative of solacing himself with what the more fortunate individual has rejected. Yes; it was out of a foolish bitterness of heart that I had spoken.

"Go on before!" said Priscilla, abruptly, and with true feminine imperiousness, which heretofore I had never seen her exercise. "It pleases me best to loiter along by myself. I do not walk so fast as you."

With her hand, she made a little gesture of dismissal. It provoked me, yet, on the whole, was the most bewitching thing that Priscilla had ever done. I obeyed her, and strolled moodily homeward, wondering—as I had wondered a thousand times, already—how Hollingsworth meant to dispose of these two hearts, which (plainly to my perception, and, as I could not but now suppose, to his) he had engrossed into his own huge egotism.

There was likewise another subject, hardly less fruitful of speculation. In what attitude did Zenobia present herself to Hollingsworth? Was it in that of a free woman, with no mortgage on her affections nor claimant to her hand, but fully at liberty to surrender both, in exchange for the heart and hand which she apparently expected to receive? But, was it a vision that I had witnessed in the wood? Was Westervelt a goblin? Were those words of passion and agony, which Zenobia had uttered in my hearing, a mere stage-declamation? Were they formed of a material lighter than common air? Or, supposing them to bear sterling weight, was it not a perilous and dreadful wrong, which she was meditating towards herself and Hollingsworth?

Arriving nearly at the farm-house, I looked back over the long slope of pasture-land, and beheld them standing together, in the light of sunset, just on the spot where, according to the gossip of the Community, they meant to build their cottage. Priscilla, alone and forgotten, was lingering in the shadow of the wood.

XV

A CRISIS

THUS the summer was passing away; a summer of
toil, of interest, of something that was not pleasure,
but which went deep into my heart, and there became
a rich experience. I found myself looking forward to years,
if not to a lifetime, to be spent on the same system. The
Community were now beginning to form their permanent
plans. One of our purposes was to erect a Phalanstery (as
I think we called it, after Fourier; but the phraseology of
those days is not very fresh in my remembrance) where the
great and general family should have its abiding-place. Individual members, too, who made it a point of religion to pre-
serve the sanctity of an exclusive home, were selecting sites
for their cottages, by the wood-side, or on the breezy swells,
or in the sheltered nook of some little valley, according as
their taste might lean towards snugness or the picturesque.
Altogether, by projecting our minds outward, we had imparted a show of novelty to existence, and contemplated it
as hopefully as if the soil, beneath our feet, had not been
fathom-deep with the dust of deluded generations, on every
one of which, as on ourselves, the world had imposed itself
as a hitherto unwedded bride.

Hollingsworth and myself had often discussed these prospects. It was easy to perceive, however, that he spoke with

little or no fervor, but either as questioning the fulfilment of our anticipations, or, at any rate, with a quiet consciousness that it was no personal concern of his. Shortly after the scene at Eliot's pulpit, while he and I were repairing an old stone-fence, I amused myself with sallying forward into the future time.

"When we come to be old men," I said, "they will call us Uncles, or Fathers—Father Hollingsworth and Uncle Coverdale—and we will look back cheerfully to these early days, and make a romantic story for the young people (and if a little more romantic than truth may warrant, it will be no harm) out of our severe trials and hardships. In a century or two, we shall every one of us be mythical personages, or exceedingly picturesque and poetical ones, at all events. They will have a great public hall, in which your portrait, and mine, and twenty other faces that are living now, shall be hung up; and as for me, I will be painted in my shirt-sleeves, and with the sleeves rolled up, to show my muscular development. What stories will be rife among them about our mighty strength," continued I, lifting a big stone and putting it into its place; "though our posterity will really be far stronger than ourselves, after several generations of a simple, natural, and active life! What legends of Zenobia's beauty, and Priscilla's slender and shadowy grace, and those mysterious qualities which make her seem diaphanous with spiritual light! In due course of ages, we must all figure heroically in an Epic Poem; and we will ourselves—at least, I will—bend unseen over the future poet, and lend him inspiration, while he writes it."

"You seem," said Hollingsworth, "to be trying how much nonsense you can pour out in a breath."

"I wish you would see fit to comprehend," retorted I, "that the profoundest wisdom must be mingled with nine-tenths of nonsense; else it is not worth the breath that utters it. But I do long for the cottages to be built, that the creeping plants may begin to run over them, and the moss to gather on the walls, and the trees—which we will set out—to cover them with a breadth of shadow. This spick-and-span novelty does not quite suit my taste. It is time, too, for children to be born among us. The first-born child is still to come! And I shall never feel as if this were a real, practical, as well as poetical, system of human life, until somebody has sanctified it by death."

"A pretty occasion for martyrdom, truly!" said Hollingsworth.

"As good as any other!" I replied. "I wonder, Hollingsworth, who, of all these strong men, and fair women and maidens, is doomed the first to die. Would it not be well, even before we have absolute need of it, to fix upon a spot for a cemetery? Let us choose the rudest, roughest, most uncultivable spot, for Death's garden-ground; and Death shall teach us to beautify it, grave by grave. By our sweet, calm way of dying, and the airy elegance out of which we will shape our funeral rites, and the cheerful allegories which we will model into tombstones, the final scene shall lose its terrors; so that, hereafter, it may be happiness to live, and bliss to die. None of us must die young. Yet, should Providence ordain it so, the event shall not be sorrowful, but affect us with a tender, delicious, only half-melancholy, and almost smiling pathos!"

"That is to say," muttered Hollingsworth, "you will die like a Heathen, as you certainly live like one! But, listen to me, Coverdale. Your fantastic anticipations make me discern, all the more forcibly, what a wretched, unsubstantial scheme is this, on which we have wasted a precious summer of our lives. Do you seriously imagine that any such realities as you, and many others here, have dreamed of, will ever be brought to pass?"

"Certainly, I do," said I. "Of course, when the reality comes, it will wear the every-day, common-place, dusty, and rather homely garb, that reality always does put on. But, setting aside the ideal charm, I hold, that our highest anticipations have a solid footing on common-sense."

"You only half believe what you say," rejoined Hollingsworth; "and as for me, I neither have faith in your dream, nor would care the value of this pebble for its realization, were that possible. And what more do you want of it? It has given you a theme for poetry. Let that content you. But, now, I ask you to be, at last, a man of sobriety and earnestness, and aid me in an enterprise which is worth all our strength, and the strength of a thousand mightier than we!"

There can be no need of giving, in detail, the conversation that ensued. It is enough to say, that Hollingsworth once more brought forward his rigid and unconquerable idea; a scheme for the reformation of the wicked by methods moral, intellectual, and industrial, by the sympathy of pure, humble, and yet exalted minds, and by opening to his pupils the possibility of a worthier life than that which had become their fate. It appeared, unless he over-estimated his own means, that Hollingsworth held it at his choice (and he did so choose) to obtain possession of the very ground on which we had planted our Community, and which had not yet been made irrevocably ours, by purchase. It was just the foundation that he desired. Our beginnings might readily be adapted to his great end. The arrangements, already completed, would work quietly into his system. So plausible looked his theory, and, more than that, so practical; such an air of reasonableness had he, by patient thought, thrown over it; each segment of it was contrived to dove-tail into all the rest, with such a complicated applicability; and so ready was he with a response for every objection—that, really, so far as logic and argument went, he had the matter all his own way.

"But," said I, "whence can you, having no means of your own, derive the enormous capital which is essential to this experiment? State-street,* I imagine, would not draw its purse-strings very liberally, in aid of such a speculation."

"I have the funds—as much, at least, as is needed for a commencement—at command," he answered. "They can be produced within a month, if necessary."

My thoughts reverted to Zenobia. It could only be her wealth which Hollingsworth was appropriating so lavishly. And on what conditions was it to be had? Did she fling it into the scheme, with the uncalculating generosity that characterizes a woman, when it is her impulse to be generous at all? And did she fling herself along with it? But Hollingsworth did not volunteer an explanation.

"And have you no regrets," I inquired, "in overthrowing this fair system of our new life, which has been planned so deeply, and is now beginning to flourish so hopefully around us? How beautiful it is, and, so far as we can yet see, how practicable! The Ages have waited for us, and here we are—the very first that have essayed to carry on our mortal existence, in love, and mutual help! Hollingsworth, I would be loth to take the ruin of this enterprise upon my conscience!"

"Then let it rest wholly upon mine!" he answered, knitting his black brows. "I see through the system. It is full of defects—irremediable and damning ones!—from first to last, there is nothing else! I grasp it in my hand, and find no substance whatever. There is not human nature in it!"

"Why are you so secret in your operations?" I asked. "God forbid that I should accuse you of intentional wrong; but the besetting sin of a philanthropist, it appears to me, is apt to be a moral obliquity. His sense of honor ceases to be the sense of other honorable men. At some point of his course—I know not exactly when nor where—he is tempted to palter with the right, and can scarcely forbear persuading himself that the importance of his public ends renders it allowable to throw aside his private conscience. Oh, my dear friend, beware this error! If you meditate the overthrow of this establishment, call together our companions, state your design, support it with all your eloquence, but allow them an opportunity of defending themselves!"

"It does not suit me," said Hollingsworth. "Nor is it my duty to do so."

"I think it is!" replied I.

Hollingsworth frowned; not in passion, but like Fate, inexorably.

"I will not argue the point," said he. "What I desire to know of you is—and you can tell me in one word—whether I am to look for your co-operation in this great scheme of good. Take it up with me! Be my brother in it! It offers you (what you have told me, over and over again, that you most need) a purpose in life, worthy of the extremest self-devotion —worthy of martyrdom, should God so order it! In this view, I present it to you. You can greatly benefit mankind. Your peculiar faculties, as I shall direct them, are capable of being so wrought into this enterprise, that not one of them need lie idle. Strike hands with me; and, from this moment, you shall never again feel the languor and vague wretchedness of an indolent or half-occupied man! There may be no more aimless beauty in your life; but, in its stead, there shall be strength, courage, immitigable will—everything that a manly and generous nature should desire! We shall succeed! We shall have done our best for this miserable world; and happiness (which never comes but incidentally) will come to us unawares!"

It seemed his intention to say no more. But, after he had quite broken off, his deep eyes filled with tears, and he held out both his hands to me.

"Coverdale," he murmured, "there is not the man in this wide world, whom I can love as I could you. Do not forsake me!"

As I look back upon this scene, through the coldness and dimness of so many years, there is still a sensation as if

Hollingsworth had caught hold of my heart, and were pulling it towards him with an almost irresistible force. It is a mystery to me, how I withstood it. But, in truth, I saw in his scheme of philanthropy nothing but what was odious. A loathsomeness that was to be forever in my daily work! A great, black ugliness of sin, which he proposed to collect out of a thousand human hearts, and that we should spend our lives in an experiment of transmuting it into virtue! Had I but touched his extended hand, Hollingsworth's magnetism would perhaps have penetrated me with his own conception of all these matters. But I stood aloof. I fortified myself with doubts whether his strength of purpose had not been too gigantic for his integrity, impelling him to trample on considerations that should have been paramount to every other.

"Is Zenobia to take a part in your enterprise?" I asked.

"She is," said Hollingsworth.

"She!—the beautiful!—the gorgeous!" I exclaimed. "And how have you prevailed with such a woman to work in this squalid element?"

"Through no base methods, as you seem to suspect," he answered, "but by addressing whatever is best and noblest in her."

Hollingsworth was looking on the ground. But, as he often did so—generally, indeed, in his habitual moods of thought—I could not judge whether it was from any special unwillingness now to meet my eyes. What it was that dictated my next question, I cannot precisely say. Nevertheless, it rose so inevitably into my mouth, and, as it were, asked itself, so involuntarily, that there must needs have been an aptness in it.

"What is to become of Priscilla?"

Hollingsworth looked at me fiercely, and with glowing eyes. He could not have shown any other kind of expression than that, had he meant to strike me with a sword.

"Why do you bring in the names of these women?" said he, after a moment of pregnant silence. "What have they to do with the proposal which I make you? I must have your answer! Will you devote yourself, and sacrifice all to this great end, and be my friend of friends, forever?"

"In Heaven's name, Hollingsworth," cried I, getting angry, and glad to be angry, because so only was it possible to oppose his tremendous concentrativeness and indomitable will, "cannot you conceive that a man may wish well to the world, and struggle for its good, on some other plan than precisely that which you have laid down? And will you cast off a friend, for no unworthiness, but merely because he stands upon his right, as an individual being, and looks at matters through his own optics, instead of yours?"

"Be with me," said Hollingsworth, "or be against me! There is no third choice for you."

"Take this, then, as my decision," I answered. "I doubt the wisdom of your scheme. Furthermore, I greatly fear that the methods, by which you allow yourself to pursue it, are such as cannot stand the scrutiny of an unbiassed conscience."

"And you will not join me?"

"No!"

I never said the word—and certainly can never have it to say, hereafter—that cost me a thousandth part so hard an effort as did that one syllable. The heart-pang was not merely figurative, but an absolute torture of the breast. I was gazing steadfastly at Hollingsworth. It seemed to me that it struck him, too, like a bullet. A ghastly paleness—always so terrific on a swarthy face—overspread his features. There was a convulsive movement of his throat, as if he were forcing down some words that struggled and fought for utterance. Whether words of anger, or words of grief, I cannot tell; although, many and many a time, I have vainly tormented myself with conjecturing which of the two they were. One other appeal to my friendship—such as once, already, Hollingsworth had made—taking me in the revulsion that followed a strenuous exercise of opposing will, would completely have subdued me. But he left the matter there.

"Well!" said he.

And that was all! I should have been thankful for one word more, even had it shot me through the heart, as mine did him. But he did not speak it; and, after a few moments, with one accord, we set to work again, repairing the stone-fence. Hollingsworth, I observed, wrought like a Titan;* and, for my own part, I lifted stones which, at this day—or, in a calmer mood, at that one—I should no more have thought it possible to stir, than to carry off the gates of Gaza*on my back.

XVI

LEAVE-TAKINGS

A FEW DAYS after the tragic passage-at-arms between Hollingsworth and me, I appeared at the dinner-table, actually dressed in a coat, instead of my customary blouse; with a satin cravat, too, a white vest, and several other things that made me seem strange and outlandish to myself. As for my companions, this unwonted spectacle caused a great stir upon the wooden benches, that bordered either side of our homely board.

"What's in the wind now, Miles?" asked one of them. "Are you deserting us?"

"Yes, for a week or two," said I. "It strikes me that my health demands a little relaxation of labor, and a short visit to the seaside, during the dog-days."

"You look like it!" grumbled Silas Foster, not greatly pleased with the idea of losing an efficient laborer, before the stress of the season was well over. "Now, here's a pretty fellow! His shoulders have broadened, a matter of six inches, since he came among us; he can do his day's work, if he likes, with any man or ox on the farm;—and yet he talks about going to the seashore for his health! Well, well, old woman," added he to his wife, "let me have a platefull of that pork and cabbage! I begin to feel in a very weakly way. When

the others have had their turn, you and I will take a jaunt
to Newport or Saratoga!"*

"Well, but, Mr. Foster," said I, "you must allow me to
take a little breath."

"Breath!" retorted the old yeoman. "Your lungs have the
play of a pair of blacksmith's bellows, already. What on earth
do you want more? But go along! I understand the business.
We shall never see your face here again. Here ends the
reformation of the world, so far as Miles Coverdale has a
hand in it!"

"By no means," I replied. "I am resolute to die in the last
ditch, for the good of the cause."

"Die in a ditch!" muttered gruff Silas, with genuine Yankee
intolerance of any intermission of toil, except on Sunday, the
Fourth of July, the autumnal Cattle-show, Thanksgiving, or
the annual Fast.* "Die in a ditch! I believe in my conscience
you would, if there were no steadier means than your own
labor to keep you out of it!"

The truth was, that an intolerable discontent and irksomeness had come over me. Blithedale was no longer what it
had been. Everything was suddenly faded. The sun-burnt and
arid aspect of our woods and pastures, beneath the August
sky, did but imperfectly symbolize the lack of dew and moisture that, since yesterday, as it were, had blighted my fields
of thought, and penetrated to the innermost and shadiest of
my contemplative recesses. The change will be recognized
by many, who, after a period of happiness, have endeavored
to go on with the same kind of life, in the same scene, in
spite of the alteration or withdrawal of some principal circumstance. They discover (what heretofore, perhaps, they
had not known) that it was this which gave the bright color
and vivid reality to the whole affair.

I stood on other terms than before, not only with Hollingsworth, but with Zenobia and Priscilla. As regarded the two
latter, it was that dreamlike and miserable sort of change that

denies you the privilege to complain, because you can assert no positive injury, nor lay your finger on anything tangible. It is a matter which you do not see, but feel, and which, when you try to analyze it, seems to lose its very existence, and resolve itself into a sickly humor of your own. Your understanding, possibly, may put faith in this denial. But your heart will not so easily rest satisfied. It incessantly remonstrates, though, most of the time, in a bass-note, which you do not separately distinguish; but, now-and-then, with a sharp cry, importunate to be heard, and resolute to claim belief. 'Things are not as they were!'—it keeps saying—'You shall not impose on me! I will never be quiet! I will throb painfully! I will be heavy, and desolate, and shiver with cold! For I, your deep heart, know when to be miserable, as once I knew when to be happy! All is changed for us! You are beloved no more!' And,.were my life to be spent over again, I would invariably lend my ear to this Cassandra*of the inward depths, however clamorous the music and the merriment of a more superficial region.

My outbreak with Hollingsworth, though never definitely known to our associates, had really an effect upon the moral atmosphere of the Community. It was incidental to the closeness of relationship, into which we had brought ourselves, that an unfriendly state of feeling could not occur between any two members, without the whole society being more or less commoted*and made uncomfortable thereby. This species of nervous sympathy (though a pretty characteristic enough, sentimentally considered, and apparently betokening an actual bond of love among us) was yet found rather inconvenient in its practical operation; mortal tempers being so infirm and variable as they are. If one of us happened to give his neighbor a box on the ear, the tingle was immediately felt, on the same side of everybody's head. Thus, even on the supposition that we were far less quarrelsome than the rest of the world, a great deal of time was necessarily wasted in rubbing our ears.

Musing on all these matters, I felt an inexpressible longing for at least a temporary novelty. I thought of going across the Rocky Mountains, or to Europe, or up the Nile—of offering myself a volunteer on the Exploring Expedition—of taking a ramble of years, no matter in what direction, and coming back on the other side of the world. Then, should the colonists of Blithedale have established their enterprise on a permanent basis, I might fling aside my pilgrim-staff and dusty shoon, and rest as peacefully here as elsewhere. Or, in case Hollingsworth should occupy the ground with his School of Reform, as he now purposed, I might plead earthly guilt enough, by that time, to give me what I was inclined to think the only trustworthy hold on his affections. Meanwhile, before deciding on any ultimate plan, I determined to remove myself to a little distance, and take an exterior view of what we had all been about.

In truth, it was dizzy work, amid such fermentation of opinions as was going on in the general brain of the Community. It was a kind of Bedlam, for the time being; although, out of the very thoughts that were wildest and most destructive, might grow a wisdom, holy, calm, and pure, and that should incarnate itself with the substance of a noble and happy life. But, as matters now were, I felt myself (and having a decided tendency towards the actual, I never liked to feel it) getting quite out of my reckoning, with regard to the existing state of the world. I was beginning to lose the sense of what kind of a world it was, among innumerable schemes of what it might or ought to be. It was impossible, situated as we were, not to imbibe the idea that everything in nature and human existence was fluid, or fast becoming so; that the crust of the Earth, in many places, was broken, and its whole surface portentously upheaving; that it was a day of crisis, and that we ourselves were in the critical vortex. Our great globe floated in the atmosphere of infinite space like an unsubstantial bubble. No sagacious man will long retain his sagacity, if he live exclusively among reformers and progressive people, without periodically returning into the settled system of things, to correct himself by a new observation from that old stand-point.

It was now time for me, therefore, to go and hold a little talk with the conservatives, the writers of the North American Review,* the merchants, the politicians, the Cambridge men,* and all those respectable old blockheads, who still, in this intangibility and mistiness of affairs, kept a death-grip on one or two ideas which had not come into vogue since yesterday-morning.

The brethren took leave of me with cordial kindness; and as for the sisterhood, I had serious thoughts of kissing them all round, but forbore to do so, because, in all such general salutations, the penance is fully equal to the pleasure. So I kissed none of them, and nobody, to say the truth, seemed to expect it.

"Do you wish me," I said to Zenobia, "to announce, in town, and at the watering-places, your purpose to deliver a course of lectures on the rights of women?"

"Women possess no rights," said Zenobia, with a half-melancholy smile; "or, at all events, only little girls and grandmothers would have the force to exercise them."

She gave me her hand, freely and kindly, and looked at me, I thought, with a pitying expression in her eyes; nor was there any settled light of joy in them, on her own behalf, but a troubled and passionate flame, flickering and fitful.

"I regret, on the whole, that you are leaving us," she said; "and all the more, since I feel that this phase of our life is finished, and can never be lived over again. Do you know, Mr. Coverdale, that I have been several times on the point of making you my confidant, for lack of a better and wiser one? But you are too young to be my Father Confessor; and you would not thank me for treating you like one of those good little handmaidens, who share the bosom-secrets of a tragedy-queen!"

"I would at least be loyal and faithful," answered I, "and would counsel you with an honest purpose, if not wisely."

"Yes," said Zenobia, "you would be only too wise—too honest. Honesty and wisdom are such a delightful pastime, at another person's expense!"

"Ah, Zenobia," I exclaimed, "if you would but let me speak!"

"By no means," she replied; "especially when you have just resumed the whole series of social conventionalisms, together with that straight-bodied coat. I would as lief open my heart to a lawyer or a clergyman! No, no, Mr. Coverdale; if I choose a counsellor, in the present aspect of my affairs, it must be either an angel or a madman; and I rather apprehend that the latter would be likeliest of the two to speak the fitting word. It needs a wild steersman when we voyage through Chaos! The anchor is up! Farewell!"

Priscilla, as soon as dinner was over, had betaken herself into a corner, and set to work on a little purse. As I approached her, she let her eyes rest on me, with a calm, serious look; for, with all her delicacy of nerves, there was a singular self-possession in Priscilla, and her sensibilities seemed to lie sheltered from ordinary commotion, like the water in a deep well.

"Will you give me that purse, Priscilla," said I, "as a parting keepsake?"

"Yes," she answered; "if you will wait till it is finished."

"I must not wait, even for that," I replied. "Shall I find you here, on my return?"

"I never wish to go away," said she.

"I have sometimes thought," observed I, smiling, "that you, Priscilla, are a little prophetess; or, at least, that you have spiritual intimations respecting matters which are dark to us grosser people. If that be the case, I should like to ask you what is about to happen. For I am tormented with a strong foreboding, that, were I to return even so soon as tomorrow morning, I should find everything changed. Have you any impressions of this nature?"

"Ah, no!" said Priscilla, looking at me apprehensively. "If any such misfortune is coming, the shadow has not reached me yet. Heaven forbid! I should be glad if there might never be any change, but one summer follow another, and all just like this!"

"No summer ever came back, and no two summers ever were alike," said I, with a degree of Orphic wisdom* that astonished myself. "Times change, and people change; and if our hearts do not change as readily, so much the worse for us! Good bye, Priscilla!"

I gave her hand a pressure, which, I think, she neither resisted nor returned. Priscilla's heart was deep, but of small compass; it had room but for a very few dearest ones, among whom she never reckoned me.

On the door-step, I met Hollingsworth. I had a momentary impulse to hold out my hand, or, at least, to give a parting nod, but resisted both. When a real and strong affection has come to an end, it is not well to mock the sacred past with any show of those common-place civilities that belong to ordinary intercourse. Being dead henceforth to him, and he to me, there could be no propriety in our chilling one another with the touch of two corpse-like hands, or playing at looks of courtesy with eyes that were impenetrable beneath the glaze and the film. We passed, therefore, as if mutually invisible.

I can nowise explain what sort of whim, prank, or perversity it was, that, after all these leave-takings, induced me to go to the pig-stye and take leave of the swine! There they lay, buried as deeply among the straw as they could burrow, four huge black grunters, the very symbols of slothful ease and sensual comfort. They were asleep, drawing short and heavy breaths, which heaved their big sides up and down. Unclosing their eyes, however, at my approach, they looked dimly forth at the outer world, and simultaneously uttered a gentle grunt; not putting themselves to the trouble of an additional breath for that particular purpose, but grunting with their ordinary inhalation. They were involved, and almost stifled, and buried alive, in their own corporeal substance. The very unreadiness and oppression, wherewith these greasy citizens gained breath enough to keep their life-machinery in sluggish movement, appeared to make them only the more sensible of the ponderous and fat satisfaction of their existence. Peeping at me, an instant, out of their small, red, hardly perceptible eyes, they dropt asleep again; yet not so far asleep but that their unctuous bliss was still present to them, betwixt dream and reality.

"You must come back in season to eat part of a spare-rib," said Silas Foster, giving my hand a mighty squeeze. "I shall have these fat fellows hanging up by the heels, heads downward, pretty soon, I tell you!"

"Oh, cruel Silas, what a horrible idea!" cried I. "All the rest of us, men, women, and live-stock, save only these four porkers, are bedevilled with one grief or another; they alone are happy—and you mean to cut their throats, and eat them! It would be more for the general comfort to let them eat us; and bitter and sour morsels we should be!"

XVII

THE HOTEL

ARRIVING in town, (where my bachelor-rooms, long before this time, had received some other occupant,) I established myself, for a day or two, in a certain respectable hotel. It was situated somewhat aloof from my former track in life; my present mood inclining me to avoid most of my old companions, from whom I was now sundered by other interests, and who would have been likely enough to amuse themselves at the expense of the amateur working-man. The hotel-keeper put me into a back-room of the third story of his spacious establishment. The day was lowering, with occasional gusts of rain, and an ugly-tempered east-wind, which seemed to come right off the chill and melancholy sea, hardly mitigated by sweeping over the roofs, and amalgamating itself with the dusky element of city-smoke. All the effeminacy of past days had returned upon me at once. Summer as it still was, I ordered a coal-fire in the rusty grate, and was glad to find myself growing a little too warm with an artificial temperature.

My sensations were those of a traveller, long sojourning in remote regions, and at length sitting down again amid customs once familiar. There was a newness and an oldness, oddly combining themselves into one impression. It made me acutely sensible how strange a piece of mosaic-work had lately been wrought into my life. True; if you look at it in one way, it had been only a summer in the country. But, considered in a profounder relation, it was part of another age, a different state of society, a segment of an existence peculiar in its aims and methods, a leaf of some mysterious volume, interpolated into the current history which Time was writing off. At one moment, the very circumstances now surrounding me—my coal-fire, and the dingy room in the bustling hotel—appeared far off and intangible. The next instant, Blithedale looked vague, as if it were at a distance both in time and space, and so shadowy, that a question might be raised whether the whole affair had been anything more than the thoughts of a speculative man. I had never before experienced a mood that so robbed the actual world of its solidity. It nevertheless involved a charm, on which—a devoted epicure of my own emotions—I resolved to pause, and enjoy the moral sillabub* until quite dissolved away.

Whatever had been my taste for solitude and natural scenery, yet the thick, foggy, stifled element of cities, the entangled life of many men together, sordid as it was, and empty of the beautiful, took quite as strenuous a hold upon my mind. I felt as if there could never be enough of it. Each characteristic sound was too suggestive to be passed over, unnoticed. Beneath and around me, I heard the stir of the hotel; the loud voices of guests, landlord, or barkeeper; steps echoing on the staircase; the ringing of a bell, announcing arrivals or departures; the porter lumbering past my door with baggage, which he thumped down upon the floors of neighboring chambers; the lighter feet of chamber-maids scudding along the passages;—it is ridiculous to think what an interest they had for me. From the street, came the tumult of the pavements, pervading the whole house with a continual uproar, so broad and deep that only an unaccustomed ear would dwell upon it. A company of the city-soldiery, with a full military band, marched in front of the hotel, invisible to me, but stirringly

audible both by its foot-tramp and the clangor of its instruments. Once or twice, all the city-bells jangled together,
announcing a fire, which brought out the engine-men and
their machines, like an army with its artillery rushing to
battle. Hour by hour, the clocks in many steeples responded
one to another. In some public hall, not a great way off, there
seemed to be an exhibition of a mechanical diorama,*for, three
times during the day, occurred a repetition of obstreperous
music, winding up with the rattle of imitative cannon and
musketry, and a huge final explosion. Then ensued the
applause of the spectators, with clap of hands, and thump of
sticks, and the energetic pounding of their heels. All this
was just as valuable, in its way, as the sighing of the breeze
among the birch-trees, that overshadowed Eliot's pulpit.

Yet I felt a hesitation about plunging into this muddy tide
of human activity and pastime. It suited me better, for the
present, to linger on the brink, or hover in the air above it.
So I spent the first day, and the greater part of the second,
in the laziest manner possible, in a rocking-chair, inhaling
the fragrance of a series of cigars, with my legs and slippered
feet horizontally disposed, and in my hand a novel, purchased
of a railroad bibliopolist.* The gradual waste of my cigar
accomplished itself with an easy and gentle expenditure of
breath. My book was of the dullest, yet had a sort of sluggish
flow, like that of a stream in which your boat is as often
aground as afloat. Had there been a more impetuous rush, a
more absorbing passion of the narrative, I should the sooner
have struggled out of its uneasy current, and have given myself up to the swell and subsidence of my thoughts. But, as
it was, the torpid life of the book served as an unobtrusive
accompaniment to the life within me and about me. At intervals, however, when its effect grew a little too soporific—not
for my patience, but for the possibility of keeping my eyes
open—I bestirred myself, started from the rocking-chair, and
looked out of the window.

A gray sky; the weathercock of a steeple, that rose beyond the opposite range of buildings, pointing from the eastward; a sprinkle of small, spiteful-looking raindrops on the window-pane! In that ebb-tide of my energies, had I thought of venturing abroad, these tokens would have checked the abortive purpose.

After several such visits to the window, I found myself getting pretty well acquainted with that little portion of the backside of the universe which it presented to my view. Over against the hotel and its adjacent houses, at the distance of forty or fifty yards, was the rear of a range of buildings, which appeared to be spacious, modern, and calculated for fashionable residences. The interval between was apportioned into grass-plots, and here and there an apology for a garden, pertaining severally to these dwellings. There were apple-trees, and pear and peach-trees, too, the fruit on which looked singularly large, luxuriant, and abundant; as well it might, in a situation so warm and sheltered, and where the soil had doubtless been enriched to a more than natural fertility. In two or three places, grape-vines clambered upon trellises, and bore clusters already purple, and promising the richness of Malta or Madeira*in their ripened juice. The blighting winds of our rigid climate could not molest these trees and vines; the sunshine, though descending late into this area, and too early intercepted by the height of the surrounding houses, yet lay tropically there, even when less than temperate in every other region. Dreary as was the day, the scene was illuminated by not a few sparrows and other birds, which spread their wings, and flitted and fluttered, and alighted now here, now there, and busily scratched their food out of the wormy earth. Most of these winged people seemed to have their domicile in a robust and healthy buttonwood-tree.* It aspired upward, high above the roof of the houses, and spread a dense head of foliage half across the area,

There was a cat—as there invariably is, in such places—who evidently thought herself entitled to all the privileges of forest-life, in this close heart of city-conventionalisms. I watched her creeping along the low, flat roofs of the offices, descending a flight of wooden steps, gliding among the grass, and besieging the buttonwood-tree, with murderous purpose against its feathered citizens. But, after all, they were birds of city-breeding, and doubtless knew how to guard themselves against the peculiar perils of their position.

Bewitching to my fancy are all those nooks and crannies, where Nature, like a stray partridge, hides her head among the long-established haunts of men! It is likewise to be remarked, as a general rule, that there is far more of the picturesque, more truth to native and characteristic tendencies, and vastly greater suggestiveness, in the back view of a residence, whether in town or country, than in its front. The latter is always artificial; it is meant for the world's eye, and is therefore a veil and a concealment. Realities keep in the rear, and put forward an advance-guard of show and humbug. The posterior aspect of any old farm-house, behind which a railroad has unexpectedly been opened, is so different from that looking upon the immemorial highway, that the spectator gets new ideas of rural life and individuality, in the puff or two of steam-breath which shoots him past the premises. In a city, the distinction between what is offered to the public, and what is kept for the family, is certainly not less striking.

But, to return to my window, at the back of the hotel. Together with a due contemplation of the fruit-trees, the grape-vines, the buttonwood-tree, the cat, the birds, and many other particulars, I failed not to study the row of fashionable dwellings to which all these appertained. Here, it must be confessed, there was a general sameness. From the upper-story to the first floor, they were so much alike that I could only conceive of the inhabitants as cut out on one identical pattern, like little wooden toy-people of German manufacture.

One long, united roof, with its thousands of slates glittering in the rain, extended over the whole. After the distinctness of separate characters, to which I had recently been accustomed, it perplexed and annoyed me not to be able to resolve this combination of human interests into well-defined elements. It seemed hardly worth while for more than one of those families to be in existence; since they all had the same glimpse of the sky, all looked into the same area, all received just their equal share of sunshine through the front windows, and all listened to precisely the same noises of the street on which they bordered. Men are so much alike, in their nature, that they grow intolerable unless varied by their circumstances.

Just about this time, a waiter entered my room. The truth was, I had rung the bell and ordered a sherry-cobbler.*

"Can you tell me," I inquired, "what families reside in any of those houses opposite?"

"The one right opposite is a rather stylish boarding-house," said the waiter. "Two of the gentlemen-boarders keep horses at the stable of our establishment. They do things in very good style, sir, the people that live there."

I might have found out nearly as much for myself, on examining the house a little more closely. In one of the upper chambers, I saw a young man in a dressing-gown, standing before the glass and brushing his hair, for a quarter-of-an-hour together. He then spent an equal space of time in the elaborate arrangement of his cravat, and finally made his appearance in a dress-coat, which I suspected to be newly come from the tailor's, and now first put on for a dinner-party. At a window of the next story below, two children, prettily dressed, were looking out. By-and-by, a middle-aged gentleman came softly behind them, kissed the little girl, and playfully pulled the little boy's ear. It was a papa, no doubt, just come in from his counting-room or office; and anon appeared mamma, stealing as softly behind papa, as he had stolen behind the children, and laying her hand on his shoulder to surprise him. Then followed a kiss between papa and mamma, but a noiseless one; for the children did not turn their heads.

"I bless God for these good folks!" thought I to myself. "I have not seen a prettier bit of nature, in all my summer in the country, than they have shown me here in a rather stylish boarding-house. I will pay them a little more attention, by-and-by."

On the first floor, an iron balustrade ran along in front of the tall, and spacious windows, evidently belonging to a back drawing-room; and, far into the interior, through the arch of the sliding-doors, I could discern a gleam from the windows of the front apartment. There were no signs of present occupancy in this suite of rooms; the curtains being enveloped in a protective covering, which allowed but a small portion of their crimson material to be seen. But two housemaids were industriously at work; so that there was good prospect that the boarding-house might not long suffer from the absence of its most expensive and profitable guests. Meanwhile, until they should appear, I cast my eyes downward to the lower regions. There, in the dusk that so early settles into such places, I saw the red glow of the kitchen-range; the hot cook, or one of her subordinates, with a ladle in her hand, came to draw a cool breath at the back-door; as soon as she disappeared, an Irish man-servant, in a white jacket, crept slily forth and threw away the fragments of a china-dish, which unquestionably he had just broken. Soon afterwards, a lady, showily dressed, with a curling front of what must have been false hair, and reddish brown, I suppose, in hue—though my remoteness allowed me only to guess at such particulars—this respectable mistress of the boarding-house made a momentary transit across the kitchen-window, and appeared no more. It was her final, comprehensive glance, in order to make sure that soup, fish, and flesh, were in a proper state of readiness, before the serving up of dinner.

There was nothing else worth noticing about the house; unless it be, that, on the peak of one of the dormer-windows, which opened out of the roof, sat a dove, looking very dreary and forlorn; insomuch that I wondered why she chose to sit there, in the chilly rain, while her kindred were doubtless nestling in a warm and comfortable dove-cote. All at once, this dove spread her wings, and launching herself in the air, came flying so straight across the intervening space, that I fully expected her to alight directly on my window-sill. In the latter part of her course, however, she swerved aside, flew upward, and vanished, as did likewise the slight, fantastic pathos with which I had invested her.

XVIII

THE BOARDING-HOUSE

T HE NEXT day, as soon as I thought of looking again towards the opposite house, there sat the dove again, on the peak of the same dormer-window!

It was by no means an early hour; for, the preceding evening, I had ultimately mustered enterprise enough to visit the theatre, had gone late to bed, and slept beyond all limit, in my remoteness from Silas Foster's awakening horn. Dreams had tormented me, throughout the night. The train of thoughts which, for months past, had worn a track through my mind, and to escape which was one of my chief objects in leaving Blithedale, kept treading remorselessly to-and-fro, in their old footsteps, while slumber left me impotent to regulate them. It was not till I had quitted my three friends that they first began to encroach upon my dreams. In those of the last night, Hollingsworth and Zenobia, standing on either side of my bed, had bent across it to exchange a kiss of passion. Priscilla, beholding this—for she seemed to be peeping in at the chamber-window—had melted gradually away, and left only the sadness of her expression in my heart. There it still lingered, after I awoke; one of those unreasonable sadnesses that you know not how to deal with, because it involves nothing for common-sense to clutch.

It was a gray and dripping forenoon; gloomy enough in town, and still gloomier in the haunts to which my recollec-

tions persisted in transporting me. For, in spite of my efforts
to think of something else, I thought how the gusty rain was
drifting over the slopes and valleys of our farm; how wet must
be the foliage that overshadowed the pulpit-rock; how cheerless, in such a day, my hermitage—the tree-solitude of my
owl-like humors—in the vine-encircled heart of the tall pine!
It was a phase of home-sickness. I had wrenchéd myself too
suddenly out of an accustomed sphere. There was no choice
now, but to bear the pang of whatever heart-strings were
snapt asunder, and that illusive torment (like the ache of a
limb long ago cut off) by which a past mode of life prolongs
itself into the succeeding one. I was full of idle and shapeless
regrets. The thought impressed itself upon me, that I had left
duties unperformed. With the power, perhaps, to act in the
place of destiny, and avert misfortune from my friends, I had
resigned them to their fate. That cold tendency, between
instinct and intellect, which made me pry with a speculative
interest into people's passions and impulses, appeared to have
gone far towards unhumanizing my heart.

But a man cannot always decide for himself whether his
own heart is cold or warm. It now impresses me, that, if I
erred at all, in regard to Hollingsworth, Zenobia, and Priscilla,
it was through too much sympathy, rather than too little.

To escape the irksomeness of these meditations, I resumed
my post at the window. At first sight, there was nothing new
to be noticed. The general aspect of affairs was the same as
yesterday, except that the more decided inclemency of to-day
had driven the sparrows to shelter, and kept the cat within
doors, whence, however, she soon emerged, pursued by the
cook, and with what looked like the better half of a roast
chicken in her mouth. The young man in the dress-coat was
invisible; the two children, in the story below, seemed to be
romping about the room, under the superintendence of a
nursery-maid. The damask curtains of the drawing-room, on

the first floor, were now fully displayed, festooned gracefully from top to bottom of the windows, which extended from the ceiling to the carpet. A narrower window, at the left of the drawing-room, gave light to what was probably a small boudoir, within which I caught the faintest imaginable glimpse of a girl's figure, in airy drapery. Her arm was in regular movement, as if she were busy with her German worsted, or some other such pretty and unprofitable handiwork.

While intent upon making out this girlish shape, I became sensible that a figure had appeared at one of the windows of the drawing-room. There was a presentiment in my mind; or perhaps my first glance, imperfect and sidelong as it was, had sufficed to convey subtle information of the truth. At any rate, it was with no positive surprise, but as if I had all along expected the incident, that, directing my eyes thitherward, I beheld—like a full-length picture, in the space between the heavy festoons of the window-curtains—no other than Zenobia! At the same instant, my thoughts made sure of the identity of the figure in the boudoir. It could only be Priscilla.

Zenobia was attired, not in the almost rustic costume which she had heretofore worn, but in a fashionable morning-dress. There was, nevertheless, one familiar point. She had, as usual, a flower in her hair, brilliant, and of a rare variety, else it had not been Zenobia. After a brief pause at the window, she turned away, exemplifying, in the few steps that removed her out of sight, that noble and beautiful motion which character-ized her as much as any other personal charm. Not one woman in a thousand could move so admirably as Zenobia. Many women can sit gracefully; some can stand gracefully; and a few, perhaps, can assume a series of graceful positions. But natural movement is the result and expression of the whole being, and cannot be well and nobly performed, unless responsive to something in the character. I often used to think that music—light and airy, wild and passionate, or the full harmony of stately marches, in accordance with her varying mood—should have attended Zenobia's footsteps.

I waited for her re-appearance. It was one peculiarity, distinguishing Zenobia from most of her sex, that she needed for her moral well-being, and never would forego, a large amount of physical exercise. At Blithedale, no inclemency of sky or muddiness of earth had ever impeded her daily walks. Here, in town, she probably preferred to tread the extent of the two drawing-rooms, and measure out the miles by spaces of forty feet, rather than bedraggle her skirts over the sloppy pavements. Accordingly, in about the time requisite to pass through the arch of the sliding-doors to the front window, and to return upon her steps, there she stood again, between the festoons of the crimson curtains. But another personage was now added to the scene. Behind Zenobia appeared that face which I had first encountered in the wood-path; the man who had passed, side by side with her, in such mysterious familiarity and estrangement, beneath my vine-curtained hermitage in the tall pine-tree. It was Westervelt. And though he was looking closely over her shoulder, it still seemed to me, as on the former occasion, that Zenobia repelled him—that, perchance, they mutually repelled each other—by some incompatibility of their spheres.

This impression, however, might have been altogether the result of fancy and prejudice, in me. The distance was so great as to obliterate any play of feature, by which I might otherwise have been made a partaker of their counsels.

There now needed only Hollingsworth and old Moodie to complete the knot of characters, whom a real intricacy of events, greatly assisted by my method of insulating them from other relations, had kept so long upon my mental stage, as actors in a drama. In itself, perhaps, it was no very remarkable event, that they should thus come across me, at the moment when I imagined myself free. Zenobia, as I well knew, had retained an establishment in town, and had not unfrequently withdrawn herself from Blithedale, during brief intervals, on one of which occasions she had taken Priscilla along with her. Nevertheless, there seemed something fatal in the coincidence that had borne me to this one spot, of all others in a great city, and transfixed me there, and compelled me again to waste my already wearied sympathies on affairs which were none of mine, and persons who cared little for me. It irritated my nerves; it affected me with a kind of heart-sickness. After the effort which it cost me to fling them off—after consummating my escape, as I thought, from these goblins of flesh and blood, and pausing to revive myself with a breath or two of an atmosphere in which they should have no share—it was a positive despair, to find the same figures arraying themselves before me, and presenting their old problem in a shape that made it more insoluble than ever.

I began to long for a catastrophe. If the noble temper of Hollingsworth's soul were doomed to be utterly corrupted by the too powerful purpose, which had grown out of what was noblest in him; if the rich and generous qualities of Zenobia's womanhood might not save her; if Priscilla must perish by her tenderness and faith, so simple and so devout;—then be it so! Let it all come! As for me, I would look on, as it seemed my part to do, understandingly, if my intellect could fathom the meaning and the moral, and, at all events, reverently and sadly. The curtain fallen, I would pass onward with my poor individual life, which was now attenuated of much of its proper substance, and diffused among many alien interests.

Meanwhile, Zenobia and her companion had retreated from the window. Then followed an interval, during which I directed my eyes towards the figure in the boudoir. Most certainly it was Priscilla, although dressed with a novel and fanciful elegance. The vague perception of it, as viewed so far off, impressed me as if she had suddenly passed out of a chrysalis state and put forth wings. Her hands were not now in motion. She had dropt her work, and sat with her head thrown back, in the same attitude that I had seen several times before, when she seemed to be listening to an imperfectly distinguished sound.

Again the two figures in the drawing-room became visible. They were now a little withdrawn from the window, face to face, and, as I could see by Zenobia's emphatic gestures, were discussing some subject in which she, at least, felt a passionate concern. By-and-by, she broke away, and vanished beyond my ken. Westervelt approached the window, and leaned his forehead against a pane of glass, displaying the sort of smile on his handsome features which, when I before met him, had let me into the secret of his gold-bordered teeth. Every human being, when given over to the Devil, is sure to have the wizard mark upon him, in one form or another. I fancied that this smile, with its peculiar revelation, was the Devil's signet on the Professor.

This man, as I had soon reason to know, was endowed with a cat-like circumspection; and though precisely the most unspiritual quality in the world, it was almost as effective as spiritual insight, in making him acquainted with whatever it suited him to discover. He now proved it, considerably to my discomfiture, by detecting and recognizing me, at my post of observation. Perhaps I ought to have blushed at being caught in such an evident scrutiny of Professor Westervelt and his affairs. Perhaps I did blush. Be that as it might, I retained presence of mind enough not to make my position yet more irksome, by the poltroonery of drawing back.

Westervelt looked into the depths of the drawing-room, and beckoned. Immediately afterwards, Zenobia appeared at the window, with color much heightened, and eyes which, as my conscience whispered me, were shooting bright arrows, barbed with scorn, across the intervening space, directed full at my sensibilities as a gentleman. If the truth must be told, far as her flight-shot was, those arrows hit the mark. She signified her recognition of me by a gesture with her head and hand, comprising at once a salutation and dismissal. The next moment, she administered one of those pitiless rebukes which a woman always has at hand, ready for an offence, (and which she so seldom spares, on due occasion,) by letting down a white linen curtain between the festoons of the damask ones. It fell like the drop-curtain of a theatre, in the interval between the acts.

Priscilla had disappeared from the boudoir. But the dove still kept her desolate perch, on the peak of the attic-window.

XIX

ZENOBIA'S DRAWING-ROOM

THE REMAINDER of the day, so far as I was concerned, was spent in meditating on these recent incidents. I contrived, and alternately rejected, innumerable methods of accounting for the presence of Zenobia and Priscilla, and the connection of Westervelt with both. It must be owned, too, that I had a keen, revengeful sense of the insult inflicted by Zenobia's scornful recognition, and more particularly by her letting down the curtain; as if such were the proper barrier to be interposed between a character like hers, and a perceptive faculty like mine. For, was mine a mere vulgar curiosity? Zenobia should have known me better than to suppose it. She should have been able to appreciate that quality of the intellect and the heart, which impelled me (often against my own will, and to the detriment of my own comfort) to live in other lives, and to endeavor—by generous sympathies, by delicate intuitions, by taking note of things too slight for record, and by bringing my human spirit into manifold accordance with the companions whom God assigned me—to learn the secret which was hidden even from themselves.

Of all possible observers, methought, a woman, like Zenobia, and a man, like Hollingsworth, should have selected me. And, now, when the event has long been past, I retain the same opinion of my fitness for the office. True; I might have condemned them. Had I been judge, as well as witness, my sentence might have been stern as that of Destiny itself. But, still, no trait of original nobility of character; no struggle against temptation; no iron necessity of will, on the one hand, nor extenuating circumstance to be derived from passion and despair, on the other; no remorse that might co-exist with error, even if powerless to prevent it; no proud repentance, that should claim retribution as a meed—would go unappreciated. True, again, I might give my full assent to the punishment which was sure to follow. But it would be given mournfully, and with undiminished love. And, after all was finished, I would come, as if to gather up the white ashes of those who had perished at the stake, and to tell the world—the wrong being now atoned for—how much had perished there, which it had never yet known how to praise.

I sat in my rocking-chair, too far withdrawn from the window to expose myself to another rebuke, like that already inflicted. My eyes still wandered towards the opposite house, but without effecting any new discoveries. Late in the afternoon, the weathercock on the church-spire indicated a change of wind; the sun shone dimly out, as if the golden wine of its beams were mingled half-and-half with water. Nevertheless, they kindled up the whole range of edifices, threw a glow over the windows, glistened on the wet roofs, and, slowly withdrawing upward, perched upon the chimney-tops; thence they took a higher flight, and lingered an instant on the tip of the spire, making it the final point of more cheerful light in the whole sombre scene. The next moment, it was all gone. The twilight fell into the area like a shower of dusky snow; and before it was quite dark, the gong of the hotel summoned me to tea.

When I returned to my chamber, the glow of an astral lamp* was penetrating mistily through the white curtain of Zenobia's drawing-room. The shadow of a passing figure was now-and-then cast upon this medium, but with too vague an outline for even my adventurous conjectures to read the hieroglyphic that it presented.

All at once, it occurred to me how very absurd was my behavior, in thus tormenting myself with crazy hypotheses as to what was going on within that drawing-room, when it was at my option to be personally present there. My relations with Zenobia, as yet unchanged—as a familiar friend, and associated in the same life-long enterprise—gave me the right, and made it no more than kindly courtesy demanded, to call on her. Nothing, except our habitual independence of conventional rules, at Blithedale, could have kept me from sooner recognizing this duty. At all events, it should now be performed.

In compliance with this sudden impulse, I soon found myself actually within the house, the rear of which, for two days past, I had been so sedulously watching. A servant took my card, and immediately returning, ushered me up-stairs. On the way, I heard a rich, and, as it were, triumphant burst of music from a piano, in which I felt Zenobia's character, although heretofore I had known nothing of her skill upon the instrument. Two or three canary-birds, excited by this gush of sound, sang piercingly, and did their utmost to produce a kindred melody. A bright illumination streamed through the door of the front drawing-room; and I had barely stept across the threshold before Zenobia came forward to meet me, laughing, and with an extended hand.

"Ah, Mr. Coverdale," said she, still smiling, but, as I thought, with a good deal of scornful anger underneath, "it has gratified me to see the interest which you continue to take in my affairs! I have long recognized you as a sort of transcendental Yankee, with all the native propensity of your countrymen to investigate matters that come within their range, but rendered almost poetical, in your case, by the refined methods which you adopt for its gratification. After all, it was an unjustifiable stroke, on my part—was it not?—to let down the window-curtain!"

"I cannot call it a very wise one," returned I, with a secret bitterness which, no doubt, Zenobia appreciated. "It is really impossible to hide anything, in this world, to say nothing of the next. All that we ought to ask, therefore, is, that the witnesses of our conduct, and the speculators on our motives, should be capable of taking the highest view which the circumstances of the case may admit. So much being secured, I, for one, would be most happy in feeling myself followed, everywhere, by an indefatigable human sympathy."

"We must trust for intelligent sympathy to our guardian angels, if any there be," said Zenobia. "As long as the only spectator of my poor tragedy is a young man, at the window of his hotel, I must still claim the liberty to drop the curtain."

While this passed, as Zenobia's hand was extended, I had applied the very slightest touch of my fingers to her own. In spite of an external freedom, her manner made me sensible that we stood upon no real terms of confidence. The thought came sadly across me, how great was the contrast betwixt this interview and our first meeting. Then, in the warm light of the country fireside, Zenobia had greeted me cheerily and hopefully, with a full sisterly grasp of the hand, conveying as much kindness in it as other women could have evinced by the pressure of both arms around my neck, or by yielding a cheek to the brotherly salute. The difference was as complete as between her appearance, at that time—so simply attired, and with only the one superb flower in her hair—and now, when her beauty was set off by all that dress and ornament could do for it. And they did much. Not, indeed, that they created, or added anything to what Nature had lavishly done for Zenobia. But, those costly robes which she had on, those flaming jewels on her neck, served as lamps to display the personal advantages which required nothing less than such an illumination, to be fully seen. Even her characteristic flower, though it seemed to be still there, had undergone a cold and bright transfiguration; it was a flower exquisitely imitated in jeweller's work, and imparting the last touch that transformed Zenobia into a work of art.

"I scarcely feel," I could not forbear saying, "as if we had ever met before. How many years ago it seems, since we last sat beneath Eliot's pulpit, with Hollingsworth extended on the fallen leaves, and Priscilla at his feet! Can it be, Zenobia, that you ever really numbered yourself with our little band of earnest, thoughtful, philanthropic laborers?"

"Those ideas have their time and place," she answered, coldly. "But, I fancy, it must be a very circumscribed mind that can find room for no others."

Her manner bewildered me. Literally, moreover, I was dazzled by the brilliancy of the room. A chandelier hung down in the centre, glowing with I know not how many lights; there were separate lamps, also, on two or three tables, and on marble brackets, adding their white radiance to that of the chandelier. The furniture was exceedingly rich. Fresh from our old farm-house, with its homely board and benches in the dining-room, and a few wicker-chairs in the best parlor, it struck me that here was the fulfilment of every fantasy of an imagination, revelling in various methods of costly self-indulgence and splendid ease. Pictures, marbles, vases; in brief, more shapes of luxury than there could be any object in enumerating, except for an auctioneer's advertisement—and the whole repeated and doubled by the reflection of a great mirror, which showed me Zenobia's proud figure, likewise, and my own. It cost me, I acknowledge, a bitter sense of shame, to perceive in myself a positive effort to bear up against the effect which Zenobia sought to impose on me. I reasoned against her, in my secret mind, and strove so to keep my footing. In the gorgeousness with which she had surrounded herself—in the redundance of personal ornament, which the largeness of her physical nature and the rich type of her beauty caused to seem so suitable—I malevolently beheld the true character of the woman, passionate, luxurious, lacking simplicity, not deeply refined, incapable of pure and perfect taste.

But, the next instant, she was too powerful for all my opposing struggles. I saw how fit it was that she should make herself as gorgeous as she pleased, and should do a thousand things that would have been ridiculous in the poor, thin, weakly characters of other women. To this day, however, I hardly know whether I then beheld Zenobia in her truest attitude, or whether that were the truer one in which she had presented herself at Blithedale. In both, there was something like the illusion which a great actress flings around her.

"Have you given up Blithedale forever?" I inquired.

"Why should you think so?" asked she.

"I cannot tell," answered I; "except that it appears all like a dream that we were ever there together."

"It is not so to me," said Zenobia. "I should think it a poor and meagre nature, that is capable of but one set of forms, and must convert all the past into a dream, merely because the present happens to be unlike it. Why should we be content with our homely life of a few months past, to the exclusion of all other modes? It was good; but there are other lives as good or better. Not, you will understand, that I condemn those who give themselves up to it more entirely than I, for myself, should deem it wise to do."

It irritated me, this self-complacent, condescending, qualified approval and criticism of a system to which many individuals—perhaps as highly endowed as our gorgeous Zenobia—had contributed their all of earthly endeavor, and their loftiest aspirations. I determined to make proof if there were any spell that would exorcise her out of the part which she seemed to be acting. She should be compelled to give me a glimpse of something true; some nature, some passion, no matter whether right or wrong, provided it were real.

"Your allusion to that class of circumscribed characters, who can live only in one mode of life," remarked I, coolly, "reminds me of our poor friend Hollingsworth. Possibly, he was in your thoughts, when you spoke thus. Poor fellow! It is a pity that, by the fault of a narrow education, he should have so completely immolated himself to that one idea of his; especially as the slightest modicum of common-sense would teach him its utter impracticability. Now that I have returned into the world, and can look at his project from a distance, it requires quite all my real regard for this respectable and well-intentioned man to prevent me laughing at him—as, I find, society at large does!"

Zenobia's eyes darted lightning; her cheeks flushed; the vividness of her expression was like the effect of a powerful light, flaming up suddenly within her. My experiment had fully succeeded. She had shown me the true flesh and blood of her heart, by thus involuntarily resenting my slight, pitying, half-kind, half-scornful mention of the man who was all in all with her. She herself, probably, felt this; for it was hardly a moment before she tranquillized her uneven breath, and seemed as proud and self-possessed as ever.

"I rather imagine," said she, quietly, "that your appreciation falls short of Mr. Hollingsworth's just claims. Blind enthusiasm, absorption in one idea, I grant, is generally ridiculous, and must be fatal to the respectability of an ordinary man; it requires a very high and powerful character, to make it otherwise. But a great man—as, perhaps, you do not know—attains his normal condition only through the inspiration of one great idea. As a friend of Mr. Hollingsworth, and, at the same time, a calm observer, I must tell you that he seems to me such a man. But you are very pardonable for fancying him ridiculous. Doubtless, he is so—to you! There can be no truer test of the noble and heroic, in any individual, than the degree in which he possesses the faculty of distinguishing heroism from absurdity."

I dared make no retort to Zenobia's concluding apothegm. In truth, I admired her fidelity. It gave me a new sense of Hollingsworth's native power, to discover that his influence was no less potent with this beautiful woman, here, in the midst of artificial life, than it had been, at the foot of the gray rock, and among the wild birch-trees of the wood-path, when she so passionately pressed his hand against her heart. The great, rude, shaggy, swarthy man! And Zenobia loved him!

"Did you bring Priscilla with you?" I resumed. "Do you know, I have sometimes fancied it not quite safe, considering the susceptibility of her temperament, that she should be so constantly within the sphere of a man like Hollingsworth? Such tender and delicate natures, among your sex, have often, I believe, a very adequate appreciation of the heroic element in men. But, then, again, I should suppose them as likely as any other women to make a reciprocal impression. Hollingsworth could hardly give his affections to a person capable of taking an independent stand, but only to one whom he might absorb into himself. He has certainly shown great tenderness for Priscilla."

Zenobia had turned aside. But I caught the reflection of her face in the mirror, and saw that it was very pale;—as pale, in her rich attire, as if a shroud were round her.

"Priscilla is here," said she, her voice a little lower than usual. "Have not you learnt as much, from your chamber-window? Would you like to see her?"

She made a step or two into the back drawing-room, and called:—

"Priscilla! Dear Priscilla!"

XX

THEY VANISH

P RISCILLA immediately answered the summons, and made her appearance through the door of the boudoir. I had conceived the idea—which I now recognized as a very foolish one—that Zenobia would have taken measures to debar me from an interview with this girl, between whom and herself there was so utter an opposition of their dearest interests, that, on one part or the other, a great grief, if not likewise a great wrong, seemed a matter of necessity. But, as Priscilla was only a leaf, floating on the dark current of events, without influencing them by her own choice or plan—as she probably guessed not whither the stream was bearing her, nor perhaps even felt its inevitable movement—there could be no peril of her communicating to me any intelligence with regard to Zenobia's purposes.

On perceiving me, she came forward with great quietude of manner; and when I held out my hand, her own moved slightly towards it, as if attracted by a feeble degree of magnetism.

"I am glad to see you, my dear Priscilla," said I, still holding her hand. "But everything that I meet with, now-a-days, makes me wonder whether I am awake. You, especially, have always seemed like a figure in a dream—and now more than ever."

"Oh, there is substance in these fingers of mine!" she answered, giving my hand the faintest possible pressure, and then taking away her own. "Why do you call me a dream? Zenobia is much more like one than I; she is so very, very beautiful! And, I suppose," added Priscilla, as if thinking aloud, "everybody sees it, as I do."

But, for my part, it was Priscilla's beauty, not Zenobia's, of which I was thinking, at that moment. She was a person who could be quite obliterated, so far as beauty went, by anything unsuitable in her attire; her charm was not positive and material enough to bear up against a mistaken choice of color, for instance, or fashion. It was safest, in her case, to attempt no art of dress; for it demanded the most perfect taste, or else the happiest accident in the world, to give her precisely the adornment which she needed. She was now dressed in pure white, set off with some kind of a gauzy fabric, which—as I bring up her figure in my memory, with a faint gleam on her shadowy hair, and her dark eyes bent shyly on mine, through all the vanished years—seems to be floating about her like a mist. I wondered what Zenobia meant by evolving so much loveliness out of this poor girl. It was what few women could afford to do; for, as I looked from one to the other, the sheen and splendor of Zenobia's presence took nothing from Priscilla's softer spell, if it might not rather be thought to add to it.

"What do you think of her?" asked Zenobia.

I could not understand the look of melancholy kindness with which Zenobia regarded her. She advanced a step, and beckoning Priscilla near her, kissed her cheek; then, with a slight gesture of repulse, she moved to the other side of the room. I followed.

"She is a wonderful creature," I said. "Ever since she came among us, I have been dimly sensible of just this charm which you have brought out. But it was never absolutely visible till now. She is as lovely as a flower!"

"Well; say so, if you like," answered Zenobia. "You are a poet—at least, as poets go, now-a-days—and must be allowed to make an opera-glass of your imagination, when you look at women. I wonder, in such Arcadian freedom of falling in love as we have lately enjoyed, it never occurred to you to fall in love with Priscilla! In society, indeed, a genuine American never dreams of stepping across the inappreciable air-line* which separates one class from another. But what was rank to the colonists of Blithedale?"

"There were other reasons," I replied, "why I should have demonstrated myself an ass, had I fallen in love with Priscilla. By-the-by, has Hollingsworth ever seen her in this dress?"

"Why do you bring up his name, at every turn?" asked Zenobia, in an undertone, and with a malign look which wandered from my face to Priscilla's. "You know not what you do! It is dangerous, sir, believe me, to tamper thus with earnest human passions, out of your own mere idleness, and for your sport. I will endure it no longer! Take care that it does not happen again! I warn you!"

"You partly wrong me, if not wholly," I responded. "It is an uncertain sense of some duty to perform, that brings my thoughts, and therefore my words, continually to that one point."

"Oh, this stale excuse of duty!" said Zenobia, in a whisper so full of scorn that it penetrated me like the hiss of a serpent. "I have often heard it before, from those who sought to interfere with me, and I know precisely what it signifies. Bigotry; self-conceit; an insolent curiosity; a meddlesome temper; a cold-blooded criticism, founded on a shallow interpretation of half-perceptions; a monstrous scepticism in regard to any conscience or any wisdom, except one's own; a most irreverent propensity to thrust Providence aside, and substitute one's self in its awful place—out of these, and other motives as miserable as these, comes your idea of duty!

But beware, sir! With all your fancied acuteness, you step blindfold into these affairs. For any mischief that may follow your interference, I hold you responsible!"

It was evident, that, with but a little further provocation, the lioness would turn to bay; if, indeed, such were not her attitude, already. I bowed, and, not very well knowing what else to do, was about to withdraw. But, glancing again towards Priscilla, who had retreated into a corner, there fell upon my heart an intolerable burthen of despondency, the purport of which I could not tell, but only felt it to bear reference to her. I approached her, and held out my hand; a gesture, however, to which she made no response. It was always one of her peculiarities that she seemed to shrink from even the most friendly touch, unless it were Zenobia's or Hollingsworth's. Zenobia, all this while, stood watching us, but with a careless expression, as if it mattered very little what might pass.

"Priscilla," I inquired, lowering my voice, "when do you go back to Blithedale?"

"Whenever they please to take me," said she.

"Did you come away of your own free-will?" I asked.

"I am blown about like a leaf," she replied. "I never have any free-will."

"Does Hollingsworth know that you are here?" said I.

"He bade me come," answered Priscilla.

She looked at me, I thought, with an air of surprise, as if the idea were incomprehensible, that she should have taken this step without his agency.

"What a gripe*this man has laid upon her whole being!" muttered I, between my teeth. "Well; as Zenobia so kindly intimates, I have no more business here. I wash my hands of it all. On Hollingsworth's head be the consequences! Priscilla," I added, aloud, "I know not that ever we may meet again. Farewell!"

As I spoke the word, a carriage had rumbled along the street, and stopt before the house. The door-bell rang, and steps were immediately afterwards heard on the staircase. Zenobia had thrown a shawl over her dress.

"Mr. Coverdale," said she, with cool courtesy, "you will perhaps excuse us. We have an engagement, and are going out."

"Whither?" I demanded.

"Is not that a little more than you are entitled to inquire?" said she, with a smile. "At all events, it does not suit me to tell you."

The door of the drawing-room opened, and Westervelt appeared. I observed that he was elaborately dressed, as if for some grand entertainment. My dislike for this man was infinite. At that moment, it amounted to nothing less than a creeping of the flesh, as when, feeling about in a dark place, one touches something cold and slimy, and questions what the secret hatefulness may be. And, still, I could not but acknowledge, that, for personal beauty, for polish of manner, for all that externally befits a gentleman, there was hardly another like him. After bowing to Zenobia, and graciously saluting Priscilla in her corner, he recognized me by a slight, but courteous inclination.

"Come, Priscilla," said Zenobia, "it is time. Mr. Coverdale, good evening!"

As Priscilla moved slowly forward, I met her in the middle of the drawing-room.

"Priscilla," said I, in the hearing of them all, "do you know whither you are going?"

"I do not know," she answered.

"Is it wise to go?—and is it your choice to go?" I asked. "If not—I am your friend, and Hollingsworth's friend—tell me so, at once!"

"Possibly," observed Westervelt, smiling, "Priscilla sees in me an older friend than either Mr. Coverdale or Mr. Hollingsworth. I shall willingly leave the matter at her option."

While thus speaking, he made a gesture of kindly invitation; and Priscilla passed me, with the gliding movement of a sprite, and took his offered arm. He offered the other to Zenobia. But she turned her proud and beautiful face upon him, with a look which—judging from what I caught of it in profile—would undoubtedly have smitten the man dead, had he possessed any heart, or had this glance attained to it. It seemed to rebound, however, from his courteous visage, like an arrow from polished steel. They all three descended the stairs; and when I likewise reached the street-door, the carriage was already rolling away.

XXI

AN OLD ACQUAINTANCE

THUS excluded from everybody's confidence, and attaining no further, by my most earnest study, than to an uncertain sense of something hidden from me, it would appear reasonable that I should have flung off all these alien perplexities. Obviously, my best course was, to betake myself to new scenes. Here, I was only an intruder. Elsewhere, there might be circumstances in which I could establish a personal interest, and people who would respond, with a portion of their sympathies, for so much as I should bestow of mine.

Nevertheless, there occurred to me one other thing to be done. Remembering old Moodie, and his relationship with Priscilla, I determined to seek an interview, for the purpose of ascertaining whether the knot of affairs was as inextricable, on that side, as I found it on all others. Being tolerably well acquainted with the old man's haunts, I went, the next day, to the saloon of a certain establishment about which he often lurked. It was a reputable place enough, affording good entertainment in the way of meat, drink, and fumigation;* and there, in my young and idle days and nights, when I was neither nice nor wise, I had often amused myself with watching the staid humors and sober jollities of the thirsty souls around me.

At my first entrance, old Moodie was not there. The more patiently to await him, I lighted a cigar, and establishing myself in a corner, took a quiet, and, by sympathy, a boozy kind of pleasure in the customary life that was going forward. Human nature, in my opinion, has a naughty instinct that approves of wine, at least, if not of stronger liquor. The temperance-men may preach till doom's day; and still this cold and barren world will look warmer, kindlier, mellower, through the medium of a toper's glass; nor can they, with all their efforts, really spill his draught upon the floor, until some hitherto unthought-of discovery shall supply him with a truer element of joy. The general atmosphere of life must first be rendered so inspiriting that he will not need his delirious solace. The custom of tippling has its defensible side, as well as any other question. But these good people snatch at the old, time-honored demijohn, and offer nothing—either sensual or moral—nothing whatever to supply its place; and human life, as it goes with a multitude of men, will not endure so great a vacuum as would be left by the withdrawal of that big-bellied convexity. The space, which it now occupies, must somehow or other be filled up. As for the rich, it would be little matter if a blight fell upon their vineyards; but the poor man—whose only glimpse of a better state is through the muddy medium of his liquor—what is to be done for him? The reformers should make their efforts positive, instead of negative; they must do away with evil by substituting good.*

The saloon was fitted up with a good deal of taste. There were pictures on the walls, and among them an oil-painting of a beef-steak, with such an admirable show of juicy tenderness, that the beholder sighed to think it merely visionary, and incapable of ever being put upon a gridiron. Another work of high art was the lifelike representation of a noble sirloin; another, the hind-quarters of a deer, retaining the hoofs and tawny fur; another, the head and shoulders of a salmon; and, still more exquisitely finished, a brace of canvass-back ducks, in which the mottled feathers were depicted with the accuracy of a daguerreotype.* Some very hungry painter, I suppose, had wrought these subjects of still life, heightening his imagination with his appetite, and earning, it is to be hoped, the privilege of a daily dinner off whichever of his pictorial viands he liked best. Then there was a fine old cheese, in which you could almost discern the mites; and some sardines, on a small plate, very richly done, and looking as if oozy with the oil in which they had been smothered. All these things were so perfectly imitated, that you seemed to have the genuine article before you, and yet with an indescribable, ideal charm; it took away the grossness from what was fleshiest and fattest, and thus helped the life of man, even in its earthliest relations, to appear rich and noble, as well as warm, cheerful, and substantial. There were pictures, too, of gallant revellers, those of the old time, Flemish, apparently, with doublets and slashed sleeves, drinking their wine out of fantastic, long-stemmed glasses; quaffing joyously, quaffing forever, with inaudible laughter and song; while the champagne bubbled immortally against their moustaches, or the purple tide of Burgundy ran inexhaustibly down their throats.

But, in an obscure corner of the saloon, there was a little picture—excellently done, moreover—of a ragged, bloated, New England toper, stretched out on a bench, in the heavy, apoplectic sleep of drunkenness. The death-in-life was too well portrayed. You smelt the fumy liquor that had brought on this syncope.* Your only comfort lay in the forced reflection, that, real as he looked, the poor caitiff was but imaginary, a bit of painted canvass, whom no delirium tremens, nor so much as a retributive headache, awaited, on the morrow.

By this time, it being past eleven o'clock, the two bar-keepers of the saloon were in pretty constant activity. One of these young men had a rare faculty in the concoction of gin-cocktails. It was a spectacle to behold, how, with a tumbler in each hand, he tossed the contents from one to the other. Never conveying it awry, nor spilling the least drop, he compelled the frothy liquor, as it seemed to me, to spout forth from one glass and descend into the other, in a great parabolic curve, as well-defined and calculable as a planet's orbit. He had a good forehead, with a particularly large development just above the eyebrows; fine intellectual gifts, no doubt, which he had educated to this profitable end; being famous for nothing but gin-cocktails, and commanding a fair salary by his one accomplishment. These cocktails, and other artificial combinations of liquor, (of which there were at least a score, though mostly, I suspect, fantastic in their differences,) were much in favor with the younger class of customers, who, at farthest, had only reached the second stage of potatory life. The staunch, old soakers, on the other hand— men who, if put on tap, would have yielded a red alcoholic liquor, by way of blood—usually confined themselves to plain brandy-and-water, gin, or West India rum; and, oftentimes, they prefaced their dram with some medicinal remark as to the wholesomeness and stomachic qualities of that particular drink. Two or three appeared to have bottles of their own, behind the counter; and winking one red eye to the bar-keeper, he forthwith produced these choicest and peculiar cordials, which it was a matter of great interest and favor, among their acquaintances, to obtain a sip of.

Agreeably to the Yankee habit, under whatever circumstances, the deportment of all these good fellows, old or young, was decorous and thoroughly correct. They grew only the more sober in their cups; there was no confused babble, nor boisterous laughter. They sucked in the joyous fire of the decanters, and kept it smouldering in their inmost recesses, with a bliss known only to the heart which it warmed and comforted. Their eyes twinkled a little, to be sure; they hemmed vigorously, after each glass, and laid a hand upon the pit of the stomach, as if the pleasant titillation, there, was what constituted the tangible part of their enjoyment. In that spot, unquestionably, and not in the brain, was the acme of the whole affair. But the true purpose of their drinking—and one that will induce men to drink, or do something equivalent, as long as this weary world shall endure—was the renewed youth and vigor, the brisk, cheerful sense of things present and to come, with which, for about a quarter-of-an-hour, the dram permeated their systems. And when such quarters-of-an-hour can be obtained in some mode less baneful to the great sum of a man's life—but, nevertheless, with a little spice of impropriety, to give it a wild flavor—we temperance-people may ring out our bells for victory!

The prettiest object in the saloon was a tiny fountain, which threw up its feathery jet, through the counter, and sparkled down again into an oval basin, or lakelet, containing several gold-fishes. There was a bed of bright sand, at the bottom, strewn with coral and rock-work; and the fishes went gleaming about, now turning up the sheen of a golden side, and now vanishing into the shadows of the water, like the fanciful thoughts that coquet with a poet in his dream. Never before, I imagine, did a company of water-drinkers remain so entirely uncontaminated by the bad example around them; nor could I help wondering that it had not occurred to any freakish inebriate, to empty a glass of liquor into their lakelet. What a delightful idea! Who would not be a fish, if he could inhale jollity with the essential element of his existence!

I had begun to despair of meeting old Moodie, when, all at once, I recognized his hand and arm, protruding from behind a screen that was set up for the accommodation of bashful topers. As a matter of course, he had one of Priscilla's little purses, and was quietly insinuating it under the notice of a person who stood near. This was always old Moodie's way. You hardly ever saw him advancing towards you, but became aware of his proximity without being able to guess how he had come thither. He glided about like a spirit, assuming visibility close to your elbow, offering his petty trifles of merchandise, remaining long enough for you to purchase, if so disposed, and then taking himself off, between two breaths, while you happened to be thinking of something else.

By a sort of sympathetic impulse that often controlled me, in those more impressible days of my life, I was induced to approach this old man in a mode as undemonstrative as his own. Thus, when, according to his custom, he was probably just about to vanish, he found me at his elbow.

"Ah!" said he, with more emphasis than was usual with him. "It is Mr. Coverdale!"

"Yes, Mr. Moodie, your old acquaintance," answered I. "It is some time now since we ate our luncheon together, at Blithedale, and a good deal longer since our little talk together, at the street-corner."

"That was a good while ago," said the old man.

And he seemed inclined to say not a word more. His existence looked so colorless and torpid—so very faintly shadowed on the canvass of reality—that I was half afraid lest he should altogether disappear, even while my eyes were fixed full upon his figure. He was certainly the wretchedest old ghost in the world, with his crazy hat, the dingy handkerchief about his throat, his suit of threadbare gray, and especially that patch over his right eye,* behind which he always seemed to be hiding himself. There was one method, however, of bringing him out into somewhat stronger relief. A glass of brandy would effect it. Perhaps the gentler influence of a bottle of claret might do the same. Nor could I think it a matter for the recording angel to write down against me, if—with my painful consciousness of the frost in this old man's blood, and the positive ice that had congealed about his heart—I should thaw him out, were it only for an hour, with the summer warmth of a little wine. What else could possibly be done for him? How else could he be imbued with energy enough to hope for a happier state, hereafter? How else be inspirited to say his prayers? For there are states of our spiritual system, when the throb of the soul's life is too faint and weak to render us capable of religious aspiration.

"Mr. Moodie," said I, "shall we lunch together? And would you like to drink a glass of wine?"

His one eye gleamed. He bowed; and it impressed me that he grew to be more of a man at once, either in anticipation of the wine, or as a grateful response to my good-fellowship in offering it.

"With pleasure," he replied.

The barkeeper, at my request, showed us into a private room, and, soon afterwards, set some fried oysters and a bottle of claret on the table; and I saw the old man glance curiously at the label of the bottle, as if to learn the brand.

"It should be good wine," I remarked, "if it have any right to its label."

"You cannot suppose, sir," said Moodie, with a sigh, "that a poor old fellow, like me, knows any difference in wines."

And yet, in his way of handling the glass, in his preliminary snuff at the aroma, in his first cautious sip of the wine, and the gustatory skill with which he gave his palate the full advantage of it, it was impossible not to recognize the connoisseur.

"I fancy, Mr. Moodie," said I, "you are a much better judge of wines than I have yet learned to be. Tell me fairly—did you never drink it where the grape grows?"

"How should that have been, Mr. Coverdale?" answered old Moodie, shyly; but then he took courage, as it were, and uttered a feeble little laugh. "The flavor of this wine," added he, "and its perfume, still more than its taste, makes me remember that I was once a young man!"

"I wish, Mr. Moodie," suggested I—not that I greatly cared about it, however, but was only anxious to draw him into some talk about Priscilla and Zenobia—"I wish, while we sit over our wine, you would favor me with a few of those youthful reminiscences."

"Ah," said he, shaking his head, "they might interest you more than you suppose. But I had better be silent, Mr. Coverdale. If this good wine—though claret, I suppose, is not apt to play such a trick—but if it should make my tongue run too freely, I could never look you in the face again."

"You never did look me in the face, Mr. Moodie," I replied, "until this very moment."

"Ah!" sighed old Moodie.

It was wonderful, however, what an effect the mild grape-juice wrought upon him. It was not in the wine, but in the associations which it seemed to bring up. Instead of the mean, slouching, furtive, painfully depressed air of an old city-vagabond, more like a gray kennel-rat* than any other living thing, he began to take the aspect of a decayed gentleman. Even his garments—especially after I had myself quaffed a glass or two—looked less shabby than when we first sat down. There was, by-and-by, a certain exuberance and elaborateness of gesture, and manner, oddly in contrast with all that I had hitherto seen of him. Anon, with hardly any impulse from me, old Moodie began to talk. His communications referred exclusively to a long past and more fortunate period of his life, with only a few unavoidable allusions to the circumstances that had reduced him to his present state. But, having once got the clue, my subsequent researches acquainted me with the main facts of the following narrative; although, in writing it out, my pen has perhaps allowed itself a trifle of romantic and legendary license, worthier of a small poet than of a grave biographer.

XXII

FAUNTLEROY

FIVE-AND-TWENTY years ago, at the epoch of this story, there dwelt, in one of the middle states, a man whom we shall call Fauntleroy;* a man of wealth, and magnificent tastes, and prodigal expenditure. His home might almost be styled a palace; his habits, in the ordinary sense, princely. His whole being seemed to have crystallized itself into an external splendor, wherewith he glittered in the eyes of the world, and had no other life than upon this gaudy surface. He had married a lovely woman, whose nature was deeper than his own. But his affection for her, though it showed largely, was superficial, like all his other manifestations and developments; he did not so truly keep this noble creature in his heart, as wear her beauty for the most brilliant ornament of his outward state. And there was born to him a child, a beautiful daughter, whom he took from the beneficent hand of God with no just sense of her immortal value, but as a man, already rich in gems, would receive another jewel. If he loved her, it was because she shone.

After Fauntleroy had thus spent a few empty years, corruscating continually an unnatural light, the source of it—which was merely his gold—began to grow more shallow, and finally became exhausted. He saw himself in imminent peril under another name, in a squalid street, or court, of the older portion of the city. There he dwelt among poverty-stricken wretches, sinners, and forlorn, good people, Irish, and whomsoever else were neediest. Many families were clustered in each house together, above stairs and below, in the little peaked garrets, and even in the dusky cellars. The house, where Fauntleroy paid weekly rent for a chamber and a closet, had been a stately habitation, in its day. An old colonial Governor had built it, and lived there, long ago, and held his levees in a great room where now slept twenty Irish bedfellows, and died in Fauntleroy's chamber, which his embroidered and white-wigged ghost still haunted. Tattered hangings, a marble hearth, traversed with many cracks and fissures, a richly-carved oaken mantel-piece, partly hacked-away for kindling-stuff, a stuccoed ceiling, defaced with great, unsightly patches of the naked laths;—such was the chamber's aspect, as if, with its splinters and rags of dirty splendor, it were a kind of practical gibe at this poor, ruined man of show.

At first, and at irregular intervals, his relatives allowed Fauntleroy a little pittance to sustain life; not from any love, perhaps, but lest poverty should compel him, by new offences, to add more shame to that with which he had already stained them. But he showed no tendency to further guilt. His character appeared to have been radically changed (as, indeed, from its shallowness, it well might) by his miserable fate; or, it may be, the traits now seen in him were portions of the same character, presenting itself in another phase. Instead of any longer seeking to live in the sight of the world, his impulse was to shrink into the nearest obscurity, and to be unseen of men, were it possible, even while standing before their eyes. He had no pride; it was all trodden in the dust. No ostentation; for how could it survive, when there was nothing left of Fauntleroy, save penury and shame! His very gait demonstrated that he would gladly have faded out of view, and have crept about invisibly, for the sake of sheltering

himself from the irksomeness of a human glance. Hardly,
it was averred, within the memory of those who knew him
now, had he the hardihood to show his full front to the world.
He skulked in corners, and crept about in a sort of noonday
twilight, making himself gray and misty, at all hours, with
his morbid intolerance of sunshine.

In his torpid despair, however, he had done an act which
that condition of the spirit seems to prompt, almost as often
as prosperity and hope. Fauntleroy was again married. He
had taken to wife a forlorn, meek-spirited, feeble young
woman, a seamstress, whom he found dwelling with her
mother in a contiguous chamber of the old gubernatorial
residence. This poor phantom—as the beautiful and noble
companion of his former life had done—brought him a
daughter. And sometimes, as from one dream into another,
Fauntleroy looked forth out of his present grimy environment,
into that past magnificence, and wondered whether the
grandee of yesterday or the pauper of to-day were real. But,
in my mind, the one and the other were alike impalpable.
In truth, it was Fauntleroy's fatality to behold whatever he
touched dissolve. After a few years, his second wife (dim
shadow that she had always been) faded finally out of the
world, and left Fauntleroy to deal as he might with their
pale and nervous child. And, by this time, among his distant
relatives—with whom he had grown a weary thought, linked
with contagious infamy, and which they were only too willing
to get rid of—he was himself supposed to be no more.

The younger child, like his elder one, might be considered as the true offspring of both parents, and as the
reflection of their state. She was a tremulous little creature,
shrinking involuntarily from all mankind, but in timidity,
and no sour repugnance. There was a lack of human substance in her; it seemed as if, were she to stand up in a
sunbeam, it would pass right through her figure, and trace
out the cracked and dusty window-panes upon the naked

floor. But, nevertheless, the poor child had a heart; and from her mother's gentle character, she had inherited a profound and still capacity of affection. And so her life was one of love. She bestowed it partly on her father, but, in greater part, on an idea.

For Fauntleroy, as they sat by their cheerless fireside—which was no fireside, in truth, but only a rusty stove—had often talked to the little girl about his former wealth, the noble loveliness of his first wife, and the beautiful child whom she had given him. Instead of the fairy tales, which other parents tell, he told Priscilla this. And, out of the loneliness of her sad little existence, Priscilla's love grew, and tended upward, and twined itself perseveringly around this unseen sister; as a grape-vine might strive to clamber out of a gloomy hollow among the rocks, and embrace a young tree, standing in the sunny warmth above. It was almost like worship, both in its earnestness and its humility; nor was it the less humble, though the more earnest, because Priscilla could claim human kindred with the being whom she so devoutly loved. As with worship, too, it gave her soul the refreshment of a purer atmosphere. Save for this singular, this melancholy, and yet beautiful affection, the child could hardly have lived; or, had she lived, with a heart shrunken for lack of any sentiment to fill it, she must have yielded to the barren miseries of her position, and have grown to womanhood, characterless and worthless. But, now, amid all the sombre coarseness of her father's outward life, and of her own, Priscilla had a higher and imaginative life within. Some faint gleam thereof was often visible upon her face. It was as if, in her spiritual visits to her brilliant sister, a portion of the latter's brightness had permeated our dim Priscilla, and still lingered, shedding a faint illumination through the cheerless chamber, after she came back.

As the child grew up, so pallid and so slender, and with much unaccountable nervousness, and all the weaknesses of neglected infancy still haunting her, the gross and simple neighbors whispered strange things about Priscilla. The big, red, Irish matrons, whose innumerable progeny swarmed out of the adjacent doors, used to mock at the pale Western child. They fancied—or, at least, affirmed it, between jest and 'earnest—that she was not so solid flesh and blood as other children, but mixed largely with a thinner element. They called her ghost-child, and said that she could indeed vanish, when she pleased, but could never, in her densest moments, make herself quite visible. The sun, at mid-day, would shine through her; in the first gray of the twilight, she lost all the distinctness of her outline; and, if you followed the dim thing into a dark corner, behold! she was not there. And it was true, that Priscilla had strange ways; strange ways, and stranger words, when she uttered any words at all. Never stirring out of the old Governor's dusky house, she sometimes talked of distant places and splendid rooms, as if she had just left them. Hidden things were visible to her, (at least, so the people inferred from obscure hints, escaping unawares out of her mouth,) and silence was audible. And, in all the world, there was nothing so difficult to be endured, by those who had any dark secret to conceal, as the glance of Priscilla's timid and melancholy eyes.

Her peculiarities were the theme of continual gossip among the other inhabitants of the gubernatorial mansion. The rumor spread thence into a wider circle. Those who knew old Moodie—as he was now called—used often to jeer him, at the very street-corners, about his daughter's gift of second-sight and prophecy. It was a period when science (though mostly through its empirical professors) was bringing forward, anew, a hoard of facts and imperfect theories, that had partially won credence, in elder times, but which modern scepticism had swept away as rubbish. These things were now tossed up again, out of the surging ocean of human thought and experience. The story of Priscilla's preternatural manifestations, therefore, attracted a kind of notice of which it would have been deemed wholly unworthy, a few years earlier. One day, a gentleman ascended the creaking staircase, and inquired which was old Moodie's chamber-door. And, several times, he came again. He was a marvellously handsome man, still youthful, too, and fashionably dressed. Except that Priscilla, in those days, had no beauty, and, in the languor of her existence, had not yet blossomed into womanhood, there would have been rich food for scandal in these visits; for the girl was unquestionably their sole object, although her father was supposed always to be present. But, it must likewise be added, there was something about Priscilla that calumny could not meddle with; and thus far was she privileged, either by the preponderance of what was spiritual, or the thin and watery blood that left her cheek so pallid.

Yet, if the busy tongues of the neighborhood spared Priscilla, in one way, they made themselves amends by renewed and wilder babble, on another score. They averred that the strange gentleman was a wizard, and that he had taken advantage of Priscilla's lack of earthly substance to subject her to himself, as his familiar spirit, through whose medium he gained cognizance of whatever happened, in regions near or remote. The boundaries of his power were defined by the verge of the pit of Tartarus, on the one hand, and the third sphere of the celestial world, on the other. Again, they declared their suspicion that the wizard, with all his show of manly beauty, was really an aged and wizened figure, or else that his semblance of a human body was only a necromantic, or perhaps a mechanical contrivance, in which a demon walked about. In proof of it, however, they could merely instance a gold band around his upper teeth, which had once been visible to several old women, when he smiled at them from the top of the Governor's staircase. Of course, this was all absurdity, or mostly so. But, after every possible deduction, there remained certain very mysterious points about the stranger's character, as well as the connection that he established with Priscilla. Its nature, at that period, was even less understood than now, when miracles of this kind have grown so absolutely stale, that I would gladly, if the truth allowed, dismiss the whole matter from my narrative.

We must now glance backward, in quest of the beautiful daughter of Fauntleroy's prosperity. What had become of her? Fauntleroy's only brother, a bachelor, and with no other relative so near, had adopted the forsaken child. She grew up in affluence, with native graces clustering luxuriantly about her. In her triumphant progress towards womanhood, she was adorned with every variety of feminine accomplishment. But she lacked a mother's care. With no adequate control, on any hand, (for a man, however stern, however wise, can never sway and guide a female child,) her character was left to shape itself. There was good in it, and evil. Passionate, self-willed, and imperious, she had a warm and generous nature; showing the richness of the soil, however, chiefly by the weeds that flourished in it, and choked up the herbs of grace. In her girlhood, her uncle died. As Fauntleroy was supposed to be likewise dead, and no other heir was known to exist, his wealth devolved on her, although, dying suddenly, the uncle left no will. After his death, there were obscure passages in Zenobia's history. There were whispers of an attachment, and even a secret marriage, with a fascinating and accomplished, but unprincipled young man. The incidents and appearances, however, which led to this surmise, soon passed away and were forgotten.

Nor was her reputation seriously affected by the report. In fact, so great was her native power and influence, and such seemed the careless purity of her nature, that whatever Zenobia did was generally acknowledged as right for her to do. The world never criticised her so harshly as it does most women who transcend its rules. It almost yielded its assent, when it beheld her stepping out of the common path, and asserting the more extensive privileges of her sex, both theoretically and by her practice. The sphere of ordinary womanhood was felt to be narrower than her development required.

A portion of Zenobia's more recent life is told in the foregoing pages. Partly in earnest—and, I imagine, as was her disposition, half in a proud jest, or in a kind of recklessness that had grown upon her, out of some hidden grief—she had given her countenance, and promised liberal pecuniary aid, to our experiment of a better social state. And Priscilla followed her to Blithedale. The sole bliss of her life had been a dream of this beautiful sister, who had never so much as known of her existence. By this time, too, the poor girl was enthralled in an intolerable bondage, from which she must either free herself or perish. She deemed herself safest near Zenobia, into whose large heart she hoped to nestle.

One evening, months after Priscilla's departure, when Moodie (or shall we call him Fauntleroy?) was sitting alone in the state-chamber of the old Governor, there came footsteps up the staircase. There was a pause on the landing-place. A lady's musical, yet haughty accents were heard making an inquiry from some denizen of the house, who had thrust a head out of a contiguous chamber. There was then a knock at Moodie's door.

"Come in!" said he.

And Zenobia entered. The details of the interview that followed, being unknown to me—while, notwithstanding, it would be a pity quite to lose the picturesqueness of the situation—I shall attempt to sketch it, mainly from fancy, although with some general grounds of surmise in regard to the old man's feelings.

She gazed, wonderingly, at the dismal chamber. Dismal to her, who beheld it only for an instant, and how much more so to him, into whose brain each bare spot on the ceiling, every tatter of the paper-hangings, and all the splintered carvings of the mantel-piece, seen wearily through long years, had worn their several prints! Inexpressibly miserable is this familiarity with objects that have been, from the first, disgustful.

"I have received a strange message," said Zenobia, after a moment's silence, "requesting, or rather enjoining it upon me, to come hither. Rather from curiosity than any other motive—and because, though a woman, I have not all the timidity of one—I have complied. Can it be you, sir, who thus summoned me?"

"It was," answered Moodie.

"And what was your purpose?" she continued. "You require charity, perhaps? In that case, the message might have been more fitly worded. But you are old and poor; and age and poverty should be allowed their privileges. Tell me, therefore, to what extent you need my aid."

"Put up your purse," said the supposed mendicant, with an inexplicable smile. "Keep it—keep all your wealth—until I demand it all, or none! My message had no such end in view. You are beautiful, they tell me; and I desired to look at you!"

He took the one lamp that showed the discomfort and sordidness of his abode, and approaching Zenobia, held it up, so as to gain the more perfect view of her, from top to toe. So obscure was the chamber, that you could see the reflection of her diamonds thrown upon the dingy wall, and flickering with the rise and fall of Zenobia's breath. It was the splendor of those jewels on her neck, like lamps that burn before some fair temple, and the jewelled flower in her hair, more than the murky yellow light, that helped him to see her beauty. But he beheld it, and grew proud at heart; his own figure, in spite of his mean habiliments, assumed an air of state and grandeur.

"It is well!" cried old Moodie. "Keep your wealth. You are right worthy of it. Keep it, therefore, but with one condition, only!"

Zenobia thought the old man beside himself, and was moved with pity.

"Have you none to care for you?" asked she. "No daughter? —no kind-hearted neighbor?—no means of procuring the attendance which you need? Tell me, once again, can I do nothing for you?"

"Nothing," he replied. "I have beheld what I wished. Now, leave me! Linger not a moment longer; or I may be tempted to say what would bring a cloud over that queenly brow. Keep all your wealth, but with only this one condition. Be kind—be no less kind than sisters are—to my poor Priscilla!"

And, it may be, after Zenobia withdrew, Fauntleroy paced his gloomy chamber, and communed with himself, as follows: —or, at all events, it is the only solution, which I can offer, of the enigma presented in his character.

"I am unchanged—the same man as of yore!" said he. "True; my brother's wealth, he dying intestate, is legally my own. I know it; yet, of my own choice, I live a beggar, and go meanly clad, and hide myself behind a forgotten ignominy. Looks this like ostentation? Ah, but, in Zenobia, I live again! Beholding her so beautiful—so fit to be adorned with all imaginable splendor of outward state—the cursed vanity, which, half-a-lifetime since, dropt off like tatters of once gaudy apparel from my debased and ruined person, is all renewed for her sake! Were I to re-appear, my shame would go with me from darkness into daylight. Zenobia has the splendor, and not the shame. Let the world admire her, and be dazzled by her, the brilliant child of my prosperity! It is Fauntleroy that still shines through her!"

But, then, perhaps, another thought occurred to him.

"My poor Priscilla! And am I just, to her, in surrendering all to this beautiful Zenobia? Priscilla! I love her best—I love her only!—but with shame, not pride. So dim, so pallid, so shrinking—the daughter of my long calamity! Wealth were but a mockery in Priscilla's hands. What is its use, except to fling a golden radiance around those who grasp it? Yet, let Zenobia take heed! Priscilla shall have no wrong!"

But, while the man of show thus meditated—that very evening, so far as I can adjust the dates of these strange incidents—Priscilla—poor, pallid flower!—was either snatched from Zenobia's hand, or flung wilfully away!

XXIII

A VILLAGE-HALL

WELL! I betook myself away, and wandered up and
down, like an exorcised spirit that had been driven
from its old haunts, after a mighty struggle. It takes
down the solitary pride of man, beyond most other things, to
find the impracticability of flinging aside affections that have
grown irksome. The bands, that were silken once, are apt
to become iron fetters, when we desire to shake them off.
Our souls, after all, are not our own. We convey a property
in them to those with whom we associate, but to what extent
can never be known, until we feel the tug, the agony, of our
abortive effort to resume an exclusive sway over ourselves.
Thus, in all the weeks of my absence, my thoughts continually
reverted back, brooding over the by-gone months, and bringing
up incidents that seemed hardly to have left a trace of themselves, in their passage. I spent painful hours in recalling
these trifles, and rendering them more misty and unsubstantial
than at first, by the quantity of speculative musing, thus
kneaded in with them. Hollingsworth, Zenobia, Priscilla!
These three had absorbed my life into themselves. Together
with an inexpressible longing to know their fortunes, there
was likewise a morbid resentment of my own pain, and a
stubborn reluctance to come again within their sphere.

• 194 •

All that I learned of them, therefore, was comprised in a few brief and pungent squibs, such as the newspapers were then in the habit of bestowing on our socialist enterprise. There was one paragraph which, if I rightly guessed its purport, bore reference to Zenobia, but was too darkly hinted to convey even thus much of certainty. Hollingsworth, too, with his philanthropic project, afforded the penny-a-liners*a theme for some savage and bloody-minded jokes; and, considerably to my surprise, they affected me with as much indignation as if we had still been friends.

Thus passed several weeks; time long enough for my brown and toil-hardened hands to re-accustom themselves to gloves. Old habits, such as were merely external, returned upon me with wonderful promptitude. My superficial talk, too, assumed altogether a worldly tone. Meeting former acquaintances, who showed themselves inclined to ridicule my heroic devotion to the cause of human welfare, I spoke of the recent phase of my life as indeed fair matter for a jest. But I also gave them to understand that it was, at most, only an experiment, on which I had staked no valuable amount of hope or fear; it had enabled me to pass the summer in a novel and agreeable way, had afforded me some grotesque specimens of artificial simplicity, and could not, therefore, so far as I was concerned, be reckoned a failure. In no one instance, however, did I voluntarily speak of my three friends. They dwelt in a profounder region. The more I consider myself, as I then was, the more do I recognize how deeply my connection with those three had affected all my being.

As it was already the epoch of annihilated space, I might, in the time I was away from Blithedale, have snatched a glimpse at England, and been back again. But my wanderings were confined within a very limited sphere. I hopped and fluttered, like a bird with a string about its leg, gyrating round a small circumference, and keeping up a restless activity to no purpose. Thus, it was still in our familiar Massachusetts—

in one of its white country-villages—that I must next particu-
larize an incident.

The scene was one of those Lyceum-halls,*of which almost
every village has now its own, dedicated to that sober and
pallid, or, rather, drab-colored, mode of winter-evening entertainment, the Lecture. Of late years, this has come strangely
into vogue, when the natural tendency of things would seem
to be, to substitute lettered for oral methods of addressing
the public. But, in halls like this, besides the winter course
of lectures, there is a rich and varied series of other exhibitions.
Hither comes the ventriloquist, with all his mysterious tongues;
the thaumaturgist,* too, with his miraculous transformations of
plates, doves, and rings, his pancakes smoking in your hat,
and his cellar of choice liquors, represented in one small bottle.
Here, also, the itinerant professor instructs separate classes
of ladies and gentlemen in physiology, and demonstrates his
lessons by the aid of real skeletons, and mannikins in wax,
from Paris. Here is to be heard the choir of Ethiopian melo-
dists, and to be seen, the diorama of Moscow or Bunker Hill,
or the moving panorama of the Chinese wall. Here is displayed the museum of wax figures, illustrating the wide
catholicism of earthly renown by mixing up heroes and
statesmen, the Pope and the Mormon Prophet,* kings, queens,
murderers, and beautiful ladies; every sort of person, in short,
except authors, of whom I never beheld even the most
famous, done in wax. And here, in this many-purposed hall,
(unless the selectmen of the village chance to have more
than their share of the puritanism, which, however diversified
with later patchwork, still gives its prevailing tint to New
England character,) here the company of strolling players
sets up its little stage, and claims patronage for the legitimate
drama.

But, on the autumnal evening which I speak of, a number
of printed handbills—stuck up in the bar-room and on the
sign-post of the hotel, and on the meeting-house porch, and

distributed largely through the village—had promised the inhabitants an interview with that celebrated and hitherto inexplicable phenomenon, the Veiled Lady!

The hall was fitted up with an amphitheatrical descent of seats towards a platform, on which stood a desk, two lights, a stool, and a capacious, antique chair. The audience was of a generally decent and respectable character; old farmers, in their Sunday black coats, with shrewd, hard, sun-dried faces, and a cynical humor, oftener than any other expression, in their eyes; pretty girls, in many-colored attire; pretty young men—the schoolmaster, the lawyer, or student-at-law, the shopkeeper—all looking rather suburban than rural. In these days, there is absolutely no rusticity, except when the actual labor of the soil leaves its earth-mould on the person. There was likewise a considerable proportion of young and middle-aged women, many of them stern in feature, with marked foreheads, and a very definite line of eyebrow; a type of womanhood in which a bold intellectual development seems to be keeping pace with the progressive delicacy of the physical constitution. Of all these people I took note, at first, according to my custom. But I ceased to do so, the moment that my eyes fell on an individual who sat two or three seats below me, immoveable, apparently deep in thought, with his back, of course, towards me, and his face turned stead-fastly upon the platform.

After sitting awhile, in contemplation of this person's familiar contour, I was irresistibly moved to step over the intervening benches, lay my hand on his shoulder, put my mouth close to his ear, and address him in a sepulchral, melo-dramatic whisper:—

"Hollingsworth! Where have you left Zenobia!"

His nerves, however, were proof against my attack. He turned half around, and looked me in the face, with great, sad eyes, in which there was neither kindness nor resentment, nor any perceptible surprise.

"Zenobia, when I last saw her," he answered, "was at Blithedale."

He said no more. But there was a great deal of talk going on, near me, among a knot of people who might be considered as representing the mysticism, or, rather, the mystic sensuality, of this singular age. The nature of the exhibition, that was about to take place, had probably given the turn to their conversation.

I heard, from a pale man in blue spectacles, some stranger stories than ever were written in a romance; told, too, with a simple, unimaginative steadfastness, which was terribly effica- cious in compelling the auditor to receive them into the category of established facts. He cited instances of the miracu- lous power of one human being over the will and passions of another; insomuch that settled grief was but a shadow, beneath the influence of a man possessing this potency, and the strong love of years melted away like a vapor. At the bidding of one of these wizards, the maiden, with her lover's kiss still burning on her lips, would turn from him with icy indifference; the newly made widow would dig up her buried heart out of her young husband's grave, before the sods had taken root upon it; a mother, with her babe's milk in her bosom, would thrust away her child. Human character was but soft wax in his hands; and guilt, or virtue, only the forms into which he should see fit to mould it. The religious sentiment was a flame which he could blow up with his breath, or a spark that he could utterly extinguish. It is un- utterable, the horror and disgust with which I listened, and saw, that, if these things were to be believed, the individual soul was virtually annihilated, and all that is sweet and pure, in our present life, debased, and that the idea of man's eternal responsibility was made ridiculous, and immortality rendered, at once, impossible, and not worth acceptance. But I would have perished on the spot, sooner than believe it.

The epoch of rapping spirits,* and all the wonders that

have followed in their train—such as tables, upset by invisible agencies, bells, self-tolled at funerals, and ghostly music, performed on jewsharps—had not yet arrived. Alas, my countrymen, methinks we have fallen on an evil age! If these phenomena have not humbug at the bottom, so much the worse for us. What can they indicate, in a spiritual way, except that the soul of man is descending to a lower point than it has ever before reached, while incarnate? We are pursuing a downward course, in the eternal march, and thus bring ourselves into the same range with beings whom death, in requital of their gross and evil lives, has degraded below humanity. To hold intercourse with spirits of this order, we must stoop, and grovel in some element more vile than earthly dust. These goblins, if they exist at all, are but the shadows of past mortality, outcasts, mere refuse-stuff, adjudged unworthy of the eternal world, and, on the most favorable supposition, dwindling gradually into nothingness. The less we have to say to them, the better; lest we share their fate!

The audience now began to be impatient; they signified their desire for the entertainment to commence, by thump of sticks and stamp of boot-heels. Nor was it a great while longer, before, in response to their call, there appeared a bearded personage in Oriental robes, looking like one of the enchanters of the Arabian Nights. He came upon the platform from a side-door—saluted the spectators, not with a salaam, but a bow—took his station at the desk—and first blowing his nose with a white handkerchief, prepared to speak. The environment of the homely village-hall, and the absence of many ingenious contrivances of stage-effect, with which the exhibition had heretofore been set off, seemed to bring the artifice of this character more openly upon the surface. No sooner did I behold the bearded enchanter, than laying my hand again on Hollingsworth's shoulder, I whispered in his ear:—

"Do you know him?"

"I never saw the man before," he muttered, without turning his head.

But I had seen him, three times, already. Once, on occasion of my first visit to the Veiled Lady; a second time, in the wood-path at Blithedale; and, lastly, in Zenobia's drawing-room. It was Westervelt. A quick association of ideas made me shudder, from head to foot; and, again, like an evil spirit, bringing up reminiscences of a man's sins, I whispered a question in Hollingsworth's ear.

"What have you done with Priscilla?"

He gave a convulsive start, as if I had thrust a knife into him, writhed himself round on his seat, glared fiercely into my eyes, but answered not a word.

The Professor began his discourse, explanatory of the psychological phenomena, as he termed them, which it was his purpose to exhibit to the spectators. There remains no very distinct impression of it on my memory. It was eloquent, ingenious, plausible, with a delusive show of spirituality, yet really imbued throughout with a cold and dead materialism. I shivered, as at a current of chill air, issuing out of a sepulchral vault and bringing the smell of corruption along with it. He spoke of a new era that was dawning upon the world; an era that would link soul to soul, and the present life to what we call futurity, with a closeness that should finally convert both worlds into one great, mutually conscious brotherhood. He described (in a strange, philosophical guise, with terms of art, as if it were a matter of chemical discovery) the agency by which this mighty result was to be effected; nor would it have surprised me, had he pretended to hold up a portion of his universally pervasive fluid, as he affirmed it to be, in a glass phial.

At the close of his exordium, the Professor beckoned with his hand—one, twice, thrice—and a figure came gliding upon the platform, enveloped in a long veil of silvery whiteness. It fell about her, like the texture of a summer cloud, with a kind of vagueness, so that the outline of the form, beneath it, could not be accurately discerned. But the movement of the Veiled Lady was graceful, free, and unembarrassed, like that of a person accustomed to be the spectacle of thousands. Or, possibly, a blindfold prisoner within the sphere with which this dark, earthly magician had surrounded her, she was wholly unconscious of being the central object to all those straining eyes.

Pliant to his gesture, (which had even an obsequious courtesy, but, at the same time, a remarkable decisiveness,) the figure placed itself in the great chair. Sitting there, in such visible obscurity, it was perhaps as much like the actual presence of a disembodied spirit as anything that stage-trickery could devise. The hushed breathing of the spectators proved how high-wrought were their anticipations of the wonders to be performed, through the medium of this incomprehensible creature. I, too, was in breathless suspense, but with a far different presentiment of some strange event at hand.

"You see before you the Veiled Lady," said the bearded Professor, advancing to the verge of the platform. "By the agency of which I have just spoken, she is, at this moment, in communion with the spiritual world. That silvery veil is, in one sense, an enchantment, having been dipt, as it were, and essentially imbued, through the potency of my art, with the fluid medium of spirits. Slight and ethereal as it seems, the limitations of time and space have no existence within its folds. This hall—these hundreds of faces, encompassing her within so narrow an amphitheatre—are of thinner substance, in her view, than the airiest vapor that the clouds are made of. She beholds the Absolute!"

As preliminary to other, and far more wonderful psychological experiments, the exhibitor suggested that some of his auditors should endeavor to make the Veiled Lady sensible of their presence by such methods—provided, only, no touch

were laid upon her person—as they might deem best adapted
to that end. Accordingly, several deep-lunged country-fellows,
who looked as if they might have blown the apparition away
with a breath, ascended the platform. Mutually encouraging
one another, they shouted so close to her ear, that the veil
stirred like a wreath of vanishing mist; they smote upon the
floor with bludgeons; they perpetrated so hideous a clamor,
that methought it might have reached, at least a little way,
into the eternal sphere. Finally, with the assent of the Professor, they laid hold of the great chair, and were startled,
apparently, to find it soar upward, as if lighter than the air
through which it rose. But the Veiled Lady remained seated
and motionless, with a composure that was hardly less than
awful, because implying so immeasurable a distance betwixt
her and these rude persecutors.

"These efforts are wholly without avail," observed the Professor, who had been looking on with an aspect of serene
indifference. "The roar of a battery of cannon would be
inaudible to the Veiled Lady. And yet, were I to will it,
sitting in this very hall, she could hear the desert-wind sweeping over the sands, as far off as Arabia; the ice-bergs grinding
one against the other, in the polar seas; the rustle of a leaf
in an East Indian forest; the lowest whispered breath of the
bashfullest maiden in the world, uttering the first confession
of her love! Nor does there exist the moral inducement, apart
from my own behest, that could persuade her to lift the
silvery veil, or arise out of that chair!"

Greatly to the Professor's discomposure, however, just as
he spoke these words, the Veiled Lady arose. There was a
mysterious tremor that shook the magic veil. The spectators,
it may be, imagined that she was about to take flight into that
invisible sphere, and to the society of those purely spiritual
beings, with whom they reckoned her so near akin. Hollingsworth, a moment ago, had mounted the platform, and now
stood gazing at the figure, with a sad intentness that brought

the whole power of his great, stern, yet tender soul, into his glance.

"Come!" said he, waving his hand towards her. "You are safe!"

She threw off the veil, and stood before that multitude of people, pale, tremulous, shrinking, as if only then had she discovered that a thousand eyes were gazing at her. Poor maiden! How strangely had she been betrayed! Blazoned abroad as a wonder of the world, and performing what were adjudged as miracles—in the faith of many, a seeress and a prophetess—in the harsher judgment of others, a mountebank —she had kept, as I religiously believe, her virgin reserve and sanctity of soul, throughout it all. Within that encircling veil, though an evil hand had flung it over her, there was as deep a seclusion as if this forsaken girl had, all the while, been sitting under the shadow of Eliot's pulpit, in the Blithedale woods, at the feet of him who now summoned her to the shelter of his arms. And the true heart-throb of a woman's affection was too powerful for the jugglery that had hitherto environed her. She uttered a shriek and fled to Hollingsworth, like one escaping from her deadliest enemy, and was safe forever!

XXIV

THE MASQUERADERS

TWO NIGHTS had passed since the foregoing occurrences, when, in a breezy September forenoon, I set forth from town, on foot, towards Blithedale.

It was the most delightful of all days for a walk, with a dash of invigorating ice-temper in the air, but a coolness that soon gave place to the brisk glow of exercise, while the vigor remained as elastic as before. The atmosphere had a spirit and sparkle in it. Each breath was like a sip of ethereal wine, tempered, as I said, with a crystal lump of ice. I had started on this expedition in an exceedingly sombre mood, as well befitted one who found himself tending towards home, but was conscious that nobody would be quite overjoyed to greet him there. My feet were hardly off the pavement, however, when this morbid sensation began to yield to the lively influences of air and motion. Nor had I gone far, with fields yet green on either side, before my step became as swift and light as if Hollingsworth were waiting to exchange a friendly hand-grip, and Zenobia's and Priscilla's open arms would welcome the wanderer's re-appearance. It has happened to me, on other occasions, as well as this, to prove how a state of physical well-being can create a kind of joy, in spite of the profoundest anxiety of mind.

The pathway of that walk still runs along, with sunny freshness, through my memory. I know not why it should be so. But my mental eye can even now discern the September grass, bordering the pleasant roadside with a brighter verdure than while the summer-heats were scorching it; the trees, too, mostly green, although, here and there, a branch or shrub has donned its vesture of crimson and gold, a week or two before its fellows. I see the tufted barberry bushes,* with their small clusters of scarlet fruit; the toadstools, likewise, some spotlessly white, others yellow or red—mysterious growths, springing suddenly from no root or seed, and growing nobody can tell how or wherefore. In this respect, they resembled many of the emotions in my breast. And I still see the little rivulets, chill, clear, and bright, that murmured beneath the road, through subterranean rocks, and deepened into mossy pools where tiny fish were darting to-and-fro, and within which lurked the hermit-frog. But, no—I never can account for it—that, with a yearning interest to learn the upshot of all my story, and returning to Blithedale for that sole purpose, I should examine these things so like a peaceful-bosomed naturalist. Nor why, amid all my sympathies and fears, there shot, at times, a wild exhilaration through my frame!

Thus I pursued my way, along the line of the ancient stone-wall that Paul Dudley*built, and through white villages, and past orchards of ruddy apples, and fields of ripening maize, and patches of woodland, and all such sweet rural scenery as looks the fairest, a little beyond the suburbs of a town. Hollingsworth, Zenobia, Priscilla! They glided mistily before me, as I walked. Sometimes, in my solitude, I laughed with the bitterness of self-scorn, remembering how unreservedly I had given up my heart and soul to interests that were not mine. What had I ever had to do with them? And why, being now free, should I take this thraldom on me, once again? It was both sad and dangerous, I whispered to myself, to be in too close affinity with the passions, the errors, and the misfortunes, of individuals who stood within a circle of their own, into which, if I stept at all, it must be as an intruder, and at a peril that I could not estimate.

Drawing nearer to Blithedale, a sickness of the spirits kept alternating with my flights of causeless buoyancy. I indulged in a hundred odd and extravagant conjectures. Either there was no such place as Blithedale, nor ever had been, nor any brotherhood of thoughtful laborers, like what I seemed to recollect there; or else it was all changed, during my absence. It had been nothing but dream-work and enchantment. I should seek in vain for the old farm-house, and for the greensward, the potatoe-fields, the root-crops, and acres of Indian corn, and for all that configuration of the land which I had imagined. It would be another spot, and an utter strangeness.

These vagaries were of the spectral throng, so apt to steal out of an unquiet heart. They partly ceased to haunt me, on my arriving at a point whence, through the trees, I began to catch glimpses of the Blithedale farm. That, surely, was something real. There was hardly a square foot of all those acres, on which I had not trodden heavily in one or another kind of toil. The curse of Adam's posterity—and, curse or blessing be it, it gives substance to the life around us—had first come upon me there. In the sweat of my brow, I had there earned bread and eaten it, and so established my claim to be on earth, and my fellowship with all the sons of labor. I could have knelt down, and have laid my breast against that soil. The red clay, of which my frame was moulded, seemed nearer akin to those crumbling furrows than to any other portion of the world's dust. There was my home; and there might be my grave.

I felt an invincible reluctance, nevertheless, at the idea of presenting myself before my old associates, without first ascertaining the state in which they were. A nameless fore-boding weighed upon me. Perhaps, should I know all the

circumstances that had occurred, I might find it my wisest
course to turn back, unrecognized, unseen, and never look
at Blithedale more. Had it been evening, I would have stolen
softly to some lighted window of the old farm-house, and
peeped darkling in, to see all their well-known faces round
the supper-board. Then, were there a vacant seat, I might
noiselessly unclose the door, glide in, and take my place
among them, without a word. My entrance might be so quiet,
my aspect so familiar, that they would forget how long I had
been away, and suffer me to melt into the scene, as a wreath
of vapor melts into a larger cloud. I dreaded a boisterous
greeting. Beholding me at table, Zenobia, as a matter of
course, would send me a cup of tea, and Hollingsworth fill
my plate from the great dish of pan-dowdy, and Priscilla, in
her quiet way, would hand the cream, and others help me
to the bread and butter. Being one of them again, the knowledge of what had happened would come to me, without a
shock. For, still, at every turn of my shifting fantasies, the
thought stared me in the face, that some evil thing had
befallen us, or was ready to befall.

Yielding to this ominous impression, I now turned aside
into the woods, resolving to spy out the posture of the Community, as craftily as the wild Indian before he makes his
onset. I would go wandering about the outskirts of the farm,
and, perhaps catching sight of a solitary acquaintance, would
approach him amid the brown shadows of the trees, (a kind
of medium fit for spirits departed and revisitant, like myself,)
and entreat him to tell me how all things were.

The first living creature that I met, was a partridge, which
sprung up beneath my feet, and whirred away; the next was
a squirrel, who chattered angrily at me, from an overhanging
bough. I trod along by the dark, sluggish river, and remember
pausing on the bank, above one of its blackest and most placid
pools—(the very spot, with the barkless stump of a tree aslantwise over the water, is depicting itself to my fancy, at this

instant)—and wondering how deep it was, and if any over-
laden soul had ever flung its weight of mortality in thither,
and if it thus escaped the burthen, or only made it heavier.
And perhaps the skeleton of the drowned wretch still lay
beneath the inscrutable depth, clinging to some sunken log
at the bottom with the gripe of its old despair. So slight,
however, was the track of these gloomy ideas, that I soon
forgot them in the contemplation of a brood of wild ducks,
which were floating on the river, and anon took flight, leaving
each a bright streak over the black surface. By-and-by, I came
to my hermitage, in the heart of the white-pine tree, and
clambering up into it, sat down to rest. The grapes, which I
had watched throughout the summer, now dangled around
me in abundant clusters of the deepest purple, deliciously
sweet to the taste, and though wild, yet free from that un-
gentle flavor which distinguishes nearly all our native and
uncultivated grapes. Methought a wine might be pressed out
of them, possessing a passionate zest, and endowed with a
new kind of intoxicating quality, attended with such bacchanalian ecstasies as the tamer grapes of Madeira, France,
and the Rhine, are inadequate to produce. And I longed to
quaff a great goblet of it, at that moment!

While devouring the grapes, I looked on all sides out of
the peep-holes of my hermitage, and saw the farm-house, the
fields, and almost every part of our domain, but not a single
human figure in the landscape. Some of the windows of the
house were open, but with no more signs of life than in a
dead man's unshut eyes. The barn-door was ajar, and swinging in the breeze. The big, old dog—he was a relic of the
former dynasty of the farm—that hardly ever stirred out of
the yard, was nowhere to be seen. What, then, had become
of all the fraternity and sisterhood? Curious to ascertain this
point, I let myself down out of the tree, and going to the
edge of the wood, was glad to perceive our herd of cows,
chewing the cud, or grazing, not far off. I fancied, by their

manner, that two or three of them recognized me, (as, indeed, they ought, for I had milked them, and been their chamberlain, times without number;) but, after staring me in the face, a little while, they phlegmatically began grazing and chewing their cuds again. Then I grew foolishly angry at so cold a reception, and flung some rotten fragments of an old stump at these unsentimental cows.

Skirting farther round the pasture, I heard voices and much laughter proceeding from the interior of the wood. Voices, male and feminine; laughter, not only of fresh young throats, but the bass of grown people, as if solemn organ-pipes should pour out airs of merriment. Not a voice spoke, but I knew it better than my own; not a laugh, but its cadences were familiar. The wood, in this portion of it, seemed as full of jollity as if Comus*and his crew were holding their revels, in one of its usually lonesome glades. Stealing onward as far as I durst, without hazard of discovery, I saw a concourse of strange figures* beneath the overshadowing branches; they appeared, and vanished, and came again, confusedly, with the streaks of sunlight glimmering down upon them.

Among them was an Indian chief, with blanket, feathers and war-paint, and uplifted tomahawk; and near him, looking fit to be his woodland-bride, the goddess Diana, with the crescent on her head, and attended by our big, lazy dog, in lack of any fleeter hound. Drawing an arrow from her quiver, she let it fly, at a venture, and hit the very tree behind which I happened to be lurking. Another group consisted of a Bavarian broom-girl,* a negro of the Jim Crow*order, one or two foresters of the middle-ages, a Kentucky woodsman in his trimmed hunting-shirt and deerskin leggings, and a Shaker* elder, quaint, demure, broad-brimmed, and square-skirted. Shepherds of Arcadia, and allegoric figures from the Faerie Queen,* were oddly mixed up with these. Arm in arm, or otherwise huddled together, in strange discrepancy, stood grim Puritans, gay Cavaliers, and Revolutionary officers, with three-cornered cocked-hats, and queues longer than their swords. A bright-complexioned, dark-haired, vivacious little gipsy, with a red shawl over her head, went from one group to another, telling fortunes by palmistry; and Moll Pitcher,* the renowned old witch of Lynn, broomstick in hand, showed herself prominently in the midst, as if announcing all these apparitions to be the offspring of her necromantic art. But Silas Foster, who leaned against a tree near by, in his customary blue frock, and smoking a short pipe, did more to disenchant the scene, with his look of shrewd, acrid, Yankee observation, than twenty witches and necromancers could have done, in the way of rendering it weird and fantastic.

A little further off, some old-fashioned skinkers and drawers,* all with portentously red noses, were spreading a banquet on the leaf-strewn earth; while a horned and long-tailed gentleman (in whom I recognized the fiendish musician, erst seen by Tam O'Shanter)*tuned his fiddle, and summoned the whole motley rout to a dance, before partaking of the festal cheer. So they joined hands in a circle, whirling round so swiftly, so madly, and so merrily, in time and tune with the Satanic music, that their separate incongruities were blended all together; and they became a kind of entanglement that went nigh to turn one's brain, with merely looking at it. Anon, they stopt, all of a sudden, and staring at one another's figures, set up a roar of laughter; whereat, a shower of the September leaves (which, all day long, had been hesitating whether to fall or no) were shaken off by the movement of the air, and came eddying down upon the revellers.

Then, for lack of breath, ensued a silence; at the deepest point of which, tickled by the oddity of surprising my grave associates in this masquerading trim, I could not possibly refrain from a burst of laughter, on my own separate account.

"Hush!" I heard the pretty gipsy fortuneteller say. "Who is that laughing?"

"Some profane intruder!" said the goddess Diana. "I shall send an arrow through his heart, or change him into a stag, as I did Actaeon,* if he peeps from behind the trees!"

"Me take his scalp!" cried the Indian chief, brandishing his tomahawk, and cutting a great caper in the air.

"I'll root him in the earth, with a spell that I have at my tongue's end!" squeaked Moll Pitcher. "And the green moss shall grow all over him, before he gets free again!"

"The voice was Miles Coverdale's," said the fiendish fiddler, with a whisk of his tail and a toss of his horns. "My music has brought him hither. He is always ready to dance to the devil's tune!"

Thus put on the right track, they all recognized the voice at once, and set up a simultaneous shout.

"Miles! Miles! Miles Coverdale, where are you?" they cried. "Zenobia! Queen Zenobia! Here is one of your vassals lurking in the wood. Command him to approach, and pay his duty!"

The whole fantastic rabble forthwith streamed off in pursuit of me, so that I was like a mad poet hunted by chimaeras. Having fairly the start of them, however, I succeeded in making my escape, and soon left their merriment and riot at a good distance in the rear. Its fainter tones assumed a kind of mournfulness, and were finally lost in the hush and solemnity of the wood. In my haste, I stumbled over a heap of logs and sticks that had been cut for firewood, a great while ago, by some former possessor of the soil, and piled up square, in order to be carted or sledded away to the farm-house. But, being forgotten, they had lain there, perhaps fifty years, and possibly much longer; until, by the accumulation of moss, and the leaves falling over them and decaying there, from autumn to autumn, a green mound was formed, in which the softened outline of the wood-pile was still perceptible. In the fitful mood that then swayed my mind, I found something strangely affecting in this simple circumstance. I imagined the long-dead woodman, and his long-dead wife and children, coming out of their chill graves, and essaying to make a fire with this heap of mossy fuel!

From this spot I strayed onward, quite lost in reverie, and neither knew nor cared whither I was going, until a low, soft, well-remembered voice spoke, at a little distance.

"There is Mr. Coverdale!"

"Miles Coverdale!" said another voice—and its tones were very stern—"Let him come forward, then!"

"Yes, Mr. Coverdale," cried a woman's voice—clear and melodious, but, just then, with something unnatural in its chord—"You are welcome! But you come half-an-hour too late, and have missed a scene which you would have enjoyed!"

I looked up, and found myself nigh Eliot's pulpit, at the base of which sat Hollingsworth, with Priscilla at his feet, and Zenobia standing before them.

XXV

THE THREE TOGETHER

HOLLINGSWORTH was in his ordinary working-
dress. Priscilla wore a pretty and simple gown, with
a kerchief about her neck, and a calash,* which she
had flung back from her head, leaving it suspended by the
strings. But Zenobia (whose part among the masquers, as
may be supposed, was no inferior one) appeared in a costume
of fanciful magnificence, with her jewelled flower as the
central ornament of what resembled a leafy crown, or coronet.
She represented the Oriental princess, by whose name we
were accustomed to know her. Her attitude was free and
noble, yet, if a queen's, it was not that of a queen triumphant,
but dethroned, on trial for her life, or perchance condemned,
already. The spirit of the conflict seemed, nevertheless, to
be alive in her. Her eyes were on fire; her cheeks had each a
crimson spot, so exceedingly vivid, and marked with so definite an outline, that I at first doubted whether it were not
artificial. In a very brief space, however, this idea was shamed
by the paleness that ensued, as the blood sank suddenly away.
Zenobia now looked like marble.

One always feels the fact, in an instant, when he has
intruded on those who love, or those who hate, at some acme
of their passion that puts them into a sphere of their own,
where no other spirit can pretend to stand on equal ground

with them. I was confused—affected even with a species of terror—and wished myself away. The intentness of their feelings gave them the exclusive property of the soil and atmosphere, and left me no right to be or breathe there.

"'Hollingsworth—Zenobia—I have just returned to Blithedale," said I, "and had no thought of finding you here. We shall meet again at the house. I will retire."

"This place is free to you," answered Hollingsworth.

"As free as to ourselves," added Zenobia. "This long while past, you have been following up your game, groping for human emotions in the dark corners of the heart. Had you been here a little sooner, you might have seen them dragged into the daylight. I could even wish to have my trial over again, with you standing by, to see fair-play! Do you know, Mr. Coverdale, I have been on trial for my life?"

She laughed, while speaking thus. But, in truth, as my eyes wandered from one of the group to another, I saw in Hollingsworth all that an artist could desire for the grim portrait of a Puritan magistrate, holding inquest of life and death in a case of witchcraft;—in Zenobia, the sorceress herself, not aged, wrinkled, and decrepit, but fair enough to tempt Satan with a force reciprocal to his own;—and, in Priscilla, the pale victim, whose soul and body had been wasted by her spells. Had a pile of faggots been heaped against the rock, this hint of impending doom would have completed the suggestive picture.

"It was too hard upon me," continued Zenobia, addressing Hollingsworth, "that judge, jury, and accuser, should all be comprehended in one man! I demur, as I think the lawyers say, to the jurisdiction. But let the learned Judge Coverdale seat himself on the top of the rock, and you and me stand at its base, side by side, pleading our cause before him! There might, at least, be two criminals, instead of one."

"You forced this on me," replied Hollingsworth, looking her sternly in the face. "Did I call you hither from among the masqueraders yonder? Do I assume to be your judge? No; except so far as I have an unquestionable right of judgment, in order to settle my own line of behavior towards those, with whom the events of life bring me in contact. True; I have already judged you, but not on the world's part—neither do I pretend to pass a sentence!"

"Ah, this is very good!" said Zenobia, with a smile. "What strange beings you men are, Mr. Coverdale!—is it not so? It is the simplest thing in the world, with you, to bring a woman before your secret tribunals, and judge and condemn her, unheard, and then tell her to go free without a sentence. The misfortune is, that this same secret tribunal chances to be the only judgment-seat that a true woman stands in awe of, and that any verdict short of acquittal is equivalent to a death-sentence!"

The more I looked at them, and the more I heard, the stronger grew my impression that a crisis had just come and gone. On Hollingsworth's brow, it had left a stamp like that of irrevocable doom, of which his own will was the instrument. In Zenobia's whole person, beholding her more closely, I saw a riotous agitation; the almost delirious disquietude of a great struggle, at the close of which, the vanquished one felt her strength and courage still mighty within her, and longed to renew the contest. My sensations were as if I had come upon a battle-field, before the smoke was as yet cleared away.

And what subjects had been discussed here? All, no doubt, that, for so many months past, had kept my heart and my imagination idly feverish. Zenobia's whole character and history; the true nature of her mysterious connection with Westervelt; her later purposes towards Hollingsworth, and, reciprocally, his in reference to her; and, finally, the degree in which Zenobia had been cognizant of the plot against Priscilla, and what, at last, had been the real object of that scheme. On these points, as before, I was left to my own conjectures. One thing, only, was certain. Zenobia and Hollingsworth were friends no longer. If their heart-strings were ever intertwined, the knot had been adjudged an entanglement, and was now violently broken.

But Zenobia seemed unable to rest content with the matter, in the posture which it had assumed.

"Ah! Do we part so?" exclaimed she, seeing Hollingsworth about to retire.

"And why not?" said he, with almost rude abruptness. "What is there further to be said between us?"

"Well; perhaps nothing!" answered Zenobia, looking him in the face, and smiling. "But we have come, many times before, to this gray rock, and we have talked very softly, among the whisperings of the birch-trees. They were pleasant hours! I love to make the latest of them, though not altogether so delightful, loiter away as slowly as may be. And, besides, you have put many queries to me, at this, which you design to be our last interview; and being driven, as I must acknowledge, into a corner, I have responded with reasonable frankness. But, now, with your free consent, I desire the privilege of asking a few questions in my turn."

"I have no concealments," said Hollingsworth.

"We shall see!" answered Zenobia. "I would first inquire, whether you have supposed me to be wealthy?"

"On that point," observed Hollingsworth, "I have had the opinion which the world holds."

"And I held it, likewise," said Zenobia. "Had I not, Heaven is my witness, the knowledge should have been as free to you as me. It is only three days since I knew the strange fact that threatens to make me poor; and your own acquaintance with it, I suspect, is of at least as old a date. I fancied myself affluent. You are aware, too, of the disposition which I purposed making of the larger portion of my imaginary opulence;—nay, were it all, I had not hesitated. Let me ask you further, did

I ever propose or intimate any terms of compact, on which depended this—as the world would consider it—so important sacrifice?"

"You certainly spoke of none," said Hollingsworth.

"Nor meant any," she responded. "I was willing to realize your dream, freely—generously, as some might think—but, at all events, fully—and heedless though it should prove the ruin of my fortune. If, in your own thoughts, you have imposed any conditions of this expenditure, it is you that must be held responsible for whatever is sordid and unworthy in them. And, now, one other question! Do you love this girl?"

"Oh, Zenobia!" exclaimed Priscilla, shrinking back, as if longing for the rock to topple over, and hide her.

"Do you love her?" repeated Zenobia.

"Had you asked me that question, a short time since," replied Hollingsworth, after a pause, during which, it seemed to me, even the birch-trees held their whispering breath, "I should have told you—'No!' My feelings for Priscilla differed little from those of an elder brother, watching tenderly over the gentle sister whom God has given him to protect."

"And what is your answer, now?" persisted Zenobia.

"I do love her!" said Hollingsworth, uttering the words with a deep, inward breath, instead of speaking them outright. "As well declare it thus, as in any other way. I do love her!"

"Now, God be judge between us," cried Zenobia, breaking into sudden passion, "which of us two has most mortally offended Him! At least, I am a woman—with every fault, it may be, that a woman ever had, weak, vain, unprincipled, (like most of my sex; for our virtues, when we have any, are merely impulsive and intuitive,) passionate, too, and pursuing my foolish and unattainable ends, by indirect and cunning, though absurdly chosen means, as an hereditary bond-slave must—false, moreover, to the whole circle of good, in my reckless truth to the little good I saw before me—but still a woman! A creature, whom only a little change of earthly fortune, a little kinder smile of Him who sent me hither, and one true heart to encourage and direct me, might have made all that a woman can be! But how is it with you? Are you a man? No; but a monster! A cold, heartless, self-beginning and self-ending piece of mechanism!"

"With what, then, do you charge me?" asked Hollingsworth, aghast, and greatly disturbed at this attack. "Show me one selfish end in all I ever aimed at, and you may cut it out of my bosom with a knife!"

"It is all self!" answered Zenobia, with still intenser bitterness. "Nothing else; nothing but self, self, self! The fiend, I doubt not, has made his choicest mirth of you, these seven years past, and especially in the mad summer which we have spent together. I see it now! I am awake, disenchanted, disenthralled! Self, self, self! You have embodied yourself in a project. You are a better masquerader than the witches and gipsies yonder; for your disguise is a self-deception. See whither it has brought you! First, you aimed a death-blow, and a treacherous one, at this scheme of a purer and higher life, which so many noble spirits had wrought out. Then, because Coverdale could not be quite your slave, you threw him ruthlessly away. And you took me, too, into your plan, as long as there was hope of my being available, and now fling me aside again, a broken tool! But, foremost, and blackest of your sins, you stifled down your inmost consciousness!—you did a deadly wrong to your own heart!—you were ready to sacrifice this girl, whom, if God ever visibly showed a purpose, He put into your charge, and through whom He was striving to redeem you!"

"This is a woman's view," said Hollingsworth, growing deadly pale—"a woman's, whose whole sphere of action is in the heart, and who can conceive of no higher nor wider one!"

"Be silent!" cried Zenobia, imperiously. "You know neither man nor woman! The utmost that can be said in your behalf—and because I would not be wholly despicable in my own eyes, but would fain excuse my wasted feelings, nor own it wholly a delusion, therefore I say it—is, that a great and rich heart has been ruined in your breast. Leave me, now! You have done with me, and I with you. Farewell!"

"Priscilla," said Hollingsworth, "come!"

Zenobia smiled; possibly, I did so too. Not often, in human life, has a gnawing sense of injury found a sweeter morsel of revenge, than was conveyed in the tone with which Hollingsworth spoke those two words. It was the abased and tremulous tone of a man, whose faith in himself was shaken, and who sought, at last, to lean on an affection. Yes; the strong man bowed himself, and rested on this poor Priscilla. Oh, could she have failed him, what a triumph for the lookers-on!

And, at first, I half imagined that she was about to fail him. She rose up, stood shivering, like the birch-leaves that trembled over her head, and then slowly tottered, rather than walked, towards Zenobia. Arriving at her feet, she sank down there, in the very same attitude which she had assumed on their first meeting, in the kitchen of the old farm-house. Zenobia remembered it.

"Ah, Priscilla," said she, shaking her head, "how much is changed since then! You kneel to a dethroned princess. You, the victorious one! But he is waiting for you. Say what you wish, and leave me."

"We are sisters!" gasped Priscilla.

I fancied that I understood the word and action; it meant the offering of herself, and all she had, to be at Zenobia's disposal. But the latter would not take it thus.

"True; we are sisters!" she replied; and, moved by the sweet word, she stooped down and kissed Priscilla—but not lovingly;

for a sense of fatal harm, received through her, seemed to be lurking in Zenobia's heart—"We had one father! You knew it from the first; I, but a little while—else some things, that have chanced, might have been spared you. But I never wished you harm. You stood between me and an end which I desired. I wanted a clear path. No matter what I meant. It is over now. Do you forgive me?"

"Oh, Zenobia," sobbed Priscilla, "it is I that feel like the guilty one!"

"No, no, poor little thing!" said Zenobia, with a sort of contempt. "You have been my evil fate; but there never was a babe with less strength or will to do an injury. Poor child! Methinks you have but a melancholy lot before you, sitting all alone in that wide, cheerless heart, where, for aught you know—and as I, alas! believe—the fire which you have kindled may soon go out. Ah, the thought makes me shiver for you! What will you do, Priscilla, when you find no spark among the ashes?"

"Die!" she answered.

"That was well said!" responded Zenobia, with an approving smile. "There is all a woman in your little compass, my poor sister. Meanwhile, go with him, and live!"

She waved her away, with a queenly gesture, and turned her own face to the rock. I watched Priscilla, wondering what judgment she would pass, between Zenobia and Hollingsworth; how interpret his behavior, so as to reconcile it with true faith both towards her sister and herself; how compel her love for him to keep any terms whatever with her sisterly affection! But, in truth, there was no such difficulty as I imagined. Her engrossing love made it all clear. Hollingsworth could have no fault. That was the one principle at the centre of the universe. And the doubtful guilt or possible integrity of other people, appearances, self-evident facts, the testimony of her own senses—even Hollingsworth's self-accusation, had he volunteered it—would have weighed not the value of a mote of thistle-down, on the other side. So secure was she of his right, that she never thought of comparing it with another's wrong, but left the latter to itself.

Hollingsworth drew her arm within his, and soon disappeared with her among the trees. I cannot imagine how Zenobia knew when they were out of sight; she never glanced again towards them. But, retaining a proud attitude, so long as they might have thrown back a retiring look, they were no sooner departed—utterly departed—than she began slowly to sink down. It was as if a great, invisible, irresistible weight were pressing her to the earth. Settling upon her knees, she leaned her forehead against the rock, and sobbed convulsively; dry sobs, they seemed to be, such as have nothing to do with tears.

XXVI

ZENOBIA AND COVERDALE

ENOBIA had entirely forgotten me. She fancied herself alone with her great grief. And had it been only a common pity that I felt for her—the pity that her proud nature would have repelled, as the one worst wrong which the world yet held in reserve—the sacredness and awfulness of the crisis might have impelled me to steal away, silently, so that not a dry leaf should rustle under my feet. I would have left her to struggle, in that solitude, with only the eye of God upon her. But, so it happened, I never once dreamed of questioning my right to be there, now, as I had questioned it, just before, when I came so suddenly upon Hollingsworth and herself, in the passion of their recent debate. It suits me not to explain what was the analogy that I saw, or imagined, between Zenobia's situation and mine; nor, I believe, will the reader detect this one secret, hidden beneath many a revelation which perhaps concerned me less. In simple truth, however, as Zenobia leaned her forehead against the rock, shaken with that tearless agony, it seemed to me that the self-same pang, with hardly mitigated torment, leaped thrilling from her heart-strings to my own. Was it wrong, therefore, if I felt myself consecrated to the priesthood, by sympathy like this, and called upon to minister to this woman's affliction, so far as mortal could?

But, indeed, what could mortal do for her? Nothing! The attempt would be a mockery and an anguish. Time, it is true, would steal away her grief, and bury it, and the best of her heart in the same grave. But Destiny itself, methought, in its kindliest mood, could do no better for Zenobia, in the way of quick relief, than to cause the impending rock to impend a little further, and fall upon her head. So I leaned against a tree, and listened to her sobs, in unbroken silence. She was half prostrate, half kneeling, with her forehead still pressed against the rock. Her sobs were the only sound; she did not groan, nor give any other utterance to her distress. It was all involuntary.

At length, she sat up, put back her hair, and stared about her with a bewildered aspect, as if not distinctly recollecting the scene through which she had passed, nor cognizant of the situation in which it left her. Her face and brow were almost purple with the rush of blood. They whitened, however, by-and-by, and, for some time, retained this deathlike hue. She put her hand to her forehead, with a gesture that made me forcibly conscious of an intense and living pain there.

Her glance, wandering wildly to-and-fro, passed over me, several times, without appearing to inform her of my presence. But, finally, a look of recognition gleamed from her eyes into mine.

"Is it you, Miles Coverdale?" said she, smiling. "Ah, I perceive what you are about! You are turning this whole affair into a ballad. Pray let me hear as many stanzas as you happen to have ready!"

"Oh, hush, Zenobia!" I answered. "Heaven knows what an ache is in my soul!"

"It is genuine tragedy, is it not?" rejoined Zenobia, with a sharp, light laugh. "And you are willing to allow, perhaps, that I have had hard measure. But it is a woman's doom, and I have deserved it like a woman; so let there be no pity, as, on my part, there shall be no complaint. It is all right now, or will shortly be so. But, Mr. Coverdale, by all means, write this ballad, and put your soul's ache into it, and turn your sympathy to good account, as other poets do, and as poets must, unless they choose to give us glittering icicles instead of lines of fire. As for the moral, it shall be distilled into the final stanza, in a drop of bitter honey."

"What shall it be, Zenobia?" I inquired, endeavoring to fall in with her mood.

"Oh, a very old one will serve the purpose," she replied. "There are no new truths, much as we have prided ourselves on finding some. A moral? Why, this:—that, in the battle-field of life, the downright stroke, that would fall only on a man's steel head-piece, is sure to light on a woman's heart, over which she wears no breastplate, and whose wisdom it is, therefore, to keep out of the conflict. Or this:—that the whole universe, her own sex and yours, and Providence, or Destiny, to boot, make common cause against the woman who swerves one hair's breadth out of the beaten track. Yes; and add, (for I may as well own it, now,) that, with that one hair's breadth, she goes all astray, and never sees the world in its true aspect, afterwards!"

"This last is too stern a moral," I observed. "Cannot we soften it a little?"

"Do it, if you like, at your own peril, not on my responsi-bility," she answered; then, with a sudden change of subject, she went on:—"After all, he has flung away what would have served him better than the poor, pale flower he kept. What can Priscilla do for him? Put passionate warmth into his heart, when it shall be chilled with frozen hopes? Strengthen his hands, when they are weary with much doing and no per-formance? No; but only tend towards him with a blind, instinctive love, and hang her little, puny weakness for a clog upon his arm! She cannot even give him such sympathy as is worth the name. For will he never, in many an hour of darkness, need that proud, intellectual sympathy which he might have had from me?—the sympathy that would flash light along his course, and guide as well as cheer him? Poor Hollingsworth! Where will he find it now?"

"Hollingsworth has a heart of ice!" said I, bitterly. "He is a wretch!"

"Do him no wrong!" interrupted Zenobia, turning haughtily upon me. "Presume not to estimate a man like Hollingsworth! It was my fault, all along, and none of his. I see it now! He never sought me. Why should he seek me? What had I to offer him? A miserable, bruised, and battered heart, spoilt long before he met me! A life, too, hopelessly entangled with a villain's! He did well to cast me off. God be praised, he did it! And yet, had he trusted me, and borne with me a little longer, I would have saved him all this trouble."

She was silent, for a time, and stood with her eyes fixed on the ground. Again raising them, her look was more mild and calm.

"Miles Coverdale!" said she.

"Well, Zenobia!" I responded. "Can I do you any service?"

"Very little," she replied. "But it is my purpose, as you may well imagine, to remove from Blithedale; and, most likely, I may not see Hollingsworth again. A woman in my position, you understand, feels scarcely at her ease among former friends. New faces—unaccustomed looks—those only can she tolerate. She would pine, among familiar scenes; she would be apt to blush, too, under the eyes that knew her secret; her heart might throb uncomfortably; she would mortify herself, I suppose, with foolish notions of having sacrificed the honor of her sex, at the foot of proud, contumacious man. Poor womanhood, with its rights and wrongs! Here will be new matter for my course of lectures, at the idea of which you smiled, Mr. Coverdale, a month or two ago. But, as you have really a heart and sympathies, as far as they go, and as I shall depart without seeing Hollingsworth, I must entreat you to be a messenger between him and me."

"Willingly," said I, wondering at the strange way in which her mind seemed to vibrate from the deepest earnest to mere levity. "What is the message?"

"True;—what is it?" exclaimed Zenobia. "After all, I hardly know. On better consideration, I have no message. Tell him—tell him something pretty and pathetic, that will come nicely and sweetly into your ballad—anything you please, so it be tender and submissive enough. Tell him he has murdered me! Tell him that I'll haunt him!"—she spoke these words with the wildest energy—"And give him—no, give Priscilla—this!"

Thus saying, she took the jewelled flower out of her hair; and it struck me as the act of a queen, when worsted in a combat, discrowning herself, as if she found a sort of relief in abasing all her pride.

"Bid her wear this for Zenobia's sake," she continued. "She is a pretty little creature, and will make as soft and gentle a wife as the veriest Bluebeard could desire. Pity that she must fade so soon! These delicate and puny maidens always do. Ten years hence, let Hollingsworth look at my face and Priscilla's, and then choose betwixt them. Or, if he pleases, let him do it now!"

How magnificently Zenobia looked, as she said this! The effect of her beauty was even heightened by the over-consciousness and self-recognition of it, into which, I suppose, Hollingsworth's scorn had driven her. She understood the look of admiration in my face; and—Zenobia to the last— it gave her pleasure.

"It is an endless pity," said she, "that I had not bethought myself of winning your heart, Mr. Coverdale, instead of Hollingsworth's. I think I should have succeeded; and many women would have deemed you the worthier conquest of the two. You are certainly much the handsomest man. But there is a fate in these things. And beauty, in a man, has been of little account with me, since my earliest girlhood, when, for once, it turned my head. Now, farewell!"

"Zenobia, whither are you going?" I asked.

"No matter where," said she. "But I am weary of this place, and sick to death of playing at philanthropy and progress. Of all varieties of mock-life, we have surely blundered into the very emptiest mockery, in our effort to establish the one true system. I have done with it; and Blithedale must find another woman to superintend the laundry, and you, Mr. Coverdale, another nurse to make your gruel, the next time you fall ill. It was, indeed, a foolish dream! Yet it gave us some pleasant summer days, and bright hopes, while they lasted. It can do no more; nor will it avail us to shed tears over a broken bubble. Here is my hand! Adieu!"

She gave me her hand, with the same free, whole-souled gesture as on the first afternoon of our acquaintance; and being greatly moved, I bethought me of no better method of expressing my deep sympathy than to carry it to my lips. In so doing, I perceived that this white hand—so hospitably warm when I first touched it, five months since—was now cold as a veritable piece of snow.

"How very cold!" I exclaimed, holding it between both my own, with the vain idea of warming it. "What can be the reason? It is really deathlike!"

"The extremities die first, they say," answered Zenobia, laughing. "And so you kiss this poor, despised, rejected hand! Well, my dear friend, I thank you! You have reserved your homage for the fallen. Lip of man will never touch my hand again. I intend to become a Catholic, for the sake of going into a nunnery. When you next hear of Zenobia, her face will be behind the black-veil; so look your last at it now—for all is over! Once more, farewell!"

She withdrew her hand, yet left a lingering pressure, which I felt long afterwards. So intimately connected, as I had been, with perhaps the only man in whom she was ever truly interested, Zenobia looked on me as the representative of all the past, and was conscious that, in bidding me adieu, she likewise took final leave of Hollingsworth, and of this whole epoch of her life. Never did her beauty shine out more lustrously, than in the last glimpse that I had of her. She departed, and was soon hidden among the trees.

But, whether it was the strong impression of the foregoing scene, or whatever else the cause, I was affected with a fantasy that Zenobia had not actually gone, but was still hovering about the spot, and haunting it. I seemed to feel her eyes upon me. It was as if the vivid coloring of her character had left a brilliant stain upon the air. By degrees, however, the impression grew less distinct. I flung myself upon the fallen leaves, at the base of Eliot's pulpit. The sunshine withdrew up the tree-trunks, and flickered on the topmost boughs; gray twilight made the wood obscure; the stars brightened out; the pendent boughs became wet with chill autumnal dews. But I was listless, worn-out with emotion on my own behalf, and sympathy for others, and had no heart to leave my comfortless lair, beneath the rock.

I must have fallen asleep, and had a dream, all the circumstances of which utterly vanished at the moment when they converged to some tragical catastrophe, and thus grew too powerful for the thin sphere of slumber that enveloped them. Starting from the ground, I found the risen moon shining upon the rugged face of the rock, and myself all in a tremble.

XXVII

MIDNIGHT

I T COULD not have been far from midnight, when I came beneath Hollingsworth's window, and finding it open, flung in a tuft of grass, with earth at the roots, and heard it fall upon the floor. He was either awake, or sleeping very lightly; for scarcely a moment had gone by, before he looked out and discerned me standing in the moonlight.

"Is it you, Coverdale?" he asked. "What is the matter?"

"Come down to me, Hollingsworth!" I answered. "I am anxious to speak with you."

The strange tone of my own voice startled me, and him, probably, no less. He lost no time, and soon issued from the house-door, with his dress half-arranged.

"Again, what is the matter?" he asked, impatiently.

"Have you seen Zenobia," said I, "since you parted from her, at Eliot's pulpit?"

"No," answered Hollingsworth; "nor did I expect it."

His voice was deep, but had a tremor in it. Hardly had he spoken, when Silas Foster thrust his head, done up in a cotton handkerchief, out of another window, and took what he called—as it literally was—a squint at us.

"Well, folks, what are ye about here?" he demanded. "Aha, are you there, Miles Coverdale? You have been turning night into day, since you left us, I reckon; and so you find it quite natural to come prowling about the house, at this time o' night, frightening my old woman out of her wits, and making her disturb a tired man out of his best nap. In with you, you vagabond, and to bed!"

"Dress yourself quietly, Foster," said I. "We want your assistance."

I could not, for the life of me, keep that strange tone out of my voice. Silas Foster, obtuse as were his sensibilities, seemed to feel the ghastly earnestness that was conveyed in it, as well as Hollingsworth did. He immediately withdrew his head, and I heard him yawning, muttering to his wife, and again yawning heavily, while he hurried on his clothes. Meanwhile, I showed Hollingsworth a delicate handkerchief, marked with a well-known cypher, and told where I had found it, and other circumstances which had filled me with a suspicion so terrible, that I left him, if he dared, to shape it out for himself. By the time my brief explanation was finished, we were joined by Silas Foster, in his blue woollen frock.

"Well, boys," cried he, peevishly, "what is to pay now?"

"Tell him, Hollingsworth!" said I.

Hollingsworth shivered, perceptibly, and drew in a hard breath betwixt his teeth. He steadied himself, however, and looking the matter more firmly in the face than I had done, explained to Foster my suspicions and the grounds of them, with a distinctness from which, in spite of my utmost efforts, my words had swerved aside. The tough-nerved yeoman, in his comment, put a finish on the business, and brought out the hideous idea in its full terror, as if he were removing the napkin from the face of a corpse.

"And so you think she's drowned herself!"*he cried.

I turned away my face.

"What on earth should the young woman do that for?" exclaimed Silas, his eyes half out of his head with mere surprise. "Why, she has more means than she can use or waste, and lacks nothing to make her comfortable, but a husband—and that's an article she could have, any day! There's some mistake about this, I tell you!"

"Come," said I, shuddering. "Let us go and ascertain the truth."

"Well, well," answered Silas Foster, "just as you say. We'll take the long pole, with the hook at the end, that serves to get the bucket out of the draw-well, when the rope is broken. With that, and a couple of long-handled hay-rakes, I'll answer for finding her, if she's anywhere to be found. Strange enough! Zenobia drown herself! No, no, I don't believe it. She had too much sense, and too much means, and enjoyed life a great deal too well."

When our few preparations were completed, we hastened, by a shorter than the customary route, through fields and pastures, and across a portion of the meadow, to the particular spot, on the river-bank, which I had paused to contemplate, in the course of my afternoon's ramble. A nameless presentiment had again drawn me thither, after leaving Eliot's pulpit. I showed my companions where I had found the handkerchief, and pointed to two or three footsteps, impressed into the clayey margin, and tending towards the water. Beneath its shallow verge, among the water-weeds, there were further traces, as yet unobliterated by the sluggish current, which was there almost at a stand-still. Silas Foster thrust his face down close to these footsteps, and picked up a shoe, that had escaped my observation, being half imbedded in the mud.

"There's a kid-shoe that never was made on a Yankee last," observed he. "I know enough of shoemaker's craft to tell that. French manufacture; and see what a high instep!—and how evenly she trod in it! There never was a woman that stept handsomer in her shoes than Zenobia did. Here," he added, addressing Hollingsworth, "would you like to keep the shoe?"

Hollingsworth started back.

"Give it to me, Foster," said I.

I dabbled it in the water, to rinse off the mud, and have
kept it ever since. Not far from this spot, lay an old, leaky
punt, drawn up on the oozy river-side, and generally half-full
of water. It served the angler to go in quest of pickerel, or
the sportsman to pick up his wild-ducks. Setting this crazy
barque afloat, I seated myself in the stern, with the paddle,
while Hollingsworth sat in the bows, with the hooked pole,
and Silas Foster amidships, with a hay-rake.

"It puts me in mind of my young days," remarked Silas,
"when I used to steal out of bed to go bobbing for horn-pouts*
and eels. Heigh-ho!—well!—life and death together make sad
work for us all. Then, I was a boy, bobbing for fish; and now
I am getting to be an old fellow, and here I be, groping for
a dead body! I tell you what, lads, if I thought anything had
really happened to Zenobia, I should feel kind o' sorrowful."

"I wish, at least, you would hold your tongue!" muttered I.

The moon, that night, though past the full, was still large
and oval, and having risen between eight and nine o'clock,
now shone aslantwise over the river, throwing the high, opposite bank, with its woods, into deep shadow, but lighting up
the hither shore pretty effectually. Not a ray appeared to fall
on the river itself. It lapsed imperceptibly away, a broad,
black, inscrutable depth, keeping its own secrets from the
eye of man, as impenetrably as mid-ocean could.

"Well, Miles Coverdale," said Foster, "you are the helms-
man. How do you mean to manage this business?"

"I shall let the boat drift, broadside foremost, past that
stump," I replied. "I know the bottom, having sounded it in
fishing. The shore, on this side, after the first step or two,
goes off very abruptly; and there is a pool, just by the stump,
twelve or fifteen feet deep. The current could not have force
enough to sweep any sunken object—even if partially buoyant
—out of that hollow."

"Come, then," said Silas. "But I doubt whether I can
touch bottom with this hay-rake, if it's as deep as you say.

Mr. Hollingsworth, I think you'll be the lucky man, to-night, such luck as it is!"

We floated past the stump. Silas Foster plied his rake manfully, poking it as far as he could into the water, and immersing the whole length of his arm besides. Hollingsworth at first sat motionless, with the hooked-pole elevated in the air. But, by-and-by, with a nervous and jerky movement, he began to plunge it into the blackness that upbore us, setting his teeth, and making precisely such thrusts, methought, as if he were stabbing at a deadly enemy. I bent over the side of the boat. So obscure, however, so awfully mysterious, was that dark stream, that—and the thought made me shiver like a leaf—I might as well have tried to look into the enigma of the eternal world, to discover what had become of Zenobia's soul, as into the river's depths, to find her body. And there, perhaps, she lay, with her face upward, while the shadow of the boat, and my own pale face peering downward, passed slowly betwixt her and the sky.

Once, twice, thrice, I paddled the boat up stream, and again suffered it to glide, with the river's slow, funereal motion, downward. Silas Foster had raked up a large mass of stuff, which, as it came towards the surface, looked somewhat like a flowing garment, but proved to be a monstrous tuft of water-weeds. Hollingsworth, with a gigantic effort, upheaved a sunken log. When once free of the bottom, it rose partly out of water—all weedy and slimy, a devilish-looking object, which the moon had not shone upon for half a hundred years —then plunged again, and sullenly returned to its old resting-place, for the remnant of the century.

"That looked ugly!" quoth Silas. "I half thought it was the Evil One on the same errand as ourselves—searching for Zenobia!"

"He shall never get her!" said I, giving the boat a strong impulse.

"That's not for you to say, my boy!" retorted the yeoman. "Pray God he never has, and never may! Slow work this, however! I should really be glad to find something. Pshaw! What a notion that is, when the only good-luck would be, to paddle, and drift and poke, and grope, hereabouts, till morning, and have our labor for our pains! For my part, I shouldn't wonder if the creature had only lost her shoe in the mud, and saved her soul alive, after all. My stars, how she will laugh at us, tomorrow morning!"

It is indescribable what an image of Zenobia—at the breakfast-table, full of warm and mirthful life—this surmise of Silas Foster's brought before my mind. The terrible phantasm of her death was thrown by it into the remotest and dimmest back-ground, where it seemed to grow as improbable as a myth.

"Yes, Silas; it may be as you say!" cried I.

The drift of the stream had again borne us a little below the stump, when I felt—yes, felt, for it was as if the iron hook had smote my breast—felt Hollingsworth's pole strike some object at the bottom of the river. He started up, and almost overset the boat.

"Hold on!" cried Foster. "You have her!"

Putting a fury of strength into the effort, Hollingsworth heaved amain, and up came a white swash to the surface of the river. It was the flow of a woman's garments. A little higher, and we saw her dark hair, streaming down the current. Black River of Death, thou hadst yielded up thy victim Zenobia was found!

Silas Foster laid hold of the body—Hollingsworth, likewise, grappled with it—and I steered towards the bank, gazing, all the while, at Zenobia, whose limbs were swaying in the current, close at the boat's side. Arriving near the shore, we all three stept into the water, bore her out, and laid her on the ground, beneath a tree.

"Poor child!" said Foster—and his dry old heart, I verily believe, vouchsafed a tear—"I'm sorry for her!"

Were I to describe the perfect horror of the spectacle, the reader might justly reckon it to me for a sin and shame. For more than twelve long years I have borne it in my memory, and could now reproduce it as freshly as if it were still before my eyes. Of all modes of death, methinks it is the ugliest. Her wet garments swathed limbs of terrible inflexibility. She was the marble image of a death-agony. Her arms had grown rigid in the act of struggling, and were bent before her, with clenched hands; her knees, too, were bent, and—thank God for it!—in the attitude of prayer. Ah, that rigidity! It is impossible to bear the terror of it. It seemed—I must needs impart so much of my own miserable idea—it seemed as if her body must keep the same position in the coffin, and that her skeleton would keep it in the grave, and that when Zenobia rose, at the Day of Judgment, it would be in just the same attitude as now!

One hope I had; and that, too, was mingled half with fear. She knelt, as if in prayer. With the last, choking consciousness, her soul, bubbling out through her lips, it may be, had given itself up to the Father, reconciled and penitent. But her arms! They were bent before her, as if she struggled against Providence in never-ending hostility. Her hands! They were clenched in immitigable defiance. Away with the hideous thought! The flitting moment, after Zenobia sank into the dark pool—when her breath was gone, and her soul at her lips—was as long, in its capacity of God's infinite forgiveness, as the lifetime of the world.

Foster bent over the body, and carefully examined it.

"You have wounded the poor thing's breast," said he to Hollingsworth. "Close by her heart, too!"

"Ha!" cried Hollingsworth, with a start.

And so he had, indeed, both before and after death.

"See!" said Foster. "That's the place where the iron struck her. It looks cruelly, but she never felt it!"

He endeavored to arrange the arms of the corpse decently by its side. His utmost strength, however, scarcely sufficed to bring them down; and rising again, the next instant, they bade him defiance, exactly as before. He made another effort, with the same result.

"In God's name, Silas Foster," cried I, with bitter indignation, "let that dead woman alone!"

"Why, man, it's not decent!" answered he, staring at me in amazement. "I can't bear to see her looking so! Well, well," added he, after a third effort, "'tis of no use, sure enough; and we must leave the women to do their best with her, after we get to the house. The sooner that's done, the better."

We took two rails from a neighboring fence, and formed a bier by laying across some boards from the bottom of the boat. And thus we bore Zenobia homeward. Six hours before, how beautiful! At midnight, what a horror! A reflection occurs to me, that will show ludicrously, I doubt not, on my page, but must come in, for its sterling truth. Being the woman that she was, could Zenobia have foreseen all these ugly circumstances of death, how ill it would become her, the altogether unseemly aspect which she must put on, and, especially, old Silas Foster's efforts to improve the matter, she would no more have committed the dreadful act, than have exhibited herself to a public assembly in a badly-fitting garment! Zenobia, I have often thought, was not quite simple in her death. She had seen pictures, I suppose, of drowned persons, in lithe and graceful attitudes. And she deemed it well and decorous to die as so many village-maidens have, wronged in their first-love, and seeking peace in the bosom of the old, familiar stream—so familiar that they could not dread it—where, in childhood, they used to bathe their little feet, wading mid-leg deep, unmindful of wet skirts. But, in Zenobia's case, there was some tint of the Arcadian affectation that had been visible enough in all our lives, for a few months past.

This, however, to my conception, takes nothing from the tragedy. For, has not the world come to an awfully sophisticated pass, when, after a certain degree of acquaintance with it, we cannot even put ourselves to death in whole-hearted simplicity?

Slowly, slowly, with many a dreary pause—resting the bier often on some rock, or balancing it across a mossy log, to take fresh hold—we bore our burthen onward, through the moonlight, and, at last, laid Zenobia on the floor of the old farm-house. By-and-by, came three or four withered women, and stood whispering around the corpse, peering at it through their spectacles, holding up their skinny hands, shaking their night-capt heads, and taking counsel of one another's experience what was to be done.

With those tire-women,* we left Zenobia!

XXVIII

BLITHEDALE-PASTURE

BLITHEDALE, thus far in its progress, had never found the necessity of a burial-ground. There was some consultation among us, in what spot Zenobia might most fitly be laid. It was my own wish, that she should sleep at the base of Eliot's pulpit, and that, on the rugged front of the rock, the name by which we familiarly knew her— ZENOBIA—and not another word, should be deeply cut, and left for the moss and lichens to fill up, at their long leisure. But Hollingsworth (to whose ideas, on this point, great deference was due) made it his request that her grave might be dug on the gently sloping hill-side, in the wide pasture, where, as we once supposed, Zenobia and he had planned to build their cottage. And thus it was done, accordingly.

She was buried very much as other people have been, for hundreds of years gone by. In anticipation of a death, we Blithedale colonists had sometimes set our fancies at work to arrange a funereal ceremony, which should be the proper symbolic expression of our spiritual faith and eternal hopes; and this we meant to substitute for those customary rites, which were moulded originally out of the Gothic gloom, and, by long use, like an old velvet-pall, have so much more than their first death-smell in them. But, when the occasion came, we found it the simplest and truest thing, after all, to content ourselves with the old fashion, taking away what we could, but interpolating no novelties, and particularly avoiding all frippery of flowers and cheerful emblems. The procession moved from the farm-house. Nearest the dead walked an old man in deep mourning, his face mostly concealed in a white handkerchief, and with Priscilla leaning on his arm. Hollingsworth and myself came next. We all stood around the narrow niche in the cold earth; all saw the coffin lowered in; all heard the rattle of the crumbly soil upon its lid—that final sound, which mortality awakens on the utmost verge of sense, as if in the vain hope of bringing an echo from the spiritual world.

I noticed a stranger—a stranger to most of those present, though known to me—who, after the coffin had descended, took up a handful of earth, and flung it first into the grave. I had given up Hollingsworth's arm, and now found myself near this man.

"It was an idle thing—a foolish thing—for Zenobia to do!" said he. "She was the last woman in the world to whom death could have been necessary. It was too absurd! I have no patience with her."

"Why so?" I inquired, smothering my horror at his cold comment in my eager curiosity to discover some tangible truth, as to his relation with Zenobia. "If any crisis could justify the sad wrong she offered to herself, it was surely that in which she stood. Everything had failed her—prosperity, in the world's sense, for her opulence was gone—the heart's prosperity, in love. And there was a secret burthen on her, the nature of which is best known to you. Young as she was, she had tried life fully, had no more to hope, and something, perhaps, to fear. Had Providence taken her away in its own holy hand, I should have thought it the kindest dispensation that could be awarded to one so wrecked."

"You mistake the matter completely," rejoined Westervelt.

"What, then, is your own view of it?" I asked.

"Her mind was active, and various in its powers," said he; "her heart had a manifold adaptation; her constitution an infinite buoyancy, which (had she possessed only a little patience to await the reflux of her troubles) would have borne her upward, triumphantly, for twenty years to come. Her beauty would not have waned—or scarcely so, and surely not beyond the reach of art to restore it—in all that time. She had life's summer all before her, and a hundred varieties of brilliant success. What an actress Zenobia might have been! It was one of her least valuable capabilities. How forcibly she might have wrought upon the world, either directly in her own person, or by her influence upon some man, or a series of men, of controlling genius! Every prize that could be worth a woman's having—and many prizes which other women are too timid to desire—lay within Zenobia's reach."

"In all this," I observed, "there would have been nothing to satisfy her heart."

"Her heart!" answered Westervelt, contemptuously. "That troublesome organ (as she had hitherto found it) would have been kept in its due place and degree, and have had all the gratification it could fairly claim. She would soon have established a control over it. Love had failed her, you say! Had it never failed her before? Yet she survived it, and loved again—possibly, not once alone, nor twice either. And now to drown herself for yonder dreamy philanthropist!"

"Who are you," I exclaimed, indignantly, "that dare to speak thus of the dead? You seem to intend a eulogy, yet leave out whatever was noblest in her, and blacken, while you mean to praise. I have long considered you as Zenobia's evil fate. Your sentiments confirm me in the idea, but leave me still ignorant as to the mode in which you have influenced her life. The connection may have been indissoluble, except by death. Then, indeed—always in the hope of God's infinite mercy—I cannot deem it a misfortune that she sleeps in yonder grave!"

"No matter what I was to her," he answered, gloomily, yet without actual emotion. "She is now beyond my reach. Had she lived, and hearkened to my counsels, we might have served each other well. But there Zenobia lies, in yonder pit, with the dull earth over her. Twenty years of a brilliant lifetime thrown away for a mere woman's whim!"

Heaven deal with Westervelt according to his nature and deserts!—that is to say, annihilate him. He was altogether earthy, worldly, made for time and its gross objects, and incapable—except by a sort of dim reflection, caught from other minds—of so much as one spiritual idea. Whatever stain Zenobia had, was caught from him; nor does it seldom happen that a character of admirable qualities loses its better life, because the atmosphere, that should sustain it, is rendered poisonous by such breath as this man mingled with Zenobia's. Yet his reflections possessed their share of truth. It was a woful thought, that a woman of Zenobia's diversified capacity should have fancied herself irretrievably defeated on the broad battle-field of life, and with no refuge, save to fall on her own sword, merely because Love had gone against her. It is nonsense, and a miserable wrong—the result, like so many others, of masculine egotism—that the success or failure of woman's existence should be made to depend wholly on the affections, and on one species of affection; while man has such a multitude of other chances, that this seems but an incident. For its own sake, if it will do no more, the world should throw open all its avenues to the passport of a woman's bleeding heart.

As we stood around the grave, I looked often towards Priscilla, dreading to see her wholly overcome with grief. And deeply grieved, in truth, she was. But a character, so simply constituted as hers, has room only for a single predominant affection. No other feeling can touch the heart's inmost core, nor do it any deadly mischief. Thus, while we see that such a being responds to every breeze, with tremulous vibration, and imagine that she must be shattered by the first rude blast, we find her retaining her equilibrium amid shocks that might have overthrown many a sturdier frame. So with Priscilla! Her one possible misfortune was Hollingsworth's unkindness; and that was destined never to befall her—never yet, at least—for Priscilla has not died.

But, Hollingsworth! After all the evil that he did, are we to leave him thus, blest with the entire devotion of this one true heart, and with wealth at his disposal, to execute the long contemplated project that had led him so far astray? What retribution is there here? My mind being vexed with precisely this query, I made a journey, some years since, for the sole purpose of catching a last glimpse at Hollingsworth, and judging for myself whether he were a happy man or no. I learned that he inhabited a small cottage, that his way of life was exceedingly retired, and that my only chance of encountering him or Priscilla was, to meet them in a secluded lane, where, in the latter part of the afternoon, they were accustomed to walk. I did meet them, accordingly. As they approached me, I observed in Hollingsworth's face a depressed and melancholy look, that seemed habitual; the powerfully built man showed a self-distrustful weakness, and a childlike, or childish, tendency to press close, and closer still, to the side of the slender woman whose arm was within his. In Priscilla's manner, there was a protective and watchful quality, as if she felt herself the guardian of her companion, but, likewise, a deep, submissive, unquestioning reverence, and also a veiled happiness in her fair and quiet countenance.

Drawing nearer, Priscilla recognized me, and gave me a kind and friendly smile, but with a slight gesture which I could not help interpreting as an entreaty not to make myself known to Hollingsworth. Nevertheless, an impulse took possession of me, and compelled me to address him.

"I have come, Hollingsworth," said I, "to view your grand edifice for the reformation of criminals. Is it finished yet?"

"No—nor begun!" answered he, without raising his eyes. "A very small one answers all my purposes."

Priscilla threw me an upbraiding glance. But I spoke again, with a bitter and revengeful emotion, as if flinging a poisoned arrow at Hollingsworth's heart.

"Up to this moment," I inquired, "how many criminals have you reformed?"

"Not one!" said Hollingsworth, with his eyes still fixed on the ground. "Ever since we parted, I have been busy with a single murderer!"

Then the tears gushed into my eyes, and I forgave him. For I remembered the wild energy, the passionate shriek, with which Zenobia had spoken those words—'Tell him he has murdered me! Tell him that I'll haunt him!'—and I knew what murderer he meant, and whose vindictive shadow dogged the side where Priscilla was not.

The moral which presents itself to my reflections, as drawn from Hollingsworth's character and errors, is simply this:—that, admitting what is called Philanthropy, when adopted as a profession, to be often useful by its energetic impulse to society at large, it is perilous to the individual, whose ruling passion, in one exclusive channel, it thus becomes. It ruins, or is fearfully apt to ruin, the heart; the rich juices of which God never meant should be pressed violently out, and distilled into alcoholic liquor, by an unnatural process; but should render life sweet, bland, and gently beneficent, and insensibly influence other hearts and other lives to the same blessed end. I see in Hollingsworth an exemplification of the most awful truth in Bunyan's book* of such;—from the very gate of Heaven, there is a by-way to the pit!

But, all this while, we have been standing by Zenobia's grave. I have never since beheld it, but make no question that the grass grew all the better, on that little parallelogram of pasture-land, for the decay of the beautiful woman who slept beneath. How much Nature seems to love us! And how readily, nevertheless, without a sigh or a complaint, she converts us to a meaner purpose, when her highest one—that of conscious, intellectual life, and sensibility—has been untimely baulked! While Zenobia lived, Nature was proud of her, and directed all eyes upon that radiant presence, as her fairest handiwork. Zenobia perished. Will not Nature shed a tear? Ah, no! She adopts the calamity at once into her system, and is just as well pleased, for aught we can see, with the tuft of ranker vegetation that grew out of Zenobia's heart, as with all the beauty which has bequeathed us no earthly representative, except in this crop of weeds. It is because the spirit is inestimable, that the lifeless body is so little valued.

that we had struck upon what ought to be a truth. Posterity may dig it up, and profit by it. The experiment, so far as its original projectors were concerned, proved long ago a failure, first lapsing into Fourierism, and dying, as it well deserved, for this infidelity to its own higher spirit. Where once we toiled with our whole hopeful hearts, the town-paupers, aged, nerveless, and disconsolate, creep sluggishly afield. Alas, what faith is requisite to bear up against such results of generous effort!

My subsequent life has passed—I was going to say, happily—but, at all events, tolerably enough. I am now at middle-age—well, well, a step or two beyond the midmost point, and I care not a fig who knows it!—a bachelor, with no very decided purpose of ever being otherwise. I have been twice to Europe, and spent a year or two, rather agreeably, at each visit. Being well to do in the world, and having nobody but myself to care for, I live very much at my ease, and fare sumptuously every day. As for poetry, I have given it up, notwithstanding that Doctor Griswold*—as the reader, of course, knows—has placed me at a fair elevation among our minor minstrelsy, on the strength of my pretty little volume, published ten years ago. As regards human progress, (in spite of my irrepressible yearnings over the Blithedale reminiscences,) let them believe in it who can, and aid in it who choose! If I could earnestly do either, it might be all the better for my comfort. As Hollingsworth once told me, I lack a purpose. How strange! He was ruined, morally, by an overplus of the very same ingredient, the want of which, I occasionally suspect, has rendered my own life all an emptiness. I by no means wish to die. Yet, were there any cause, in this whole chaos of human struggle, worth a sane man's dying for, and which my death would benefit, then—provided, however, the effort did not involve an unreasonable amount of trouble—methinks I might be bold to offer up my life. If Kossuth,* for example, would pitch the battle-field of Hun-

garian rights within an easy ride of my abode, and choose a
mild, sunny morning, after breakfast, for the conflict, Miles
Coverdale would gladly be his man, for one brave rush upon
the levelled bayonets. Farther than that, I should be loth to
pledge myself.

I exaggerate my own defects. The reader must not take
my own word for it, nor believe me altogether changed from
the young man, who once hoped strenuously, and struggled,
not so much amiss. Frostier heads than mine have gained
honor in the world; frostier hearts have imbibed new warmth,
and been newly happy. Life, however, it must be owned,
has come to rather an idle pass with me. Would my friends
like to know what brought it thither? There is one secret—I
have concealed it all along, and never meant to let the least
whisper of it escape—one foolish little secret, which possibly
may have had something to do with these inactive years of
meridian manhood, with my bachelorship, with the unsatis-
fied retrospect that I fling back on life, and my listless glance
towards the future. Shall I reveal it? It is an absurd thing
for a man in his afternoon—a man of the world, moreover,
with these three white hairs in his brown moustache, and that
deepening track of a crow's foot on each temple—an absurd
thing ever to have happened, and quite the absurdest for an
old bachelor, like me, to talk about. But it rises in my throat;
so let it come.

I perceive, moreover, that the confession, brief as it shall
be, will throw a gleam of light over my behavior throughout
the foregoing incidents, and is, indeed, essential to the full
understanding of my story. The reader, therefore, since I
have disclosed so much, is entitled to this one word more. As
I write it, he will charitably suppose me to blush, and turn
away my face:—

I—I myself—was in love—with—PRISCILLA!

THE END.

EXPLANATORY NOTES

1   *Brook Farm*: co-operative community (1841–7), near West Roxbury, Mass., 9 miles from Boston. It was established by the Transcendentalist movement (see note to p. 115), but leading figures like Emerson, Channing, Alcott, and Margaret Fuller were regular visitors rather than members. Hawthorne was a founding member, residing at Brook Farm from April to November 1841.

fancy-sketch: whimsical picture.

2   *the American romancer*: Hawthorne makes similar pleas for the nature of his fiction in other prefaces, notably in *The House of the Seven Gables* (1851).

Sibylline: prophetic; from the sibyls of classical mythology.

3   *Ripley ... Dana, Dwight, Channing, Burton, Parker*: George Ripley (1802–80) was a religious thinker who founded Brook Farm on leaving his Unitarian ministry in 1841. Among the original members were Charles Dana (1819–97), later a newspaper editor; John Dwight (1813–93), a music critic, and Warren Burton (1800–60), a minister and teacher. The Channing associated with the community was the Christian socialist William Henry Channing (1810–84), rather than his uncle Ellery Channing. Theodore Parker (1810–60), another Transcendentalist, was an unorthodox Unitarian minister.

Howadji: George Curtis (1824–92), travel writer and later social reformer, attended the school at Brook Farm in the community's early years. Hawthorne refers to the pen-name used in his books *Nile Notes of a Howadji* (1851) and *The Howadji in Syria* (1852).

5   *Mr. Coverdale*: Hawthorne names his narrator after a historical figure, Miles Coverdale (1488–1568), a priest and biblical scholar who produced an important translation of the Bible into English during the reign of Henry VIII.

a phenomenon in the mesmeric line: Franz Mesmer (1734–1815), an Austrian physician, became an international celebrity after announcing his theory of 'animal magnetism' in Paris in 1778. His influence continued throughout the first half of the nineteenth century, and the word 'mesmerism' came to be used of all phenomena now identified as 'spiritualism', and of hypnotism (hence our word 'mesmerize'). In the 1830s the mesmerist Charles Poyen toured New England, lecturing on animal magnetism and giving demonstrations of hypnotism, using his 'trance-maidens' as subjects. Elizabeth Peabody, Hawthorne's future sister-in-law, was among the many who heard him speak.

8   *Zenobia*: the name of a famous Queen of Palmyra in the third century AD. She was defeated by the Roman Emperor Aurelian in 272, after extending the territories under her control, and led captive through Rome.

      cannel coal: bright-burning candle coal.

10   *Esquimaux*: Eskimo.

      and somewhat of proof ... a big demijohn: these words were omitted in the first edition, apparently at the instigation of the author's wife, who was strongly opposed to drinking. A demijohn is a large bottle enclosed in wickerwork, probably containing whisky.

15   *dry-goods people*: drapers.

17   *I almost fancied myself actually beholding it*: also omitted from the first edition, probably at Sophia Hawthorne's request.

19   *phalansteries*: the phalanstery was the multiple-purpose central building in the ideal community envisaged by Charles Fourier; see below, note to p. 52.

21   *Arcadia*: region of Greece inhabited largely by shepherds; associated in poetic tradition with the pastoral ideal.

23   *California gold*: still a relatively new phenomenon when the novel was written. Gold was discovered in January 1848, and the first great wave of migrants (the 'forty-niners') arrived in the following year.

24   *Pandora*: the first mortal woman in Greek mythology, parallel to Eve. Created by the blacksmith god Vulcan at Zeus's request, she opened a box the latter had given her, and thereby released all the troubles of the world.

      the millennium of love: the second golden age which Utopian socialism sought to create.

33   *a seamstress from the city*: in his *American Notebooks* (9 October 1841), Hawthorne describes the arrival at Brook Farm of 'a little sempstress from Boston'.

34 *salamander-stove*: small portable stove for heating rooms.

37 *Blithedale*: the name hints at the 'happy valley' of the hero in Samuel Johnson's long prose romance *Rasselas* (1759).

38 *Sisera's brain*: fleeing after defeat by the Israelite armies, the Canaanite general Sisera took refuge in the tent of a woman called Jael. As foretold, she drove a tent nail into his skull. Judges 4: 21.

   How cold an Arcadia: the Forest of Arden in Shakespeare's *As You Like It*, another modern Arcadia, is also cold; e.g. II. i. 6–9, II. v. 42. The play is referred to again in Ch. XI.

40 *Michael Scott*: Scottish scholar, astrologer, and reputed magician (*c.*1175–1230) with an international reputation. He was said to be able to conjure food for his dinner guests from the kitchens of the royal courts of Europe.

41 *homeopathic*: invented in the eighteenth century, homeopathic treatment prescribes small doses of curatives related in some way to the illness.

46 *vegetable diet*: such a diet was thought at the time to result in 'ether' entering the system, making the person more spiritual, less fleshly.

52 *Miss Margaret Fuller*: essayist, teacher, and pioneering feminist (1810–50) associated with the Transcendentalist movement, and a friend of the Hawthornes (her famous conversational classes for women took place between 1839 and 1844 at the Boston home of Sophia's sister Elizabeth Peabody). Zenobia is usually taken to be in part a portrait of her, although Hawthorne seeks to head off such an inference in this passage, and gives Priscilla her squinting gaze and hunched posture. Fuller died tragically in a shipwreck off the American coast as she returned to the country after several years in Europe.

   Mr. Emerson's essays, ... the Dial, Carlyle's works, George Sand's romances: the works read by Coverdale represent the progressive thinking of the 1840s. The *Essays* of Ralph Waldo Emerson (1803–82), the central figure of the Transcendentalist movement, were published in collections in 1841 and 1844. They reflect his belief in the supreme value of the individual soul, and its kinship with the divine spirit. He succeeded Margaret Fuller as editor of the *Dial*, a Transcendentalist quarterly which appeared between 1840 and 1844. Emerson met the Scottish essayist, historian, and translator Thomas

Carlyle (1795–1881) during his European tour of 1832–3, and admired his passionate individualism and hostility to material-ism, the prophetic force of his writing, and the breadth of his intellectual interests. They corresponded, and supported one another's work. George Sand was the pen-name of the French authoress Amandine Dudevant (1804–76). Her novels of the early 1830s, such as *Lélia* (1833), are extravagant romances concerned with love, reflecting her hostile view of marriage. In the 1840s she turned to works looking towards a future egalitarian golden age, and to studies of rural life. The attractions for Zenobia of Sand—feminist, socialist, roman-tic—are obvious. Hawthorne gives his character a name which could belong to a Sand heroine.

Fourier: Charles Fourier (1772–1837), French social theorist who advanced ideas closer to anarchism than socialism. Start-ing with *Théorie des quatre mouvements et des destinées générales* (1808), he developed a vision of society moving towards harmony through self-sufficient co-operative units (pha-langes) of 1,500 people. The members would all live in a single building (phalanstery), receiving an equal basic wage. Brook Farm became Fourierist in some respects after 1843, but was not so while Hawthorne belonged to the community.

53 *limonade à cèdre*: a slightly distorted version of a passage in Fourier's *Théorie*. See *American Notebooks* entry, 7 August 1851.

the selfish principle: Fourier believed that a harmonious society would emerge if personal needs and desires were no longer repressed.

54 *Swedenborg*: the Swedish theologian Emanuel Swedenborg (1688–1772), a mystic who taught that natural objects are symbols of higher realities. His ideas influenced Emerson and the other Transcendentalists, notably the concept of 'corres-pondence' between the natural, the human, and the divine.

Gehenna: a hellish region, from Jeremiah via Milton.

58 *houstonias*: the four-petalled flowers of the genus Rubiaceae; the bluet is the best-known variety.

60 *frock*: rough outer shirt.

'*airy tongues that syllable men's names*': quoting *Comus* (1634), l. 209. There are clear parallels between Priscilla and the virtuous heroine of Milton's masque, held fast in her seat by a sorcerer's magic.

64   *Grub-street*: London street associated with impoverished writers from the seventeenth century onwards.

Pantisocracy: in the 1790s, in the aftermath of the French Revolution, Coleridge and his fellow-poet Southey planned to found a Utopian community in Pennsylvania. The Greek name means 'all to rule equally'.

Candide: Voltaire's satirical novella (1759) attacking optimistic philosophy and religion. The protagonists return from their travels to cultivate their garden.

Falstaff: in *1 Henry IV*, IV. ii, the fat knight musters some unlikely soldiers in Gloucestershire in order to aid the royal campaign against the rebels.

linsey-woolsey: coarse fabric mixing linen and wool, or cotton and wool.

'*Ara nudus; sere nudus*': Virgil, *Georgics*, I, l. 299: 'Plow naked; sow naked'.

66   *Burns*: the Scottish poet Robert Burns (1759–96) worked as an agricultural labourer before seeking fame in Edinburgh, and as a farmer after his failure. Although the poems present him as happy, he found the work harsh.

72   *Golden Age*: in classical myth, the period after the creation of the world, in which mankind lived in perfect happiness and harmony.

73   *caprioles*: leaps, capers.

Atalanta: in Greek myth, a princess of Arcadia who was the swiftest of mortals. Suitors for her hand were required to race her, accepting the penalty of death if they lost.

75   *Goldsmith's old folks*: in Oliver Goldsmith's pastoral elegy 'The Deserted Village' (1770), ll. 13–24.

91   *forest of Arden*: the pastoral refuge of all those banished or estranged from the court in *As You Like It*.

salvage man: savage man, exemplified by Caliban in *The Tempest*; traditionally depicted in antiquity and the Renaissance as hairy and covered in foliage.

94   *quixotism*: extravagant romanticism, like that of the hero of Cervantes's *Don Quixote*, who, *inter alia*, appoints himself guardian of Dulcinea.

97   *the Chorus*: in Greek tragedy a group of ordinary citizens who act as commentators on the dramatic action.

98   *Robinson Crusoe*: the hero of Daniel Defoe's novel (1719) has a look-out platform in a tree.

     King Charles: Charles II, fleeing from the Parliamentarian army after the Battle of Worcester (1851), reputedly hid in a tree.

99   *allegorical figure of rich October*: Spenser, *The Faerie Queene* (1590), VII. vii. 39.

100 *fancy-work*: ornamental needlework.

103 *Dante's ghostly forest*: at the start of the *Inferno*, in the *Divine Comedy*.

106 *Tableaux vivants*: Fr. living pictures; standing motionless and wearing appropriate costumes, the participants re-create famous paintings. Hawthorne describes a *tableaux vivants* evening at Brook Farm in a letter to Sophia (4 May 1841).

110 *Medusa*: in Greek myth, the snake-haired Gorgon, whose gaze was fatal; Perseus was able to kill her because he looked only at her reflection in his shield.

115 *transcendentalists*: a New England literary and philosophical movement which flourished in the period between the publication of Emerson's *Nature* (1836) and the outbreak of the Civil War. Besides Emerson, the leading figures included Thoreau, Fuller, Bronson Alcott, Ellery Channing, and George Ripley. German philosophy and English Romanticism were important influences; there was no common credo, but members of the group shared a suspicion of organized religion, and a belief that the divine could also be found in nature, or in great art and thought. Transcendentalists were frequently associated with progressive causes, such as the anti-slavery struggle, or the campaign for women's rights.

118 *Apostle Eliot*: John Eliot (1604–90), a missionary who emigrated from England to Boston in 1631, had some success in converting the Indians of Massachusetts, and translated the Bible into their language.

120 *when my sex shall achieve its rights*: Margaret Fuller, the partial model for the character of Zenobia, was the author of *Women in the Nineteenth Century* (1845), and played an important role in the movement for social, educational, and political equality. Elizabeth Peabody, Hawthorne's sister-in-law, was another leading figure.

132 *State-street*: the Boston equivalent of Wall Street.

136 *Titan*: a member of the gigantic race defeated by Zeus and his brothers in Greek myth. The mighty Atlas was their war leader.

carry off the gates of Gaza: as Samson does in Judges 16: 1–3, foiling the attempt by the Philistines to trap him in the city.

138 *Newport or Saratoga*: fashionable resorts in Rhode Island and upstate New York, respectively.

the annual Fast: a custom in Puritan New England; later the day became a public holiday in many states.

139 *Cassandra*: the wild prophetess, accurate but unheeded, of Homer's *Iliad*.

commoted: disturbed (cf. 'commotion').

141 *the North American Review*: a conservative Bostonian quarterly.

Cambridge men: members of Harvard University, situated in Cambridge, near Boston.

143 *Orphic wisdom*: oracular, esoteric, prophetic; from Orpheus, the inspired musician of Greek myth, who was said to have founded a mystery religion.

146 *sillabub*: frothy cream dessert.

147 *diorama*: a miniature scene on public display; here depicting a battle, as in Ch. XXIII ('the diorama of Moscow or Bunker Hill'). A successful diorama made the nineteenth-century spectator feel part of the spectacle.

bibliopolist: bookseller.

148 *Malta or Madeira*: both islands were famous for producing wine.

buttonwood-tree: plane.

150 *sherry-cobbler*: drink mixing sherry, lemon, sugar, and ice.

161 *astral lamp*: type of oil lamp.

170 *air-line*: imaginary line in the air.

171 *gripe*: grip.

174 *fumigation*: smoking.

175 *Human nature . . . substituting good*: restored by the editors of the *Centenary Edition*, this whole passage was crossed out in manuscript, and absent from editions published in the author's lifetime. Sophia Hawthorne's strong disapproval of alcohol is again assumed to have been decisive.

176 *daguerreotype*: the earliest form of photograph, invented by Louis Daguerre (1789–1851) in the 1820s.

syncope: fainting fit, black-out.

179 *patch over his right eye*: previously over the left eye.

181 *kennel-rat*: gutter rat; cf. canal, channel.

182 *Fauntleroy*: a probable allusion to the well-known case of the English banker Henry Fauntleroy, hanged for forgery in 1824 (see Introduction, pp. xiv–xviii).

183 *the New England metropolis*: Boston.

195 *penny-a-liners*: journalists paid at this rate.

196 *Lyceum-halls*: founded in the 1820s, and flourishing by the 1840s, the lyceum movement established colleges for adult education, which also served as venues for visiting lecturers and the kinds of entertainment Hawthorne describes.

thaumaturgist: magician.

the Mormon Prophet: Joseph Smith (1805–44), who founded the Church of Latter-Day Saints and published the *Book of Mormon* in 1830.

198 *the epoch of rapping spirits*: American spiritualism only became a widespread phenomenon in the late 1840s, after the publication of Andrew Jackson Davis's book *The Principles of Nature* (1847).

205 *barberry bushes*: Berberis.

Paul Dudley: Massachusetts landowner, judge, and legislator (1675–1751), credited with erecting such walls throughout the colony.

209 *Comus*: the sorcerer in Milton's masque, already referred to in Ch. VIII.

a concourse of strange figures: the source of this passage was a masquerade party at Brook Farm, recorded in Hawthorne's *American Notebooks* (28 September 1841).

Bavarian broom-girl: witch.

Jim Crow: a dancing negro character in minstrel shows who made his first appearance in the song 'Jim Crow' (1830), performed by T. D. Rice, the father of minstrelsy. The body of racist laws brought in in the latter part of the nineteenth century became known as the 'Jim Crow laws'.

Shaker: the Shakers were a millenarian Protestant sect

founded in the eighteenth century; Ann Lee, the church's leader, emigrated from England to America in 1774.

the Faerie Queen: Edmund Spenser's long poem, left incomplete at his death in 1598. Six of the planned twelve books were published in 1596.

210   *Moll Pitcher*: a famous Massachusetts fortune-teller and reputed witch, who died in 1813.

skinkers and drawers: men serving drinks.

Tam O'Shanter: the hero of a Robert Burns poem (1791), who is pursued by the Devil when drunk.

211   *Actaeon*: in Greek myth, a hunter who watched Artemis (Diana) and her attendants bathing; she changed him into a stag, and he was killed by his own hounds.

213   *calash*: hooped sun-bonnet.

214   *a Puritan magistrate, holding inquest ... in a case of witchcraft*: as one of Hawthorne's ancestors had done in the Salem witch trials of 1692.

230   *so you think she's drowned herself!*: in the *American Notebooks* (9 July 1845) Hawthorne records taking part in 'a search for the body of a drowned girl'.

232   *horn-pouts*: catfish.

237   *tire-women*: those who prepare (attire) the body for burial.

243   *Bunyan's book*: *The Pilgrim's Progress* (1678); an allegorical work, like Spenser's *Faerie Queene*, referred to in Ch. XXIV.

246   *Doctor Griswold*: Rufus Griswold (1815–57), literary journalist best known as the biographer of Poe, and the editor of his poetry; Coverdale refers to his survey *The Poets and Poetry of America* (1842).

Kossuth: Lajos Kossuth (1802–94), leader of the Hungarian Revolution of 1848, and head of the republic he had proclaimed until defeat in 1849. Hawthorne heard him speak in Boston in 1851.

The Oxford World's Classics Website

www.worldsclassics.co.uk

- Information about new titles
- Explore the full range of Oxford World's Classics
- Links to other literary sites and the main OUP webpage
- Imaginative competitions, with bookish prizes
- Peruse *Compass*, the Oxford World's Classics magazine
- Articles by editors
- Extracts from Introductions
- A forum for discussion and feedback on the series
- Special information for teachers and lecturers

www.worldsclassics.co.uk

American Literature

British and Irish Literature

Children's Literature

Classics and Ancient Literature

Colonial Literature

Eastern Literature

European Literature

History

Medieval Literature

Oxford English Drama

Poetry

Philosophy

Politics

Religion

The Oxford Shakespeare

A complete list of Oxford Paperbacks, including Oxford World's Classics, OPUS, Past Masters, Oxford Authors, Oxford Shakespeare, Oxford Drama, and Oxford Paperback Reference, is available in the UK from the Academic Division Publicity Department, Oxford University Press, Great Clarendon Street, Oxford OX2 6DP.

In the USA, complete lists are available from the Paperbacks Marketing Manager, Oxford University Press, 198 Madison Avenue, New York, NY 10016.

Oxford Paperbacks are available from all good bookshops. In case of difficulty, customers in the UK can order direct from Oxford University Press Bookshop, Freepost, 116 High Street, Oxford OX1 4BR, enclosing full payment. Please add 10 per cent of published price for postage and packing.